FANNY TROLLOPE

THE VICAR OF WREXHILL

ALAN SUTTON PUBLISHING LIMITED

First published in 1837

First published in this edition in the United Kingdom in 1996
Alan Sutton Publishing Limited
Phoenix Mill · Far Thrupp · Stroud · Gloucestershire

British Library Cataloguing in Publication Data

A catalogue record of this book is available from the British Library.

ISBN 0-7509-1156-5

Cover picture: detail from A Woman by a Fireside *(1864) by Marcus Stone (1840–1921) (Agnew & Sons, London/Bridgeman Art Library, London)*

Typeset in 10/11 Bembo.
Typesetting and origination by
Alan Sutton Publishing Limited.
Printed in Great Britain by
The Guernsey Press Company Limited,
Guernsey, Channel Islands.

INTRODUCTION

The Vicar of Wrexhill was written in 1837 when Fanny Trollope was renting a house at Hadley, a village north-west of London. Living with her were her daughter Cecilia and youngest son Anthony, who at that time was employed as a post office clerk in London. Tom, the eldest son, was teaching in Birmingham.

The previous three years had been traumatic. Deeply in debt and under threat of imprisonment in England, the family had fled to Bruges in 1834. There they stayed for two years, while Fanny nursed her sick and dying family during the daylight hours and wrote books at night to earn money for clothes, food and medicines. In their miserable rented rooms in Bruges her beloved second son, Henry, died in December 1834; Mr Trollope died in October 1835 and Emily, the youngest, died in February 1836.

The Vicar of Wrexhill was Fanny Trollope's ninth book and was written early in her widowhood while she was reshaping her own life and learning to live without the protection of a husband. She writes with savage satire of the paternalistic attitudes of English society with which she was all too familiar; she draws a chilling picture of the devious misuse of evangelical power and the vulnerability of an unworldly widow who has not yet learnt to protect herself from predatory vicars.

The critics were horrified. The *Athenaeum* wrote in the autumn of 1837: 'Handsome, silkily-spoken . . . with his black eyes and caressing hands, which make such sad havoc among the bevy of admiring village ladies, he glides on his way, like a serpent – glossy, silent and poisonous – throwing out hints here, innuendos there; blighting with the language of brotherly love, and under the mask of Scriptural sanctity, creeping steadily upward towards wealth and power. His is a fearful character; and some of his later doings are too dark and terrible to have been written down by a woman, – aye, or a man either; but Mrs Trollope loves debateable ground.'

In her son Anthony's book, *Barchester Towers*, written 20 years later in 1857, the character of Mr Slope has much in common with that of the Vicar of Wrexhill. Mr Slope 'can reprove faults with so much flattery, and utter censure in so caressing a manner, that the female heart, if it glow with a spark of low church susceptibility, cannot withstand him. . . . He has, however, a pawing, greasy way with him, which does not endear him to those who do not value him for their soul's sake'.

Fanny Trollope was a remarkable woman who commenced writing at the late age of fifty-three from economic necessity, became an instant best seller, and in the space of 25 years produced forty-one books in 115 volumes.

She was born Frances Milton on 10 March 1779 in Stapleton, a village just north of Bristol. Her father, the Reverend William Milton, held the living of Heckfield in Hampshire and was also a Clerk of Holy Orders at Saint Michael's church in Bristol. It was in Stapleton that all six Milton children were born, though only three survived, Mary, Frances (called Fanny) and the youngest, Henry.

Their mother died after the birth of Henry, and the children were brought up by their father, who was more inclined towards mathematics and mechanical inventions than religion, and from whom they received a somewhat unorthodox education. Fluent in Latin, French and Italian, and at ease with her father's scientific friends, Fanny was less familiar with the more feminine requirements of a young lady of the eighteenth century. After their father remarried in 1800 he resumed his duties as parish priest at Heckfield and his family went with him. Life in the quiet country vicarage must have seemed very slow after the bustle of Bristol, and when brother Henry took up his new appointment at the War Office in London, twenty-two-year-old Fanny and her older sister Mary were happy to go and keep house for him at Keppel Street.

There they enjoyed dinner parties, whist, charades, and visits to the theatre and art galleries; but in spite of the social whirl Fanny at the age of twenty-nine was unmarried. In 1808 she met a friend of Henry's, a barrister, Thomas Anthony Trollope, who lent her some books of verse which marked the beginning of a courtship. In 1909, thirty-five-year-old Mr Trollope married thirty-year-old Miss Milton in Heckfield parish church. Their early married life in Keppel Street was very happy, and they had seven children in eight years. Tom, born in 1810, was followed by Henry in 1811, Arthur in 1812, Emily 1, who was born and died on the same day in 1813, Anthony in 1815, Cecilia in 1816 and Emily 2 in 1818.

When the family outgrew Keppel Street, they leased a farmhouse, Julian Hill, at Harrow, and after the birth of Anthony in 1815 they made this their main home. In the expectation of an inheritance from Uncle Adolphus Meetkerke, the Trollopes built an imposing house, Julians, on a nearby hill, but when the inheritance failed to materialise the family was forced to move back to their smaller farmhouse. Julians was then leased to the Vicar of Harrow, the Revd Dr J.W. Cunningham. He was an evangelical and much disliked by the Established Church faction to which the Trollopes belonged. He was viewed with suspicion as being too suave and soft, too apt to bestow 'the kiss of peace' on the young women of his parish, and lacking in sincerity. Fanny's contemporaries thought that she had made the Revd J.W. Cunningham the model for the Revd W.J. Cartwright, the Vicar of Wrexhill, an allegation which Fanny always denied.

Life became much harder for the family when after a few years Mr Trollope began to show signs of the irritability and disabling sick headaches which were to plague him for the rest of his life. He was a strict father demanding from his boys that they waste no time in 'idling', and initiating the rudiments of Latin into them as soon as they began to read. The boys were educated first at Harrow, where they were able to go as 'town boys', and later at Winchester and New College, Oxford, where their father and grandfather had been before them.

For several years all went well with the family; Fanny had many friends and enjoyed the social life of Harrow and London. In 1823 she and Mr Trollope visited Paris where they met Fanny's childhood friends the Garnetts and a mutual friend Frances Wright, and were invited to stay by General Lafayette.

The Trollopes began to experience money problems and as Henry was achieving little at Winchester, it was decided to find employment for the sixteen-year-old boy in a counting house in Paris. In early 1827, Anthony was awarded a place at Winchester, and Mr Trollope, who was determined to send all his sons to a public school, decided that in order to pay the fees the family must move to a smaller dilapidated farmhouse three miles from Harrow at Harrow Weald, where they would pay less rent. Fanny was appalled at the prospect of having to move from her friends and her beloved Julian Hill. She visited Paris in the summer of 1827 to attend Julia Garnett's wedding and to see Henry. Here she again met the charismatic young reformer Frances Wright who had founded an idealistic settlement at Nashoba in Tennessee where slaves worked to earn their freedom. Frances Wright was now in Paris to look for new settlers for her community and to recover from the American fever. She suggested to Fanny that she and Henry become part of the Nashoba experiment; American living was cheaper and Henry could find employment.

Fanny was enthusiastic, and eventually obtained Mr Trollope's permission on condition that Thomas Adolphus and Anthony remained as boarders at Winchester. She took with her Henry, Cecilia and Emily, and their drawing master, a young Frenchman, Auguste Hervieu.

They arrived in America at the mouth of the Mississippi in December 1827, and reached the Utopian settlement of Nashoba in January. Fanny was devastated upon her arrival to find it nothing but a collection of miserable wooden huts, built on partly cleared land in a fever-ridden swamp. What to do now? She was without funds, marooned in a strange land with three children, a drawing master, two servants and a quantity of luggage. With all possible speed she took her party to Cincinnati, where, supported by Auguste Hervieu, she planned to wait for the arrival of her husband to transport them home.

Bedevilled by his own financial worries, it was nearly a year before Mr Trollope could join them, and by then Fanny had decided to remain in Cincinnati and build a bazaar. It was to be a community centre where the sexes could mingle socially, with a saloon, art gallery, coffee house and ball room. Managing this establishment was to be Henry's future. The bazaar was a disaster; unscrupulous contractors walked off with the money, and instead of sending money from England to pay the workmen, Mr Trollope sent out trumpery store goods for sale. The bazaar, later nicknamed 'Trollope's Folly' was seized by the creditors before it was completed and all the Trollopes' possessions were sold to pay their debts. There were another two years of hardship before Fanny and Hervieu between them could save and borrow enough money to get them back to England. Fanny resolved on writing a book of her adventures in the hope that it might bring her some much needed income.

They returned to England in 1831 to the run-down farmhouse where Mr Trollope was now living. Fanny's book was in the hands of the publishers by the autumn of that year. *Domestic Manners of the Americans* was published in March 1832, and became an instant bestseller. In the first year it went into four editions in England, and a further four editions in America. A truthful, witty, sardonic tale of Fanny's experiences of the equality of American life, it made the Americans howl with rage. In England the Tories hailed it as a dire warning of the pitfalls of freedom, and the Whigs spluttered that it was a pack of lies. Overnight, at the age of fifty-three, Fanny became a celebrity.

Domestic Manners of the Americans was followed by an unending stream of books. From now on she became the family's main income earner, and sometimes wrote as many as three three-volume novels in one year, driven by the need to earn money for the support of herself and her family. Fanny wrote not only travel books, but romances, murder mysteries, gothic novels and satires. Some of her most powerful books were written to expose social injustice; the evils of slavery; the injustice of the poor laws; the exploitation of children in the factories and, in *The Vicar of Wrexhill*, the dangers of excessive evangelicalism. She became one of the nineteenth century's most popular writers and was acquainted with, among others, Wordsworth, Dickens, Elizabeth Barrett Browning and George Eliot.

Fanny spent the last few years of her life living among the expatriate literary community in Florence where, at the age of seventy-seven, she wrote her last book, *Fashionable Life: or Paris and London*. She died in Florence in 1863, and is buried there in the English Cemetery.

After her death her writing went out of fashion and she is now mainly remembered for her satirical *Domestic Manners of the Americans*. She wrote of her own Regency and early Victorian world with a sharp sense of the ridiculous in contemporary society and it is just this outspoken quality which makes her works so interesting to read today. Her quizzical sense of humour was deplored by the critics who labelled her writing 'coarse' and 'vulgar'. William Thackeray, in a review of *The Vicar of Wrexhill* for *Fraser's Magazine,* condemned the book as 'a display of licentiousness, overt and covert, such as no woman conceived before'.

But times change. When read today, the Fanny Trollope books of one hundred and fifty years ago are clever, witty, and surprisingly modern.

Teresa Ransom, 1996

Further Reading

Teresa Ransom, *Fanny Trollope: A Remarkable Life*, Alan Sutton Publishing Ltd, Stroud, 1995.

CHAPTER I

The beauties of an English village have been so often dwelt upon, so often described, that I dare not linger long upon the sketch of Wrexhill, which must of necessity precede my introduction of its vicar. And yet not even England can show many points of greater beauty than this oak-sheltered spot can display. Its peculiar style of scenery, half garden, half forest in aspect, is familiar to all who are acquainted with the New Forest, although it has features entirely its own. One of these is an overshot mill, the sparkling fall of which is accurately and most nobly overarched by a pair of oaks which have long been the glory of the parish. Another is the grey and mellow beauty of its antique church, itself unencumbered by ivy, while the wall and old stone gateway of the churchyard look like a line and knot of sober green, enclosing it with such a rich and unbroken luxuriance of foliage 'never sear,' as seems to show that it is held sacred, and that no hand profane ever ventured to rob its venerable mass of a leaf or a berry. Close beside the church, and elevated by a very gentle ascent, stands the pretty Vicarage, as if placed expressly to keep watch and ward over the safety and repose of its sacred neighbour. The only breach in the ivy-bound fence of the churchyard, is the little wicket gate that opens from the Vicarage garden; but even this is arched over by the same immortal and unfading green, – a fitting emblem of that eternity, the hope of which emanates from the shrine it encircles. At this particular spot, indeed, the growth of the plant is so vigorous, that it is controlled with difficulty, and has not obeyed the hand which led it over the rustic arch without dropping a straggling wreath or two, which if a vicar of the nineteenth century could wear a wig, might leave him in the state coveted for Absalom by his father. The late Vicar of Wrexhill, however, – I speak of him who died a few weeks before my story begins, – would never permit these graceful pendants to be shorn, declaring that the attitude they enforced on entering the churchyard was exactly such as befitted a Christian when passing the threshold of the court of God.

Behind the Vicarage, and stretching down the side of the little hill on which it stood, so as to form a beautiful background to the church rose a grove of lofty forest-trees, that seemed to belong to its garden, but which in fact was separated from it by the road which led to Mowbray Park, on the outskirts of which noble domain they were situated. This same road, having passed behind the church and Vicarage, led to the village street of Wrexhill, and thence, towards various other parishes, over a common, studded with oaks and holly bushes, on one side of which, with shelving grassy banks that gave to the scene the appearance of noble pleasure-grounds, was a sheet of water large enough to be dignified by the appellation of Wrexhill Lake. Into this, the little stream that turned the mill emptied itself, after meandering very prettily through Mowbray Park, where, by the help of a little artifice, it became wide enough at one spot to deserve a boat and boat-house, and at another to give occasion for the erection of one of the most graceful park-bridges in the county of Hampshire.

On one side of the common stands what might be called an alehouse, did not the exquisite neatness of every feature belonging to the little establishment render this vulgar appellation inappropriate. It was in truth just such a place as a town-worn and fastidious invalid might have fixed his eyes upon and said, 'How I should like to lodge in that house for a week or two!' Roses and honeysuckles battled together for space to display themselves over the porch, and above the windows. The little enclosure on each side the post whence swung the 'Mowbray Arms' presented to the little bay windows of the mansion such a collection of odorous plants, without a single weed to rob them of their strength, that no lady in the land, let her flower-garden be what it may, but would allow that Sally Freeman, the daughter, bar-maid, waiter, gardener at the 'Mowbray Arms,' understood how to manage common flowers as well as any Scotchman in her own scientific establishment.

Industry, neatness, and their fitting accompaniment and reward, comfort, were legible throughout the small domain. John Freeman brewed his own beer, double and single; Dorothy, his loving wife, baked her own bread, cured her own bacon, churned her own butter, and poached her own eggs, or roasted her own chicken, when they were called for by any wandering lover of woodland scenery who was lucky enough to turn his steps towards Wrexhill. The other labours of the household were performed by Sally, except indeed the watering of horses, and the like, for which services a stout, decent peasant-boy received a shilling a week, and three good meals a day: and happy was the cottager whose son got the appointment, for both in morals and manners the horseboy at the Mowbray Arms might have set an example to his betters.

There are many other pretty spots and many more good people at Wrexhill; but they must show themselves by degrees, as it is high time the business of my story should begin.

The 2nd of May 1833 was a gay day at Wrexhill, for it was that on which Charles Mowbray came of age, and the fête given on the occasion was intended to include every human being in the parish, besides about a hundred more, neighbours and friends, who came from a greater distance to witness and share in the festivities.

A merrier, or in truth a happier set of human beings, than those assembled round the breakfast-table at Mowbray Park on the morning of that day, could hardly be found any where. This important epoch in the young heir's life had been long anticipated with gay impatience, and seemed likely to be enjoyed with a fulness of contentment that should laugh to scorn the croaking prophecy which speaks of hopes fulfilled as of something wherein doubtful good is ever blended with certain disappointment. The Mowbray family had hoped to wake upon a joyous morning, and they did so: no feeling of anxiety, no touch of disease, no shadow of unkindness to any being who shared with them the breath of life, came to blight the light-hearted glee which pervaded the whole circle.

Charles Mowbray senior had hardly passed the prime of life, though a constitutional tendency to something like corpulency made him look older than he really was. Throughout his fifty summers he had scarcely known an ailment or a grief, and his spirit was as fresh within him as that of the noble-looking young man on whom his eyes rested with equal pride and love.

Mrs Mowbray, just seven years his junior, looked as little scathed by time as himself; her slight and graceful figure, indeed, gave her almost the appearance of youth; and though her delicate face had lost its bloom, there was enough of beauty left to render her still a very lovely woman.

Charles Mowbray junior, the hero of the day, was, in vulgar but expressive phrase, as fine a young fellow as ever the sun shone upon. His mind, too, was in excellent accordance with the frame it inhabited, – powerful, elastic, unwearying, and almost majestic in its unbroken vigour and still-increasing power.

'Aux cœurs heureux les vertus sont faciles,' says the proverb; and as Charles Mowbray was certainly as happy as it was well possible for a man to be, he must not be overpraised for the fine qualities that warmed his heart and brightened his eye. Nevertheless, it is only justice to declare, that few human beings ever passed through twenty-one years of life with less of evil and more of good feeling than Charles Mowbray.

Helen, his eldest sister, was a fair creature of nineteen, whose history had hitherto been, and was probably ever doomed to be, dependent upon her affections. As yet, these had been wholly made up of warm and well-requited attachment to her own family; but few people capable of loving heartily, are without the capacity of suffering heartily also, if occasion calls for it, and this strength of feeling rarely leaves its possessor long in the enjoyment of such pure and unmixed felicity as that which shone in Helen's hazel eye as she threw her arms around her brother's neck, and wished him a thousand and a thousand times joy!

Fanny Mowbray, the youngest of the family, wanted three months of sixteen. Poets have often likened young creatures of this age to an opening rose-bud, and it was doubtless just such a being as Fanny Mowbray that first suggested the simile. Anything more bright, more delicate, more attractive in present loveliness, or more full of promise for loveliness more perfect still, was never seen.

In addition to this surprising beauty of form and feature, she possessed many of those qualities of mind which are attributed to genius. Meditative and imaginative in no common degree, with thoughts occasionally both soaring and profound, she passed many hours of her existence in a manner but little understood by her family – sometimes devouring with unwearying ardour the miscellaneous contents of the large library, and sometimes indulging in the new delight of pouring forth her own wild, rambling thoughts in prose or rhyme. Unfortunately, the excellent governess who had attended the two girls from the time that Helen attained her eighth year died when Fanny was scarcely fourteen; and the attachment of the whole family being manifested by a general declaration that it would be impossible to permit any one to supply her place, the consequence was, that the cadette of the family had a mind less well and steadily regulated than it might have been, had her good governess been spared to her a few years longer.

Though so many persons were expected before night to share the hospitalities of Mowbray Park, that, notwithstanding the ample size of its mansion, both the lady and her housekeeper were obliged to exert considerable skill in arranging their accommodation, there was but one person besides the family present at the happy breakfast-table; and she was not a guest but an inmate.

Rosalind Torrington was a young Irish girl from the province of Ulster, who had passed the first seventeen years of her life in great retirement, in a village not far distant from the coast, with no other society than the immediate neighbourhood afforded. Since that time her destiny had undergone a great change. She was an only child, and lost both father and mother in one of those pestilential fevers which so frequently ravage the populous districts of Ireland. Her father was one of that frightfully-wronged and much-enduring race of Protestant clergy, who, during the last few years, have suffered a degree of oppression and persecution unequalled for its barefaced injustice by anything that the most atrocious page of history can record.

Her mother, of high English descent, had been banished from all intercourse with her patrician family, because she refused to use her influence with her exemplary husband to induce him to abandon his profitless and often perilous preferment in Ireland, where he felt he had the power as well as the will to do good, in order to place himself in dependence upon his wife's brother, a bachelor viscount who had invited the impoverished family to his house, and promised some time or other to do something for him in his profession – if he could. This invitation was politely but most positively refused, and for the last three years no intercourse of any kind had taken place between them. At the end of that time, Mr Torrington and his exemplary wife, while sedulously administering to the sick souls of their poor parishioners, caught the fever that raged among them, and perished. Mrs Torrington survived her husband three days; and during that time her thoughts were painfully occupied by the future prospects of her highly-connected but slenderly portioned girl.

All she could do for her she did. She wrote to her haughty brother in such a manner as she thought, from her deathbed must produce some effect; but lest it should not, she addressed another letter to Mrs Mowbray, the favourite friend of her youth, entreating her protection for her orphan child.

This letter enclosed a will fully executed, by which she left to her daughter whatever property she might die possessed of, (amounting at the utmost, as she supposed, to about five thousand pounds,) and constituting Mrs Mowbray sole guardian of her person and property.

During the interval which had elapsed since Mrs Torrington's estrangement from her noble brother, his lordship had contrived to quarrel also with his nephew and heir, and in the height of his resentment against him, made a will, leaving the whole of his unentailed property, amounting to above eighty thousand pounds, to his sister. By a singular coincidence, Lord Trenct died two days before Mrs Torrington; so that her will was made exactly one day after she had unconsciously become the possessor of this noble fortune. Had this most unexpected event been made known to her, however, it would probably have made no other alteration in her will than the addition of the name of some male friend, who might have taken care of the property during the minority of her child: and even this would only have been done for the purpose of saving her friend trouble; for such was her opinion of Mrs Mowbray, that no circumstances attending her daughter's fortune could have induced her to place the precious deposit of her person in other hands.

The poor girl herself, while these momentous events were passing, was stationed at the house of an acquaintance at a few miles' distance, whither she had been sent at the first appearance of infection; and thus in the short space of ten days, from the cherished, happy darling of parents far from rich, she became an heiress and an orphan.

Rosalind Torrington was a warm-hearted, affectionate girl, who had fondly loved her parents, and she mourned for them with all her soul. But the scene around her was so rapidly and so totally changed, and so much that was delightful mixed with the novelty, that it is not wonderful if at her age her grief wore away, and left her, sooner than she could have believed the change possible, the gay and happy inmate of Mowbray Park.

About four months had elapsed since her arrival, and she was already greatly beloved by the whole family. In age she was about halfway between the two sisters; and as she did not greatly resemble either of them in temper or acquirements, she was at this time equally the friend of both.

In most branches of female erudition Miss Torrington was decidedly inferior to the Miss Mowbrays: but nature had given her a voice and a taste for music which led her to excel in it; and so much spirit and vivacity supplied on other points the want of regular study, that by the help of her very pretty person, her good birth, and her large fortune, nobody but Charles Mowbray ever discovered deficiency or inferiority of any kind in Rosalind Torrington: but he had declared vehemently, the moment she arrived, that she was not one quarter so pretty as his sister Fanny, nor one thousandth part so angelic in all ways as his sister Helen.

Such was the party who, all smiles and felicitations, first crowded clamorously round the hero of the fête which now occupied the thoughts of all, and then seated themselves at the breakfast-table, more intent upon talking of its coming glories than on doing justice to the good things before them.

'Oh, you lucky twenty-one!' exclaimed Miss Torrington, addressing young Mowbray, 'Did any one ever see such sunshine! . . . And just think what it would have been if all the tents for the people had been drenched with rain! The inward groans for best bonnets would have checked the gratulations in their throats, and we should have had sighs perchance for cheers.'

'I do not believe any single soul would have cared for rain, or thought for one moment of the weather, let it have been what it would, Rosalind,' observed Helen. 'Charles,' she continued, 'is so adored and doted upon by all the people round, both rich and poor, that I am persuaded, while they were drinking his health, there would not have been a thought bestowed on the weather.'

'Oh! . . . To be sure, dear Helen. . . . I quite forgot that. Of course, a glance at the Mowbray would be worth all the Mackintosh cloaks in the world, for keeping a dry skin in a storm; – but then, you know, the hero himself might have caught cold when he went out to shine upon them – and the avoiding this is surely a blessing for which we all ought to be thankful: not but what I would have held an umbrella over him with the greatest pleasure, of course . . . but, altogether, I think it is quite as well as it is.'

'You won't quiz my Helen out of her love for me, Miss Rosalind Torrington,' replied Charles, laughing; 'so do not hope it.'

'Miss Rosalind Torrington!' . . . repeated the young lady indignantly. Then rising and approaching Mrs Mowbray, she said very solemnly, 'Is that my style and title, madam? Is there any other Miss Torrington in all the world? . . . Is there any necessity, because he is one-and-twenty, that he should call me Miss Rosalind? . . . And is it not your duty, oh! my guardianess! to support me in all my rights and privileges? And won't you please to scold him if he calls me Miss Rosalind again?'

'Beyond all question you are Miss Torrington, my dear,' replied Mrs Mowbray; 'and were not Charles unfortunately of age, and therefore legally beyond all control, I would certainly command him never to say Rosalind again.'

'That is not exactly what I said, Most Respected!' replied the young lady. 'He may call me Rosalind if he will; but if I am Miss any thing, I am Miss Torrington.'

'You certainly are a lucky fellow, Charles,' said his father, 'and Rosalind is quite right in praising the sunshine. Helen with her coaxing ways may say what she will, but our fête would have been spoilt without it.'

'Indeed I think so, sir. . . . Pray do not believe me ungrateful. Besides, I like to see everything accord – and your bright beaming faces would have been completely out of keeping with a dark frowning sky.'

'You are quite right. . . . But come, make haste with your breakfast . . . let us leave the ladies to give an inquiring glance to the decorations of the ball-room, and let you and I walk down to the walnut-trees, and see how they are getting on with the tents and the tables, and all the rest of it.'

'I shall be ready in a minute, sir; but I have been scampering round the whole park already this morning, and I am as hungry as a hound. Give me one more egg, Helen, and then . . .'

'It is really a comfort to see what a fine appetite he has! – is it not, Helen?' said Rosalind, surrounding his plate with rolls of all sorts and sizes.

'I will call you "*Wild Irish Girl*" in the very midst of the ball this evening if you do not behave better,' said young Mowbray.

'And if you do, I will . . .'

'Come along, Charles,' said his father, 'her threats may put you out of heart for the whole day.'

'And might not we too take a walk before any of the people arrive?' said Fanny. 'I have heard the cuckoo this morning for the first time. He was certainly thanking God for the sunshine; and I really think we ought to go out, and then we shall do so too.'

'A most delightful proposal!' cried Rosalind; 'and if the birds should happen to introduce a jig movement, we can practise our dancing steps as we go along.'

'Wait half an hour for me,' said Charles, rising to accompany his father, 'and I will join your party. Let us go to the Pebble-Ford, Rosalind; and you shall all three drink my health out of that clear pool beside it, that Ros . . . Miss Torrington – admired so much the other day.'

'No, no, we can't wait a moment, Char . . . Mr Mowbray ——' said Rosalind. 'Come, dear girls, let us be gone instantly.'

'Not wait for him on his birthday!' cried Helen. 'But you are not in earnest, Rosalind?'

'How you do labour and toil to spoil that man, Helen!' said Miss Torrington, raising her hands and eyes as he left the room. 'It is a great blessing for him that I am come amongst you! If anything can save him from utter destruction, it is I shall do it.'

Charles however was waited for, and that for at least three times the period he had named; but he came at last, and the walk was taken, and the birds sang, and the brook sparkled, and the health was drunk cordially, even by Rosalind; and the gay party returned in time to see the first carriage approach, bearing guests invited to be present at the tenants' dinner in the Park. Their morning toilet was hastily readjusted, as another and another equipage rolled onwards towards the house; and then the business of the day began. Lords and ladies, knights and squires, yeomen and peasants, were seen riding, driving, running, and walking through the spacious park in all directions. Then followed the rustic fête, and the joyous carouse, in which the name of Charles Mowbray made the welkin ring; and then, the company having retreated to the house, came the hurried steps of a dozen lady's-maids hastening to the various scenes of action, and valets converting closets of all sorts and sizes into dressing-rooms for unnumbered gentlemen; and then the banquet, and then the coffee and the short repose – and then the crowded ball.

All this came and went in order, and without the intervention of a single circumstance that might mar the enjoyment of a day long set apart for happiness, and which began and ended more exactly according to the wishes and intentions of those who arranged its festivities than often falls out at galas planned by mortals.

At five o'clock on the following morning the joyous din at length sank into silence, and as many as hospitable ingenuity could find room for lay down at Mowbray Park to enjoy again in dreams the untarnished gaiety of that happy day.

CHAPTER II

THE MORNING AFTER THE BIRTHDAY

Even the stable-boys deemed themselves privileged to sleep later than usual on the day after; and the ploughboy, as he went afield, missed the merry smile of the Park dairy-maid, who, like her superiors, seemed to think on such an occasion time was made for very vulgar souls indeed, and that none who had joined in so illustrious a gala could be expected to recover the full possession of their waking senses for some hours after the usual time.

By slow degrees, however, the different members of the establishment began to stretch themselves and give sign of reviving animation. The housemaids yawningly opened the window-shutters; the footmen crept after them to aid in removing from one room at least the traces of the jubilee, which, like the relics of a lamp that has burnt out, showed but the more unsightly from its past splendour; and at length, to a superficial eye, the breakfast-room looked like the breakfast-room of former years; though a more discriminating glance might have detected girandoles where no such things had ever glittered before, card-tables in the place of work-tables, and flowers, still blooming in situations as little usual to them as a bed of strawberries would have been the day before.

But it was long after these hireling efforts of forced labour had prepared the table for the morning meal, that any one of the favoured sleepers destined to partake of it left his or her downy pillow. . . . In short . . . it was past mid-day before the family and their guests began to assemble; and even then many stragglers were still waited for before they appeared, and Mrs Mowbray and Helen began at length to talk of breaking up the long session, and of giving orders to the butler to take care of all those who should come after.

'It is not very surprising that the Davenports, who never ceased dancing till long after the sun came to look at them,' said Helen, – 'it is not at all wonderful that they should sleep late, and I believe Mr Vivian makes it a principle to be the last on all occasions. But I am quite astonished that papa does not appear: was he asleep, mamma, when you came down this morning?'

'No, Helen, not quite asleep, for he spoke to me. But I think he was very sleepy, for I hardly understood what he said; and as he appeared extremely tired when he went to bed, I told Curtis to darken the room again and leave him quiet.'

Another half-hour brought forth the Davenports and Mr Vivian; but still Mr Mowbray did not appear, and Helen, though hitherto she had been quite satisfied by her mother's account of his prolonged slumbers, again began to feel uneasy about him.

'Do you not think, mamma,' said she, 'that I might venture to go up to him?'

'I see not the least objection to it, Helen; especially as we know that if it were you who happened to wake him out of the soundest sleep he ever enjoyed, the pleasure of seeing you near him would quite atone for it.'

'Very well, mamma, – then I shall certainly let him sleep no longer now;' and so saying, Helen left the room.

'Is not Helen Mowbray a charming creature?' said a gentleman who was seated next Miss Torrington, and who, being neither young, handsome, rich, nor noble, felt that he could wound no feelings by expressing his admiration of one young lady to another.

'I will tell you what she is,' answered Rosalind warmly: 'she is just as much better than everybody else in the world, as her sister, there, is more beautiful.'

'And you are . . .' said the middle-aged gentleman, fixing a pair of very intelligent eyes on her face, – 'you are . . .'

But notwithstanding the look of curiosity with which Miss Torrington listened, the speaker suddenly stopped, for a bell was rung with that sort of sudden and continued vehemence which denotes haste and agitation in the hand that gives it movement.

'That is my father's bell!' said Charles in an accent of alarm; and starting up, he was out of the room in an instant.

Mrs Mowbray immediately followed him, and for several minutes a sort of heavy silence seemed to have fallen on every individual present – not a word being uttered by any one, and the eyes of all fixing themselves on the face of Fanny, who kept her place as if spell-bound, but with a countenance that expressed a feeling approaching to terror.

'This is not to be borne!' exclaimed Rosalind abruptly. 'Excuse us for a moment,' she added, addressing those who still remained in the breakfast-room. – 'Come with me, Fanny, and let us know the worst at once.'

The two girls left the room together; and in a very few minutes afterwards a servant entered, the violent agitation of whose manner announced the news he brought before he spoke it.

'My master . . . my poor master is dead!' were the words he uttered; and their effect upon a party assembled for an occasion of so much festivity, and who had so lately parted with their kind and happy host in perfect health, may be easily imagined.

One single word in reply to the eager chorus of inquiry told the manner of his death——

'Apoplexy!'

The scene which followed was what such an event must necessarily produce. No single creature present, except one pretty portionless young lady who thought it very likely that Mr Charles might now fall in love with her, could by possibility be benefited by the death of the amiable man who had just breathed his last, and it is therefore probable that the universal expression of regret was sincere in quality, though its quantity might have been somewhat preternaturally increased by the circumstances in which the parties were relatively placed when the awful event was made known. Several tears were shed and some glasses of cold water called for while the carriages were getting ready; the gentlemen all looked grave, and many of the ladies pale; but in less than half an hour they had all left the house, not one of them, as it happened, being on terms of sufficient intimacy with the family to justify their offering to remain at such a moment.

It is easy enough to dismiss from the scene persons whose feelings were so slightly interested in it; but far different would be the task were I to attempt painting the heartfelt anguish of those who remained. Mr Mowbray had been so deeply yet so tranquilly loved by every member of his family – his intercourse with them had been so uniformly that of constant endearment, unchequered by any mixture of rough temper or unreasonable caprice, that their love for him was so natural and inevitable, that they had never reasoned upon it, or were fully aware of its intensity, till the dreadful moment in which they learned that they had lost him for ever.

The feelings of Mrs Mowbray for many hours amounted to agony; for till a medical gentleman who examined the body at length succeeded in convincing her that she was mistaken, she felt persuaded that her beloved husband owed his death to her neglect, and that if, when she mistook his unintelligible speech for sleepiness, she had discovered his condition and caused him to be bled, his precious life might have been saved. It was evident, however, from many circumstances, that the seizure was of a nature not to be baffled or parried by art; and the relief this conviction at length afforded the widow was so great, that her having first formed a contrary opinion was perhaps a blessing to her.

The grief of Charles was that of a young, ardent, and most affectionate spirit; but his mother and his sisters now seemed to hang upon him wholly, and the Being who alone can read all hearts only knew how deep was the sorrow he felt. The young Fanny, stealing away to her chamber, threw herself in an agony of tears upon her bed, and, forgotten in the general dismay that had fallen upon all, wept herself into a sleep that lasted till she awakened on the following morning to a renewed sense of sorrow which came over her like the dreadful memory of some frightful dream.

But of all those whom poor Mowbray had left to deplore his loss, it was Helen – his darling Helen – who unquestionably felt it the most profoundly. His love for her had all that is most touching in partiality, without one atom of the injustice which renders such a feeling criminal; and its effect upon her loving and enthusiastic temper was stronger than any words can describe.

Miss Torrington was perhaps beyond any other member of the family aware of this, and the tenderest pity for the silent, suffering Helen took possession of her. She was in truth a looker-on upon the melancholy scene, and as such, was more qualified to judge how sorrow worked in each of them than any other could be. Her residence in the family, though sufficient to impress her with the kindest feelings towards its chief, and the deepest impression of his worth, had hardly been long enough to awaken thoroughly her affections towards him, and she wept more in pity for those around her than from any personal feeling of grief for the loss she had herself sustained. To soothe poor Helen, to lead her thoughts even for a moment from the subject that engrossed them, and to keep her as much as possible from gazing in vain tenderness and hopeless agony upon the body of her father, became the sole occupation of Rosalind during the dreadful interval between the real loss of the beloved being to whom the soul of his child still fondly clung, and the apparently more final separation still which took place when all that was left of him was borne from the house.

Helen made little apparent return to all these tender cares, but she was fully conscious of them. She felt that Rosalind read her heart, and knew how to pity her; and the conviction turned liking into love, of that enduring kind which such hearts as Helen's alone know how to give.

CHAPTER III

THE VICAR OF WREXHILL

On the day preceding that appointed for the funeral, Mrs Mowbray received the following letter:–

'Madam,

'I trust that, as the minister of your parish, my venturing to break in upon your grief will not be considered as an intrusion. In the festivities which have ended so awfully, your hospitality invited me and my children to bear a part; and although I declined the invitation, I am most anxious to prove to you, madam, and to your family, that no deficiency of friendly feeling induced me to do so. But "it is better to go to the house of mourning than to the house of feasting," and I now therefore ask your permission to wait on you, with the most earnest hope that the sacred office I hold may enable you to receive me rather with a feeling of comfort than of pain. Be assured, madam, that short as the period of my ministry in the parish of Wrexhill has been, it is with deep sympathy in the grief that afflicts you that I subscribe myself, madam,

'Your humble servant and friend,

'WILLIAM JACOB CARTWRIGHT.

'Wrexhill Vicarage, May 9th, 1833.'

Little calculated as this letter may seem to excite violent emotion, it threw poor Mrs Mowbray into an agony of renewed grief. The idea of seeing for the first time since her loss a person who, however well-meaning in his wish to visit her, must be classed as a stranger, was inexpressibly painful; and, unused to encounter difficulty or inconvenience of any kind, she shrank from receiving Mr Cartwright with a degree of weakness which made her son, who had seldom left her side, tremble to think how little she was calculated to endure with firmness the desolation that had fallen upon her.

'Oh! no! no! no!' she exclaimed vehemently, 'I cannot see him – I can see no one! – keep him from me, Charles, – keep every one from me, if you would not see me sink to the earth before your eyes!'

'My poor mother! . . .' said Charles, tenderly taking her hand, 'do not let me see you tremble thus – you will make me tremble too! and we have need of strength – we have all great need of strength in this time of trial.'

'But you will not let this clergyman come to me, Charles? . . . Oh, no! you cannot be so cruel!'

'The very weakness which makes you shrink from this, my dearest mother, is the strongest proof that such a visit should be sought, and not avoided. Where, mother, are we any of us to look for the strength we want, except from Him whose minister now seeks to comfort us?'

'He cannot comfort me! . . . Can you, can Helen, can my pretty Fanny comfort me? . . . Then how should he? . . . Charles, Charles, there is no comfort in seeing this strange man; you cannot think there is: then why do you still stand with his note in your hand as if doubtful how you ought to answer it?'

'No, mother, I am not doubtful: my very soul seems to sink within me, when I think that he whose precepts . . .'

Tears – copious woman-like tears choked the utterance of the athletic youth, who looked as if he could fight and conquer in any strife to which fortune or misfortune could lead him. But the softness that now mastered him came not of weakness, but of strength – strength of every feeling that might do honour to a man. For a few moments he gave way to this burst of passionate sorrow, and the mother and son wept together.

'My own dear Charles!' said Mrs Mowbray, taking his hand and pressing it to her heart, 'how could I think for a moment that you would urge me to do what was so very painful?'

'It can hardly be so painful for you to do as for me to urge it, dearest mother; and yet I must do so . . . because I think it right. There is no other person in the world, I think, of what rank or station soever, for whose admittance I would plead so earnestly, unless it were one who, like this gentleman, offered to visit you as the minister of God.'

Mrs Mowbray buried her face in her handkerchief, and turned from him with a movement of impatience. At this moment, Helen, and her constant attendant Rosalind entered the room. Mr Cartwright's note was still in Charles's hand, and he gave it to his sister, saying, 'Helen, I think my mother ought not to refuse this visit; but she is very averse to it. God knows, I would not pain her for the world; but this is not a moment to refuse any one who offers to visit us as the minister from Heaven.'

Helen read the note, and her pale cheeks were washed anew with tears as she did so.

'It is meant kindly,' she said as she laid it upon the table; 'but it is very soon for my poor mother to meet a stranger.'

Rosalind's eyes rested on the folded note, and some feeling suggested by the consciousness that she too was almost a stranger brought a flush to her cheek, and led her to step back towards a distant sofa. Whether Charles observed or understood the movement, she knew not; but he followed and placed the letter in her hand.

The words of Helen seemed to comfort her mother for she again looked up, and addressing Charles almost reproachfully, said,

'Your sister Helen thinks as I do Charles: it would almost be an outrage against decency to receive a stranger on such a day as this.'

'Had the request to wait upon you come from our late clergyman, mother, would you have refused it?'

'Certainly not: but he was a friend of long standing, not a stranger, Charles.'

'But had he not been a clergyman, mother, you would hardly have wished him to choose such a time to make a visit here; and our not having yet become familiar with Mr Cartwright in the common intercourse of society, seems to me no sufficient reason for refusing to see him in the sacred character in which he has offered to come——'

Some powerful emotion checked his utterance; but in a moment he added,

'I would wish once more to pray beside my father before he goes hence to be no more seen by us on earth.'

'Mother! . . .' cried Helen, dropping on her knees and throwing her arms round her.

The appeal was answered by an embrace in which their tears mingled, and poor Mrs Mowbray, whose aching heart seemed to dread every new emotion, said, while something like a shudder ran through her frame, 'Do with me as you will, my children . . . I cannot bear much more. . . . But perhaps it would be better for me that I should sink to rest beside him!'

'My dearest friend!' exclaimed Rosalind, coming softly towards her and impressing a kiss upon her forehead, 'you have not lost all for which you might wish to live.'

'Oh, true . . . most true! . . . Where is my poor Fanny, Rosalind? You will answer this letter for me, Charles? . . . I will be ready to see Mr Cartwright whenever he chooses to come. . . . It will be a dreadful trial – but I am willing to endure it.'

The young man left the room, and such an answer was returned to the clergyman's note as brought him to the door within an hour after it was despatched.

Rosalind, in obedience to Mrs Mowbray's hint, had sought Fanny in her chamber, where she seemed to find a sad consolation in versifying all the tender recollections of her lost father that her memory could supply; but she instantly obeyed the summons, and when Mr Cartwright arrived, the whole family were assembled in the drawing-room to receive him.

The person, voice, and address of the gentleman were singularly well calculated to touch and soothe hearts suffering from affliction; and after the first painful moment in which they raised their eyes to meet those of the first stranger who had been admitted to look upon their sorrow, there was nothing in the interview to justify the terror with which the thought of it had inspired the poor widow.

Either from tact or feeling, Mr Cartwright seemed to avoid speaking to Mrs Mowbray, and it was to her son that he addressed such words as the occasion called for. Meanwhile, from time to time his eyes rested with gentle pity on the three beautiful girls, whose tears flowed silently as they listened to him.

But though the manner of Mr Cartwright was full of the tenderest kindness, it was apparently embarrassed. He evidently feared to touch or to dwell upon the agonizing subject which occupied all their thoughts, and it was Charles who had the courage to turn this melancholy meeting to the only purpose for which it could be desirable, by saying, though with a faltering voice,–

'Mr Cartwright . . . may we ask you to pray with us beside the coffin that contains the body of my father?'

The clergyman started, and his countenance expressed a mixture of satisfaction and surprise, his manner instantly became more solemn – more devout, and he replied eagerly, rising from his chair as he spoke, as if willing to hasten to the scene to which he was called,

'Most gladly – most joyfully, my dear sir, will I kneel with you and your amiable family to implore the divine grace. I did not know . . . I had hardly dared to hope. . . . Indeed I feared from the festivities . . . from the style in which . . .'

'I trust, sir,' interrupted young Mowbray almost in a whisper, 'that you do not suppose us unused to prayer, because we have rejoiced in the blessings which Heaven has bestowed?'

'I thank my God and Saviour that it is not so,' replied the clergyman, pressing the young man's hand affectionately; 'and I will praise His holy name for every symptom I find that the world, my dear young friend, has not taken too strong a hold upon your heart. May we through His grace walk righteously together in the path in which it hath pleased Him to place us side by side!'

Charles Mowbray's heart was ever open to every expression of kindness; and now, softened by sorrow, and warmed by a feeling of the purest piety, he returned the friendly pressure with interest, and then, taking his poor mother's arm within his own, led the way to the chamber of death.

The mourning family knelt beside the coffin, and listened with suppressed sobs to an extempore prayer, by no means ill suited to the occasion, though it was not, as poor Charles had expected, chosen from among the many solemn and beautiful orisons which the Church has furnished or which the Scriptures might supply for such an hour of need. But he was not disposed at this moment to cavil at any words calculated to raise his thoughts and those of the beings he most fondly loved to that Power which had hitherto blessed their existence, and from whence alone they could hope for support under the affliction with which He had now visited them. Fervently and earnestly he prayed for them and for himself; and when he rose from his knees and again pressed his suffering mother to his heart, it was with a feeling of renovated hope and confidence in the future protection of Heaven which nothing but prayer uttered with genuine piety can give.

Mr Cartwright did not take his leave till he had spoken an individual blessing to each of them, which was accompanied by a pressure of the hand that seemed to express more sympathy in what each felt than any words could have done.

Young Mowbray then retired with him to arrange everything respecting the ceremony which was to take place on the morrow. His mother expressed a wish to lie down for an hour; and the three girls, after attending her to her room, carefully shutting out the light in the hope that she might sleep, and each one bidding her do so with a fond caress, retreated to the dressing-room of Helen, when their conversation naturally turned on Mr Cartwright.

This gentleman had taken possession of the little living of Wrexhill only one month before the death of his most distinguished parishioner. During the week which followed his first performance of duty in the church, the family at the Park made a visit at the Vicarage: for though Mr Cartwright was a widower, he had a daughter nearly twenty years of age, who, as mistress of her father's house, was of course visited by the ladies. When this visit was returned, the Mowbray family were all absent; and during the short interval which followed before the day on which young Mowbray came of age, the preparations for the fête by which this event was to be celebrated had prevented Mr Cartwright and his family from receiving any other invitation than that which requested their attendance at it. This having been declined, he was as nearly as possible a personal stranger to the whole Mowbray family.

'What exquisite benevolence his countenance expresses!' exclaimed Fanny; 'I never saw eyes so full of gentleness.'

'His eyes are remarkably handsome,' replied Rosalind; 'but I am not quite sure that I like him.'

'The moments we passed with him were moments of agony,' said Helen. 'It would hardly be fair to pronounce any judgment upon him from such an interview.'

'Perhaps you are right, dear Helen, and I will endeavour to suspend mine,' replied Rosalind. 'But at least I may venture to remark that he is a very young-looking father for the full-grown son and daughter we have seen.'

'I do not think he can be their father,' observed Fanny. 'Perhaps he is only the husband of their mother? . . . Don't you think that is most likely, Helen?'

'I don't know, dear,' answered Helen: 'I believe I hardly saw him.'

'I really doubt if you did, my poor Helen,' said Rosalind; 'but if he speak sooth, he could not say the same of us. If the reverend gentleman be given to sketching of portraits, he might, I think, produce a good likeness of either of us, for, like Hamlet when he looked at Ophelia, "he fell to such perusal of our faces, as he would draw them" . . . I do not think I shall like this Mr Cartwright. . . . I do not mean now, Helen; I speak only of what I think I shall do when I know more of him.'

'Do you call that suspending your judgment, Rosalind?' said Helen with a feeble smile.

'Well, then, do not try to make a hypocrite of me, dearest: it will never answer. Wisdom is of too slow a growth for my little unprofitable hotbed of an intellect, which forces every thought to run up to full growth, lanky and valueless, as soon as it is sown. But by-and-by you shall transplant some of my notions, Helen, into the fine natural soil of your brain; and then, if they flourish, we shall see what they are really worth.'

For all reply, the pale Helen shook her head, as one who knows not well what has been said to him; and the conversation languished and dropped, as every other had done since the blow had fallen which had levelled her young and joyous spirit to the dust.

CHAPTER IV

THE WILL

The day which saw the honoured remains of Mr Mowbray committed to the tomb was one of dreadful suffering to his family, and to none more than to his son, who, with a heart swelling with the most genuine grief, was obliged to assume the garb of ceremony, and do the now gloomy honours of the mansion to many of the same friends and neighbours who had so recently received the joyous greeting of his father. Most thankful was he for the relief which followed the departure of the last of those who came to do honour to these splendid obsequies; and most soothing was it to his wounded and weary spirits to find himself once more surrounded only by those who could read in a look all he wished to express, and who required no welcome to share in the sorrow of that bitter day.

But, like all other periods of human life, whether marked by sorrow or by joy, it passed away with as even and justly-measured a pace as if no event distinguished it from its fellow days; and then, by slow but sure degrees, the little trifling ordinary routine of daily circumstance came with its invisible and unnoticed magic, to efface, or at least to weaken, feelings which seemed to have been impressed by the stamp of burning iron on their souls.

Charles Mowbray had not yet taken his degree, and wishing to do so as soon as possible, he was anxious to return to Christ Church without delay; but his father's will had not yet been opened, and, at the request of his mother, he postponed his departure till this could be done. This important document was in the hands of Sir Gilbert Harrington, an intimate friend and neighbour, who being in London at the time of Mr Mowbray's death, had been unable to obey the summons sent to him in time to attend the funeral; but within a week after, he arrived, and the following morning was fixed upon for this necessary business.

The persons present were Sir Gilbert Harrington, Mr Cartwright, a respectable solicitor from the country town who had himself drawn the instrument, and Charles Mowbray.

It was dated rather more than ten years back, and, after the usual preamble, ran thus:

'In order that my children, or any other persons whom it may concern, may know the reason and motive of the disposition of my property which I am about to make, it is necessary that I should therewith state the manner of my marriage with Clara Helena Frances, my dearly-beloved wife. Notwithstanding her vast possessions, I wooed and married her solely because I loved her; and this she had the generosity to believe, though I was nearly penniless, having nothing but my true affection and good blood to offer in return for all the wealth she brought. For several months she withstood my earnest solicitations for an immediate union, because, had she married before she became of age, her guardian would have insisted upon settlements and restrictions, which would have deprived me of all control over her property; nor would she subsequently sign any document whatever previous to her marriage, thereby rendering me the sole possessor of her fortune. WHEREFORE, to show my sense of this unparalleled confidence and generosity, I hereby make her the sole inheritrix of all I possess, to be ultimately disposed of according wholly and solely to her own will and pleasure.' . . . And then followed, with every necessary and unnecessary technicality of the law, such a disposition of his property as left his children entirely dependant on their mother both for their present and future subsistence.

That this will was very different from anything that Charles Mowbray expected, is most certain, and there might perhaps have been some slight feeling of disappointment at finding himself dependant even upon his mother; but if such there were, it was not sufficiently strong to prevent his doing justice to the noble feeling which had led to it; and, in truth, he felt so certain of the fond affection of his mother, that not a shadow of fear either for his own interest or that of his sisters crossed his mind.

The lawyer who read aloud the deed he had penned, had of course no observation to make upon it, and Mr Cartwright only remarked that it was a proof of very devoted love and confidence.

Of the small party present at this lecture, Sir Gilbert Harrington was the only one who testified any strong emotion respecting it; and his displeasure and vexation were expressed in no very measured terms. His warmth was at length checked, not because he had uttered all he had to say, but because he met the eye of Mr Cartwright fixed upon him with a sort of scrutiny that was unpleasing to his feelings. He therefore stopped short in the philippic he was pouring forth upon the infernal folly of a man's acting in matters of importance without consulting his friends, and taking the arm of Charles, walked through the hall into the grounds without appearing to remember that as he was left joint executor with Mrs Mowbray to the will, it might be expected that he should make some notification of its contents to her before he left the house.

'Shall we not speak to my mother, Sir Gilbert?' said Mowbray, endeavouring to restrain the eager step of the baronet as he was passing through the hall-door.

'No, sir,' was the laconic reply; and on he stalked with a more rapid step than before.

The conversation which passed between them during the hour which intervened before Sir Gilbert clambered up to his saddle and galloped off, was made up of something between lamentation and anathema on his side, and the most earnest assurances that no mischief could ensue from his father's will on the part of Charles. The testy old gentleman could not, however, be wrought upon to see the widow who, as he said, must have used most cursed cunning in obtaining such a will; of which, however, poor lady, she was as innocent as the babe unborn; and he at length left the Park, positive that he should have a fit of the gout, and that the widow Mowbray would marry within a year.

As soon as he had got rid of his warm-hearted but passionate old friend, Mowbray hastened to repair the neglect he had been forced into committing, and sought his mother in the drawing-room. But she was no longer there.

The room, indeed, appeared to be wholly untenanted, and he was on the point of leaving it to seek his mother elsewhere, when he perceived that Miss Torrington was seated at the most distant corner of it, almost concealed by the folds of the farthest window-curtain.

'Rosalind!' . . . he exclaimed, 'are you hid there? . . . Where are all the rest? and how come you to be left alone?'

'I am left alone, Mr Mowbray . . . because I wished it. Helen and Fanny are with your mother, I believe, in her room.'

Charles wished to see them all, and to see them together, and had almost turned to go; but there was something in the look and manner of Rosalind that puzzled him, and going up to her, he said kindly, 'Is anything the matter, Rosalind? You look as if something had vexed you.'

To his great astonishment she burst into tears, and turning from him as if to hide an emotion she could not conquer, she said, 'Go, go, Mr Mowbray – go to your mother – you ought to have gone to her instantly.'

'Instantly? . . . When? . . . What do you mean, Miss Torrington?'

'Miss Torrington means, Mr Mowbray, that it would in every way have been more proper for you to have announced to your mother yourself the strange will it has pleased your father to leave, instead of sending a stranger to do it.'

'Who then has told her of it, Rosalind? Was it the lawyer? Was it Mr Humphries?'

'No, sir, – it was Mr Cartwright.'

'But why should you be displeased with me for this, dear Rosalind? Sir Gilbert led me out of the library by force, and would not let me go to my mother as I wished to do, and I have but this instant got rid of him; but I did not commission either Mr Cartwright or any one else to make a communication to her which I was particularly desirous of making myself.'

'You did not send Mr Cartwright to her?' said Rosalind, colouring, and looking earnestly in his face.

'No, indeed I did not. Did he say I had sent him?'

'How very strange it is,' she replied after a moment's consideration, 'that I should be perfectly unable to say whether he did or did not! I certainly do not remember that he explicitly said "Madam, your son has sent me here;" but this I do remember – that somehow or other I understood that you had done so.'

'And how did he announce to my mother that she . . . I mean, how did he communicate to her the purport of my father's will?'

'Charles Mowbray!' exclaimed Rosalind passionately, clenching her small hands and stamping her little foot upon the ground – 'I may be a very, very wicked girl: I know I am wilful, headstrong, obstinate, and vain; and call me also dark-minded, suspicious, what you will; but I do hate that man!'

'Hate whom, Rosalind?' said Charles, inexpressibly astonished at her vehemence. 'What is it you mean? . . . Is it Mr Cartwright, our good friendly clergyman, that you hate so bitterly?'

'Go to your mother, Mr Mowbray. I am little more than seventeen years old, and have always been considered less instructed, and therefore sillier of course than was to be expected even from my age and sex; then will it not be worse than waste of time to inquire what I mean – especially when I confess, as I am bound to do, that I do not well know myself? . . . Go to your mother, Charles, and let her know exactly all you feel. You, at least, have no cause to hide your faults.'

'I will go – but I wish I knew what has so strangely moved you.'

'Ask your sisters – they saw and heard all that I did; at least, they were present here, as I was; – ask them, examine them, but ask me nothing; for I do believe, Charles, that I am less to be depended on than any other person in the world.'

'And why so, my dear Rosalind?' replied Mowbray, almost laughing. 'Do you mean that you tell fibs against your will?'

'Yes. . . . I believe so. At least, I feel strangely tempted to say a great deal more than I positively know to be true; and that is very much like telling fibs, I believe.'

'Well, Rosalind, I will go, for you grow more mysterious every moment: only, remember that I should greatly like to know all the thoughts that come into that strange little head of yours. Will you promise that I shall?'

'No,' was the ungracious reply; and turning away, she left the room by a door that led into a conservatory.

On entering his mother's dressing-room, Mowbray found her seated between her two daughters, and holding a hand of each.

She looked up as he entered: the traces of tears were on her cheeks, and her eyes rested on him with an expression of melancholy reproach such as he had never read in them before.

'My dear, dear mother!' he exclaimed as he approached her, 'has my absence then vexed you so grievously? . . . I could not help it, mother; Sir Gilbert literally made me his prisoner.'

'Sir Gilbert, Charles, might have shown more respect to the memory of the friend he has lost, than by keeping his son to listen to his own wild invectives against the wife that friend so loved and trusted.'

'Whoever has repeated to you the hasty expressions of Sir Gilbert, my dear mother, in such a manner as to leave a painful impression on your mind against him, has not acted well. You know his temper, but you know his heart also; and I should not have thought that it could have been in the power of any one to make you doubt the real friendship of Sir Gilbert for us all.'

'Surely, Charles, it was no symptom of friendship to me, to say that your dear father had made an accursed will!'

'Good heavens! . . . what a strange misrepresentation, mother! . . . and all hanging, as it should seem, upon one little syllable! . . . Our friend, as you well know, is what Rosalind calls a mannish man; he denies the supremacy of woman, and might, and I verily believe did say, that a will which vested power in her must be a cursed will. But we know too well his long-licensed coarseness of expression to greatly marvel at that; but for the solemn and most awful word ac-cursed, believe me, mother, he never said it.'

'It matters little, my dear son, what particular words of abuse Sir Gilbert uttered against me, provided that your heart did not echo them.'

'Mother! dearest mother!' cried Helen, rising and going towards her brother, who seemed petrified at the words he heard, 'how for a single moment could you believe that Charles's heart could echo any word that spoke not honour and love towards you!'

'He might have been mistaken, Helen,' replied her mother with a heavy sigh: 'Charles could not indeed suspect that the mother his dear father so fully trusted should prove unworthy of the trust. — But let us quit this painful theme; and believe me, my children, that the first wish of my heart is to prove myself worthy of his trust and your love.'

'Such words are just what we might expect to hear from you, mother,' said Mowbray, 'were any profession from you to us necessary; but I would gladly forget that you have ever thought such an assurance called for.'

He bent down and kissed her fervently; and then, making a sign to Helen, who seemed about to follow him, that she should remain where she was, he walked out for a couple of hours among the darkest thickets he could find, with more of melancholy feeling than had ever before rested on his spirits.

CHAPTER V

THE ARISTOCRACY OF WREXHILL

There was no longer anything to prevent Charles Mowbray's return to Oxford, and the following day the time of his departure was canvassed, and at length fixed for the early part of the following week. During the few days that intervened, Mrs Mowbray seemed quite to have forgotten their painful conversation respecting the will; she resumed all her former confiding tenderness of manner, and told him, before they parted, that henceforward his liberal allowance would be doubled.

The day preceding his departure was Sunday, and for the first time, since their heavy loss, the whole family appeared at church. They had all dreaded the moment of re-appearing before the eyes of the little village world, and of thus giving public notice, as it were, that they no longer required to be left to mourn in secret: but this painful ceremony came, and was endured, like those that had preceded it; and poor Helen, as she laid her head upon her pillow, exclaimed, 'What is there that we could not bear, and live?'

The sad parting of the next morning having also passed over them, they at once, and by necessity, fell into the mode of life which they were hereafter to pursue. But dreary and heavy was the change that had fallen on them, and it was long ere the mere act of assembling for their daily meals ceased to be a source of suffering – for fearful was the blank left by the absence of the kind, the gentle, the beloved, the venerated being, whose voice was used to speak a blessing and a welcome over every repast. But our natures seize with avidity the healing balm which time and occupation offer: much variety of disposition was, however, manifested in the manner in which each one of the family sought the consolation they needed.

Mrs Mowbray became evidently, though perhaps unconsciously, better both in health and spirits from the time that her neighbours, according to their different ranks, resumed their visits of friendship, civility, and respect. She had testified outwardly, excepting to such an eye as Rosalind's, more intense suffering than any other member of the family. Nor was this in the smallest degree the result of affectation: she felt all, and more than all, that she had ever expressed, and would gladly, for the sake of her poor children, have concealed a part of it, had the fibre of her character permitted her doing so. But she was demonstrative by nature: with great softness and sweetness of temper, was joined that species of weakness which is often said to be the most attractive feature in the female character; – a weakness that induced her to seize gladly and gratefully any hand extended to lead her, and which, while it made her distrust herself, gave most sovereign sway and masterdom to any one ready and willing to supply the strength and decision of purpose which she wanted.

Many female philippics have been penned, I believe, against that manly passion for superiority which leads our masters to covet in a companion chosen for life the temper of mind here described; but I am tempted to think that this longing to possess a being that wants protection, far from demonstrating a disposition prone to tyranny, shows a nature disposed to love and to cherish, in a manner perfectly accordant to the most perfect *beau idéal* of married life. But, on the other hand, there may perhaps be more of fondness than judgment in those who make such mallability of mind their first requisite in a choice so awfully important.

Mrs Mowbray, however, had a thousand good qualities to justify the devoted affection of her husband. Generous, unsuspicious, and confiding, she was almost as incapable of doubting the goodness of others, as of deserving such doubts herself. Though heiress to immense property, no feeling in the slightest degree approaching to pride had even for a single instant swelled her heart; and though good, beautiful, and accomplished, her estimate of herself was lower than that formed of her by any other human being. Her heart was now more than ever opened to every expression of sympathy and kindness, and she experienced the most salutary effects from admitting those who uttered such, yet she was still a mourner in her very heart and soul; and there were moments in which she felt so bitterly that all her youthful affections were buried and every hope of earthly happiness past, that the fair young faces of the three affectionate girls who were ready to devote themselves to her seemed too bright and beautiful to be kept within the influence of her melancholy, and she often sent them from her to their music-room, their flower-gardens, or the Park, with a sort of feverish anxiety, lest their youth and health should be sacrificed to their affection for her.

Helen had all the tenderness with none of the weakness of her mother's character. She soon ceased to speak of her father, except occasionally, when walking or sitting quite alone with Rosalind, when sheltering boughs or thickening twilight might conceal the working features of her face even from her. At such a moment, if some kind caress from her young companion touched unawares the feelings over which she unceasingly kept guard, as if they were a secret treasure too precious to be exposed to vulgar eyes, she would from time to time give way to the sacred pleasure of discoursing on the character of the father she had lost.

But she had resumed all her former occupations, and added to them the far from unpleasing task of imparting to Rosalind much that had either been ill taught or altogether neglected in her early education. This, as well as their daily-increasing affection for each other, kept them much together, without any blameable desertion either of Mrs Mowbray or Fanny: for the former was really wretched if she thought they confined themselves too much to her drawing-room and herself; and the latter was hourly becoming more devoted to solitary study, and to speculations too poetical and sublime to be shared by any one less romantic and imaginative than herself.

The neighbourhood was not a large one: Mowbray Park, and the estate attached to it, stretched itself so far in all directions, that Oakley, the residence of Sir Gilbert Harrington, the nearest landed proprietor, was at the distance of more than a mile. The little village of Wrexhill, however, had one or two pretty houses in it, inhabited by ladies and gentlemen of moderate but independent fortune, with whom the family at the Park associated on terms of intimacy.

Among these, the late Vicar and his family had been the decided favourites of the whole race of Mowbrays, – and most deservedly so; for the father was a man of piety, learning, and most amiable deportment; his wife, a being whose temper, to say nothing of sundry other good qualities, had made her the idol of the whole parish; and his two sons and two daughters, just such sons and daughters as such parents deserved to have. But, as Gregory Dobbs, the old parish clerk, observed after officiating at the funeral of Mr Mowbray, 'Death seemed to have taken a spite against the village of Wrexhill, for within one short month he had mowed down and swept away the two best and *most powerful* men in the parish, and 'twas no easy matter to say how long the inhabitants might be likely to wear mourning.'

The dispersion and departure of the good Vicar's family was an additional misfortune that his parishioners had not looked for. The living, more valuable for its pleasant house and pretty glebe than for its revenue, was in the gift of one who through life had been, not in appearance or profession only, but in most true sincerity the attached friend of the late incumbent; and Edward Wallace, his eldest son, was bred to the church with the express understanding that the next presentation should be his. With this persuasion, the young man's first act on the death of his father was to tell his mother and sisters that they should continue to inhabit the home they had so long loved. But this arrangement was speedily overthrown; for in reply to the letter which announced the death of his father to Sir J.C. Blackhouse, the patron of the living, he received the following answer:

'My dear fellow,

'As the devil would have it, I am now a cabinet minister, and I no more dare give the living to your Tory father's son, than I dare blow up Westminster Hall, or pull the Lord Chancellor's nose in public. I do assure you I am very sorry for this, for I believe you are likely to be as good a man as your excellent father, who, when he was my tutor, had certainly no notion that I should turn out such a first-rate Radical. However, there is no resisting destiny; and so here I am, just going to give my pretty little living to some Reverend Mr Somebody that I don't care a straw about, because my Lord M—— says, that though a bit of a saint, he is a *capital clerical Whig*. I wish, Edward, you'd try to forget all the fusty old nonesense about Church and State, – upon my soul I do. By-gones are by-gones, my dear fellow; and if you could get up a clever pamphlet on the Tithe Laws, or on the Protestant affinities to the Church of Rome, or anything else with a good rich vein of whiggery running through it, I really think I might still be able to do something for you. Do think of this and believe me,

'My dear fellow,
'Very affectionately,
'Your friend,
'J.C. BLACKHOUSE.'

This most unlooked-for disappointment of course banished the Wallace family from Wrexhill; and the regret their departure left was so general, that it would be hardly saying too much to declare that no interference of the Whig government, however personal or tyrannical, ever produced a stronger sensation of disgust in the circle to which its influence extended than this.

It was greatly owing to the influence of Mr Mowbray, that Mr Cartwright, his son and daughter, were visited by the neighbourhood on their arrival; but the obvious injustice and impropriety of treating with indignity and disrespect the clergyman who was placed among them, solely because they would have preferred one of their own choosing, had led the benevolent owner of 'the great house' to banish the painful feelings to which this unpopular appointment had given rise, and before he died, he had the satisfaction of knowing that those who looked up to him as authority had followed his example, and that the new Vicar had been called upon by all the visiting families of Wrexhill.

The handsomest house in the village was inhabited by a widow lady still young enough to be called handsome, and living with sufficient show to be supposed rich. She played a little, sang a little, sketched a little, and talked and dressed a great deal. Some people declared that when she was young, her complexion must have been as beautiful as that of Miss Fanny Mowbray: but these were only the young farmers, who did not know rouge when they saw it. This lady, whose name was Simpson, had one little girl, a pretty little creature of eight years old, who was sometimes petted and played with till she was completely spoiled, and sometimes left in the nursery for days together, while her mamma was absorbed in the perusal of a new novel or the fabrication of a new dress.

At the next turn of the village street was the entrance to a little place of much less pretension, but infinitely prettier, and in better taste: this also was tenanted by a fair widow, who, had she not been surrounded by three daughters, all taller than herself, might have passed for being as young and as handsome as Mrs Simpson. She was, however, as little like her as possible in every other respect, being subject to no caprice, remarkably simple in her dress, and her hair and her cheeks always remaining of the colour that pleased God. This lady had been early left a widow by the gallant and unfortunate Colonel Richards, who lost a life in a skirmish with the native troops of India which might have done honour to his country in a nobler field. What his young widow endured in returning from a remote part of the country to Madras, with her three infants and very little means, had doubtless contributed, with the good gifts born with her, to make her what she was; for there was a firmness and strength of mind enveloped in her miniature frame, which seemed as if her brave husband had bequeathed to her the legacy of his dauntless spirit to sustain her under all the privations and misery his early death left her to encounter alone.

The character of her three girls will be easily understood hereafter.

Mrs Richards's cottage was the only residence in Wrexhill, except the Vicar's, that did not open upon the village street, so that she had no immediate neighbour; but close to the corner of the pretty field that fronted her dwelling and fed her cow, lived a bachelor half-pay officer, who among many other excellent qualities possessed one which made him pre-eminently interesting in her eyes: – he had known Colonel Richards well, and less than half the reverence he felt for his memory has often sufficed to enrich the church of Rome with a saint. It was not Major Dalrymple's fault if the widow of his erstwhile commanding officer had not long ago exchanged her comparative poverty for his very comfortable independence; and considering that he was five years younger than the lady, was the presumptive heir to a noble Scotch cousin who was thought consumptive, played the flute exquisitely, and was moreover a tall and gentlemanly figure, with no other fault imputed to him than a somewhat obstinate pertinacity of attachment to herself, many people both in and out of Wrexhill wondered at her obduracy, especially as she had never been heard to say, even by her most intimate friends, 'that her heart was buried in the grave of her dear Richards.'

The remaining aristocracy of Wrexhill need hardly be enumerated, as they will not make any very considerable figure in the following pages. But there was an attorney, an apothecary, and a schoolmaster. The latter, indeed, was an excellent person, of whom we may hear more in the sequel; but a *catalogue raisonné* of names makes but a dull chapter.

CHAPTER VI

THE PRINCIPAL PERSON IN THE VILLAGE – THE VICAR'S FAMILY

Two days after the Mowbray family appeared at church, the village gentry began to offer their visits of condolence, which, happily however for the tranquillity of the persons chiefly concerned, were performed in the improved manner of modern times; that is to say, every allusion to the recent event being by all but their intimate friends most cautiously avoided by all parties.

The first person who entered the drawing-room was Mrs Simpson. On all occasions, indeed, this lady exerted herself to sustain the position of 'the principal person in the village.' She seldom gave an order for 'the fly,' which, weak as were its own springs, was, in truth, the main-spring of all the rural visitings; she seldom ordered this indispensable commodity without adding to her instructions, 'Pray be punctual, Mr Sims, – I say this for your sake as well as my own; for if the principal person in the village is made to wait, you may depend upon it an opposition will be started immediately, and in that case, you know, I should be obliged to give it my patronage.' In like manner, the butcher and baker in the village, the ruddy-faced milkman out of it, the shoemaker, the dressmaker, the carpenter, the glazier, the dealer in small wares and all wares, were severally and collectively given to understand that Mrs Simpson, as the principal person in the village, had a right to expect the first fruits of their civility, attention, industry, and general stock-in-trade.

Her entrance into the presence of Mrs Mowbray was as pregnant with sentiment and sympathy as the degree of intimacy to which she was admitted would permit. The hand-shaking was performed with a little pressure and a little sigh; every pause in the conversation was made to speak volumes by the sad tone in which the next sentence was spoken: in short, if the minds of Mrs Mowbray, her eldest daughter, and her ward, who kindly volunteered to sustain this ordeal with her, had not been fully occupied by the recent event, almost every word, look, and gesture of the principal person of Wrexhill were calculated to recall it.

Mrs Simpson was accompanied by her pretty little girl, flowered and furbelowed into as near a resemblance to a bantam chicken as it was possible for a pretty little girl to take.

The distance from the village to the Park was almost too great for so young a child to walk, and the poor little thing looked heated, cross, and weary; but her mamma declared that a ramble through those delicious fields was the greatest treat in the world. 'I trust in heaven,' she continued, using her near-sighted eye-glass to look at a drawing which lay on the table, 'that Mimima' (her abbreviation of Jemima,) 'will have my taste for sketching – I like to take her out with me, dear pet, she enjoys it so! but at this lovely season it is the most difficult thing in the world not to sketch as one goes. Indeed, when the mind is preoccupied' – (a sigh) – 'every object, however' – (a pause) – 'I beg your pardon, but it is so difficult——'

'Come to me, Jemima,' said Helen, holding out her hand, 'and let me take your bonnet off.'

The child put up her shoulder and pressed with distressing closeness upon the delicate lilac of her mother's new silk dress.

'It is such a shy puss!' said Mrs Simpson; 'I often think what would become of her' – (a sigh). 'I beg your pardon – but sad thoughts will press——'

'Little girl, do you love eau de Cologne?' said Rosalind, taking a bottle from the table and holding it towards her.

Either the look, the accent, or the action of Rosalind had attraction sufficient to draw the child towards her; when she good-humouredly relieved the glowing cheeks from the stifling encumbrance of a very close pink bonnet and thick green veil, and then copiously bedewed the pretty head with the fragrant and refreshing water.

'Do you like it, dear?'

'Yes, very much; do it again! again!' said the child, laughing aloud.

'Mimima! – what did I tell you, dear? Alas! – young heads – I beg your pardon——' (a sigh). 'You are too good! – I fear you will spoil her, Miss Torrington.'

'I am only trying to cool her a little, ma'am; she looks quite in a fever.'

'She has sported along before me like a little fawn! I brought my maid and the man servant, as I thought they might carry her between them if she was tired; but she would not hear of it – the step of childhood is so elastic! – Alas! – I beg your pardon!――'

'Don't you like to ride *a-cushion*, Miss Jemima?' said Rosalind, struck by the idea of the maid and the man carrying the young lady between them.

'What is that?' inquired the child.

Rosalind laughed a little, and coloured a little, at being obliged to explain herself; but, making the best of it, she took Mimima's little hands and interlaced them with her own, after the most approved manner of preparing to treat somebody with riding *a-cushion*.

No persons resent ridicule so much as those who are perpetually exposing themselves to it. Mrs Simpson out glowed her rouge as she said, 'I did not mean, Miss Torrington, that my servants were to carry the child together, – I really wonder such a very droll idea. – I beg your pardon – but at such a time――'

Miss Torrington looked at her for a moment, and then rose and left the room.

Mrs Simpson saw that she had offended the heiress, and from that moment conceived towards her one of those little feminine antipathies, which if they do not as often lead to daggers and bowls in the higher ranks of society as to black eyes and broken noses in the lower, are nevertheless seldom quite innoxious.

The conversation now began to languish, for the principal person in Wrexhill was decidedly out of humour, and Helen was painfully seeking for what she was to say next, when the door was thrown open, and Mr and Miss Cartwright, and Mr Jacob Cartwright, were announced.

No sudden and unexpected burst of sunshine ever produced a greater change in the aspect of a watery landscape, than the entrance of this party on the countenance of the handsome widow. Had Rosalind been present, she would have found some amusement, or at least some occupation, in seeking to discover whether it were the father or son who possessed this vivifying power. To the pale hollow-eyed daughter she would certainly have attributed no such influence. But as we have not her help to decide the doubt, we must leave the matter to the slower hand of time.

Mr Jacob Cartwright was a tall, straight, young man, but as yet a little inclining to that line of contour, which can only be described by the expressive word lanky. Neither was his hair handsome, for, designated as 'light' by his particular friends and admirers, it was called 'sandy' by the rest of the world. But the young gentleman had a finely-formed mouth, with a very beautiful set of teeth, and a large clear light blue eye, which many persons declared to be beautiful.

This young man was said to resemble greatly the mother he had lost: to his father he was certainly as unlike as possible. Mr Cartwright, though somewhat above the middle height, was shorter than his son, and his person incomparably better built; his features were very regularly handsome, and the habitual expression of his countenance gentle and attractive. His eyes were large, dark, and very beautifully formed, and his hair and beard as black as those of a Spaniard, save here and there a silver line which about the temples began to mix itself with the sable. His mouth and teeth perhaps might have been said to resemble those of his son, had not the expression been so different. In the son these constituted merely a well-formed feature; to the father they seemed to give a power when he spoke that might work wonders either for good or evil.

Henrietta Cartwright resembled neither of them: of the two, she would have been said to be most like her father, because her hair and eyes were dark; but the form of the head and face, and above all, the cynic expression of the mouth, were in perfect contrast to his. Like her brother, she was extremely thin; but she was not proportionably tall, and in her this ascetic form seemed rather the result of ill health than of make. She was moreover deadly pale, and seldom spoke in general society if she could possibly avoid it.

Mrs Mowbray received all the party with cordial kindness. In Helen's manner there was a shade of coldness, especially to the father, whose offered hand she did not appear to see; but the whole trio shared the affectionate greeting of Mrs Simpson.

'How *very* lucky I am to meet you! Such a dismal long walk, all alone! – but now we can return together. How are you, my dear Miss Henrietta? has your headache left you? – No? – Oh, how I grieve to see you suffer so! I need not inquire for you, Mr Jacob – what a picture of youth and activity you are! Mimima, come here. Don't you remember your friend? – don't you remember Mr Jacob Cartwright? – Ah! I thought you could not forget him! You would not be your mother's child, dearest, if you could ever forget kindness.'

In her address to the elder gentleman there seemed to be a little more caution in the expression of her affectionate feelings; but she looked at him, and she listened to him, and more than once repeated what he said, as if to impress the precious words on her memory. In short, from the moment the Vicar and his family entered the room, it was evident the ladies of the Park were completely put

—— '*In non cale;*'

and this, considering the undeviating respect which through life Mrs Simpson had ever paid to wealth and station, was no trifling proof of the sincerity of that friendship which she professed for her new friends.

'I hope your youngest daughter is well, and Miss Torrington also?' said Mr Cartwright.

'Quite well, thank you. Helen, do you know where your sister is?'

'In the library, I believe, mamma.'

'Miss Cartwright, would you not like some refreshment? . . . Do ring the bell, Helen. I am sure, Mrs Simpson, you ought to take some wine-and-water after your long walk.'

It was not difficult to see that this civility was the result of a strong and painful effort on the part of Mrs Mowbray, and Helen was provoked with the whole party for not declining it; but no choice was left her – the bell was rung, and the tray arrived. One comfort she had, and that no trifling one: neither herself nor her mother had any further occasion to seek subjects of conversation; Mrs Simpson took the whole of this troublesome business upon herself, and for the period that the luncheon lasted was so completely engaged in eating and talking, that she had not time for a single sigh.

The two gentlemen and the little girl were very nearly as busily employed as herself; but Miss Cartwright sat silently apart, and a feeling as nearly allied perhaps to curiosity as politeness induced Helen to change her place and seat herself near her.

'Will you not take some refreshment, Miss Cartwright? . . . Let me get you some grapes.'

'I thank you – none.'

'Not even a little soda-water and wine? The morning seems unusually warm.'

'Nothing, I thank you.'

'Are you a great walker?'

'Yes.'

'This is a charming country for it – such a beautiful variety of lanes and fields.'

'I seldom vary my walk.'

'Indeed! And what is the favourite spot you have chosen?'

'The ugliest and most gloomy I could find, that I might be sure of never meeting any one.'

Helen was silenced – she had not courage for another word, and in order to cover her retreat, moved towards the table, and bestowed her attention on the little girl, who, totally forgotten by her mamma, was quaffing long draughts of wine from a tumbler which Mr Jacob had been preparing for himself, but which he had willingly yielded to her, and now seemed waiting for the inevitable effect of such excess with a sort of sly and covert glee that made Helen very angry.

'Your little girl will make herself ill, I am afraid, Mrs Simpson, by the quantity of wine she is taking: I am afraid there is no water with it.'

The lady, who was talking very earnestly in an under tone to Mr Cartwright, started at this appeal, and with a glance of more anger than the age of the child could justify, drew her back from the table and made her stand at some distance from it.

'I really think that it is Mr Jacob Cartwright who should be punished,' said Helen; 'for he knew a great deal more about the matter than the little girl herself.'

'Oh no! . . . naughty little thing!' – said the mamma.

'I am very sorry if I have been the occasion of the little girl's doing what was wrong,' said Mr Jacob slowly and in a very gentle tone. 'I did not think she would have taken so much; and she looked very tired and warm.'

Mrs Simpson made some civil answer, and turned to renew her conversation with the Vicar; but he was gone. She positively started, and looked about her with great interest to discover what had become of him. The windows of the room opened upon the lawn, and though she had not seen his exit, she very naturally guessed that it must have been made in that direction. After rising from the table, and making one or two unmeaning movements about the room, taking up a book and laying it down again without looking at its title, examining a vase on the chimney-piece and a rose on the flower-stand, she gradually drew towards the open window, and after pausing for a half a minute, walked through it upon the grass.

The little girl trotted after her; Mr Jacob followed, probably hoping to see her stagger about a little; and Helen, though sadly vexed at this new device to prolong the tedious visit, could do no less than walk after them.

The conservatory, drawing-room, and library, formed this side of the house, the whole range of windows opening uniformly upon the lawn. As Helen stepped out, she perceived that the party who had preceded her were entering by the window of the library, and she quickly followed them, thinking it probable that Fanny might be startled and vexed at this unexpected interruption, when, as was very likely, she might be in the very act of invoking the 'sacred nine.'

Upon entering the room, however, she found her sister, to her great surprise, conversing earnestly with Mr Cartwright, and appearing to be hardly yet conscious of the presence of the others.

Mrs Simpson gave a little, almost imperceptible toss of the head, at discovering how the gentleman was engaged.

'We could not think whither you had vanished, Mr Cartwright,' said she in her sweetest voice; 'but you really were very lucky to ramble in this direction. Miss Fanny ought to have her picture taken in this fine room, with all her books about her.'

While she said this, Mr Cartwright continued in a whisper to finish what he was addressing to Fanny; and having done so, he turned to the party which followed him, saying, 'The bright verdure of your beautiful lawn, Miss Mowbray, tempted me out; but I hope our intrusion has not disturbed your sister?'

Fanny answered eagerly that she was very glad to see him. At that moment Helen chanced to turn her eyes towards the window by which they entered; when she perceived that Miss Cartwright had followed them. She was, however, more than half concealed by a large orange-tree which stood in a high square box beside the window; but her head was bent forward to look into the room, and a sneer of such very singular expression rested on her lip and in her eye as she looked at her father and Fanny, who were still standing close together, that Helen remained perfectly still, staring at her. In another moment Miss Cartwright changed the direction of her eyes, and encountered those of Helen fixed upon her with a look of unconcealed astonishment; but her own did not sink before them, and she turned away with a smile quite as strange and unintelligible as the look she had bestowed on Fanny.

At length this tedious visit was brought to its conclusion; the bonnet of the tipsy and now very pale little girl was replaced, a number of civil speeches spoken, and the whole party walked off together across the lawn to a gate which was to take them by a short cut through the Park.

'I quite envy Mrs Simpson her walk home!' said Fanny. 'I see she has taken Mr Cartwright's arm: I really do think he is the very handsomest and most agreeable man I ever saw in my life!'

CHAPTER VII

THE FIRST IMPRESSIONS MADE BY MR CARTWRIGHT – LETTER FROM LADY HARRINGTON

The three girls rallied round Mrs Mowbray as soon as the guests had departed, all kindly anxious to see how she bore this first step back into a world so wholly changed for her.

She looked pale, and there was an air of languor and weariness about her: nevertheless, to the great surprise of Helen, she expressed herself much pleased by the visit.

'Mr Cartwright,' said she, 'appears to me to be one of the most amiable men I ever saw; every tone of his voice speaks kindness, and indeed, if he did not speak at all, one look of his has more feeling and pity in it than other people could express by a volume of words.'

'Do you really think so, mamma?' said Helen eagerly, but suddenly stopped herself, aware that in truth she had no grounds whatever for the strong feeling of dislike towards him of which she was conscious. She remembered, too, that her father had expressed himself greatly pleased by the urbanity of his manners, and that the last act of the benign influence he was wont to exercise on those around him had been to conquer the prejudice against him, to which the exclusion of the Wallace family had unjustly given rise. Helen remembered all this in a moment; the colour mounted to her cheeks, and she was silent.

Rosalind, too, was silent at least from words; but her eyes could speak as many volumes at a glance as Mr Cartwright's, and she fixed them for an instant on Helen with a look that told her plainly her prejudices against their new neighbour, however unreasonable, were fully shared by her.

Meanwhile Fanny had thrown her arms round her mother's neck in a sort of rapture at hearing her own opinions confirmed by such authority. 'Oh, how true that is, dearest mamma!' she exclaimed; 'how exactly I feel the same when he speaks to me! . . . Such goodness, such gentleness, so much superiority, yet so much humility! Poor dear Mr Wallace was an excellent good man, certainly, but no more to be compared to Mr Cartwright than I to Hercules!'

'How many times have you seen Mr Cartwright, Fanny?' said Rosalind.

'I have heard him preach three times,' she replied, 'and they were all the most beautiful sermons in the world; and I have seen and spoken to him four times more.'

'Poor Mr Wallace!' said Rosalind. 'It was he who christened you, Fanny; and from that time, to the hour of his death, you seldom passed many days together, I believe, without seeing and receiving affectionate words and kind looks from him: and yet four times speaking to this gentle gentleman has driven the memory of the poor old man from your heart!'

'No, it has not, Rosalind,' replied Fanny, deeply blushing: 'I am sure I did not say that, did I, mamma? – But my loving and remembering Mr Wallace all the days of my life need not make me dislike everybody else, I suppose?'

'It would be a great misfortune to you if it did, Fanny,' said Mrs Mowbray. 'I am delighted to see, both in you and many others, that the violent and most unjustifiable prejudice which was conceived against Mr Cartwright before he was seen and known, is giving way before his amiable and excellent qualities: I have no doubt that he will soon be quite as popular in the parish as Mr Wallace was.'

'And Miss Cartwright, mamma?' said Helen; 'do you think we shall love her as well as we did Emma Wallace?'

'I know nothing whatever of Miss Cartwright as yet, Helen; she appears very shy, but we must try to give her courage, my dear girls. I hope we shall be on terms of as great intimacy with our new clergyman, as with our former one: it was a sort of association that your dear father particularly approved, and that alone is a sufficient reason for our wishing to cultivate it.'

This allusion was too solemn to admit any light conversation to follow it. Mrs Mowbray strolled with Fanny into the conservatory, and Rosalind persuaded Helen that they should find the shrubberies infinitely cooler and more agreeable than the house.

But even under the thickest cover that the grounds could offer, Helen could not be tempted fully to open her heart upon the subject of Mr Cartwright, an indulgence which Rosalind certainly expected to obtain when she proposed the walk; but the name of her father had acted like a spell on Helen, and all that she could be brought positively to advance on the subject of the Cartwright family was, that she did not think Miss Cartwright was shy.

Within the next fortnight nearly every one who claimed a visiting acquaintance with the Mowbray family, both in the village and the neighbourhood round it, had called at the Park.

'All the calling is over now,' said Helen, 'and I am very glad of it.'

'Everybody has been very kind and attentive,' replied her mother, 'and next week we must begin to return their calls. I hope nobody will be offended, for some of them must be left for many days; the weather is very hot, and the horses must not be overworked.'

'I wonder why that charming little person that I fell in love with – the widow, I mean, that lives in the cottage at Wrexhill,' said Rosalind, – 'I wonder she has not been to see you! She appeared to like you all very much.'

'I have thought of that two or three times,' replied Helen. 'I think, if they had any of them been ill, we should have heard it; and yet otherwise I cannot account for such inattention.'

'It is merely accidental, I am sure,' said Mrs Mowbray. 'But there is one omission, Helen, that cuts me to the heart.' Tears burst from her eyes as she spoke.

Poor Helen knew not how to answer: she was well aware that the omission her mother alluded to was that of Sir Gilbert and Lady Harrington; and she knew too the cause of it. Lady Harrington, who, with one of the best hearts in the world, was sometimes rather blunt in her manner of showing it, had sent over a groom with a letter to Helen, her god-daughter and especial favourite, very fully explaining the cause of their not calling, but in a manner that could in no degree enable her to remove her mother's uneasiness respecting it. This letter, which by her ladyship's especial orders was delivered privately into the hands of Helen, ran thus:

'My darling child!

'Can't you think what a way I must be in at being prevented coming to see you? Sir Gilbert excels himself this time for obstinacy and wilfulness. Every breakfast, every dinner, and every tea since it happened, William, and I do nothing but beg and entreat that I may be permitted to go over and see your poor mother! Good gracious! as I tell him, it is not her fault — though God knows I do think just as much as he does, that no man ever did make such a tom-fool of a will as your father. Such a man as Charles! as Sir Gilbert says. 'Twas made at the full of the moon, my dear, and that's the long and the short of it; he was just mad, Helen, and nothing else. But is that any reason that your poor dear mother should be neglected and forsaken this way? God bless her dear soul! she's more like a baby than anything I ever saw, about money; and as to her being an heiress, why I don't believe, upon my honour, that she has ever recollected it from the day she married to the time that your unlucky, poor dear distracted madman of a father threw all her money back at her in this wild way. He had much better have pelted her with rotten eggs, Helen! Such a friend as Sir Gilbert, so warm hearted, so steady, and so true, is not to be found every day — old tiger as he is. But what on earth am I to do about it? I shall certainly go mad too, if I can't get at you; and yet, I give you my word, I no more dare order the coachman to drive me to Mowbray Park than to the devil. You never saw such a tyrannical brute of a husband as Sir Gilbert is making himself about it! And poor William too — he really speaks to him as if he were a little beggar-boy in the streets, instead of a colonel of dragoons. William said last night something very like, "I shall ride over to Wrexhill to-morrow, and perhaps I shall see the family at Mow . . ." I wish you had seen him — I only wish you had seen Sir Gilbert, Helen, for half a moment! — you would never have forgotten it, my dear, and it might have given you a hint as to choosing a husband. Never marry a man with great, wide, open, light-coloured eyes, and enormous black eyebrows, for fear he should swallow you alive some day before you know where you are. "See them!!" roared Sir Gilbert. "If you do, by G——d, sir, I'll leave every sou I have in the world to some cursed old woman myself; but it shan't be to you, madam," turning short round as if he would bite me: — "laugh if you will, but go to Mowbray if you dare!"

'"But are we never to see any of the family again, sir?" said the colonel very meekly. "I never told you so, Colonel Booby," was the reply. "You may see that glorious fellow Charles as often as you will, and the more you see of him the better; and I'll manage if I can, as soon as he has taken this degree that his heart's set upon, to get a commission for him in your regiment; so you need not palaver about my wanting to part you from him. And as for you, my lady, I give you full leave to kidnap the poor destitute, penniless girls if you can; but if I ever catch you doing anything that can be construed into respect or civility to that sly, artful hussy who cajoled my poor friend Mowbray to make that cursed will, may I. . . . You shall see, old lady, what will come of it!"

'Now what on earth can I do, dear darling? I believe your mother's as innocent of cajoling as I am, and that's saying something; and as for your being destitute, sweethearts, you'll have fifty thousand pounds apiece if you've a farthing. I know all about the property, and so does Sir Gilbert too; only the old tiger pretends to believe, just to feed his rage, that your mother will marry her footman, and bequeath her money to all the little footboys and girls that may ensue: for one principal cause of his vengeance against your poor mother is, that she is still young enough to have children. Was there ever such a man! – But here have I, according to custom, scribbled my paper as full as it will hold, and yet have got a hundred thousand more things to say; but it would all come to this, if I were to crawl over a ream. I am miserable because I can't come to see your mother and you, and yet I can't help myself any more than if I were shut up in Bridewell: for I never did do anything that my abominable old husband desired me not to do, and I don't think I could do it even to please you, my pretty Helen; only don't fancy I have forgotten you: but for God's sake don't write to me! I am quite sure I should get my ears boxed.

'Believe me, darling child,
'Your loving friend and godmother,
'JANE MATILDA HARRINGTON.'

'P.S. I am quite sure that the colonel would send pretty messages if he knew what I was about: but I will not make him a party in my sin. I was just going to tell him this morning; but my conscience smote me, and I turned very sublimely away, muttering, in the words of Macbeth – "Be innocent of this, my dearest chuck!"'

This coarse but well-meaning letter gave inexpressible pain to Helen. She dared not show it to her mother, who, she felt quite sure, would consider the unjust suspicions of Sir Gilbert as the most cruel insult: nor could she, after Lady Harrington's prohibition, attempt to answer it, though she greatly wished to do it, in the hope that she might be able to place her mother's conduct and feelings in a proper light. But she well knew that, with all her friend's rhodomontade, she was most devotedly attached to her excellent though hot-headed husband, and that she could not disoblige her more than by betraying a secret which, under the present circumstances, would certainly make him very angry.

But the sight of her mother's tears, and her utter inability to say anything that might console her very just sorrow, inspired Helen with a bold device. To Rosalind only had she shown Lady Harrington's letter, and to Rosalind only did she communicate her project of boldly writing to the enraged baronet himself.

'Do so, Helen,' said Rosalind promptly: 'it is the only measure to pursue – unless indeed you and I were to set off and surprise him by a visit.'

'But my mother? . . .' replied Helen, evidently struck by the advantages of this bolder scheme over her own, – 'what would my mother say to our going?'

'If she knew of it, Helen, I suspect it would lose all favour in Sir Gilbert's eyes, and you would have no chance whatever of softening his rage towards her. The expedition, if undertaken at all, must be a secret one. When he learns it is so, I think it will touch his tough heart, Helen, for he knows, I fancy, that such escapades are not at all in your line. I only hope that he will not find out that I proposed it, as that might lessen your merit in his eyes.'

'No, no, that would do no harm. My doing it would be quite proof enough how near this matter is to my heart.'

'Well, then, Helen, shall we go?'

'Let me sleep upon it, Rosalind. If we do go, it must, I think, be quite early in the morning, so as to have no questions asked before we set out. It is not a long walk. Shall we see if he will give us some breakfast?'

'A most diplomatic project!' replied Rosalind; 'for it will enlist his hospitality on our side, and ten to one but the rough coating of his heart will thaw and resolve itself into a dew, as Fanny would say, by the mere act of administering coffee and hot cakes to us; and then the field is won.'

'I think we will try,' said Helen, smiling with a sort of inward strengthening, from the conviction that such would very probably be the result.

A few more words settled the exact time and manner of the expedition, and the friends parted to dress for dinner.

CHAPTER VIII

MRS RICHARDS AND HER DAUGHTERS – THE TEA-PARTY

On the evening of that day, the three girls for the first time induced Mrs Mowbray to go beyond the limits of the flower-garden, and walk under the avenue of beautiful elms in the Park. The simple and unostentatious tone of her character had influenced all her habits, and Mrs Mowbray was a better and more constant walker than ladies generally who have two or three carriages ready to attend them. She appeared to enjoy the exercise from which for several weeks she had been debarred; and when the end of the avenue was reached, and Fanny almost mechanically opened the wide gate at the bottom of it, her mother passed through it without making any observation, and in truth forgetting at that moment all that happened since she had last done so. The gate opened upon a road, which, according to long established custom, they crossed nearly at right angles, and then mounted and descended half a dozen steps, which conducted them into a wide and beautiful meadow, now fragrant with the new-made hay that several waggons were conveying to augment a lofty rick in a distant corner of it.

It was not till Mrs Mowbray perceived another party seated round the base of a haycock which an empty waggon had nearly reached, that she remembered all the circumstances which made every casual meeting a matter of importance and agitation to her. The group, which seemed a very merry one, retained their places, till two stout haymakers saucily but playfully presented their pitchforks as if to dislodge them. They then started to their feet to the number of five; and the Park family recognised Mrs Richards, her three daughters, and Major Dalrymple.

'I have not seen them yet, Helen!' said Mrs Mowbray with nervous trepidation:– 'how very wrong I have been to come so far!'

'Why so, my dearest mother?' replied Helen. 'I am sure it is less painful to meet thus, than at those dreadful visits in the drawing-room.'

'But they have not called, Helen . . . certainly, we had better go back.'

'Dear mamma, it is not possible,' said Fanny, stepping forward to meet a favourite companion in the youngest Miss Richards: 'you see Rosalind has got to them already.'

It was indeed too late to retreat; nor did the wish to do so last long. Mrs Richards pressed the hand of Rosalind, who had taken hers, but, throwing it off at the same moment, hastened forward to greet the widowed friend she had wanted courage to seek. Her colour was heightened, perhaps, from feeling it possible that the cause of her absence had been mistaken; but large tears trembled in her dark eyes, and when she silently took the hand of Mrs Mowbray and pressed it to her lips, every doubt upon the subject was removed.

Major Dalrymple and the three girls followed; and the first moment of meeting over, the two parties seemed mutually and equally pleased to join. Mrs Richards was the only person in the neighbourhood to whom Rosalind, during her six months' residence in it, had at all attached herself: there was something about her that had fascinated the young heiress's fancy, and the circumstances of her being the only good second in a duet to be found within the circle of the Mowbray Park visitings had completed the charm.

With the two eldest Misses Richards, Helen was on that sort of intimate footing which a very sweet-tempered, unpretending girl of nineteen, who knows she is of some consequence from her station, and is terribly afraid of being supposed to be proud, is sure to be with young ladies of nearly her own age, blessed with most exuberant animal spirits, and desirous of making themselves as agreeable to her as possible.

Louisa and Charlotte Richards were fine, tall, showy young women, with some aspirations after the reputation of talent; but they were neither of them at all like their mother, who was at least six inches shorter than either of them, and aspired to nothing in the world but to make her three children happy.

Little Mary, as her sisters still persisted to call her, approached much nearer to the stature, person, and character of Mrs Richards: she was not quite so *mignonne* in size, but she

> 'Had her features, wore her eye,
> Perhaps some feeling of her heart,'

and was, spite of all the struggles which her mother could make to prevent it, the darling of her eyes and the hope of her heart. Moreover, little Mary was, as we have before hinted, the especial friend of Fanny Mowbray.

The delights of a balmy evening in the flowery month of June – the superadded delights of a hay-field, and above all, the supreme delight of unexpectedly meeting a party of friends, were all enthusiastically descanted upon by the two tall Misses Richards. They had each taken one of Helen's slight arms, and borne her along over the stubble grass with a degree of vehemence which hardly left her breath to speak.

'I do not think mamma is going any farther,' she continued to utter, while Miss Louisa stopped to tie a shoe-string.

'Oh, but you must!' screamed Miss Charlotte, attempting to drag her onward singly.

'Stop, Charlotte! . . . stop!' cried the eldest sister, snapping off the shoe-string in her haste – 'you shall not carry her away from me. What a shame! Isn't it a shame, when it is such an age since we met?'

There is nothing against which it is so difficult to rally, as the exaggerated expression of feelings in which we do not share. The quiet Helen could not lash herself into answering vehemence of joy, and having smiled, and smiled till she was weary, she fairly slipped from her companions and hastened back with all the speed she could make to the tranquil party that surrounded her mother.

The lively young ladies galloped after her, declaring all the way that she was the cruellest creature in the world.

Mrs Mowbray now said that she hoped they would all accompany her home to tea; – a proposal that met no dissenting voice; but it was some time before the whole party could be collected, for Fanny Mowbray and little Mary were nowhere to be seen. Major Dalrymple, however, who was taller even than the Misses Richards, by means of standing upon the last left haycock at length discovered them sitting lovingly side by side under the shelter of a huge lime-tree that filled one corner of the field. He was dismissed to bring them up to the main body, and executed his commission with great gallantry and good-nature, but not without feeling that the two very pretty girls he thus led away captive would much rather have been without him; for as he approached their lair, he perceived not only that they were in very earnest conversation, but that various scraps of written paper lay in the lap of each, which at his approach were hastily exchanged, and conveyed to reticules, pockets, or bosoms, beyond the reach of his eye.

They nevertheless smilingly submitted themselves to his guidance, and in order to prove that he was not very troublesome, Fanny so far returned to their previous conversation as to say,

'We must ask your judgment, Major Dalrymple, upon a point on which we were disputing just before you joined us: which do you prefer in the pulpit – and out of it – Mr Wallace, or Mr Cartwright?'

'You were disputing the point, were you?' he replied. 'Then I am afraid, Miss Fanny, I must give it against you; for I believe I know Mary's opinion already, and I perfectly agree with her.'

'Then I shall say to you, as I say to her,' replied Fanny eagerly, 'that you are altogether blinded, benighted, deluded, and rapt up in prejudice! I have great faith in her sincerity and yours, major; and yet I declare to you, that it does seem to me so impossible for any one to doubt the superiority of Mr Cartwright in every way, that I can hardly persuade myself you are in earnest.'

'What do you mean by *every way*, Miss Fanny? – you cannot surely believe him to be a better man than our dear old vicar?' said the major.

'We can none of us, I think, have any right to make comparisons of their respective goodness – at least not as yet,' replied Fanny. 'When I said *every way*, I meant, in the church and in society.'

'On the latter point I suppose I ought to leave the question to be decided between you, as in all cases of the kind where gentlemen are to be tried, ladies alone, I believe, are considered competent to form the jury; – not that Mary can have much right to pronounce a verdict either, for I doubt if she has ever been in a room with Mr Cartwright in her life.'

'Yes, I have,' said Mary eagerly, 'and he is perfectly delightful!'

'Indeed! – I did not know you had seen him.'

'Yes – we met him at Smith's.'

'Oh! you saw him in a shop, did you? – and even that was sufficient to prove him delightful?'

'Quite enough!' replied Mary, colouring a little as she observed Major Dalrymple smile.

'The more you see of him, the more you will be aware of his excellence,' said Fanny, coming to the aid of her friend, and with an air of gravity that was intended to check the levity of the major. 'I have seen him repeatedly at the Park, Major Dalrymple, and under circumstances that gave sufficient opportunity to show the excellence of his heart, as well as the charm of his friendly, affectionate, and graceful manner.'

'He has certainly been a very handsome man,' said the major.

'Has been!' exclaimed both the girls at once.

'He is still very well-looking,' added the gentleman.

'Well-looking!' was again indignantly echoed by the ladies.

'You do not think the term strong enough? but when a man gets on the wrong side of forty, it is, I think, as much as he can expect.'

'I don't care a farthing what his age may be,' cried Mary; 'do you, Miss Mowbray? . . . If he were a hundred and forty, with that countenance and that manner, I should still think him the handsomest and most perfect person I ever saw.'

'Dear Mary!' replied Fanny affectionately, 'how exactly we feel alike about him! I love you dearly for fighting his battles so warmly.'

'There is surely no fighting in the case,' said Major Dalrymple, laughing, – 'at least not with me. But have a care, young ladies: such perfect conformity of taste on these subjects does not always, I believe, tend to the continuance of female friendship. What a sad thing it would be if those two little hands were some day to set pulling caps between their respective owners!'

'There is not the least danger of any such dismal catastrophe, I assure you. Is there, Mary?'

'Good heavens, no!' replied little Mary in a voice of great indignation. 'What a hateful idea!'

'One reason why it is so delightful to love and admire Mr Cartwright,' rejoined Fanny, 'is, that one may do it, and talk of it too, without any danger that *rational people*, Major Dalrymple, should make a jest of it, and talk the same sort of nonsense that everybody is so fond of doing whenever a lady is heard to express admiration for a gentleman. But we may surely love and admire the clergyman of the parish: indeed I think it is a sort of duty for every one to do so.'

'I assure you,' replied the major, 'that I both loved and admired Mr Wallace exceedingly, and that I shall gladly pay the same homage to his successor as soon as I know him to deserve it. But

"Cautious age, and youth . . ."

you know the song, Mary?'

'I know your meaning, Major Dalrymple: you are always boasting of your age; but I don't know any one but yourself who thinks so very much of . . .'

'. . . My antiquity and my wisdom.'

'Just that. . . . But, good heavens! Fanny Mowbray, who is that to whom your mother is speaking on the lawn?'

'It is Mr Cartwright!' cried Fanny with animation; 'and now, Major Dalrymple, you will have an opportunity of judging for yourself.'

'I fear not,' he replied, taking out his watch; 'it is now eight o'clock, and Mrs Richards seldom walks much after nine.'

The two girls now withdrew their arms, and hastened forward to the group of which Mr Cartwright made one. Fanny Mowbray held out her hand to him, which was taken and held very affectionately for two or three minutes.

'You have been enjoying this balmy air,' said he to her in a voice sweetly modulated to the hour and the theme. 'It is heaven's own breath, Miss Fanny, and to such a mind as yours must utter accents worthy of the source from whence it comes.'

Fanny's beautiful eyes were fixed upon his face, and almost seemed to say,

'When you speak, I'd have you do it ever.'

'I do not think he recollects me,' whispered Mary Richards in her ear: 'I wish you'd introduce me.'

Fanny Mowbray started, but recovering herself, said, 'Mr Cartwright, give me leave to introduce my friend Miss Mary Richards to you. She is one of your parishioners, and one that you will find capable of appreciating the happiness of being so.'

Mr Cartwright extended his pastoral hand to the young lady with a most gracious smile.

'God bless you both!' said he, joining their hands between both of his. 'To lead you together in the path in which we must all wish to go, would be a task that might give a foretaste of the heaven we sought! — You are not little children,' he added, again pressing each of their hands; 'but I may safely say, "of such are the kingdom of heaven."'

He then turned towards Mrs Mowbray, and with a look and tone which showed that though he never alluded to her situation, he never forgot it, he inquired how far she had extended her ramble.

'Much farther than I intended when I set out,' replied Mrs Mowbray. 'But my children, the weather, and the hay, altogether beguiled me to the bottom of Farmer Bennet's great meadow.'

'Quite right, quite right,' replied Mr Cartwright, with something approaching almost to fervour of approbation: 'this species of quiet courage, of gentle submission, is just what I expected from Mrs Mowbray. It is the sweetest incense that you can offer to Heaven; and Heaven will repay it.'

Mrs Mowbray looked up at his mild countenance, and saw a moisture in his eye that spoke more tender pity than he would permit his lips to utter. It touched her to the heart.

Mrs Richards, who was something of a florist, was examining, with the assistance of Rosalind, some new geraniums that were placed on circular stands outside the drawing-room, filling the spaces between the windows. As this occupation had drawn them from the rest of the party from the time Mr Cartwright approached to join it, they had not yet received that gentleman's salutation, and he now went up to them.

'Miss Torrington looks as if she were discoursing of her kindred. Are these fair blossoms the children of your especial care?'

'They are the children of the gardener and the greenhouse, I believe,' she replied carelessly, and stepped on to another stand.

'Mrs Richards, I believe?' said the graceful vicar, taking off his hat to her.

'I hope you are well, Mr Cartwright?' replied the lady, following the steps of Rosalind.

The two eldest Misses Richards were still assiduously besieging the two ears of Helen; but as the subjects of which they discoursed did not always require the same answers, she began to feel considerable fatigue from the exertion necessary for carrying on this double conversation, and was therefore not sorry to see Mr Cartwright approach them, which must, she thought, produce a diversion in her favour. But she found that the parties were still personally strangers to each other; for though his bow was general, his address was only to herself.

'And have you, too, Miss Mowbray, been venturing upon as long a walk as the rest of the party?'

'We have all walked the same distance, Mr Cartwright; but I believe we none of us consider it to be very far. We are all good walkers.'

'I rejoice to hear it, for it is the way to become good Christians.

Where or how can we meet and *meetly* examine the works of the great Creator so well as on the carpet he has spread, and beneath the azure canopy which his hands have reared above us? – The Misses Richards, I believe? May I beg an introduction, Miss Mowbray?'

'Mr Cartwright, Miss Richards – Miss Charlotte Richards,' said Helen, without adding another word.

'I need hardly ask if you are walkers,' said the vicar, as he passed a smiling and apparently an approving glance over their rather remarkable length of limb. 'Your friends, Miss Mowbray, look like young antelopes ready to bound over the fair face of nature; and their eyes look as if there were intelligence within wherewith to read her aright.'

'Mamma is going in to tea, I believe,' said Helen, moving off.

The whole manner and demeanour of the two Misses Richards had changed from the moment Mr Cartwright approached. They became quite silent and demure; but as they followed Helen, one on each side of him, they coloured with pleasure as he addressed a gentle word, first to one, then to the other; and when, after entering the drawing-room, he left them for the purpose of making his farewell bow, or the semblence of it, to Mrs Mowbray, Miss Louisa whispered to Miss Charlotte, 'Little Mary is quite right; he *is* the most delightful man in the world.'

'You are not going to leave us, Mr Cartwright?' said Mrs Mowbray kindly. 'We are going to tea this moment.'

'You are very obliging; but I had no intention of intruding on you thus.'

'Pray do not call it an intrusion. We shall be always most happy to see you. I only wish your son and daughter were with us also.'

'My daughter, thank you, is a sad invalid; and Jacob generally wanders farther afield in such weather as this. . . . Is that gentleman Major Dalrymple? May I ask you to introduce me?'

'I shall have much pleasure in doing so, I am sure. He is a very amiable and estimable person.'

Mrs Mowbray crossed the room towards him, followed by the vicar. The introduction took place, and the two gentlemen conversed together for a few minutes on the ordinary topics of Russia, the harvest, the slave-trade, and reform. On every subject, except the harvest, which Mr Cartwright despatched by declaring that it would be peculiarly abundant, the reverend gentleman expressed himself with an unusual flow of words, in sentences particularly well constructed; yet nevertheless his opinions seemed enveloped in a mist; and when Mrs Richards afterwards asked the major his opinion of the new vicar, he replied that he thought his manners very gentlemanlike and agreeable, but that he did not perfectly remember what opinions he had expressed on any subject.

At first the company seemed inclined to disperse themselves in knots about the room; but by degrees Mr Cartwright very skilfully contrived on one pretence or another, to collect them all round a table that was covered with the usual incitements to talk, and the conversation became general. At least Mr Cartwright was very generally listened to; the major did not speak at all; and the ladies did little more than agree with and applaud from time to time the placid, even, dulcet flow of words which fell like a gentle rivulet from the lips of their new vicar. This description indeed, would not apply quite generally to all the ladies; but the majority in his favour was five to three, and with this advantage, – that whereas his admirers were loud and eloquent in their expressions of approval, the minority contented themselves by preserving silence.

CHAPTER IX

HELEN AND ROSALIND CALL UPON SIR GILBERT HARRINGTON

Helen Mowbray knew that the choleric friend whose gentler feelings she wished to propitiate was an early riser himself, and was never better disposed to be well pleased with others than when they showed themselves capable of following his example. She was therefore anxious to arrive at his house in time to have the conversation she sought, yet dreaded, before nine o'clock, the usual family breakfast-hour; though in the shooting-season Sir Gilbert generally contrived to coax my lady and her housekeeper to have hot rolls smoking on the table by eight. But, luckily for the young ladies' morning repose, it was not shooting-season; and they calculated that if they started about half-past seven, they should have time for their walk, and a reasonably long conversation afterwards, before the breakfast to which they looked as the pacific conclusion of the negotiation should be ready.

At half-past seven, accordingly, the fair friends met at the door of Rosalind's dressing room, and set off, fearless, though unattended, through the shrubberies, the Park, the flowery lanes, and finally, across one or two hay-fields, which separated the two mansions.

Nothing can be better calculated to raise the animal spirits than an early walk in the gay month of June; and on those not accustomed to the elasticity, the freshness, the exhilarating clearness of the morning air, the effect is like enchantment. All the sad thoughts which had of late so constantly brooded round Helen's heart seemed to withdraw their painful pressure, and she again felt conscious of the luxury of life, with youth, health, and innocence, a clear sky, bright verdure, flowery banks, and shady hedgerows, to adorn it.

Rosalind, by an irresistible impulse of gaiety, joined her voice to those of the blackbirds that carolled near her, till she was stopped by Helen's exclaiming, 'Rosalind, I feel courage for anything this morning!'

'Yes,' answered her companion, 'let Sir Gilbert appear in any shape but that of the Vicar of Wrexhill, and I should greet him with a degree of confidence and kindness that I am positive would be irresistible.'

They were now within a short distance of the baronet's grounds, and another step brought their courage to the proof; for on mounting a stepping-stile which had originally been placed for the especial accommodation of the Mowbray ladies, they perceived the redoubtable Sir Gilbert at the distance of fifty paces, in the act of removing an offending dock-root with his spud.

He raised his eyes, and recognising his young visitors, stepped eagerly forward to meet them. To Rosalind, however, though usually a great favourite, he now paid not the slightest attention; but taking Helen in his arms, kissing her on both cheeks and on the forehead, and then looking her in the face very much as if he were going to weep over her, he exclaimed,

'My poor, poor child! . . . Why did not you bring poor Fanny too? . . . You are right to come away, quite right, my dear child: it's dreadful to live in dependance upon any one's caprice for one's daily bread! Your home shall be here, Helen, and Fanny's too, as long as you like. Come, my dear, take my arm: my lady will dance, you may depend upon it, when she sees you, for we have had dreadful work about keeping her from Mowbray! I'd just as soon keep a wild cat in order as your godmother, Helen, when she takes a fancy: but you know, my dear, her going to Mowbray was a thing not to be thought of. You are a good girl to come – it shows that you see the matter rightly. I wish Fanny were here too!'

All this was said with great rapidity, and without pausing for any answer. Meanwhile he had drawn Helen's arm within his, and was leading her towards the house.

Rosalind followed them quietly for a few steps; and then, either moved thereto by the feeling of courage her walk had inspired, or from some latent consciousness of the baronet's partiality to herself, she boldly stepped up and took his arm on the other side.

'God bless my soul, Miss Torrington! . . . by the honour of a knight, I never saw you; nor do I think I should have seen a regiment of young ladies, though they had been all as handsome as yourself, if they had happened to come with my poor dear Helen. It was very good of you to walk over with her, poor little thing! . . . Your fortune is quite safe and independent, my dear, isn't it? Nobody's doing a foolish thing can involve you in any way, can it?'

'Not unless the foolish thing happened to be done by myself, Sir Gilbert.'

'That's a great blessing, my dear, – a very great blessing! . . . And you'll be kind to our two poor girls, won't you, my dear?'

'I have more need that they should be kind to me – and so they are, – and we are all very kind to one another; and if you will be but very kind too, and come and see us all as you used to do, we shall be very happy again in time.'

'Stuff and nonsense, child! . . . You may come here, I tell you, and see me as much as you like, under my own roof, – because I know who that belongs to, and all about it; but I promise you that you will never see me going to houses that don't belong to their right owner, – it would not suit me in the least – quite out of my way; I should be making some devilish blunder, and talking to poor Charles about his estate and his property: – poor fellow! and he not worth sixpence in the world.'

During all this time, Helen had not spoken a word. They had now nearly reached the house; and drawing her arm away, she held out her hand to Sir Gilbert, and said in a very humble and beseeching tone,

'Sir Gilbert! . . . may I speak to you alone for a few minutes?'

'Speak to me, child? – what about? Is it about a sweetheart? Is it about wanting pocket-money, my poor child? – I'm executor to your father's will, you know, Helen, and if you were starving in a ditch, and Fanny in another, and poor Charles begging his bread on the high road, I have not the power of giving either of ye a shilling of his property, though he has left above fourteen thousand a year!'

Sir Gilbert was now lashing himself into a rage that it was evident would render the object of Helen's visit abortive if she attempted to bring it forward now. She exchanged a glance with Rosalind, who shook her head, and the next moment contrived to whisper in her ear, 'Wait till after breakfast.'

Sir Gilbert was now striding up the steps to the hall-door: the two girls silently followed him, and were probably neither of them sorry to see Colonel Harrington coming forward to meet them.

This young man had for the two or three last years seen but little of the Mowbray family, having been abroad during nearly the whole of that time; but he returned with something very like a tender recollection of Helen's having been the prettiest little nymph at fifteen that he had ever beheld, and her appearance at this moment was not calculated to make him think she had lost her delicate beauty during his absence. Her slight tall figure was shown to great advantage by her mourning dress; and the fair and abundant curls that crowded round her face, now a little flushed by exercise and agitation, made her altogether as pretty a creature in her peculiar style as a young soldier would wish to look upon.

The coal-black hair and sparkling dark eyes of Rosalind, her ruby lips and pearl-like teeth, her exquisite little figure, and the general air of piquant vivacity which made her perfectly radiant when animated, rendered her in most eyes the more attractive of the two; but Colonel Harrington did not think so; and giving her one glance of curiosity, – for he had never seen her before, – he decided that neither she, nor any other woman he had ever beheld, could compare in loveliness with his former friend and favourite.

His greeting to Helen was just what might be expected from a man who had known her with great intimacy when she was some half-dozen inches shorter, and who felt the strongest possible desire to renew the acquaintance with as little delay as possible.

'Helen Mowbray!' he exclaimed, springing forward and seizing her hand, 'how delighted I am to see you! How is dear little Fanny? – how is Charles? I trust you have none of you forgotten me!'

Helen blushed deeply at the unexpected ardour of this address from a very tall, handsome, fashionable-looking personage, whose face she certainly would not have recognised had she met him accidentally: but a happy smile accompanied the blush, and he had no reason to regret the politic freedom of his first salutation, which had thus enabled him to pass over an infinity of gradations towards the intimacy he coveted, at one single step placing him at once on the footing of a familiar friend. It was indeed nearly impossible that Helen could be offended by the freedom; for not only was it sanctioned by the long-established union of their two families, but at this moment she could not but be pleased at finding another dear old friend in the garrison, who would be sure to add his influence to that of her godmother, that what she so greatly wished to obtain should not be refused.

Before they reached the breakfast-room, therefore, the most perfect understanding was established between them. Her friend Miss Torrington was gaily introduced, for her heart felt gladdened by this important addition to her supporters in the cause she had undertaken; and she was disposed to believe that Rosalind's proposal to make this alarming visit would turn out to have been one of the most fortunate things that ever happened.

Within the breakfast-room, and approachable by no other access, was a small room, known throughout the mansion, and indeed throughout the neighbourhood also, as 'My Lady's Closet.' This sacred retreat was an oblong room, about eighteen feet by eight; a large and lofty window occupied nearly one end of it, across which was placed a deal-dresser, or table of three feet wide, filling the entire space between the walls. The whole room was lined with shelves and drawers, the former of which were for the most part sheltered by heavy crimson damask curtains. A few small tables stood scattered here and there; and the sole accommodation for sitting consisted of one high stool, such as laundresses use when ironing.

To the door of this apartment Sir Gilbert approached, and there reverently stopped; for by the law of the land, even he, though a pretty extensively privileged personage, was permitted to go no farther, unless licensed by an especial warrant from its mistress.

'My lady,' he said, in the cheerful lusty voice that announces agreeable tidings, – 'My lady, I have brought home company to breakfast.'

'Have you, Sir Knight?' replied Lady Harrington, without turning her head, or otherwise interrupting herself in the performance of some apparently delicate process upon which she was occupied.

'I'd rather have Mrs Lot for a wife than such an incurious old soul as you are!' said the testy baronet. – 'And so you have not even the grace to ask who it is?'

'Why, my dear Sir Tiger, I shall be sure to know within two minutes after Tompkins gives his passing thump to announce that he is carrying in the coffee; then why should I disturb this fairest of the Pentandria class? – my charming high-dried mirabilis?'

'The devil take you, and all your classes, orders, and tribes, to his own hothouse! – I'll be hanged if I don't lock you into your den while I breakfast with her; – you shan't see her at all, by G——d!'

'Mother! mother!' exclaimed the colonel hastily, to anticipate the execution of the threat – 'it is Helen Mowbray!'

'Helen Mowbray!' cried the old lady, thrusting her hot smoothing-iron on one side, and her blossom blotting-paper on the other, while the precious mirabilis fell to the ground; 'Helen Mowbray!' and pushing aside the baronet by no very gentle movement of her tall and substantial person, she rushed forward, and Helen was speedily folded in a very close embrace.

'There, there, there! don't stifle the girl, old lady! – And supposing you were to bestow one little monosyllable of civility upon this pretty creature, Miss Torrington, who stands smiling at us all like an angel, though every soul amongst us is as rude as a bear to her. – I don't believe you ever found yourself so entirely neglected before, my dear?'

'I have never witnessed attention more gratifying to me than that which I have seen displayed this morning,' replied Rosalind.

'You are a good girl, a very good girl, my dear, and I shall always love you for coming over with this poor dear disinherited child.'

'Miss Torrington, I am delighted to see you, now and ever, my dear young lady,' said Lady Harrington, who, when she chose it, could be as dignified, and as courteous too, as any lady in the land.

'You have walked over, I am sure, by the bright freshness of your looks.

Now, then, sit down one on each side of me, that I may be able to see you without hoisting a *lunette d'approche* across this prodigious table.'

'And so, because your ladyship is near-sighted,' said Sir Gilbert, 'William and I are to sit at this awful distance from these beautiful damsels? You are a tiresome old soul as ever lived!'

'And that's the reason you appear so profoundly melancholy and miserable at this moment,' said Lady Harrington, looking with no trifling degree of satisfaction at the radiant good-humour and happiness which the unexpected arrival of Helen had caused to be visible in the countenance of her boisterous husband. 'Do you find William much altered, Helen?' she continued. 'I wonder if any one has had the grace to present Colonel Harrington to Miss Torrington?'

'Helen did me that kind office,' said the colonel, 'and I suppose she must do the same for me to little Fanny. I long to see if she continues as surpassingly beautiful as she was when I took my sad, reluctant leave of Mowbray Park.'

Rosalind immediately became answerable for the undiminished beauty of Fanny, adding to her report on this point a declaration that the whole family were anxious to renew their acquaintance with him.

This was the nearest approach that any of the party ventured to make towards the mention of Mowbray Park or its inhabitants. Nevertheless, the breakfast passed cheerfully, and even without a word from Sir Gilbert in allusion to the destitute condition of Helen, and her brother and sister. But when even the baronet had disposed of his last egg-shell, pushed the ham fairly away from him, and swallowed his last bowl of tea, the beautiful colour of Helen began gradually to deepen; she ceased to speak, and hardly seemed to hear what was said to her.

Rosalind took the hint, and with more tact than is usually found in the possession of seventeen and a half, she said to Lady Harrington,

'If I promise to keep my hands not only from picking and stealing, but from touching, will your ladyship indulge me with a sight of your press, and your boxes, and a volume or two of your *hortus siccus?* for I feel considerable aspirations after the glory of becoming a botanist myself.'

'My ladyship will show you something infinitely more to the purpose, then, if you will come to the hothouse with me,' replied Lady Harrington, rising, and giving an intelligible glance to her son as she did so, which immediately caused him to rise and follow her. 'I cannot take you where I should be sure to overhear them, my dear,' she added in a whisper as she led Rosalind from the room; 'for if my rough diamond should chance to be too rough with her, I should infallibly burst out upon them; and yet I know well enough that I should do nothing but mischief.'

Helen was thus left alone with the kind-hearted but pertinacious baronet. He seemed to have a misgiving of the attack that was about to be opened upon him; for he made a fidgetty movement in his chair, pushed it back, and looked so very much inclined to run away, that Helen saw no time was to be lost, and, in a voice not over-steady, said,

'I want to speak to you, Sir Gilbert, about my dear mamma. I fear from what you said to Charles, and more still by nobody's coming from Oakley to see us, that you are angry with her. – If it is about the will, Sir Gilbert, you do her great injustice: I am very, very sure that she neither wished for such a will, nor knew anything about it.'

'It is very pretty and dutiful in you, Miss Helen, to say so, and to think so too if you can. Perhaps I might have done the same at nineteen; but at sixty-five, child, one begins to know a little better what signs and tokens mean. – There is no effect without a cause, Miss Helen. The effect in this affair is already pretty visible to all eyes, and will speedily become more so, you may depend upon it. The cause may be still hid from babes and sucklings, but not from an old fellow like me, who knew your poor father, girl, before you were hatched or thought of, – and knew him to be both a good and a wise man, who would never have done the deed he did unless under the influence of one as ever near and ever dear to him as your mother.'

'You have known my mother too, Sir Gilbert, for many, many years: – did you ever see in her any symptom of the character you now attribute to her?'

'If I had, Miss Helen, I should not loathe and abominate her hypocrisy as I now do. I will never see her more – for all our sakes: for if I did, I know right well that I could not restrain my indignation within moderate bounds.'

'Then certainly it would be better that you should not see her,' said the weeping Helen: 'for indeed, sir, I think such unmerited indignation would almost kill her.'

'If you knew anything about the matter, child, you would be aware that *merited* indignation would be more likely to disagree with her. Unmerited indignation does one no harm in the world, as I can testify from experience; for my lady is dreadfully indignant, as I dare say you guess, at my keeping her and William away from Mowbray Park: and it's ten to one but you will be indignant too, child; – but I can't help it. I love you all three very much, Helen; but I must do what I think right, for all that.'

'Not indignant, Sir Gilbert; – at least, that would not be the prevailing feeling with me, though a sense of injustice might make it so with my poor mother. What I shall feel will be grief – unceasing grief, if the friend my beloved father most valued and esteemed continues to refuse his countenance and affection to the bereaved family he has left.'

From the time this conversation began, Sir Gilbert had been striding up and down the room, as it was always his custom to do when he felt himself in a rage, or was conscious that he was about to be so. He now stopped opposite Helen; and while something very like tenderness almost impeded his utterance, he said,

'That's trash – damnable false trash! Miss Helen. After what's passed to-day, to say nothing of times past, you must know well enough that I'm not likely to refuse my countenance and affection to your father's children; – bereaved they are, sure enough! You know as well as I do, that I love you all three – for your own sakes, girl, as well as for his; – and your pretending to doubt it, was a bit of trumpery womanhood, Helen, – so never make use of it again: for you see I understand the sex, – and that's just the reason why I like my old woman better than any other *she* in the wide world; – she never tries any make-believe tricks upon me.'

'Believe me, Sir Gilbert,' said Helen, smiling, 'I hate tricks as much as my godmother can: and if it were otherwise, you are the last person I should try them upon. But how can we think you love us, if you will not come near Mowbray?'

'You may think it, and know it, very easily, child, by the welcome you shall always find here. It is very likely that you may not be long comfortable at home; and before it happens, remember I have told you that you shall always have a home at Oakley: but it must not be on condition of bringing your mother with you; for see her I will not, – and there's an end.'

Helen remained silent. She felt painfully convinced that, at least for the present, she should gain nothing by arguing the cause of her mother any further; and after a long pause, during which Sir Gilbert continued to pace up and down before her, she rose, and sighing deeply, said,

'I believe it is time for us to return. – Goodb'ye, Sir Gilbert.'

There was something in the tone of her voice which very nearly overset all the sturdy resolution of the baronet; but instead of yielding to the weakness, as he would have called it, like a skilful general he marched off the field with his colours still flying, and certainly without giving his adversary any reasonable ground to hope for victory.

'They are all in the hothouse, I believe,' said he, walking before Helen to a door of the hall which opened upon the beautiful gardens. 'You have not seen my lady's heaths for many a day, Helen; – she'll be savage if you go without taking a look at them.'

Helen followed without saying a word in reply, for her heart was full; and when she joined the trio who had so considerately left her to the uninterrupted possession of Sir Gilbert's ear, there was no need of any questioning on their part, or answering on hers, to put them all in full possession of the result of the tête-à-tête.

It would be difficult to say which of the three looked most vexed: perhaps Lady Harrington gave the strongest outward demonstrations of what she felt on the occasion.

She glanced frowningly at Sir Gilbert, who looked as if he intended to say something amiable, and seizing upon Helen's two hands, kissed them both, exclaiming, 'Dearest and best! what a heart of flint must that being have who could find the cruel strength to pain thee!'

Colonel Harrington, who, discomposed and disappointed, had thrown himself on a bench, gave his mother a very grateful look for this; while Rosalind, after examining her sad countenance for a moment, pressed closely to her friend and whispered, 'Let us go, Helen.'

Poor Helen had no inclination to delay her departure; and knowing that her partial godmother was fully capable of understanding her feelings, she said, returning her caresses,

'Do not keep me a moment longer, dearest friend, for fear I should weep! and then I am sure he would call it a trick.'

'I will not keep you, Helen,' replied Lady Harrington aloud. 'You have come on a mission of love and peace; and if I mistake not that heavy eye and feverish cheek, you have failed. Poor child! she does not look like the same creature that she did an hour and a half ago – does she, William?'

'Adieu, Lady Harrington!' said Helen, the big tears rolling down her cheeks despite her struggles to prevent them. 'Good morning Colonel Harrington; – farewell, Sir Gilbert!'

'This is d——d hard, Miss Torrington!' said the baronet, turning from Helen's offered hand; 'this is confounded hard! I'm doing my duty, and acting according to my conscience as a man of honour, and yet I shall be made to believe that Nero was a dove, and Bluebeard a babe of grace, compared to me!'

But Miss Torrington being in no humour to answer him playfully, said gravely,

'I am very sorry we broke in upon you so unadvisedly, Sir Gilbert. It is plain our hopes have not been realised.'

The young lady bowed silently to the colonel, and taking a short farewell of Lady Harrington, but one in which mutual kindness was mutually understood, she took the arm of her discomfited friend, and they proceeded towards a little gate in the iron fencing which divided the garden from the paddock in front of the house.

'And you won't shake hands with me, Helen!' said Sir Gilbert, following.

'Do not say so, sir,' replied Helen, turning back and holding out her hand.

'And when shall we see you here again?'

'Whenever you will come and fetch me, Sir Gilbert,' she replied, endeavouring to look cheerful. He took her hand, wrung it, and turned away without speaking.

'Your interdict, sir,' said Colonel Harrington, 'does not, I hope, extend beyond Mowbray Park paling? – I trust I may be permitted to take care of these young ladies as far as the lodges?'

'If you did not do it, you know very well that I should, you puppy!' replied his father: and so saying, he turned into a walk which led in a direction as opposite as possible from that which his ireful lady had chosen.

Colonel Harrington felt that it required some exertion of his conversational powers to bring his fair companions back to the tone of cheerful familiarity which had reigned among them all at the breakfast-table; but the exertion was made, and so successfully, that before the walk was ended a feeling of perfect confidence was established between them. When they were about to part, he said,

'My mother and I shall labour, and cease not, to work our way through the *écorce* to the kernel of my good father's heart; and there we shall find exactly the material we want, of which to form a reconciliation between your mother and him. – Farewell, Helen! – farewell, Miss Torrington! I trust that while the interdict lasts, chance will sometimes favour our meeting beyond the forbidden precincts.'

He stepped foward to open the Park gate for them, shook hands, uttered another 'Farewell!' and departed.

CHAPTER X

MRS MOWBRAY CONSULTS MR CARTWRIGHT UPON THE SUBJECT OF HER LATE
HUSBAND'S WILL

The first person they encountered on entering the house was Fanny.

'Where *have* you been!' she exclaimed. 'My mother is half frightened to death. Do go to her this moment, Helen, to set her heart at ease.'

'Where is she, Fanny?' inquired Helen, with a sigh, as she remembered how little the answers she must necessarily give to the questions she would be sure to ask were likely to produce that effect.

'In her dressing-room, Helen. But where *have* you been?'

'To Oakley.'

'Good gracious, Helen! – and without asking mamma's leave?'

'I did it with a good intention, Fanny. Do you think I was wrong in endeavouring to restore the intimacy that has been so cruelly interrupted? Do you think mamma will be very angry? I am sure it was chiefly for her sake that I went.'

'No, I am sure she will not when you tell her that. But come directly: I do assure you she has been seriously uneasy. Did you find Sir Gilbert very savage, Rosalind?'

'*Pas mal*, my dear.'

Another moment brought them to Mrs Mowbray. 'Thank God!' was her first exclamation on seeing them; and the repetition of Fanny's emphatic 'Where *have* you been?' followed it.

'Dearest mother!' said Helen, fondly embracing her, 'do not chide us very severely, even if we have been wrong; for indeed we meant to be very, very right; and when we set out the expedition appeared to us anything but a pleasant one. We have been to Oakley.'

'I am too thankful at seeing you returned in safety, my dear girls, to be very angry at anything. But do tell me, Helen, what could have induced you to volunteer a visit to the only people who have been unkind to us since your poor father's death?'

'In the hope, mamma, of putting an end to an estrangement which I thought was very painful to you.'

'Dearest Helen! it was just like you! And have you succeeded, my love?'

'No, mamma, I have not.'

Mrs Mowbray coloured.

'And pray, Helen, have they explained to you the cause of their extraordinary and most unfeeling conduct?'

'Do not say *they*, dearest mother! Lady Harrington is greatly distressed at Sir Gilbert's conduct: so is the colonel, who is just come home. Whatever fault there may be, it is Sir Gilbert's alone.'

'Did he, then, explain himself to you?'

Helen remained silent.

'I must request, Helen,' resumed her mother, 'that you make no farther mystery about the Harringtons. I am willing to excuse the strange step you took this morning; but I shall be seriously displeased if you refuse to tell me what passed during your visit. Of what is it that Sir Gilbert accuses me?'

'I pointed out to him, mamma, the injustice of being angry with you because papa made a will that he did not approve.'

'Well, Helen! and what did he say to that?'

'Upon my word, mamma, I could not find a shadow of reason in anything he said.'

'You evade my questions, Helen. I insist upon knowing what it is that Sir Gilbert lays to my charge. – Helen! – do you refuse to answer me?'

'Oh no, mamma! – but you cannot think how painful it would be for me to repeat it!'

'I cannot help it, Helen: you have brought this pain on yourself by your very unadvised visit of this morning. But since you have gone to the house of one who has declared himself my enemy, you must let me know exactly what it is he has chosen to accuse me of; unless you mean that I should imagine you wish to shield him from my resentment because you think him right.'

'Oh, my mother!' cried Helen; 'what a word is that!'

'Well, then, do not trifle with me any longer, but repeat at once all that you heard him say.'

Thus urged, poor Helen stated Sir Gilbert's very unjust suspicions respecting the influence used to induce Mr Mowbray to make the will he had left. It was in vain she endeavoured to modify and soften the accusation, – the resentment and indignation of Mrs Mowbray were unbounded; and Helen had the deep mortification of perceiving that the only result of her enterprise was to have rendered the breach she so greatly wished to repair a hundred times wider than before.

'And this man, with these base and vile suspicions, is the person your father has left as join executor with me! – What a situation does this place me in! Did he make any allusion to this, Helen? – did he say anything of the necessary business that we have, most unfortunately, to transact together?'

'No, mamma, he did not.'

A long silence followed this question and answer. Mrs Mowbray appeared to suffer greatly, and in fact she did so. Nothing could be farther from the truth than the idea Sir Gilbert Harrington had conceived, and its injustice revolted and irritated her to a degree that she never before experienced against any human being. That Helen should have listened to such an accusation, pained her extremely; and a feeling in some degree allied to displeasure against her mingled with the disagreeable meditations in which she was plunged.

'My head aches dreadfully!' she said at last. 'Fanny, give me my shawl and parasol: I will try what a walk in the fresh air will do for me.'

'May I go with you, mamma?' said Helen.

'No, my dear: you have had quite walking enough. Fanny has not been out at all: she may come with me.'

These words were both natural and reasonable, but there was something in them that smote Helen to the heart. She fondly loved her mother, and, for the first time, she suspected that her heart and feelings were not understood.

Mrs Mowbray and Fanny had just walked through the library windows into the garden, when they perceived Mr Cartwright approaching the house. They both uttered an exclamation of pleasure at perceiving him, and Fanny said eagerly, 'He must see us, mamma! Do not let him go all the way round to the hall-door! May we not walk across and meet him?'

'To be sure. Run forward, Fanny; and when he sees you coming to him, he will turn this way.'

She was not mistaken: Fanny had not made three steps in advance of her mother, before Mr Cartwright turned from the road, and passing through a gate in the invisible fence, joined her in a moment.

'How kind this is of you!' said he as he drew near; – 'to appear thus willing to receive again an intruder, whose quick return must lead you to suspect that you are in danger of being haunted by him! And so I think you are, Miss Fanny; and I will be generous enough to tell you at once, that if you greet me thus kindly, I shall hardly know how to keep away from Mowbray Park.'

'But mamma is so glad to see you,' said Fanny, blushing beautifully, 'that I am sure you need not try to keep away!'

Mrs Mowbray now drew near to answer for herself; which she did very cordially, assuring him that she considered these friendly and unceremonious visits as the greatest kindness he could show her.

'It will be long, I think,' said she, 'before I shall have courage sufficient to invite any one to this mournful and sadly altered mansion: but those whose friendship I really value will I trust, have the charity to come to us without waiting for an invitation.'

'I wish I could prove to you, my dear madam,' replied Mr Cartwright with respectful tenderness, 'how fervently I desire to serve you: but, surrounded by old and long-tried friends as you must be, how can a new comer and stranger hope to be useful?'

This was touching a very tender point – and it is just possible that Mr Cartwright was aware of it, as he was present at the reading of the will, and heard Sir Gilbert Harrington's first burst of rage on becoming acquainted with its contents. But Mrs Mowbray had either forgotten this circumstance, or, feeling deeply disturbed at the fresh proof which Helen had brought her of the falling off of an old friend, was disposed to revert anew to it, in the hope of moving the compassion and propitiating the kindness of a new one.

'Alas! my dear sir,' said she feelingly, 'even old friends will sometimes fail us; and then it is that we ought to thank God for such happy accidents as that which has placed near us one so able and kindly willing to supply their place as yourself. – Fanny, my love, the business on which I have to speak is a painful one: go to your sister, dearest, while I ask our kind friend's advice respecting this unhappy business.'

'Goodb'ye then, Mr Cartwright,' said Fanny, holding out her hand to him. – 'But perhaps I shall see you again as you go away, for I shall be in the garden.'

'God bless you, my dear child!' said he fervently, as he led her a few steps towards the shrubberies; 'God bless, and have you in his holy keeping!'

'What an especial blessing have you, my dear friend,' he said, returning to Mrs Mowbray, 'in that charming child! – Watch over her, and guard her from all evil! for she is one who, if guided in that only path which leads to good, will be a saving and a precious treasure to all who belong to her; but if led astray - alas! the guilt that the downfall of so pure a spirit would entail on those whose duty it is to watch over her!'

'She is indeed an excellent young creature!' said the proud mother, whose darling the lovely Fanny had ever been; 'but I think she wants less guiding than any child I ever saw, – and it has always been so. She learned faster than she could be taught; and her temper is so sweet, and her heart so affectionate, that I really do not remember that she has ever deserved a reprimand in her life.'

'May the precepts of her admirable mother ever keep her thus!' said Mr Cartwright, as they seated themselves in the library, into which they had entered. 'But, oh! my dear lady! know you not that it is just such sweet and gifted creatures as your Fanny that the Evil One seeks for his own? – Nay, look not thus terrified, my excellent, my exemplary friend, – look not thus terrified: if it be thus, as most surely it is – if Satan doth indeed first seek to devour those that God seems to mark more especially for his own, think you he has left us without help to resist? My dear, my admirable Mrs Mowbray! yours is the hand appointed to lead this fair and attractive being unspotted through the world. If great – awfully great, as assuredly it is, be the responsibility, great – unspeakably great, will be the reward. Then tremble not, dear friend! watch and pray, and this unmeasurable reward shall be yours!'

Mrs Mowbray, however, did tremble; but her trembling was accompanied by a sweet and well-pleased consciousness of being considered by the excellent man beside her as capable of leading this darling child to eternal happiness and glory. The look, the accent of Mr Cartwright went farther than his words to convince her that he believed this power to be hers, and she gazed at him with something of the reverence and humble love with which Catholics contemplate the effigies of the saints they worship.

'But what was the business, the painful business, my poor friend, upon which you wished to consult me, before that vision of light had drawn all our attention upon herself? What was it, my dear Mrs Mowbray, you wished to say to me?'

'I am hardly justified, I fear, Mr Cartwright, thus early in our acquaintance, in taking up your valuable time in listening to my sorrows and my wrongs; but in truth I have both to bear; and I have at this moment no friend near me to whom I can apply for advice how to proceed with business that puzzles almost as much as it distresses me. May I, then, my dear sir, intrude on your kindness for half an hour, while I state to you the singular predicament in which I am placed?'

'Were it not, as most assuredly it is – were it not, dearest Mrs Mowbray, a true and deep-felt pleasure to me to believe that I might possibly be useful to you, it would be my especial and bounden duty to strive to be so. For what are the ministers of the Most High placed amidst the people? wherefore are their voices raised, so that all should hear them? Is it not, my friend, because their lives, their souls, their bodies, are devoted to the service of those committed by Providence to their care? And, trust me, the minister who would shrink from this is unworthy − utterly unworthy the post to which he has been called. Speak, then, dearest Mrs Mowbray, as to one bound alike by duty and the most fervent good-will to aid and assist you to the utmost extent of his power.'

The great natural gift of Mr Cartwright was the power of making his voice, his eye, and the flexible muscles of his handsome mouth, echo, and, as it were, reverberate and reiterate every word he spoke, giving to his language a power beyond its own. What he now said was uttered rapidly, but with an apparent depth and intensity of feeling that brought tears of mingled gratitude and admiration to the eyes of Mrs Mowbray. After a moment given to this not unpleasing emotion, she said,

'It was from you, Mr Cartwright, if I remember rightly, that I first heard the enactments of my husband's will. When I give you my word, as I now most solemnly do, that I had never during his life the slightest knowledge of what that will was to be, I think you will believe me.'

'Believe you!' exclaimed Mr Cartwright. 'Is there on earth a being sufficiently depraved to doubt an assertion so vouched by you?'

'Oh, Mr Cartwright! if all men had your generous, and, I will say, just confidence in me, I should not now be in the position I am! But Sir Gilbert Harrington, the person most unhappily chosen by Mr Mowbray as joint executor with myself, is persuaded that this generous will was made in my favour solely in consequence of my artful influence over him; and so deeply does he resent this imputed crime, that instead of standing forward, as he ought to do, as the protector and agent of his friend's widow, he loads the memory of that friend with insult, and oppresses me with scorn and revilings, the more bitter because conveyed to me by my own child.'

Mrs Mowbray wept. − Mr Cartwright hid his face with his hands, and for some moments seemed fearful of betraying all he felt. At length he fixed his eyes upon her − eyes moistened by a tear, and in a low, deep voice that seemed to indicate an inward struggle, he uttered, '*Vengeance is mine saith the Lord!*'

He closed his eyes, and sat for a moment silent, − then added, 'Perhaps of all the trials to which we are exposed in this world of temptation, the obeying this mandate is the most difficult! But, like all uttered by its Divine Author, it is blessed alike by its authority and its use. Without it! − my friend! without it, would not my hand be grappling the throat of your malignant enemy? – Without it, should I not even now be seeking to violate the laws of God and man, to bring the wretch who can thus stab an angel woman's breast to the dust before her? But, thanks to the faith that is in me, I *know* that this suspicious heart and cruel soul shall meet a vengeance as much greater than any I could inflict, as the hand that wields it is more powerful than mine! I humbly thank my God for this, and remembering it, turn with chastened spirit from the forbidden task of punishing him, to the far more Christian one of offering aid to the gentle being he would crush. – Was it indeed from the lips of your child, my poor friend, that these base aspersions reached you?'

'It was indeed, Mr Cartwright; and it was this which made them cut so deeply. Poor Helen knew not what she was about when she secretly left her mother's roof to visit this man, in the hope of restoring the families to their former habits of intimacy!'

'Did Helen do this?' said Mr Cartwright with a sort of shiver.

'Yes, poor thing, she did; and perhaps for her pains may have won caresses for herself. But, by her own statement – most reluctantly given, certainly, – she seems to have listened to calumnies against her mother, which I should have thought no child of mine would have borne to hear;' and again Mrs Mowbray shed tears.

'Great God of heaven!' exclaimed Mr Cartwright, fervently clasping his hands, 'wilt thou not visit for these things! – He will, he will, my friend! Dear, tortured Mrs Mowbray, turn your weeping eyes to Heaven! those drops shall not fall in vain. It was your child – a child nurtured in that gentle bosom, who repeated to you this blasphemy? Oh fie! fie! fie! But let us not think of this, – at least, not at this trying moment. Hereafter means must be taken to stay this plague-spot from spreading over the hearts of all whom nature has given to love and honour you. Your pretty, gentle Fanny! she at least will not, I think, be led to listen to any voice that shall speak ill of you: – sweet child! let her be near your heart, and that will comfort you. – But, alas! my poor friend, this maternal disappointment, grievous as it is, will not be all you have to bear from this wretch whom the Most High, for his own good but inscrutable purposes, permits to persecute you. There must be business, my dear Mrs Mowbray, business of great importance that this man must be immediately called upon to execute with you, – the proving the will, for instance; he must either do this, or refuse to act.'

'Would to Heaven he might refuse!' said Mrs Mowbray eagerly; 'what a relief would this be to me, Mr Cartwright! Do you think there would be any possibility of leading him to it?'

'Of leading him, – certainly not; for it is very clear from his conduct that whatever you appeared to wish, *that* he would be averse to do. Your only hope of obtaining what would most assuredly be an especial blessing for you, his formal renunciation of the executorship, would, I think, be from writing to him immediately, and imperatively demanding his joining you forthwith in proving the will. In such a state of mind as he must be in before he would bear to utter his vile suspicions to your daughter, I think it very likely he may refuse.'

'And what would happen then, Mr Cartwright?'

'You must place yourself in the hands of a respectable lawyer, totally a stranger and unconnected with him, and he would put you in the way to prove it yourself; after which he could give you no further trouble of any kind: unless, indeed, your misguided children should continue to frequent his house, and so become the means of wounding your ears and your heart by repeating his calumnies. But this I trust the God of all wisdom and goodness will give you power to prevent.'

'With your help and counsel, Mr Cartwright, I may yet hope to weather the storm that seems to have burst upon me; but indeed it could hardly have burst upon any one less capable of struggling with it! In what language should I write to this cruel man, who has so undeservedly become my enemy?'

'There is no difficulty there, my friend. The shortest and most strictly ceremonious form must be the best.'

Mrs Mowbray drew towards her materials for writing – opened the portfolio, which between its leaves of blotting-paper contained sundry sheets of wire-wove, black-edged post, – placed one of them before her, – took a pen and curiously examined its tip – dipped it delicately in the ink, and finally turned to Mr Cartwright, saying,

'How very grateful I should be if you would have the great kindness to write it for me!'

'But the hand-writing, my dear lady, must be yours.'

'Oh, yes! I know. But it would be so much more satisfactory if you would sketch the form!'

'Then I am sure I will do it most readily.' He drew the paper to him and wrote,

'Mrs Mowbray presents her compliments to Sir Gilbert Harrington, and requests to know on what day it will suit him to meet her and her lawyer in London, for the purpose of proving her late husband's will at Doctors' Commons. The amount of the real property may be ascertained from the rent-roll; that of the personal, by means of papers left by the deceased, and a valuation of the effects made by competent persons. Mrs Mowbray begs leave to intimate that she wishes as little delay as possible to intervene before the completion of this transaction.'

Mr Cartwright turned what he had written towards her saying, 'This is the sort of letter which I should think it advisable to send.'

Mrs Mowbray drew forth another sheet, and transcribed it so rapidly that it might be doubted whether she allowed herself time to read it as she did so.

'And this should be despatched instantly, should it not?' she said, folding and directing it.

'Indeed, I think so.'

'Then will you have the kindness to ring the bell, Mr Cartwright?'

'Bring me a lighted taper, John,' said Mrs Mowbray to the servant who entered: 'and let Thomas get a horse ready to take this letter immediately to Oakley.'

The taper was brought, the letter sealed and delivered, with instructions that the bearer was to wait for an answer.

This important business concluded, Mr Cartwright rose to go, saying, 'You have filled my heart and my head so completely by the communication of Sir Gilbert Harrington's conduct, that I protest to you I do not at this moment recollect why it was I troubled you with a visit this morning. I shall recollect it, I dare say, when I see you no longer; and if I do, you must let me come back before very long to tell you.'

'But whether you recollect it or not,' replied Mrs Mowbray in a plaintive tone, 'I trust you will not let it be long before I see you: otherwise, Mr Cartwright, I shall not know how to proceed when I receive Sir Gilbert's answer.'

This appeal was answered by an assurance, uttered in a tone of the most soothing kindness, that he would never be far from her when she wished him near; and then, with a pastoral and affectionate pressure of her hand, he left her.

Fanny kept her word, and was walking up and down about a dozen yards from that end of the shrubbery which terminated in the road leading to the house. Mr Cartwright looked in that direction as he stepped from the library window, and walking quickly to the spot, conversed with her for several minutes as she stood leaning over the gate. Fanny smiled, blushed, and looked delighted: her hand, too, was pressed with affectionate kindness; and Mr Cartwright returned to his vicarage and his early dinner.

CHAPTER XI

HELEN'S MISERY AT HER MOTHER'S DISPLEASURE – SIR G. HARRINGTON'S LETTER
ON THE SUBJECT OF THE WILL

When Miss Torrington and Helen retreated to the dressing-room appropriated to the former, which was the apartment in which they generally pursued their morning studies, they sat down disconsolately enough to review the results of their enterprise.

'Everything is ten times worse than it was before, Helen!' said her friend; 'and it is all my fault!'

'Your fault? – Oh, no! But I believe we are both of us too young to interfere, with any reasonable hope of doing good, between those who in age and wisdom are so greatly our superiors. Oh, Rosalind! I fear, I fear that my dearest mother is very angry with me!'

'I cannot believe it, Helen. I hardly know how far a dutiful daughter may be permitted to act like a rational human being; but, to the best of my knowledge and belief, your conduct has been such as to ensure you the approbation and gratitude of any mother in the world – at least of any reasonable mother. You know, Helen, how truly fond I have become of my sweet-tempered guardianess. – Is there such a word? – I believe not; – of my guardian, then. During the eight months that I have made one of her family, I have never yet received a harsh word or unkind look from her, though I have not the slightest doubt that I have deserved many: but nevertheless, my own dear Helen, if she should blunder so egregiously as to be really angry with you for acting with such zealous, tender affection as you have done this morning, merely because that obstinate old brute Sir Gilbert was not to be brought to reason; if she should really act thus – which I trust in God she will not – but if she should, I do verily believe, in all sincerity, that I should hate her.'

'No, you would not, – you would not be so unjust, Rosalind. What right had we to volunteer our silly services? What right had I, in particular, to fancy that if Sir Gilbert would not listen to the remonstrances of his excellent and very clever wife, he would listen to mine? – I really am ashamed of my silly vanity and most gross presumption; and if my dear, dearest mother will but forgive me this once, as all naughty children say, I do not believe she will ever have cause to chide me for meddling again. Oh, Rosalind! if she did but know how I love her, she could never have looked so coldly on me as she did when she told me I had had walking enough!'

'I hope you are mistaken; I hope she did not look coldly on you. I hope she is not angry; for if she be . . . I shall go over to the enemy, Helen, as sure as my name is Rosalind, and you may live to see me patting the rough hide of that very shaggy British bull-dog, Sir Gilbert, every time he says something impertinent against your mother.'

'There is one thing,' said Helen, slightly colouring, 'that does in some little degree reconcile me to the unfortunate visit of this morning – and that is . . .'

'The having met Colonel Harrington!' cried Rosalind, interrupting her. 'Is it not so?'

'You are right,' replied her friend composedly. 'William Harrington, when he was simply William Harrington, and not a dashing colonel of dragoons, was kindness itself to me, when I was a puny, fretful girl, that cried when I ought to have laughed. I cannot forget his good-natured protecting ways with me, and I should have been truly sorry if he had left the country again, as I suppose he will soon do, without my seeing him.'

'Truly, I believe you, my dear,' replied Rosalind, laughing. 'And your plain William Harrington, too, seemed as willing to renew the acquaintance as yourself. To tell you the truth, Helen, I thought I saw symptoms of a mighty pretty little incipient flirtation.'

'How can you talk such nonsense, when we have so much to make us sad! Don't you think I had better go and see if mamma is come in, Rosalind? I cannot express to you how miserable I shall be as long as I think that she is angry with me.'

At this moment the bell which announced that the luncheon was ready, sounded, and poor Helen exclaimed, 'Oh, I am so sorry! I ought to have sought her again, before meeting her in this manner. But come! perhaps her dear face will look smilingly at me again: how I will kiss her if it does!'

But the warm heart was again chilled to its very core by the look Mrs Mowbray wore as the two girls entered the room. Fanny was already seated next her. This was a place often playfully contested between the sisters, and Helen thought, as she approached the door, that if she could get it, and once more feel her mother's hand between her own, she should be the happiest creature living.

But nothing could be less alike, than what followed her entrance, to the imaginings which preceded it. Mrs Mowbray was unusually silent to them all, but to Helen she addressed not a single word. This was partly owing to the feeling of displeasure which had recently been so skilfully fastened in her breast, and partly to the anxiety she felt respecting the answer of Sir Gilbert to her note.

In the middle of the silent and nearly untasted meal, the poetical Fanny being in truth the only one who appeared to have much inclination to eat, a salver was presented to Mrs Mowbray, from whence, with a heightened colour and almost trembling hand, she took a note. She instantly rose from table and left the room. Helen rose too, but not to follow her: she could no longer restrain her tears, and it was to hide this from Fanny, and if possible from Rosalind, that she hastened to leave them both, and shut herself in her own chamber to weep alone.

The present emotion of Helen cannot be understood without referring to the manner in which she had hitherto lived with her mother, and indeed to the general habits of the family. Mystery of any kind was unknown among them; and to those who have observed the effect of this, its prodigious influence on the general tone of family intercourse must be well known. To those who have not, it would be nearly impossible to convey in words an adequate idea of the difference which exists in a household where the parents make a secret of all things of important interest, and where they do not. It is not the difference between ease and restraint, or even that more striking still, between sweet and sour tempers in the chief or chiefs of the establishment; it is a thousand times more vital than either. Without this easy, natural, spontaneous confidence, the family union is like a rope of sand, that will fall to pieces and disappear at the first touch of anything that can attract and draw off its loose and unbound particles. But if it be important as a general family habit, it is ten thousand times more so in the intercourse between a mother and her daughters. Let no parent believe that affection can be perfect without it; and let no mother fancy that the heart of her girl can be open to her if it find not an open heart in return. Mothers! if you value the precious deposit of your dear girls' inmost thoughts, peril not the treasure by chilling them with any mystery of your own! It is not in the nature of things that confidence should exist on one side only: it must be mutual.

Never was there less of this hateful mildew of mystery than in the Mowbray family during the life of their father. Whatever were the questions that arose, – whether they concerned the purchase of an estate, or the giving or accepting an invitation to dinner, – whether it were a discussion respecting the character of a neighbour, or the flavour of the last packet of tea, – they were ever and always canvassed in full assembly; or if any members were wanting, it was because curiosity, which lives only by searching for what is hid, lacking its proper aliment, had perished altogether, and so set the listeners free.

This new-born secrecy in her mother struck therefore like a bolt of ice into the very heart of the sensitive Helen. 'Have I lost her for ever!' she exclaimed aloud, though in solitude. 'Mother! mother! – is it to be ever thus! – If this be the consequence of my poor father's will, well might Sir Gilbert deplore it! How happily could I have lived for ever, dependent on her for my daily bread, so I could have kept her heart for ever as open as my own!'

At this period, Helen Mowbray had much suffering before her; but she never perhaps felt a pang more bitter in its newness than that which accompanied the conviction that her mother had a secret which she meant not to communicate to her. She felt the fact to be what it really was, neither more nor less; she felt that it announced the dissolution of that sweet and perfect harmony which had hitherto existed between them.

The note from Sir Gilbert Harrington was as follows:

'Sir Gilbert Harrington presents his compliments to Mrs Mowbray, and
begs to inform her that he has not the slightest intention of ever acting as
executor to the very singular and mysterious document opened in his
presence on the 12th of May last past, purporting to be the last will and
testament of his late friend, Charles Mowbray, Esquire.

'Oakley, June 29th, 1834.'

'The lady had gone to her secret bower' to peruse this scroll; and it was
fortunate perhaps that she did so, for it produced in her a sensation of
anger so much more violent than she was accustomed to feel, that she
would have done herself injustice by betraying it.

Mrs Mowbray had passed her life in such utter ignorance of every kind
of business, and such blind and helpless dependence, first on her
guardians, and then on her husband, that the idea of acting for herself was
scarcely less terrible than the notion of navigating a seventy-four would
be to ladies in general. Her thoughts now turned towards Mr Cartwright,
as to a champion equally able and willing to help and defend her, and she
raised her eyes to Heaven with fervent gratitude for the timely happiness
of having met with such a friend.

That friend had pointed out to her the fault committed by Helen in a
manner that made it appear to her almost unpardonable. To have doubted
the correctness of his judgment on this, or any point, would have been to
doubt the stability of that staff which Providence had sent her to lean
upon in this moment of her utmost need. She doubted him not: and
Helen was accordingly thrust out, not without a pang perhaps, from that
warm and sacred station in her mother's heart that it had been the first
happiness of her existence to fill. Poor Helen! matters were going worse
for her – far worse than she imagined, though she was unhappy and out
of spirits. She believed, indeed, that her mother was really angry; but,
terrible as her forebodings were, she dreamed not that she was already
and for ever estranged.

As soon as the first burst of passionate anger had been relieved by a
solitary flood of tears, Mrs Mowbray called a council with herself, as to
whether she should immediately despatch a messenger to request Mr
Cartwright to call upon her in the evening, or whether she should trust
to the interest he had so warmly expressed, which, if sincere, must bring
him to her, she thought, on the morrow.

After anxiously debating this point for nearly an hour, and deciding
first on one line of conduct, and then on the other, at least six different
times within that period, she at last determined to await his coming; and
concealing the doubts and fears which worried her by confining herself

to her room under pretence of headache, the three girls were left to pass the remainder of the day by themselves, when, as may easily be imagined, the important events of the morning were fully discussed among them.

Fanny, after the motives of the visit to Oakley had been fully explained to her, gave it as her opinion that Helen was wrong in going without the consent of her mother, but that her intention might plead in atonement for it. But her indignation at hearing of the pertinacious obstinacy of Sir Gilbert was unbounded.

'Oh! how my poor father was deceived in him!' she exclaimed. 'He must have a truly bad heart to forsake and vilify my mother at the time she most wants the assistance of a friend. For you know there is business, Helen, relative to the will, and the property, and all that – Sir Gilbert understands it all, – hard-hearted wretch! and I doubt not he thinks he shall crush poor mamma to the dust by thus leaving her, as he believes, without a friend. But, thank God! he will find he is mistaken.'

'What do you mean, Fanny?' said Rosalind sharply.

'I mean, Rosalind, that mamma is *not* without a friend,' replied Fanny with emphasis. 'It has pleased God in his mercy to send her one when she most needed it.'

'I trust that God will restore to her and to us the old, well-known, and trusted friend of my father,' said Helen gravely. 'On none other can we rest our hope for counsel and assistance, when needed, so safely.'

'Even if you were right, Helen,' replied her sister, 'there would be small comfort in your observation. Of what advantage to mamma, or to us, would the good qualities of Sir Gilbert be, if it be his will, as it evidently is, to estrange himself from us? What a contrast is the conduct of Mr Cartwright to his!'

'Mr Cartwright!' cried Rosalind, distorting her pretty features into a grimace that intimated abundant scorn, – 'Mr Cartwright! There is much consolation, to be sure, in what an acquaintance of yesterday can do or say, for the loss of such an old friend as Sir Gilbert Harrington!'

'It would be a sad thing for poor mamma if there were not,' replied Fanny. 'Of what advantage to her, I ask you, is the long standing of her acquaintance with Sir Gilbert, if his caprice and injustice are to make him withdraw himself at such a time as this? – And how unreasonable and unchristian-like would it be, Rosalind, were she to refuse the friendship of Mr Cartwright, because she has not known him as long?'

'The only objection I see to her treating Mr Cartwright as a confidential friend is, that she does not know him at all,' said Rosalind.

'Nor ever can, if she treats him as you do, Miss Torrington,' answered Fanny, colouring. 'I believe Mr Edward Wallace was an especial favourite of yours, my dear; and that perhaps may in some degree account for your prejudice against our good Mr Cartwright. – Confess, Rosalind; – is it not so?'

'He was indeed an especial favourite with me!' replied Rosalind gravely; 'and for the love I bear you all, and more particularly for your sake, Fanny, and your poor mother's, I would give much – much – much, that he were in the place which Mr Cartwright holds.'

'But if mamma is in want of a man to transact her business, why does she not write to Charles and desire him to return?' said Helen. 'The taking his degree a few months later would be of little consequence.'

'Charles?' said Fanny with a smile that seemed to mean a great deal. – 'Charles is one of the most amiable beings in the world, but the most incapable of undertaking the management of business.'

'How can you know anything about it, Fanny?' said Helen, looking at her with surprise.

'I heard Mr Cartwright say to mamma, that Charles was quite a boy, though a very charming one.'

Helen looked vexed, and Rosalind fixed her eyes upon Fanny as if wishing she would say more.

'In short,' continued Fanny, 'if Sir Gilbert chooses to cut us, I don't see what mamma *can* do so proper and so right as to make a friend of the clergyman of the parish.'

Her two companions answered not a word, and the conversation was brought to a close by Fanny's drawing from her pocket, her bag, and her bosom, sundry scraps of paper, on which many lines of unequal length were scrawled; and on these she appeared inclined to fix her whole attention. This was always considered by Helen and Rosalind as a signal for departure: for then Fanny was in a poetic mood; a word spoken or a movement made by those around her produced symptoms of impatience and suffering which they did not like to witness. Their absence was indeed a relief: for pretty Fanny, during the few moments of conversation which she had enjoyed at the gate of the shrubbery in the morning, had promised Mr Cartwright to compose a hymn. To perform this promise to the best of her power, was at this moment the first wish of her heart: for the amiable vicar had already contrived to see some of those numerous offerings to Apollo with which this fairest and freshest of Sapphos beguiled her too abundant leisure. He had pronounced her poetic powers great, and worthy of higher themes than any she had hitherto chosen: it was most natural, therefore, that she should now tax her genius to the utmost, to prove that his first judgment had not been too favourable: so the remainder of that long day passed in melancholy enough *tête-à-tête* between Rosalind and Helen, and in finding rhymes for all the epithets of heaven on the part of Fanny.

CHAPTER XII

MR CARTWRIGHT'S LETTER TO HIS COUSIN – COLONEL HARRINGTON

The intelligent reader will not be surprised to hear that Mr Cartwright did not suffer himself to be long expected in vain on the following morning. Fanny, however, was already in the garden when he arrived; and as it so happened that he saw her as she was hovering near the shrubbery gate, he turned from the carriage-road and approached her.

'How sweetly does youth, when blessed with such a cheek and eye as yours, Miss Fanny, accord with the fresh morning of such a day as this! – I feel,' he added, taking her hand and looking in her blushing face, 'that my soul never offers adoration more worthy of my Maker than when inspired by intercourse with such a being as you!'

'Oh! Mr Cartwright!' cried Fanny, avoiding his glance by fixing her beautiful eyes upon the ground.

'My dearest child! fear not to look at me – fear not to meet the eye of a friend, who would watch over you, Fanny, as the minister of God should watch over that which is best and fairest, to make and keep it holy to the Lord. Let me have that innocent heart in my keeping, my dearest child, and all that is idle, light, and vain shall be banished thence, while heavenward thoughts and holy musings shall take its place. Have you essayed to hymn the praises of your Saviour and your God, Fanny, since we parted yesterday?'

This question was accompanied by an encouraging pat upon her glowing cheek; and Fanny, her heart beating with vanity, shyness, hope, fear, and sundry other feelings, drew the MS containing a fairly-written transcript of her yesterday's labours from her bosom, and placed it in his hand.

Mr Cartwright pressed it with a sort of pious fervour to his lips, and enclosing it for greater security in a letter which he drew from his pocket, he laid it carefully within his waistcoat, on the left side of his person, and as near as possible to that part of it appropriated for the residence of the heart.

'This must be examined in private, my beloved child,' said he solemnly. 'The first attempt to raise such a spirit as yours to God the Saviour in holy song, has to my feelings something as awful in it as the first glad moment of a seraph's wing! . . . Where is your mother, Fanny?'

'She is in the library.'

'Alone?'

'Oh yes! – at least I should think so, for I am sure she is expecting you.'

'Farewell, then, my dear young friend! – Pursue your solitary musing walk; and remember, Fanny, that as by your talents you are marked and set apart, as it were, from the great mass of human souls, so will you be looked upon the more fixedly by the searching eye of God. It is from him you received this talent – keep it sacred to his use, as David did, and great shall be your reward! – Shall I startle your good mother, Fanny, if I enter by the library window?'

'Oh, no! Mr Cartwright – I am sure mamma would be quite vexed if you always went round that long way up to the door, especially in summer, you know, when the windows are always open.'

'Once more, farewell, then!'

Fanny's hand was again tenderly pressed, and they parted.

It would be a needless lengthening of my tale, were I to record all that passed at this and three or four subsequent interviews which took place between the vicar and Mrs Mowbray on the subject of proving the will. Together with the kindest and most soothing demonstrations of rapidly-increasing friendship and esteem, Mr Cartwright conveyed to her very sound legal information respecting what it was necessary for her to do. The only difficulty remaining seemed to arise from Mrs Mowbray's dislike to apply to any friend in London, either for their hospitality or assistance, during the visit it was necessary she should make there for the completion of the business. This dislike arose from the very disagreeable difficulties which had been thrown in her way by Sir Gilbert Harrington's refusing to act. It would have been very painful to her, as she frankly avowed to her new friend, to announce and explain this refusal to any one; and it was therefore finally arranged between them, that he should give her a letter of introduction to a most excellent and trustworthy friend and relation of his, who was distinguished, as he assured her, for being the most honourable and conscientious attorney in London, – and perhaps, as he added with a sigh, the only one who constantly acted with the fear of the Lord before his eyes.

Gladly did Mrs Mowbray accede to this proposal, for in truth it removed a world of anxiety from her mind; and urged as much by a wish to prove how very easy it was to be independent of Sir Gilbert, as by the strenuous advice of Mr Cartwright to lose no time in bringing the business to a conclusion, she fixed upon the following week for this troublesome but necessary expedition.

It may serve to throw a light upon the kind and anxious interest which the Vicar of Wrexhill took in the affairs of his widowed parishioner, if a copy of his letter to his cousin and friend Mr Stephen Corbold be inserted.

To Stephen Corbold, esq. solicitor,

Gray's Inn, London.

'My dear and valued friend and cousin,

'It has at length pleased to God to enable me to prove to you how sincere is the gratitude which I have ever professed for the important service your father conferred upon me by the timely loan of two hundred pounds, when I was, as I believe you know, inconvenienced by a very troublesome claim. It has been a constant matter of regret to me that I should never, through the many years which have since passed, have been able to repay it; but, if I mistake not, the service which I am now able to render you will eventually prove such as fairly to liquidate your claim upon me; and from my knowledge of your pious and honourable feelings, I cannot doubt your being willing to deliver to me my bond for the same, should your advantages from the transaction in hand prove at all commensurate to my expectations.'

[Here followed a statement of the widow Mowbray's business in London, with the commentary upon the ways and means which she possessed to carry that, and all other business in which she was concerned, to a satisfactory conclusion, much to the contentment of all those fortunate enough to be employed as her assistants therein. The reverend gentleman then proceeded thus.]

'Nor is this all I would wish to say to you, cousin Stephen, on the subject of the widow Mowbray's affairs, and the advantages which may arise to you from the connexion which equally, of course, for her advantage as for yours, I am desirous of establishing between you.

'I need not tell *you*, cousin Stephen, who, by the blessing of a gracious Saviour upon your worthy endeavours, have already been able in a little way to see what law is, – I need, not, I say, point out to you at any great length, how much there must of necessity be to do in the management of an estate and of funds which bring in a net income somewhat exceeding fourteen thousand pounds per annum. Now I learn from my excellent friend Mrs Mowbray, that her late husband transacted the whole of this business himself; an example which it is impossible, as I need not remark, for his widow and sole legatee to follow. She is quite aware of this, and, by a merciful dispensation of the Most High, her mind appears to be singularly ductile, and liable to receive such impressions as a pious and attentive friend would be able to enforce on all points. In addition to this great and heavy charge, which it has pleased an all-wise God, doubtless for his own good purposes, to lay upon her, she has also the entire management, as legal and sole guardian of a young Irish heiress, of another prodigiously fine property, consisting, like her own, partly of money in the English funds, and partly in houses and lands in the north part of Ireland. The business connected with the Torrington property is therefore at this moment, as well as everything concerning the widow Mowbray's affairs, completely without any agent whatever; and I am not without hopes, cousin Stephen, that by the blessing of God to usward, I may be enabled to obtain the same for you.

'I know the pious habit of your mind, cousin, and that you, like myself, never see any remarkable occurrence without clearly tracing therein the immediate finger of God. I confess that throughout the whole of this affair; – the sudden death of the late owner of this noble fortune; the singular will he left, by which it all has become wholly and solely at the disposal of his excellent widow; the hasty and not overwise determination to renounce the executorship on the part of this petulant Sir Gilbert Harrington; the accident, or rather series of accidents, by which I have become at once and so unexpectedly, the chief stay, support, comfort, consolation, and adviser of this amiable but very helpless lady; – throughout the whole of this, I cannot, I say, but observe the gracious providence of my Lord, who wills that I should obtain power and mastery even over the things of this world, worthless though they be, cousin Stephen, when set in comparison with those of the world to come. It is my clear perception of the will of God in this matter which renders me willing, – yea, ardent in my desire to obtain influence over the Mowbray family. They are not all, however, equally amiable to the wholesome guidance I would afford them: on the contrary, it is evident to me that the youngest child is the only one on whom the Lord is at present disposed to pour forth a saving light. Nevertheless I will persevere. Peradventure the hearts of the disobedient may in the end be turned to the wisdom of the just; and we know right well who it is that can save from all danger, even though a man went to sea without art; a tempting of Providence which would in my case be most criminal, – for great in that respect has been the mercy of the Lord to his servant, giving unto me that light which is needful to guide us through the rocks and shoals for ever scattered amidst worldly affairs.

'Thus much have I written to you, cousin Stephen, with my own hand, that you might fully comprehend the work that lies before us. But I will not with pen and ink write more unto you, for I trust I shall shortly see you, and that we shall speak face to face.

'I am now and ever, cousin Stephen, your loving kinsman and Christian friend,

'WILLIAM JACOB CARTWRIGHT.

'Wrexhill Vicarage, 9th July, 1834.

'P.S. Since writing the above, the widow Mowbray has besought me to instruct *the gentleman who is to act as her agent* to obtain lodgings for her in a convenient quarter of the town; and therefore this letter will precede her. Nor can she indeed set forth till you shall have written in return to inform her whereunto her equipage must be instructed to drive. Remember, cousin, that the apartments be suitable; and in choosing them recollect that it is neither you nor I who will pay for the same.

Farewell. If I mistake not, the mercy of the Lord overshadows you, my cousin.'

Poor Mrs Mowbray would have rejoiced exceedingly had it been possible for her kind and ever-ready adviser and friend to accompany her to London; but as he did not himself propose this, she would not venture to do it, and only asked him, such as an obedient child might ask a parent, whether he thought she ought to go attended only by a man and a maid servant, or whether she might have the comfort of taking one of her daughters with her.

Mr Cartwright looked puzzled; indeed the question involved considerable difficulties. It was by no means the vicar's wish to appear harsh or disagreeable in his enactments; yet neither did he particularly desire that the eldest Miss Mowbray should be placed in circumstances likely to give her increased influence over her mother: and as to Fanny, his conscience reproached him for having for an instant conceived the idea of permitting one to whom the elective finger of grace had so recently pointed to be removed so far from his fostering care.

After a few minutes of silent consideration, he replied,

'No! my dearest lady, you ought not to be without the soothing presence of a child; and if I might advise you on the subject, I should recommend your being accompanied by Miss Helen, – both because, as being the eldest, she might expect this preference, and because, likewise, I should deem it prudent to remove her from the great risk and danger of falling into the society of your base and injurious enemy during your absence.'

'You are quite right about that, as I'm sure you are about everything, Mr Cartwright. I really would not have Helen see more of Sir Gilbert's family for the world! She has such wild romantic notions about old friendships being better than new ones, that I am sure it would be the way to make terrible disputes between us. She has never yet known the misery of having an old friend turn against her, – nor the comfort, Mr Cartwright, of finding a new one sent by Providence to supply his place!'

'My dearest lady! I shall ever praise and bless the dispensation that has placed me near you during this great trial; – and remember always, that those whom the Lord loveth he chasteneth!'

'Ah! Mr Cartwright, I fear that I have not been hitherto sufficiently mindful of this, and that I have repined where I ought to have blessed. But I trust that a more Christian spirit is now awakened within me, and that henceforward, with your aid, and by the blessing of God upon my humble endeavours, I may become worthy of the privilege I enjoy as being one of your congregation.'

'May the Lord hear, receive, record, and bless that hope!' cried the vicar fervently, seizing her hand and kissing it with holy zeal.

Mrs Mowbray coloured slightly; but feeling ashamed of the weak and unworthy feeling that caused this, she made a strong effort to recover from the sort of embarrassment his action caused, and said, with as much ease as she could assume,

'Rosalind and Fanny are both very young and very giddy, Mr Cartwright. May I hope that during my short absence – which I shall make as short as possible, – may I hope, my kind friend, that you will look in upon them every day?'

'You cannot doubt it! – what is there I would not do to spare you an anxious thought! – They are young and thoughtless, particularly your ward. Miss Torrington is just the girl, I think, to propose some wild frolic – perhaps another visit to Sir Gilbert; and your sweet Fanny is too young and has too little authority to prevent it.'

'Good Heaven! do you think so? Then what can I do?'

'An idea has struck me, my dear friend, which I will mention to you with all frankness, certain that if you disapprove it, you will tell me so with an openness and sincerity equal to my own. – I think that if my staid and quiet daughter Henrietta were to pass the short interval of your absence here, you might be quite sure that nothing gay or giddy would be done:– her delicate health and sober turn of mind preclude the possibility of this; – and her being here would authorize my daily visit.'

'There is nothing in the world I should like so well,' replied Mrs Mowbray. 'Anything likely to promote an intimacy between my young people and a daughter brought up by you must be indeed a blessing to us. Shall I call upon her? – or shall I write the invitation?'

'You are very kind, dear lady! – very heavenly-minded; – but there is no sort of necessity that you should take the trouble of doing either. I will mention to Henrietta your most flattering wish that she should be here during your absence; and believe me, she will be most happy to comply with it.'

'I shall be very grateful to her. – But will it not be more agreeable to her, and for us also, that she should come immediately? I cannot go before Monday – this is Thursday; might she not come to us to-morrow?'

'How thoughtful is that! – how like yourself! – Certainly it will be pleasanter for her, and I will therefore bring her.'

The conversation was here interrupted by the entrance of a servant with a note. But for the better understanding its effect both on the lady and gentleman, it will be necessary to recount one or two circumstances which had occurred to the anti-Cartwright party in the Mowbray family subsequent to their visit to Oakley.

A few days after that which witnessed poor Helen's disgrace, after entering the drawing-room and receiving a hint from her mother (whom she found there in close conclave with the vicar) that she had better take her morning walk, it happened that she and Rosalind, as they were earnestly discoursing of their yesterday's visit, and enjoying the perfect shade of a lane leading to the village of Wrexhill, perceived a horseman approaching them as slowly as it was possible to make a fine horse walk. In the next moment, however, something appeared to have pricked the sides of his intent, as well as those of his horse; for with a bound or two he was close to them, and in the next instant dismounted and by their side.

The gentleman proved to be Colonel Harrington, who immediately declared, with very soldierly frankness, that he had been riding through every avenue leading to Mowbray Park, in the hope of being fortunate enough to meet them.

Rosalind smiled; while Helen, without knowing too well what she said, answered with a deep blush, 'You are very kind.'

Colonel Harrington carefully tied up his reins and so arranged them as to leave no danger of their getting loose; then giving his steed a slight cut with his riding-whip the obedient animal set off at an easy trot for Oakley.

'He knows his way at least as well as I do,' said the Colonel. 'It is my father's old hunter, and I selected him on purpose, that if I were lucky enough to meet you, I might have no trouble about getting rid of him. And now tell me, Helen, how did your mother bear the answer my father sent to her note?'

'An answer from Sir Gilbert? – and to a note from my mother?' said Helen. 'Alas! it was kept secret from me; and therefore, Colonel Harrington, I had rather you should not talk of it to me.'

'It is hardly reasonable that you should insist upon my keeping secret what I have to tell you, Helen, because others are less communicative. The letters he receives and writes are surely my father's business either to impart or conceal, as he thinks best; and he is extremely anxious to learn your opinion respecting your mother's letter, and his answer to it. He certainly did not imagine that they had been kept secret from you.'

'Indeed I have never heard of either.'

'Do you suppose, then, that she has mentioned them to no one?'

Helen did not immediately reply, but Rosalind did. 'I am very particularly mistaken, Colonel Harrington,' said she, 'if the Reverend William Jacob Cartwright, vicar of Wrexhill, and privy counsellor at Mowbray Park, did not superintend the writing of the one and the reading of the other.'

'Do you really think so, Miss Torrington? What do you say, Helen? do you believe this to have been the case?'

'He is very often at the Park,' replied Helen.

'But do you think it possible that Mrs Mowbray would communicate to him what she would conceal from you?' said Colonel Harrington.

This question was also left unanswered by Helen; but Rosalind again undertook to reply. 'You will think me a very interfering person, I am afraid, Colonel Harrington,' said she; 'but many feelings keep Helen silent which do not influence me; and as far as I am capable of judging, it is extremely proper, and perhaps important, that Sir Gilbert should know that this holy vicar never passes a day without finding or making an excuse for calling at the Park. I can hardly tell how it is, but it certainly does happen that these visits generally take place when we – that is, Helen and I – are not in the house; but . . . to confess my sins and make a clear breast at once, I will tell you what I have never yet told Helen, and that is, that I have ordered my maid to find out, if she can, when Mr Cartwright comes. He slipped in, however, through the library window twice yesterday, so it is possible that he may sometimes make good an entry without being observed; for it is impossible that my Judy can be always on the watch, though she is so fond of performing her needlework in that pretty trellised summer-house in the Park.'

'What an excellent vidette you would make, Miss Torrington,' said the young man, laughing. 'But will you tell me, sincerely and without any shadow of jesting, why it is that you have been so anxious to watch the movements of this reverend gentleman?'

'If I talk on the subject at all,' she replied, 'it will certainly be without any propensity to jesting; for I have seldom felt less inclined to be merry than while watching the increasing influence of Mr Cartwright over Mrs Mowbray and Fanny. It was because I remarked that they never mentioned his having called, when I knew he had been there, that I grew anxious to learn, if possible, how constant his visits had become; and the result of my *espionage* is, that no day passes without a visit.'

'But what makes you speak of this as of an evil, Miss Torrington?'

'That is more than I have promised to tell you,' replied Rosalind; 'but, as we *have* become so very confidential, I have no objection to tell you all – and that, remember, for the especial use of Sir Gilbert, who perhaps, if he knew all that I guess, would *not* think he was doing right to leave Mrs Mowbray, in such hands.'

'And what then, Miss Torrington, is there, *as you guess*, against this gentleman?'

Rosalind for an instant looked puzzled; but, by the rapidity with which she proceeded after she began, the difficulty seemed to arise solely from not knowing what to say first. 'There is against him,' said she, 'the having hurried away from hearing the will read to the presence of Mrs Mowbray, and not only announcing its contents to her with what might well be called indecent haste, considering that there were others to whom the task more fitly belonged, and who would have performed it too, had they not been thus forestalled; – not only did he do this, but he basely, and I do believe most falsely, gave her to understand that her son, the generous, disinterested, warm-hearted, Charles Mowbray, had manifested displeasure at it. Further, he has turned the head of poor little Fanny, by begging copies of her verses to send – Heaven knows where; and he moreover has, I am sure, persuaded Mrs Mowbray to think that my peerless Helen is in fault for something – Heaven knows what. He has likewise, as your account of those secret letters renders certain, dared to step between an affectionate mother and her devoted child, to destroy their dear and close union by hateful and poisonous mystery. He has also fomented the unhappy and most silly schism between your pettish father and my petted guardian; and moreover, with all his far-famed beauty and saint-like benignity of aspect, his soft crafty eyes dare not look me in the face. And twelfthly and lastly, I hate him.'

'After this, Miss Torrington,' said the colonel, laughing, 'no man assuredly could be sufficiently hardy to say a word in his defence; – and, all jesting apart,' he added very seriously, 'I do think you have made out a very strong case against him. If my good father sees this growing intimacy between the Vicarage and the Park with the same feelings that you do, I really think it might go farther than any other consideration towards inducing him to rescind his refusal – for he *has* positively refused to act as executor – and lead him at once and for ever to forget the unreasonable cause of anger he has conceived against your mother, Helen.'

'Then let him know it without an hour's delay,' said Helen. 'Dear Colonel Harrington! why did you let your horse go? Walk you must, but let it be as fast as you can, and let your father understand exactly everything that Rosalind has told you; for though I should hardly have ventured to say as much myself, I own that I think she is not much mistaken in any of her conclusions.'

'And do you follow her, Helen, up to her twelfthly and lastly? Do you too *hate* this reverend gentleman?'

Helen sighed. 'I hope not, Colonel Harrington,' she replied; 'I should be sorry to believe myself capable of hating, but surely I do not love him.'

The young ladies, in their eagerness to set the colonel off on his road to Oakley, were unconsciously, or rather most obliviously, guilty of the indecorum of accompanying him at least half the distance; and at last it was Rosalind, and not the much more shy and timid Helen, who became aware of the singularity of the proceeding.

'And where may *we* be going, I should like to know?' she said, suddenly stopping short. 'Helen! is it the fashion for the Hampshire ladies to escort home the gentlemen they chance to meet in their walks? We never do that in my country.'

Colonel Harrington looked positively angry, and Helen blushed celestial rosy red, but soon recovered herself, and said, with that species of frankness which at once disarms quizzing,

'It is very true, Rosalind; we seem to be doing a very strange thing: but we have had a great deal to say that was really important; yet nothing so much so, as leading Colonel Harrington to his father with as little delay as possible. – But now I think we have said all. Good-b'ye, Colonel Harrington: I need not tell you how grateful we shall all be if you can persuade Sir Gilbert to restore us all to favour.'

'The all is but one, Helen; but the doing so I now feel to be very important. Farewell! Take care of yourselves; for I will not vex you, Helen, by turning back again. Farewell!'

The letter which interrupted the tête-à-tête between Mrs Mowbray and the vicar was an immediate consequence of this conversation, and was as follows:–

'Madam,

'Upon a maturer consideration of the possible effects to the family of my late friend which my refusal to act as his executor may produce, I am willing, notwithstanding my repugnance to the office, to perform the duties of it, and hereby desire to revoke my late refusal to do so.

(Signed)
'GILBERT HARRINGTON.

'Oakley, July 12th, 1833.'

'Thank Heaven,' exclaimed Mrs Mowbray as soon as she had read the note, – 'Thank Heaven that I have no longer any occasion to submit myself to the caprices of any man! – And yet,' she added, putting the paper into Mr Cartwright's hands, 'I suppose it will be best for me to accept his reluctant and ungracious offer?'

Mr Cartwright took the paper and perused it with great attention, and more than once. At length he said,

'I trust I did not understand you. What was it you said, dearest Mrs Mowbray, respecting this most insulting communication?'

'I hardly know, Mr Cartwright, what I said,' replied Mrs Mowbray, colouring. 'How can I know what to say to a person who can treat a woman in my painful situation with such cruel caprice, such unfeeling inconsistency?'

'Were I you, my valued friend, I should make the matter very easy, for I should say nothing to him.'

'Nothing? – Do you mean that you would not answer the letter?'

'Certainly: that is what I should recommend as the only mode of noticing it, consistently with the respect you owe yourself.'

'I am sure you are quite right,' replied Mrs Mowbray, looking relieved from a load of difficulty.

'It certainly does not deserve an answer,' said she, 'and I am sure I should not in the least know what to say to him.'

'Then let us treat the scroll as it does deserve to be treated,' said the vicar with a smile. 'Let the indignant wind bear it back to the face of the hard-hearted and insulting writer!'

And so saying, he eagerly tore the paper into minute atoms, and appeared about to consign them to the conveyance he mentioned, but suddenly checked himself, and with thoughtful consideration for the gardener, added,

'But no, we will not disfigure your beautiful lawn by casting these fragments upon it: I will dispose of them on the other side of the fence.'

CHAPTER XIII

MRS MOWBRAY'S DEPARTURE FOR TOWN – AN EXTEMPORARY PRAYER

It was about nine o'clock in the evening of this same day, that Mr Cartwright was seen approaching across the lawn towards the drawing-room windows, – and that not only by Judy, but by the whole family, who were assembled there and preparing to take their tea. His daughter Henrietta was on his arm; yet still she rather followed than walked with him, so evidently did she hang back, while he as evidently endeavoured to quicken his pace and draw her forward.

The eyes of the whole party were attracted to the windows. Mrs Mowbray and Fanny, approaching different sashes, each stepped out to welcome them; while Miss Torrington and Helen were content to watch the meeting from their places on the sofa.

'Did you ever see a man drive a pig to market, Helen?' said Rosalind. 'In my country they do it so much more cleverly! for look you, if that man were half as clever as he thinks himself, he would just go behind the young lady and pull her backwards.'

'I am not quite sure that the scheme would answer in this case,' replied Helen. 'Look at the expression of her face, and I think you will perceive that nothing but a very straightforward pull could induce her to approach at all.'

'Perhaps she is disgusted at her odious father's presumption and forwardness?' cried Rosalind, starting up. 'If that be so, I will patronise her. – Poor thing! look at her eyes; I am positive she has been weeping.'

With this impression, Miss Torrington stepped forward, and, as the party entered, greeted the young lady very kindly: though she hardly appeared to perceive that her father entered with her.

She received in return a look which, with all her acuteness, she found it extremely difficult to interpret. There was a strong and obvious expression of surprise in it; and then, in the faint attempt at a smile about the corners of the mouth, – which attempt, however, was finally abortive, – Rosalind fancied that she traced a movement of gratitude, though not of pleasure; but over every feature a settled gloom seemed to hang, like a dark veil, obscuring, though not quite hiding every emotion.

The difficulty of understanding why and wherefore she looked as she did, was quite enough, with such a disposition as Rosalind's, to make her an object of interest; and therefore, when Mrs Mowbray made her the speech that she was expressly brought to hear, expressive of hope that she would have the great kindness to console that part of her family who were to remain at home by affording them the pleasure of her company, Rosalind relieved her from the immediate necessity of replying, by saying gaily,

'She will and she must, Mrs Mowbray, for we will take her prisoner; but I will promise, as far as I am concerned, that her durance shall be as gentle as possible.'

It was now the vicar's turn to look astonished, which he certainly did in no small degree, and ran some risk of destroying the favourable impression which his daughter's look of misery had created, by saying, in the sweet tone that Miss Torrington relished so little,

'Henrietta, my love – I trust you will be sensible of, and grateful for, the amiable and condescending kindness of this young lady.'

What the gloomy Henrietta answered, Rosalind did not stay to hear; for by a movement of that impatience with which she always listened to all that Mr Cartwright spoke, she turned from him and walked out of the window. She only stayed, however, long enough to gather a bunch of geranium blossoms, which she put into the hand of Henrietta as she placed herself beside her on re-entering.

'Are they not superb, Miss Cartwright?'

Miss Cartwright again answered by a look which once more set all Rosalind's ingenuity at defiance. It now spoke awakened interest, and an almost eager desire to look at and listen to her; but the heavy gloom remained, while her almost total silence gave her an appearance of reserve greatly at variance with the expression which, for a moment at least, she had read in her eyes.

Helen was now, in full assembly, informed for the first time that she was to attend her mother to town. Had this been told her, as everything was wont to be, in the dear seclusion of her mother's dressing-room, she would have hailed the news with joy and gratitude, and believed that it predicted a return of all the happiness she had lost: but now the effect was wholly different; and though she mastered herself sufficiently to send back the tears before they reached her eyes, and to declare, in the gentle voice of genuine unaffected obedience, that she should be delighted if she could be useful to her, the manner of the communication sank deeply and painfully into her heart.

An answer having arrived by return of post from Stephen Corbold, Esq. solicitor, stating that commodious apartments were secured in Wimpole Street, and himself ready, body and spirit, to do the lady's bidding, Mrs Mowbray fixed on the following day for her journey. Miss Cartwright gave one mutter beyond a tacit consent to remain at the Park during her absence, and the party separated; Fanny however declaring, as she wrapped a shawl of her mother's about her head, that she must enjoy the delicious moonlight by accompanying the vicar and his daughter as far as the Park gates.

'And return alone, Fanny?' said her mother.

'Why not, dear lady?' replied Mr Cartwright. 'Her eye will not be raised to the lamp of night without her heart rising also in a hymn to her Lord and Saviour; and I am willing to believe that her remaining for a few moments beside her pastor and her friend, while under its soft influence, will not be likely to make her thoughts wander in a wrong direction.'

'Oh no, Mr Cartwright,' replied the mother; 'I am sure, if you think it right, she shall go.'

At this moment Miss Torrington was giving a farewell shake of the hand to Henrietta; when, instead of receiving from her an answering 'Good night!' something very like a groan smote her ear.

'How very strange!' she exclaimed aloud, after a silence that lasted till the vicar, with Fanny leaning on his arm, and his sulky daughter following, had half traversed the lawn towards the gate that opened upon the drive.

'What is strange, Miss Torrington?' said Mrs Mowbray.

'Almost everything I see and hear, ma'am,' replied the young lady.

'At what hour are we to set off to-morrow, mamma?' inquired Helen.

'At ten o'clock, my dear. You had better give your orders to Curtis to-night, Helen, as to what she is to put up for you. I hope we shall not be obliged to remain in town above two or three days.'

'If you have anything to do in your room to-night, Helen, it is time to betake yourself to it,' observed Rosalind; 'for,' looking at her watch, 'it is very near midnight, though Miss Fanny Mowbray is walking in the Park. – Good night, Mrs Mowbray.' But Mrs Mowbray did not appear to hear her.

'Good night, mamma,' said Helen, approaching to kiss her.

She received a very cold salute upon her forehead, and a 'Good night, Helen,' in a tone that answered to it.

Rosalind took the arm of her friend within hers as they left the room together, and a silent pressure spoke her sympathy; but neither of them uttered a word that night, either concerning Mr Cartwright's increasing influence, or Mrs Mowbray's continued coldness to Helen. They both of them felt more than they wished to speak.

The following morning brought Mr Cartwright and his daughter again to the Park a few minutes before the post-horses arrived for Mrs Mowbray's carriage, and in a few minutes more everything was ready for the departure of the travellers. Helen gave a farewell embrace to Fanny and Rosalind; while the attentive vicar stepped into the carriage before Mrs Mowbray entered it, to see that as many windows were up and as many windows down as she wished, and likewise for the purpose of placing a small volume in the side pocket next the place she was to occupy. He then returned to her side, and as he handed her in, whispered, while he pressed her hand,

'Do not fatigue yourself with talking, my dear friend: it is a great while since you have taken a journey even so long as this. In the pocket next you I have placed a little volume that I wish – oh, how ardently! – that you would read with attention. Will you promise me this?'

'I will,' replied Mrs Mowbray, deeply affected by his earnestness. – 'God bless you!'

'The Lord watch over you!' responded Mr Cartwright with a sigh. He then retreated a step, and Helen sprang hastily into the carriage without assistance; the door was closed, and before the equipage reached the lodges, Mrs Mowbray had plunged into a disquisition on regeneration and faith – the glory of the new birth – and the assured damnation of all who cannot, or do not, attain thereto.

Meanwhile the party left under the shade of the portico looked at each other as if to inquire what they were to do next. On all occasions of morning departure there is generally a certain degree of *désoeuvrement* left with those who remain behind. In general, however, this is soon got over, except by a desperate idler or a very mournful residuary guest; but on the present occasion the usual occupations of the parties were put completely out of joint, and Rosalind, at least, was exceedingly well disposed to exclaim –

> —— 'Accursed spite,
> That ever I was born to set it right.'

She remained stationary for a few minutes, hoping and expecting that the reverend gentleman would depart: but as this did not happen, she quietly re-entered the house and retired to her own dressing-room.

Fanny then made a motion to enter also, but took very hospitable care that it should include both her companions. Mr Cartwright spoke not of going – he even led the way to the library himself, and having closed the door and put down the ever-open sash windows, he turned to Fanny, and, with a smile that might have accompanied a proposal to sing or dance, said,

'My dear Miss Fanny! does not your heart feel full of kind and tender wishes for the safety of your beloved mother during her absence from you?'

'It does indeed!' said Fanny, shaking back her chestnut ringlets.

'Then should we not,' rejoined the vicar, assisting her action by gently putting back her redundant curls with his own hand, – 'should we not, my dear child, implore a blessing upon her from the only source from whence it can come? – should we not ask of her Lord and Saviour to take her into his holy keeping, and guard her from every ill?'

'Oh yes,' replied Fanny, with affectionate earnestness, but by no means understanding his immediate purpose, – 'Oh yes, Mr Cartwright; I am sure I never pray so heartily as when praying for mamma.'

'Then let us kneel before the throne of Jesus and the Lamb!' said he, placing a chair before her, and kneeling down himself at the one that was next to it. Fanny instantly obeyed, covering her face with her hands, while her young heart beat with a timid and most truly pious feeling of fear lest the act was not performed with suitable deference; for hitherto her private devotions had been performed in strict obedience to the solemn and explicit words of Scripture – '*When thou prayest, enter thy closet, and when thou hast shut thy door, pray to thy Father which is in secret; and thy Father which seeth in secret shall reward thee openly.*'

But though conscious that the mode of prayer in which she was now so unexpectedly invited to join was very unlike what she was used to, her unbounded love and admiration for Mr Cartwright rendered it absolutely impossible for her to conceive it wrong, and she prepared herself to pray with all the fervour of her young and ardent spirit.

There was a moment's pause, during which a look was exchanged between the father and daughter unseen by Fanny; but had it met her eye, it would only have appeared to her as a mystery that she was incapable of comprehending. Had Rosalind caught a sight of it she might perhaps have fancied that the glance of the father spoke command, accompanied by direful threatenings, while that of his daughter betrayed disgust and bitterest contempt, mingled with fear.

Mr Cartwright began, almost in a whisper, to utter his extemporary prayer. It first invoked a blessing on *the little knot of united hearts* that now offered their homage to the Lord, and then proceeded to ask, in flowing periods, for exemption from all dangers likely to beset travellers by land

for 'our beloved sister in the Lord who is this day gone forth.' In a tone
somewhat more loud, he went on to implore especial grace for the not
yet awakened soul of the child she led with her; and then, his rich and
powerful voice resounding through the room, his eyes raised to the
ceiling, and his clasped and extended hands stretched out before him, he
burst into an ecstasy of enthusiastic rantings, in which he besought
blessings on the head of Fanny.

It is impossible to repeat such language as Mr Cartwright and those
who resemble him think fit to use in their extemporary devotions,
without offending against that sensitive horror of profanation which
happily still continues to be one of the strongest feelings in the minds of
Christians not converted – *i.e.* perverted from the solemn reverence our
church enjoins in the utterance of every word by which we venture to
approach the Deity. To such, the unweighed flippant use of those
momentous words 'LET US PRAY,' followed, as they often are, by turgid
rantings, and familiar appeals to the most High God, in volumes of rapid,
careless wordiness, is perhaps the most offensive outrage to which their
religious feelings can be exposed. One might be almost tempted to
believe that the sectarians who, rejecting the authorised forms in which
the bishops and fathers of our church have cautiously, reverently, and
succinctly rehearsed the petitions which the Scriptures permit man to
offer to his Creator; – one might, I say, almost be tempted to believe that
these men have so misunderstood the Word of God, as to read: – USE
vain repetitions as the Heathen do, for they SHALL BE *heard for their much
speaking.* But this 'much speaking,' with all its irreverent accompaniments
of familiar phraseology, is an abomination to those who have preserved
their right to sit within the sacred pale of our established church; and as it
is among such that I wish to find my readers, I will avoid, as much as
possible, offending them by unnecessary repetitions of Mr Cartwright's
rhapsodies, preserving only so much of their substance as may be
necessary to the making his character fully understood.

While imploring Heaven to soften the heart of poor Fanny, who knelt
weeping beside him like a Niobe, he rehearsed her talents and good
qualities, earnestly praying that they might not be turned by the Prince
of Darkness into a snare.

'Let not her gift – her shining gift of poesy, O Lord! lead her, as it has
so often done others, to the deepest pit of hell! Let not the gentle and
warm affections of her heart cling to those that shall carry her soul, with
their own, down to the worm that dieth not, and to the fire that cannot
be quenched! Rather, O Lord and Saviour, fix thou her love upon those
who will seek it in thy holy name. May she, O Lord! know to distinguish
between the true and the false, the holy and the unholy!'

'Amen!' was here uttered by Henrietta, but in so low a whisper that only her father's ear caught it. He paused for half a moment, and then continued with still-increasing zeal, so that his voice shook and tears fell from his eyes.

Fanny was fully aware of all this strong emotion; for though she uncovered not her own streaming eyes, she could not mistake the trembling voice that pronounced its fervent blessing on her amidst sobs.

Meanwhile Miss Torrington, who had seated herself before a book in her dressing-room, began to think that she was not acting very kindly towards Fanny, who, she knew, was so nearly childish in her manners as to render the entertaining company a very disagreeable task to her.

'Poor little soul!' she exclaimed: 'between the manna of the father, and the crabbishness of the daughter, she will be done to death if I go not to her rescue.' So she closed her book and hastened to the library.

The sound she heard on approaching the door startled her, and she paused to listen a moment before she entered; for not having the remotest idea that it was the voice of prayer, she really believed that some one had been taken ill, – and the notion of convulsions, blended with the recollection of Henrietta's sickly appearance, took possession of her fancy. She determined, however, to enter; but turned the lock with a very nervous hand, – and on beholding the scene which the opening door displayed, felt startled, awed, and uncertain whether to advance or retreat.

She immediately met Henrietta's eye, which turned towards her as she opened the door, and its expression at once explained the nature of the ceremony she so unexpectedly witnessed. Contempt and bitter scorn shot from it as she slowly turned it towards her father; and a smile of pity succeeded, as she mournfully shook her head, when, for a moment, she fixed her glance upon the figure of Fanny. Had the poor girl for whose especial sake this very unclerical rhapsody was uttered – had she been a few years older, and somewhat more advanced in the power of judging human actions, she must have been struck by the remarkable change which the entrance of Rosalind produced in the language and manner of the vicar. He did not for an instant suspend the flow of his eloquence, but the style of it altered altogether.

'Bless her, Lord! bless this lovely and beloved one!' were the words which preceded the opening of the door, accompanied by the sobbings of vehement emotion. – 'Bless all this worthy family, and all sorts and conditions of men; and so lead them home' . . . &c. were those which followed, – uttered too, with very decent sobriety and discretion.

Rosalind, however, was not quite deceived by this, though far from guessing how perfectly indecent and profane had been the impassioned language and vehement emotion which preceded her appearance.

After the hesitation of a moment, she closed the door, and walking up to the side of Fanny, stood beside her for the minute and a half which it took Mr Cartwright to bring his harangue to a conclusion. He then ceased, rose from his knees, and bowed to the intruder with an air so meek and sanctified, but yet with such a downcast avoidance of her eye withal, that Rosalind shrank from him with ill-concealed dislike, and would instantly have left the room, but that she did not choose again to leave Fanny, who still continued kneeling, beside her, to a repetition of the scene she had interrupted.

'Fanny!' she said, in an accent a little approaching to impatience.

But Fanny heeded her not. Vexed and disgusted at this display of a devotion so unlike the genuine, unaffected, well-regulated piety in which she had been herself brought up, she repeated her call, – adding, as she laid her hand lightly on her shoulder,

'This is not the sort of worship which your excellent father, or good Mr Wallace either, would have approved.'

Fanny now rose from her knees, and the cause of her not doing so before became evident. Her face was as pale as ashes, and traces of violent weeping were visible on her swollen eyelids.

'Good Heaven, Fanny! what can have affected you thus? – What, sir, have you been saying to produce so terrible an effect on Miss Mowbray? The prayers of the church, in the discipline of which she has been most carefully bred up, produce no such paroxysms as these, Mr Cartwright. – Come with me, Fanny, and do endeavour to conquer this extraordinary vehemence of emotion.'

Fanny took her arm; but she trembled so violently that she could scarcely stand.

'Mr Cartwright,' said Rosalind with a burst of indignation that she could not control, 'I must beg of you not to repeat this species of experiment on the feelings of this young lady during the absence of her mother. At her return, she will of course decide upon your continuance, or discontinuance, in the office you have been pleased to assume: but, till then, I must beg, in her name, that we may have no more of this.'

'Oh! Rosalind!' exclaimed Fanny, while a fresh shower of tears burst from her eyes, 'how can you speak so!'

'Tell me, my dear young lady,' said Mr Cartwright, addressing Miss Torrington in a voice of the gentlest kindness, 'did good Mrs Mowbray, on leaving home, place Miss Fanny under your care?'

'No, sir, she did not,' replied Rosalind, a crimson flush of anger and indignation mounting to her cheeks; 'but, being considerably older than Fanny, I deem it my duty to prevent her if possible from again becoming an actor in such a scene as this.'

Fanny withdrew her arm, and clasping her hands together, again exclaimed, 'Oh! Rosalind!'

'Do not agitate yourself, my good child,' said the vicar; 'I shall never suspect you of that hardening of the heart which would lead you to be of those who wish to banish the voice of prayer from the roof that shelters you. Nor shall I,' he continued meekly, but firmly, – 'nor shall I consider myself justified in remitting that care and attention which I promised your excellent mother to bestow on you, because this unhappy young person lifts her voice against the holy duties of my calling. I shall return to you in the evening, and then, I trust, we shall again raise our voices together in praise and prayer.'

So saying, Mr Cartwright took his hat and departed.

The three young ladies were left standing, but not in one group. Miss Cartwright, as soon as released from her kneeling position, had approached a window, and was assiduously paring her nails; Rosalind fixed her eyes upon the floor, and seemed to be resolving some question that puzzled her; and Fanny, after the interval of a moment, left the room.

Miss Torrington approached the window, and said coldly, but civilly, 'I am sorry, Miss Cartwright, to have spoken so sternly to your father, – or rather, for the cause which led me to do so, – but I really considered it as my duty.'

'Oh! pray, ma'am, do not apologise to me about it.'

'I do not wish to offer an apology for doing what I believe to be right; but only to express my sorrow to a guest, in the house that is my home, for having been obliged to say anything that might make her feel uncomfortable.'

'I do assure you, Miss Torrington,' replied the vicar's daughter, 'that my feelings are very particularly independent of any circumstance, accident, or event that may affect Mr Cartwright . . . my father.'

'Indeed!' said Rosalind, fixing on her a glance that seemed to invite her confidence.

'Indeed!' repeated Henrietta, quietly continuing the occupation furnished by her fingers' ends, but without showing any inclination to accept the invitation.

Rosalind was disconcerted. The singularity of Miss Cartwright's manner piqued her curiosity, and though by no means inclined to form a party with her against her father, she had seen enough to convince her that they were far from being on very affectionate terms together. A feeling of pity too, though for sorrows and sufferings suggested chiefly by her own imagination, gave her a kind-hearted inclination for more intimate acquaintance; but she began to suspect that the wish for this was wholly on her side, and not shared in any degree by her companion.

Chilled by this idea, and out of spirits from the prospect of being daily exposed to Mr Cartwright's visits, Rosalind prepared to leave the room; but good-nature, as was usual with her, prevailed over every other feeling, and before she reached the door, she turned and said,

'Is there anything, Miss Cartwright, that I can offer for your amusement? The books of the day are chiefly in our dressing-rooms, I believe – and I have abundance of new music – and in this room I can show you where to find a very splendid collection of engravings.'

'I wish for nothing of the kind, I am much obliged to you.'

'Shall I send Fanny to you? Perhaps, notwithstanding the ocean of tears you have seen her shed, she would prove a much more cheerful companion than I could do at this moment.'

'I do not wish for a cheerful companion,' said Henrietta.

'Is there anything, then, that I can do,' resumed Rosalind, half smiling, 'that may assist you in getting rid of the morning?'

'You may sit with me yourself.'

'May I? – Well, then, so I will. I assure you that I only thought of going because it appeared to me that you did not particularly desire my company.'

'To say the truth, Miss Torrington, I do not think there is anything on earth particularly worth desiring; but your conversation may perhaps be amongst the most endurable. Besides, it is agreeable to look at you.'

'You are very civil,' replied Rosalind, laughing. 'Perhaps you would like me to hold a nosegay in my hand, or to put on a bonnet and feathers, that I might be still better worth looking at.'

'No. – If I had a bunch of flowers before my eyes, I should not want you: no woman can be so beautiful as a collection of flowers. But I shall do very well, I dare say. Nothing, you know, lasts very long.'

'Your father, then, I presume, has taught your thoughts, Miss Cartwright, to fix themselves altogether on a future and a better world.'

'As to a future world, Miss Torrington, I must have better authority than Mr Cartwright's before I pretend to know anything about it: but if there be another, I have very little doubt, I confess, that it must be a better one.'

'We are taught by the highest authority to believe it will be so, for those who deserve it. But I hope your distaste for that which we enjoy at present does not arise from its having been unkind to you.'

'When I was a child,' answered Henrietta, 'I had a kind of sickly longing for kindness; but now that I am older and wiser, I cannot say that I think kindness or unkindness are matters of much consequence.'

'That indeed is a feeling that must put one speedily either above or below sorrow.'

'I am below it.'

'It would be just as easy to say, above, Miss Cartwright; and if you really have reached to a state of such stoical indifference, I rather wonder you should not feel that it sets you above all the poor sensitive souls whom you must see longing for a smile, and trembling at a frown.'

'Because, Miss Torrington, I have constantly felt that in approaching this state of mind I have been gradually sinking lower and lower in my own estimation. I am become so hatefully familiar with sin and wickedness, that I perfectly loathe myself – though assuredly it has ended by giving me a very pre-eminent degree of indifference concerning all that may hereafter happen to me.'

'Is it in your own person,' said Rosalind jestingly, 'that you have become thus familiar with sin?'

'No. It is in that of my father.'

Rosalind started. 'You talk strangely to me, Miss Cartwright,' said she gravely; 'and if you are playing upon my credulity or curiosity, I must submit to it. But if there be any serious meaning in what you say, it would be more generous if you would permit me to understand you. I believe you are aware that I do not esteem Mr Cartwright; an avowal which delicacy would have certainly prevented my making to you, had you not given me reason to suspect——'

' – That I do not very greatly esteem him either,' said Henrietta, interrupting her.

'Exactly so: and as I am deeply interested for the welfare and happiness of the family amongst whom he seems disposed to insinuate himself upon terms of very particular intimacy, I should consider it as a great kindness if you would tell me what his character really is.'

'The request is a very singular one, considering to whom it is addressed,' said Miss Cartwright; 'and besides, I really cannot perceive any reason in the world why I should be guilty of an indecorum in order to do you *a great kindness*.'

'The indecorum, Miss Cartwright, has been already committed,' said Rosalind. 'You have already spoken of your father as you should not have spoken, unless you had some strong and virtuous motive for it.'

'How exceedingly refreshing is the unwonted voice of truth!' exclaimed Henrietta. 'Rosalind Torrington, you are an honest girl, and will not betray me; for I do fear him – coward that I am – I do fear his cruelty, even while I despise his power. I think but lightly,' she continued, 'of the motes that people this paltry world of ours; yet there are gradations amongst us, from the pure-hearted kind fool, who, like you, Rosalind, would wish to spend their little hour of life in doing good, down to the plotting knave who, like my father, Miss Torrington, cares not what mischief he may do, so that his own unholy interest, and unholy joys, may be increased thereby: and so, look you, there are gradations also in my feelings towards them, from very light and easy indifference, down, down, down to the deepest abyss of hatred and contempt. I know not what power you may have here – not much, I should fear; for though you are rich, the Mowbrays are richer: yet it is possible, I think, that if the energy which I suspect makes part of your character be roused, you may obtain some influence. If you do, use it to keep Mr Cartwright as far distant from all you love as you can. Mistrust him yourself, and teach all others to mistrust him. – And now, never attempt to renew this conversation. I may have done you some service – do not let your imprudence make me repent it. Let us now avoid each other, if you please: I do not love talking, and would not willingly be led into it again.'

Miss Cartwright left the room as soon as these words were spoken, leaving Rosalind in a state of mind extremely painful. Through all the strange wildness of Henrietta's manner she thought that she could trace a friendly intention to put her on her guard; but she hardly knew what the mischief was which she feared, and less still perhaps what she could do to guard against it. The most obvious and the most desirable thing, if she could achieve it, was the preventing Mr Cartwright's making the constant morning and evening visits which he threatened; but she felt that her power was indeed small, and, such as it was, she knew not well how to use it.

Having remained for above an hour exactly in the place where Miss Cartwright had left her, inventing and rejecting a variety of schemes for keeping Mr Cartwright from the house during the absence of Mrs Mowbray, she at length determined to write to him, and after a good deal of meditation produced the following note:

'Miss Torrington presents her compliments to Mr Cartwright, and begs to inform him, that having been very strictly brought up by her father, a clergyman of the established church, she cannot, consistently with her ideas of what is right, continue to make her residence in a house where irregular and extempore prayer-meetings are held. She therefore takes this method of announcing to Mr Cartwright, that if he perseveres in repeating at Mowbray Park the scene she witnessed this morning, she shall be obliged to leave the house of her guardian, and will put herself under the protection of Sir Gilbert Harrington till such time as Mrs Mowbray shall return.

'Mowbray Park, 13th July, 1834.'

This note she immediately despatched to the Vicarage by her own footman, who was ordered to wait for an answer, and in the course of an hour returned with the following short epistle:

'Mr Cartwright presents his compliments to Miss Torrington, and respectfully requests permission to wait upon her for a few minutes to-morrow morning.

'Wrexhill Vicarage, July 13th, 1834.'

Nothing could be less like the answer she expected than this note, and she might possibly have been doubtful whether to grant the audience requested, or not, had she not perceived, with very considerable satisfaction, that she had already obtained a remission of the evening rhapsody he had threatened in the morning, which inspired her with reasonable hope that her remonstrance would not prove altogether in vain. She determined therefore to receive Mr Cartwright on the morrow, but did not deem it necessary to send another express to say so, feeling pretty certain that the not forbidding his approach would be quite sufficient to ensure its arrival.

The evening passed in very evident and very fidgety expectation on the part of Fanny, who more than once strolled out upon the lawn, returning with an air of restlessness and disappointment. But Rosalind was in excellent spirits, and contrived to amuse Miss Cartwright, and even elicit an expression of pleasure from her, by singing some of her sweetest native melodies, which she did with a delicacy and perfection of taste and feeling that few could listen to without delight.

CHAPTER XIV

AN INTERVIEW – THE LIME TREE – ROSALIND'S LETTER TO MR MOWBRAY

At about eleven o'clock the following morning, Miss Torrington was informed that Mr Cartwright requested to speak to her for a few minutes in the drawing-room. Henrietta was with her when the message was delivered, and seemed to await her reply with some curiosity.

'I will wait upon him immediately,' was the civil and ready answer; and as Rosalind gave it, and at the same moment rose from her chair to obey the summons, she looked in the face of her companion to see if there were any wish expressed there that the silence so strictly enjoined should be broken. But Miss Cartwright was occupied by a volume of engravings which lay before her, and Rosalind left the room without having met her eye.

It is impossible to imagine a demeanour or address more perfectly gentlemanlike and respectful than those of Mr Cartwright as he walked across the room to receive Miss Torrington. Strong as her feelings were against him, this still produced some effect; and as she seated herself and motioned to him to do the same, her mental soliloquy amounted to this: – 'At any rate, I will listen patiently to what he has to say.'

'I have taken the liberty of requesting to speak to you, Miss Torrington, because I feel persuaded that my conduct and principles have, from some accident, been misunderstood; and I cannot but hope

that it may be in my power to explain them, so as in some degree to
remove the prejudice which I fear you have conceived against me.'

'It is my duty, sir, both as a matter of courtesy and justice, to hear
whatever you wish to say in justification or excuse of the scene I
witnessed yesterday morning. Miss Fanny Mowbray is not yet recovered
from the effects of the agitation into which she was thrown by it; and I
have no objection, Mr Cartwright, to repeat to you in person my fixed
determination not to continue in the house, if that scene be repeated.'

'It is impossible,' replied Mr Cartwright, 'to find a lady of your age so
steadfast in adhering to what she believes to be right, without feeling
both admiration and respect for her; and I should think – forgive me if I
wound you – I should think that such a one cannot altogether condemn
the offering of prayer and thanksgiving to God?'

'Mr Cartwright,' replied Rosalind, her colour rising, and her voice
expressive of great agitation, 'you talk of having been misunderstood; but
it is I, sir, who have reason to make this complaint. From which of my
words, either written or spoken, do you presume to infer that I contemn
the offering of prayer and thanksgiving to God?'

'I beseech you to bear with me patiently,' said Mr Cartwright with a
look and tone of the most touching mildness; 'and be assured that by
doing so, we shall not only be more likely to make ourselves mutually
understood, but finally to arrive at that truth which, I am willing to
believe, is equally the object of both. And the theme, my dear young
lady, on which we speak should never be alluded to, – at least, I think
not, – with any mixture of temper.'

Poor Rosalind! Honest as her vehemence was, she felt that she had
been wrong to show it, and with an effort that did her honour she
contrived to say, 'You are quite right, sir. As far as manner is concerned,
you have greatly the advantage of me by your self-possession and
calmness. Herein I will endeavour to imitate you, and assure you, with a
sang froid as perfect as your own, that I consider the offering of prayer and
thanksgiving to God as the first duty of a Christian. It is in consequence
of the reverence in which I hold this sacred duty, that I shrink from
seeing it performed irreverently. I have been taught to believe, sir, that
the deepest learning, the most deliberative wisdom, and the most grave
and solemn meditation given to the subject by the fathers and founders of
our church, were not too much to bestow on the sublime and awful
attempt to address ourselves suitably to God in prayer. Prayers so framed,
and fitted for every exigency that human nature can know, have been
prepared for us with equal piety and wisdom; and while such exist, I will
never join in any crude, unweighed, unauthorised jargon addressed to the
Deity, however vehement the assumption of piety might be in the bold
man who uses it.'

'It is seldom that so young a lady,' replied the vicar, with a kind and gentle smile, 'can have found time to give this important question so much attention as you appear to have done. Yet, perhaps, – yet, perhaps, Miss Torrington, when a few years more of deep consideration have been given by you to the subject, you may be led to think that fervour of feeling may more than atone for imperfection in expression.'

'If you imagine, sir,' replied Rosalind, in a voice as tranquil and deliberate as his own, 'that I have dared to regulate my conduct and opinions on such a point as this by any wisdom of my own, you do me great injustice. Such conduct, if general, would make as many churches upon earth as there are audacious spirits who reject control. My father, Mr Cartwright, was one whose life was passed in the situation which, perhaps, beyond all others in the world, taught him the value of the establishment to which he belonged. To those of another and an adverse faith he was a kind friend and generous benefactor; but he could not be insensible, nor did he leave me so, of the superior purity and moral efficacy of his own; – and I hope not to live long enough to forget the reverence which he has left impressed upon my mind for all that our church holds sacred.'

'Not for worlds, my excellent young lady,' exclaimed Mr Cartwright with warmth, 'would I attempt to shake opinions so evidently sustained by a sense of duty! Respect for such will assuredly prevent my again attempting to perform the office which offended your opinions this morning, as long as you continue, what you certainly ought to be at this time, the mistress of this family. I will only ask, Miss Torrington, in return for the sincere veneration I feel for your conscientious scruples, that you will judge me with equal candour, and will believe that however we may differ in judgment, I am not less anxious to be right than yourself.'

Rosalind answered this appeal by a silent bow.

'May I, then, hope that we are friends?' said he, rising and presenting his hand; 'and that I may venture to call, as I promised Mrs Mowbray I would do, on yourself, Miss Fanny, and my daughter, without driving you from the house?'

'Certainly, sir,' was Rosalind's cold reply. The request appeared as reasonable in itself, as it was politely and respectfully made, and to refuse it would have been equally churlish, presumptuous and unjust. Nevertheless, there was something at the bottom of her heart that revolted against the act of shaking hands with him; and feigning to be occupied by arranging some flowers on the table, she suffered the offered hand to remain extended, till at length its patient owner withdrew it.

Though well pleased that her remonstrance had put a stop to the vicar's extempore prayings at the house, Rosalind was not altogether satisfied by the result of the interview. 'We are still upon infinitely too civil terms,' thought she; 'but I see that just at present it would be an Herculean labour to quarrel with him: – if I smite him on one cheek, he will turn himself about as unresistingly as a sucking pig upon the spit, and submit to be basted all round without uttering a single squeak. But when Mrs Mowbray returns, I suspect that it will be my turn to be basted: – *n'importe* – I am sure I have done no more than my father would have thought right.'

With this consolation she returned to her dressing-room and applied herself to her usual occupations. Henrietta was no longer there; but as the fashion of the house was for every one to find employment and amusement for themselves during the morning, she did not think it necessary to pursue her in order to prove her wish to be agreeable.

At luncheon the three young ladies met as usual in the dining-room: Fanny appeared to have recovered her spirits and good-humour, and Henrietta seemed to wish to be more conversable than usual. They then strolled into the gardens, visited the hothouses, and finally placed themselves in a shady and fragrant bower, where they discoursed of poetry and music for an hour or two.

When these subjects seemed to be well-nigh exhausted, Miss Cartwright rose and slowly walked towards the house without intimating to her companions what it was her purpose to do next.

Rosalind and Fanny being thus left tête-à-tête, the former said, 'What do you think of our new acquaintance, Fanny? – How do you like Miss Cartwright?'

'I do not think she seems at all an amiable girl,' replied Fanny. 'With such advantages as she has, it is quite astonishing that her manners are so little agreeable.'

'She is not remarkably conversable, certainly,' said Rosalind; 'but I suspect that she has very bad health. How dreadfully sallow she is!'

'I suspect that she has a worse infirmity than bad health,' answered Fanny; – 'she has, I fear, an extremely bad temper.'

'She has not a violent temper, at any rate,' observed Rosalind; 'for I never remember to have seen any one who gave me a greater idea of being subdued and spirit-broken.'

'That is not at all the impression she makes upon me,' said Fanny: 'I should call her rather sullen than gentle, and obstinate instead of subdued. But this gossiping is sad idle work, Rosalind: as Miss Henrietta has fortunately taken herself off, I may go on with what I was doing before luncheon.'

* * *

Late in the evening, Mr Cartwright and his son Jacob paid the young ladies a visit. The vicar's conversation was chiefly addressed to Miss

Torrington; and if she had never seen him before, she must have agreed with Fanny in thinking him one of the most agreeable persons in the world, – for he spoke fluently and well upon every subject, and with a person and voice calculated to please every eye and every ear. There were probably, indeed, but few who could retain as steady a dislike to him as our Rosalind did.

The young man got hold of a purse that Fanny was netting, and did his best to entangle her silks; but his chief amusement was derived from attempts to quiz and plague his sister, who treated him much as a large and powerful dog does a little one, – enduring his gambols and annoying tricks with imperturbable patience for a while, and then suddenly putting forth a heavy paw and driving him off in an instant.

The following day passed very nearly in the same manner, – excepting that the three girls separated immediately after breakfast, and did not meet again till luncheon time. On the third, Fanny was the first to leave the breakfast room; and Miss Cartwright and Rosalind being left together, the former said,

'I suppose we owe our repose from morning and evening ranting to you, Miss Torrington?'

'I certainly did not approve it, Miss Cartwright, and I took the liberty of telling your father so.'

'You were undoubtedly very right and very wise, and I dare say you feel some inward satisfaction at your success. Mr Cartwright has really shown great deference to your opinion, by so immediately abandoning, at your request, so very favourite an occupation.'

Rosalind was about to reply, when Miss Cartwright changed the conversation, by abruptly saying,

'Will you take a stroll with me this morning, Miss Torrington?'

'Yes, certainly, if you wish it; – but I think we shall find it very warm.'

'Oh! no. I will lead you a very nice shady walk to the prettiest and most sheltered little thicket in the world. Let us put on our bonnets directly; – shall we?'

'I will not delay you a moment,' said Rosalind. 'Shall I ask Fanny to go with us?'

'Why no,' replied Miss Cartwright; 'I think you had better not; – the chances are ten to one against her finding it convenient. You know she is so fond of solitary study——'

'I believe you are right,' said Rosalind; and the young ladies parted, to meet again a few minutes after, with bonnets and parasols at the hall-door.

'And which way are we to go to find this welcome shade?' said Rosalind, holding her parasol low down to shelter her pretty face. 'The sun is almost intolerable.'

'This way,' said Henrietta, turning aside from the drive in a direction
which soon brought them to a thickly-planted drive that surrounded the
Park. 'We shall find it delightful here.'

It was an hour which, in the month of July, few ladies would choose
for walking; but Miss Torrington politely exerted herself to converse,
though she secretly longed to be lying silent and alone on the sofa in her
own dressing-room, with no greater exertion than was necessary for the
perusal of –

> 'The dear pages of some new romance.'

Henrietta, however, only answered her dryly and shortly, and presently
said,

'I should be really very much obliged to you, Miss Torrington, if you
would not speak to me any more. Just listen to the blackbirds, will you? –
depend upon it we can neither of us express ourselves one half so well as
they do.'

Rosalind willingly submitted to this request; and the young ladies
walked onward, producing no other sound than the occasional brushing
of their dresses against the underwood, which at every step became
thicker, rendering the path almost too narrow for two to walk abreast.

'Now, let us just turn down through this little opening,' said Henrietta
in a whisper; 'and pray, do not speak to me.'

Rosalind, who began to believe that she must have some meaning for
her strange manner of proceeding, followed her in perfect silence; and
they had not gone far into the intricacies of the tangled copse, before she
heard the sound of a human voice at no great distance from her.
Henrietta, who was in advance, turned round and laid her finger on her
lips. The caution was not needed: Rosalind had already recognised the
tones of Mr Cartwright, and a few more silent steps brought them to a
spot thickly surrounded on all sides, but from whence they could look
out upon a small and beautiful opening, in the centre of which a majestic
lime-tree stretched its arms, in all directions over the soft green turf.

Rosalind instantly recognized the spot as one frequently resorted to in
their evening rambles, for the sake of its cool and secluded beauty, and
also because a bench, divided into commodious stalls, surrounded the
capacious tree, from whence opened a vista commanding a charming
view across the Park.

On the turf before this bench, and with their backs turned towards the
spot where Rosalind and Henrietta stood, knelt Mr Cartwright and
Fanny. His eyes were fixed upon her with passionate admiration, and the
first words they distinctly heard were these, spoken with great vehemence
by the vicar:–

'Persecuted – trampled on – turned forth from every other roof, O Lord! let thy blue vault spread over us, and while I struggle to snatch this precious brand from the eternal fire of thy wrath, pour upon our heads the dew of thy love! Grant me power, O Lord! to save this one dear soul alive, though it should seem good in thy sight that millions should perish round her! Save her, O Lord! – save her from the eternal flame that even now rises to lick her feet, and if not stayed by prayer – the prayer of thy saints, O Lord! – will speedily envelope and consume her!'

Rosalind remained to hear no more. Heartsick, indignant, disgusted, and almost terrified by what she saw and heard, she retreated hastily, and, followed by Henrietta, rapidly pursued her way to the house.

Her companion made an effort to overtake her, and, almost out of breath by an exertion to which she was hardly equal, she said,

'I have shown you this, Miss Torrington, for the sake of giving you a useful lesson. If you are wise, you will profit by it, and learn to know that it is not always safe to suppose you have produced an effect, merely because it may be worth some one's while to persuade you into believing it. Having said thus much to point the moral of our walk in the sun, you may go your way, and I will go mine. I shall not enter upon any more elaborate exposition of Mr Cartwright's character.'

So saying she fell back among the bushes, and Rosalind reached the house alone.

On entering her dressing-room, Miss Torrington sat herself down, with her eau de Cologne bottle in one hand and a large feather fan in the other, to meditate – coolly, if she could, but at any rate to meditate – upon what she ought to do in order immediately to put a stop to the very objectionable influence which Mr Cartwright appeared to exercise over the mind of Fanny.

Had she been aware of Sir Gilbert Harrington's having written to recall his refusal of the executorship, she would immediately have had recourse to him; but this fact had never transpired beyond Mrs Mowbray and the vicar; and the idea that he had resisted the representation which she felt sure his son had made to him after the conversation Helen and herself had held with him, not only made her too angry to attempt any farther to soften him, but naturally impressed her with the belief that, do or say what she would on the subject, it must be in vain.

At length it struck her that Charles Mowbray was the most proper person to whom she could address herself; yet the writing such a letter as might immediately bring him home, was a measure which, under all existing circumstances, she felt to be awkward and disagreeable. But the more she meditated, the more she felt convinced, that, notwithstanding the obvious objections to it, this was the safest course she could pursue; so, having once made up her mind upon the subject, she set about it

without farther delay, and, with the straightforward frankness and
sincerity of her character, produced the following epistle:—

'Dear Mr Mowbray,

'Your last letter to Helen, giving so very agreeable an account of the
style and manner of your *Little-go*, makes it an ungracious task to
interrupt your studies — and yet that is what I am bent on doing. You
will be rather puzzled, I suspect, at finding me assuming the rights and
privileges of a correspondent, and moreover of an adviser, or rather a
dictator: but so it is — and you must not blame me till you are quite sure
you know all my reasons for it.

'Mrs Mowbray is gone to London, accompanied by Helen, for the
purpose of proving (I think it is called) your father's will; a business in
which Sir Gilbert Harrington has, most unkindly for all of you, refused
to join her. This journey was so suddenly decided upon, that dear Helen
had no time to write to you about it: she knew not that she was to go till
about nine o'clock the evening preceding.

'The Vicar of Wrexhill was probably acquainted with the intended
movement earlier; for no day passes, or has passed for some weeks,
without his holding a private consultation with your mother.

'Oh! that vicar, Charles! I think I told you that I hated him, and you
seemed to smile at my hatred as a sort of missish impertinence and
caprice; but what was instinct then has become reason now, and I am
strangely mistaken if your hatred would not fully keep pace with mine
had you seen and heard what I have done.

'When I decided upon writing to you, I intended, I believe, to enter
into all particulars; but I cannot do this — you must see for yourself, and
draw your own inferences. My dislike for this man may carry me too far,
and you must be much more capable of forming a judgment respecting his
motives than I can be. Of this however I am quite sure, — Fanny ought at
this time to have some one near her more capable of protecting her from
the mischievous influence of this hateful man than I am. I know, Mr
Charles, that you have no very exalted idea of my wisdom; and I am not
without some fear that instead of coming home immediately, as I think
you ought to do, you may write me a very witty, clever answer, with
reasons as plenty as blackberries to prove that I am a goose. *Do not do this,
Mr Mowbray*. I do not think that you know me very well, but in common
courtesy you ought not to believe that any young lady would write you
such a summons as this without having very serious reasons for it.

'As one proof of the rapidly-increasing intimacy between the family of
the vicar and your own, you will, on your arrival, find the daughter, Miss
Cartwright, established here to console us for your mother's (and
Helen's!) absence. She is a very singular personage: but on her I pass no

judgment, sincerely feeling that I am not competent to it. If my opinion be of sufficient weight to induce you to come, Mr Mowbray, I must beg you to let your arrival appear the result of accident; and not to let any one but Helen know of this letter.

'Believe me, very sincerely,

'Your friend,

'ROSALIND TORRINGTON.'

CHAPTER XV

ROSALIND'S CONVERSATION WITH MISS CARTWRIGHT – MRS SIMPSON AND MISS RICHARDS MEET THE VICAR AT THE PARK – THE HYMN – THE WALK HOME

In the course of the morning after this letter was despatched, Miss Cartwright and Rosalind again found themselves tête-à-tête. The nature of Rosalind Torrington was so very completely the reverse of mysterious or intriguing, that far from wishing to lead Henrietta to talk of her father in that style of hints and innuendos to which the young lady seemed addicted, she determined, in future, carefully to avoid the subject; although it was very evident from the preconcerted walk to the lime-tree, that, notwithstanding her declaration to the contrary, Miss Cartwright was desirous to make her acquainted with the character and conduct of her father.

Whether it were that spirit of contradiction which is said to possess the breast of woman, or any other more respectable feeling, it may be difficult to decide, but it is certain that the less Rosalind appeared disposed to speak of the adventure of yesterday, the more desirous did Henrietta feel to lead her to it.

'You were somewhat disappointed, I fancy, Miss Torrington,' said she, 'to discover that though you had contrived to banish the conventicle from the house, it had raised its voice in the grounds.'

'Indeed I was,' replied Rosalind.

'I rather think that you are addicted to speaking truth, – and perhaps you pique yourself upon it,' resumed Miss Cartwright. 'Will you venture to tell me what you think of the scene you witnessed?'

'You are not the person I should most naturally have selected as the confidant of my opinions respecting Mr Cartwright,' said Rosalind; 'but since you put the question plainly, I will answer it plainly, and confess that I suspect him not only of wishing to inculcate his own Calvinistic doctrines on the mind of Fanny Mowbray, but moreover, notwithstanding his disproportionate age, of gaining her affections.'

'Her affections?' repeated Henrietta. 'And with what view do you imagine he is endeavouring to gain her affections?'

'Doubtless with a view to making her his wife; though, to be sure, the idea is preposterous.'

'Sufficiently. Pray, Miss Torrington, has Miss Fanny Mowbray an independent fortune?'

'None whatever. Like the rest of the family, she is become by the death of her father, entirely dependant upon Mrs Mowbray.'

'Your fortune is entirely at your own disposal, I believe?'

Rosalind looked provoked at the idle turn Miss Cartwright was giving to a conversation which, though she had not led to it, interested her deeply.

'Do not suspect me of impertinence,' said Henrietta in a tone more gentle than ordinary. 'But such is the case, is it not?'

'Yes, Miss Cartwright,' was Rosalind's grave reply.

'Then, do you know that I think it infinitely more probable Mr Cartwright may have it in contemplation to make you his wife.'

'I beg your pardon, Miss Cartwright,' said Rosalind, 'but I really thought that you were speaking of your father seriously; and it seems you are disposed to punish me for imagining you would do so, to one so nearly a stranger.'

'I never jest on any subject,' replied the melancholy-looking girl, knitting her dark brows into a frown of such austerity as almost made Rosalind tremble. 'A reasoning being who has nothing to hope among the realities on this side the grave, and hopes nothing among the visions on the other, is not very likely to be jocose.'

'Good God! Miss Cartwright,' exclaimed Rosalind, 'what dreadful language is this? Are you determined to prove to me that there may be opinions and doctrines more terrible still than those of your father?'

'I had no meaning of the kind, I assure you,' replied Henrietta, in her usual quiet manner, which always seemed to hover between the bitterness of a sneer, and the quietude or indifference of philosophy. 'Pray do not trouble yourself for a moment to think about me or my opinions. You might, perhaps, as you are a bold-spirited, honest-minded girl, do some good if you fully comprehended all that was going on around you; though it is very doubtful, for it is impossible to say to what extent the besotted folly of people may go. But don't you think it might, on the whole, be quite as probable that Mr Cartwright may wish to marry the mother, as the daughter?'

'Mrs Mowbray! – Good gracious! no.'

'Then we differ. But may I ask you why you think otherwise?'

'One reason is, that Mrs Mowbray's recent widowhood seems to put such an idea entirely out of the question; and another, that he appears to be positively making love to Fanny.'

'Oh! – is that all? I do assure you there is nothing at all particular in that. He would tell you himself, I am sure, if you were to enter upon the subject with him, that it is his duty to influence and lead the hearts of his flock into the way he would have them go, by *every* means in his power.'

'Then you really do not think he has been making love to Fanny?'

'I am sure, Miss Torrington,' replied Henrietta, very gravely, 'I did not mean to say so.'

'Indeed! indeed! Miss Cartwright,' said Rosalind with evident symptoms of impatience, 'these riddles vex me cruelly. If your father *does* make love to this dear fanciful child, he must, I suppose, have some hope that she will marry him?'

'How can I answer you?' exclaimed Henrietta with real feeling. 'You cannot be above two or three years younger than I am, yet your purity and innocence make me feel myself a monster.'

'For God's sake do not trifle with me!' cried Rosalind, her face and neck dyed with indignant blood; 'you surely do not mean that your father is seeking to seduce this unhappy child?'

'Watch Mr Cartwright a little while, Rosalind Torrington, as I have done for the six last terrible years of my hateful life, and you may obtain perhaps some faint idea of the crooked, complex machinery – the movements and counter-movements, the shiftings and the balancings, by which his zig-zag course is regulated. Human passions are in him for ever struggling with, and combating, what may be called in their strength, *superhuman* avarice and ambition.

'To touch, to influence, to lead, to rule, to tyrannise over the hearts and souls of all he approaches, is the great object of his life. He would willingly do this in the hearts of men, – but for the most part he has found them tough; and he now, I think, seems to rest all his hopes of fame, wealth, and station on the power he can obtain over women. – I say not,' she added after a pause, while a slight blush passed over her pallid cheek, 'that I believe his senses uninfluenced by beauty; – this is far, hatefully far from being the case with Mr Cartwright; – but he is careful, most cunningly careful, whatever victims he makes, never to become one in his own person.

'You would find, were you to watch him, that his system, both for pleasure and profit, consists of a certain graduated love-making to every woman within his reach, not too poor, too old, or too ugly. But if any among them fancy that he would sacrifice the thousandth part of a hair's breadth of his worldly hopes for all they could give him in return – they are mistaken.'

'The character you paint,' said Rosalind, who grew pale as she listened, 'is too terrible for me fully to understand, and I would turn my eyes from the portrait, and endeavour to forget that I had ever heard of it, were not those I love endangered by it. Hateful as all this new knowledge is to me, I must still question you further, Miss Cartwright: What do you suppose to be his object in thus working upon the mind of Fanny Mowbray?'

'His motives, depend upon it, are manifold. Religion and love, the new birth and intellectual attachment – mystical sympathy of hearts, and the certainty of eternal damnation to all that he does not take under the shadow of his wing; – these are the tools with which he works. He has got his foot – perhaps you may think it a cloven one, but, such as it is, he seems to have got it pretty firmly planted within the paling of Mowbray Park. He made me follow him hither as a volunteer visitor, very much against my inclination; but if by what I have said you may be enabled to defeat any of his various projects among ye, – for he never plots single-handed, – I shall cease to regret that I came.'

'My power of doing any good,' replied Rosalind, 'must, I fear, be altogether destroyed by my ignorance of what Mr Cartwright's intentions and expectations are. You have hinted various things, but all so vaguely, that I own I do not feel more capable of keeping my friends from any danger which may threaten them, than before this conversation took place.'

'I am sorry for it,' said Henrietta coldly, 'but I have really no information more accurate to give.'

'I truly believe that you have meant very kindly,' said Rosalind, looking seriously distressed. 'Will you go one step farther, and say what you would advise me to do, Miss Cartwright?'

'No, certainly, Miss Torrington, I will not. But I will give you a hint or two what not to do. Do not appear at all better acquainted with me than I show myself disposed to be with you. Do not make the slightest alteration in your manner of receiving Mr Cartwright; and do not, from any motive whatever, repeat one syllable of this conversation to Fanny Mowbray. Should you disobey this last injunction, you will be guilty of very cruel and ungrateful treachery towards me.' Having said this, with the appearance of more emotion than she had hitherto manifested, Henrietta rose and left the room.

'At length,' thought Rosalind, 'she has spoken out: yet what are we likely to be the better for it? It seems that there is a great net thrown over us, of which we shall feel and see the meshes by-and-by, when he who has made prey of us begins to pull the draught to shore; but how to escape from it, the oracle sayeth not!'

* * *

On the evening of that day, Mrs Simpson and the eldest Miss Richards walked over from Wrexhill to pay a visit at the Park. They were not aware of the absence of Mrs Mowbray, and seemed disposed to shorten their visit on finding she was not at home; but Rosalind, who for the last hour had been sitting on thorns expecting Mr Cartwright to make his evening call, most cordially and earnestly invited them to stay till after tea, feeling that their presence would greatly relieve the embarrassment which she feared she might betray on again seeing the vicar.

'But it will be so late!' said Miss Richards. 'How are we to get home after it is dark? Remember, Mrs Simpson, there is no moon.'

'It is very true,' said Mrs Simpson. 'I am afraid, my dear Miss Torrington, that we must deny ourselves the pleasure you offer; – but I am such a nervous creature! It is very seldom that I stir out without ordering a manservant to follow me; and I regret excessively that I omitted to do so this evening.'

'I think,' said Rosalind, colouring at her own eagerness, which she was conscious must appear rather new and rather strange to Mrs Simpson, with whom she had hardly ever exchanged a dozen words before, – 'I think Mr Cartwright will very likely be here this evening, and perhaps he might attend you home. Do you not think, Miss Cartwright,' she added, turning to Henrietta, 'that it is very likely your father will call this evening?'

'Good gracious! – Miss Cartwright – I beg your pardon, I did not know you. I hope you heard that I called; – so very happy to cultivate your acquaintance! – Oh dear! I would not miss seeing Mr Cartwright for the world! – Thank you, my dear Miss Torrington; – thank you, Miss Fanny: I will just set my hair to rights a little, if you will give me leave. Perhaps, Miss Fanny, you will permit me to go into your bed-room?' Such was the effect produced by the vicar's name upon the handsome widow.

Miss Richards coloured, smiled, spoke to Henrietta with very respectful politeness, and finally followed her friend Mrs Simpson out of the room, accompanied by Fanny, who willingly undertook to be their gentlewoman usher.

'Mr Cartwright has already made some impression on these fair ladies, or I am greatly mistaken,' said Henrietta. 'Did you remark, Miss Torrington, the effect produced by his name?'

'I did,' replied Rosalind, 'and my reasonings upon it are very consolatory; for if he has already found time and inclination to produce so great effect there, why should we fear that his labours of love here should prove more dangerous in their tendency?'

'Very true. Nor do I see any reason in the world why the Mowbray is in greater peril than the Simpson, or the Fanny than the Louisa, – excepting that one widow is about twenty times richer than the other, and the little young lady about five hundred times handsomer than the great one.'

At this moment the Mr Cartwrights, father and son, were seen turning off from the regular approach to the house, towards the little gate that opened from the lawn; a friendly and familiar mode of entrance, which seemed to have become quite habitual to them.

Rosalind, who was the first to perceive them, flew towards the door, saying, 'You must excuse me for running away, Miss Cartwright. I invited that furbelow widow to stay on purpose to spare me this almost tête-à-tête meeting. I will seek the ladies and return with them.'

'Then so will I too,' said Henrietta, hastily following her. 'I am by no means disposed to stand the cross-examination which I know will ensue if I remain here alone.'

The consequence of this movement was, that the vicar and his son prepared their smiles in vain; for, on entering the drawing-room, sofas and ottomans, foot-stools, tables, and chairs, alone greeted them.

Young Cartwright immediately began peeping into the work-boxes and portfolios which lay on the tables.

'Look here, sir,' said he, holding up a caricature of Lord B——m. 'Is not this sinful?'

'Do be quiet, Jacob! – we shall have them here in a moment; – I really wish I could teach you when your interest is at stake to make the best of yourself. You know that I should be particularly pleased by your marrying Miss Torrington; and I do beg, my dear boy, that you will not suffer your childish spirits to put any difficulties in my way.'

'I will become an example unto all men,' replied Jacob, shutting up his eyes and mouth demurely, and placing himself bolt upright upon the music-stool.

'If you and your sister could but mingle natures a little,' said Mr Cartwright, 'you would both be wonderfully improved. Nothing with which I am acquainted, however joyous, can ever induce Henrietta to smile; and nothing, however sad, can prevent your being on the broad grin from morning to night. However, of the two, I confess I think you are the most endurable.'

'A whip for the horse, a bridle for the ass, and a rod for the fool's back,' said Jacob in a sanctified tone.

'Upon my honour, Jacob, I shall be very angry with you if you do not set about this love-making as I would have you. Don't make ducks and drakes of eighty thousand pounds: – at least, not till you have got them.'

'Answer not a fool according to his folly, lest he be wise in his own conceit,' said Jacob.

Mr Cartwright smiled, as it seemed against his will, but shook his head very solemnly. 'I'll tell you what, Jacob,' said he, – 'If I see you set about this in a way to please me, I'll give you five shillings to-morrow morning.'

'Wherefore is there a price in the hand of a fool to get wisdom, seeing he hath no heart to it?' replied Jacob. 'Nevertheless, father, I will look lovingly upon the maiden, and receive thy promised gift, even as thou sayest.'

'Upon my word, Jacob, you try my patience too severely,' said the vicar; yet there was certainly but little wrath in his eye as he said so, and his chartered libertine of a son was preparing again to answer him in the words of Solomon, but in a spirit of very indecent buffoonery, when the drawing-room door opened, and Mrs Simpson, Miss Richards, and Fanny Mowbray entered.

It appeared that Rosalind and Miss Cartwright, on escaping from the drawing-room, had not sought the other ladies, but taken refuge in the dining-parlour, from whence they issued immediately after the others had passed the door, and entering the drawing-room with them, enjoyed the gratification of witnessing the meeting of the vicar and his fair parishioners.

To the surprise of Rosalind, and the great though silent amusement of her companion, they perceived that both the stranger ladies had contrived to make a very edifying and remarkable alteration in the general appearance of their dress.

Miss Richards had combed her abounding black curls as nearly straight as their nature would allow, and finally brought them into very reverential order by the aid of her ears, and sundry black pins to boot, – an arrangement by no means unfavourable to the display of her dark eyes and eyebrows.

But the change produced by the *castigato* toilet of the widow was considerably more important. A transparent blond *chemisette*, rather calculated to adorn than conceal that part of the person to which it belonged, was now completely hidden by a lavender-coloured silk handkerchief, tightly, smoothly, and with careful security pinned behind, and before, and above, and below, upon her full but graceful bust.

Rosalind had more than once of late amused herself by looking over the pages of Molière's 'Tartufe;' and a passage now occurred to her that she could not resist muttering in the ear of Henrietta:–

> 'Ah, mon Dieu! je vous prie,
> 'Avant que de parler, prenez-moi ce mouchoir' – &c.

The corner of Miss Cartwright's mouth expressed her appreciation of the quotation, but by a movement so slight that none but Rosalind could perceive it.

Meanwhile the vicar approached Mrs Simpson with a look that was full of meaning, and intended to express admiration both of her mental and personal endowments. She, too, had banished the drooping ringlets from her cheeks, and appeared before him with all the pretty severity of a Madonna band across her forehead.

Was it in the nature of man to witness such touching proofs of his influence without being affected thereby? At any rate, such indifference made no part of the character of the Vicar of Wrexhill, and the murmured 'God bless you, my dear lady!' which accompanied his neighbourly pressure of the widow Simpson's hand, gave her to understand how much his grateful and affectionate feelings were gratified by her attention to the hints he had found an opportunity to give her during a tête-à-tête conversation at her own house a few days before.

Nor was the delicate attention of Miss Richards overlooked. She, too, felt at her fingers' ends how greatly the sacrifice of her curls was approved by the graceful vicar, who now, in all the beauty of holiness, sat down surrounded by this fair bevy of ladies, smiling with bland and gentle sweetness on them all.

Mr Jacob thought of the promised five shillings, and displaying his fine teeth from ear to ear, presented a chair to Miss Torrington.

'I wish you would let us have a song, Miss Rosalind Torrington,' said he, stationing himself at the back of her chair and leaning over her shoulder. 'I am told that your voice beats all the heavenly host hollow.'

His eye caught an approving glance from his father as he took this station, and he wisely trusted to his attitude for obtaining his reward, for these words were audible only to the young lady herself.

'You are a mighty odd set of people!' said she, turning round to him. 'I cannot imagine how you all contrive to live together! There is not one of you that does not appear to be a contrast to the other two.'

'Then, at any rate, you cannot dislike us all *equally*,' said the strange lad, with a grimace that made her laugh, despite her inclination to look grave.

'I do not know that,' was the reply. 'I may dislike you all equally, and yet have a different species of dislike for each.'

'But one species must be stronger and more vigorous than the others. Besides, I will assist your judgment. I do not mean to say I am quite perfect; but, depend upon it, I'm the best of the *set*, as you call us.'

'Your authority, Mr Jacob, is the best in the world, certainly. Nevertheless, there are many who on such an occasion might suspect you of partiality.'

'Then they would do me great injustice, Miss Torrington. I am a man, or a boy, or something between both: take me for all in all, it is five hundred to one you ne'er shall look upon my like again. But that is a play-going and sinful quotation, Miss Rosalind, like your name: so be gracious and merciful unto me, and please not to tell my papa.'

'You may be very certain, Mr Jacob, that I shall obey you in this.'

> 'Sweetest nut hath sourest rind, –
> Such a nut is Rosalind,'

responded the youth; and probably thinking that he had fairly won his five shillings, he raised his tall thin person from the position which had so well pleased his father, and stole round to the sofa on which Fanny was sitting.

Fanny was looking very lovely, but without a trace of that bright and beaming animation which a few short months before had led her poor father to give her the *sobriquet* of 'Fire-fly.' He was wont to declare, and no one was inclined to contradict him, that whenever she appeared, something like a bright coruscation seemed to flash upon the eye. No one, not even a fond father, would have hit upon such a simile for her now. Beautiful she was, perhaps more beautiful than ever; but a sad and sombre thoughtfulness had settled itself on her young brow, – her voice was no longer the echo of gay thoughts, and, in a word, her whole aspect and bearing were changed.

She now sat silently apart from the company, watching, with an air that seemed to hover between abstraction and curiosity, Mrs Simpson's manner of making herself agreeable to Mr Cartwright.

This lady was seated on one side of the vicar, and Miss Richards on the other: both had the appearance of being unconscious that any other person or persons were in the room, and nothing but his consummate skill in the art of uttering an aside both with eyes and lips could have enabled him to sustain his position.

'My sisters and I are afraid you have quite forgotten us,' murmured Miss Richards; 'but we have been practising the hymns you gave us, and we are all quite perfect, and ready to sing them to you whenever you come.'

'The hearing this, my dear young lady, gives me as pure and holy a pleasure as listening to the sacred strains could do: – unless, indeed,' he added, bending his head sideways towards her so as nearly to touch her cheek, 'unless, indeed, they were breathed by the lips of Louisa herself. That must be very like hearing a seraph sing!'

Not a syllable of this was heard save by herself.

'I have thought incessantly,' said Mrs Simpson, in a very low voice, as soon as Mr Cartwright's head had recovered the perpendicular, – 'incessantly, I may truly say, on our last conversation. My life has been passed in a manner so widely different from what I am sure it will be in future, that I feel as if I were awakened to a new existence!'

'The great object of my hopes is, and will ever be,' replied the Vicar of Wrexhill almost aloud, 'to lead my beloved flock to sweet and safe pastures. – And for you,' he added, in a voice so low that she rather felt than heard his words, 'what is there I would not do?' Here his eyes spoke a commentary; and hers, a note upon it.

'Which is the hymn, Mr Cartwright, that you think best adapted to the semi-weekly Sabbath you recommended us to institute?' said Miss Richards.

'The eleventh, I think. – Yes, the eleventh; – study that, my dear child. Early and late let your sweet voice breathe those words, – and I will be with you in spirit, Louisa.'

Not even Mrs Simpson heard a word of this, beyond 'dear child.'

'But when shall I see you? – I have doubts and difficulties on some points, Mr Cartwright,' said the widow aloud. 'How shamefully ignorant – I must call it *shamefully* ignorant – did poor Mr Wallace suffer us to remain! – Is it not true, Louisa? Did he ever, through all the years we have known him, utter an awakening word to any of us?'

'No, *indeed* he never did,' replied Miss Louisa in a sort of penitent whine.

'I am rather surprised to hear you say that, Miss Richards,' said Rosalind, drawing her chair a little towards them. 'I always understood that Mr Wallace was one of the most exemplary parish priests in England. Did not your father consider him to be so, Fanny?'

'I – I believe so, – I don't know,' replied Fanny, stammering and colouring painfully.

'Not know, Fanny Mowbray!' exclaimed Rosalind; – 'not know your father's opinion of Mr Wallace! That is very singular indeed.'

'I mean,' said Fanny, struggling to recover her composure, 'that I never heard papa's opinion of him as compared with – with any one else.'

'I do not believe he would have lost by the comparison,' said Rosalind, rising and walking out of the window.

'Is not that prodigiously rich young lady somewhat of the tiger breed?' said young Cartwright in a whisper to Fanny.

'Miss Torrington is not at all a person of serious notions,' replied Fanny; 'and till one is subdued by religion, one is often very quarrelsome.'

'I am sure, serious or not, you would never quarrel with any one,' whispered Jacob.

'Indeed I should be sorry and ashamed to do so now,' she replied. 'Your father ought to cure us all of such unchristian faults as that.'

'I wish I was like my father!' said Jacob very sentimentally.

'Oh! how glad I am to hear you say that!' said Fanny, clasping her hands together. 'I am sure it would make him so happy!'

'I can't say I was thinking of making him happy, Miss Fanny: I only meant that I wished I was like anybody that you admire and approve so much.'

'A poor silly motive for wishing to be like such a father!' replied Fanny, blushing; and leaving her distant place, she established herself at the table on which the tea equipage had just been placed, and busied herself with the tea-cups.

This remove brought her very nearly opposite Mr Cartwright and the two ladies who were seated beside him, and from this moment the conversation proceeded without any 'asides' whatever.

'At what age, Mr Cartwright,' said Mrs Simpson, 'do you think one should begin to instil the doctrine of regeneration into a little girl?'

'Not later than ten, my dear lady. A very quick and forward child might perhaps be led to comprehend it earlier. Eight and three-quarters I have known in a state of the most perfect awakening; but this I hold to be rare.'

'What a spectacle!' exclaimed Miss Richards in a sort of rapture. 'A child of eight and three-quarters filled with the Holy Spirit! Did it speak its thoughts, Mr Cartwright?'

'The case I allude to, my dear young lady, was published. I will bring you the pamphlet. Nothing can be more edifying than the out-breakings of the Spirit through the organs of that chosen little vessel.'

'I hope, Mr Cartwright, that I shall have the benefit of this dear pamphlet also. Do not forget that I have a little girl exactly eight years three-quarters and six-weeks. – I beg your pardon, my dear Louisa, but this must be so much more interesting to me than it can be to you as yet, my dear, that I trust Mr Cartwright will give me the precedence in point of time. Besides, you know, that as the principal person in the village, I am a little spoiled in such matters. I confess to you, I should feel hurt if I had to wait for this till you had studied it. You have no child, you know.'

'Oh! without doubt, Mrs Simpson, you ought to have it first,' replied Miss Richards. 'I am certainly not likely as yet to have any one's soul to be anxious about but my own. – Is this blessed child alive, Mr Cartwright?'

'In heaven, Miss Louisa, – not on earth. It is the account of its last moments that have been so admirably drawn up by the Reverend Josiah Martin. This gentleman is a particular friend of mine, and I am much interested in the sale of the little work. I will have the pleasure, my dear ladies, of bringing a dozen copies to each of you; and you will give me a very pleasing proof of the pious feeling I so deeply rejoice to see, if you will dispose of them at one shilling each among your friends.'

'I am sure I will try all I can!' said Miss Richards.

'My influence could not be better employed, I am certain, than in forwarding your wishes in all things,' added Mrs Simpson.

Young Jacob, either in the hope of amusement, or of more certainly securing his five shillings, had followed the indignant Rosalind out of the window, and found her refreshing herself by arranging the vagrant tendrils of a beautiful creeping plant outside it.

'I am afraid, Miss Rosalind Torrington,' said he, 'that you would not say Amen! if I did say, May the saints have you in their holy keeping! I do believe in my heart that you would rather find yourself in the keeping of sinners.'

'The meaning of words often depends upon the character of those who utter them,' replied Rosalind. 'There is such a thing as slang, Mr Jacob; and there is such a thing as cant.'

'Did you ever mention that to my papa, Miss Rosalind?' inquired Jacob in a voice of great simplicity.

Rosalind looked at him as if she wished to discover what he was at, – whether his object were to quiz her, his father, or both. But, considering his very boyish appearance and manner, there was more difficulty in achieving this than might have been expected. Sometimes she thought him almost a fool; at others, quite a wag. At one moment she was ready to believe him more than commonly simple-minded; and at another, felt persuaded that he was an accomplished hypocrite.

It is probable that the youth perceived her purpose, and felt more gratification in defeating it than he could have done from any love-making of which she were the object. His countenance, which was certainly intended by nature to express little besides frolic and fun, was now puckered up into a look of solemnity that might have befitted one of the Newman-street congregation when awaiting an address in the unknown tongue.

'I am sure,' he said, 'that my papa would like to hear you talk about all those things very much, Miss Torrington. I do not think that he would exactly agree with you in every word you might say: but that never seems to vex him: if the talk does but go about heaven and hell, and saints and sinners, and reprobation and regeneration, and the old man and the new birth, that is all papa cares for. I think he likes to be contradicted a little; for that, you know, makes more talk again.'

'Is that the principle upon which you proceed with him yourself, Mr Jacob? Do you always make a point of contradicting everything he says?'

'Pretty generally, Miss Torrington, when there is nobody by, and when I make it all pass for joke. But there *is* a law that even Miss Henrietta has been taught to obey; and that is, never to contradict him in company. Perhaps you have found that out, Miss Rosalind?'

'Perhaps I have, Mr Jacob.'

'Will you not come in to tea, Miss Torrington?' said Henrietta, appearing at the window, with the volume in her hand which had seemed to occupy her whole attention from the time she had re-entered the drawing-room with Rosalind.

'I wish, sister,' said Jacob, affecting to look extremely cross, 'that you would not pop out so, to interrupt one's conversation! You might have a fellow feeling, I think, for a young lady, when she walks out of a window, and a young gentleman walks after her!'

Rosalind gave him a look from one side, and Henrietta from the other.

'Mercy on me!' he exclaimed, putting up his hands as if to guard the two sides of his face. 'Four black eyes at me at once! – and so very black in every sense of the word!'

The young ladies walked together into the room, and Jacob followed, seeking the eye of his father, and receiving thence, as he expected, a glance of encouragement and applause.

When the tea was removed, Mr Cartwright went to the piano-forte, and ran his fingers with an appearance of some skill over the keys.

'I hope, my dear Miss Fanny, that you intend we should have a little music this evening?'

'If Mrs Simpson, Miss Richards, and Miss Torrington will sing,' said Fanny, 'I shall be very happy to accompany them.'

'What music have you got, my dear young lady?' said the vicar.

Miss Torrington had a large collection of songs very commodiously stowed beneath the instrument; and Helen and herself were nearly as amply provided with piano-forte music of all kinds: but though this was the first time Mr Cartwright had ever approached the instrument, or asked for music, Fanny had a sort of instinctive consciousness that the collection would be found defective in his eyes.

'We have several of Handel's oratorios,' she replied; 'and I think Helen has got the "Creation."'

'Very fine music both,' replied Mr Cartwright; 'but in the social meetings of friends, where many perhaps may be able to raise a timid note toward heaven, though incapable of performing the difficult compositions of these great masters, I conceive that a simpler style is preferable. If you will permit me,' he continued, drawing a small volume of manuscript music from his pocket, 'I will point out to you some very beautiful, and, indeed, popular melodies, which have heretofore been sadly disgraced by the words applied to them. In this little book many of my female friends, to whom God has seen fit for his own especial glory to give some sparks of poetic power, have, at my request, written words fit for a Christian to sing, to notes that the sweet voice of youth and beauty may love to breathe. Miss Torrington, I have heard that you are considered to be a very superior vocalist: – will you use the power that God has given, to hymn his praise?'

There was too much genuine piety in Rosalind's heart to refuse a challenge so worded, without a better reason for doing it than personal dislike to Mr Cartwright; nevertheless, it was not without putting some constraint upon herself that she replied,

'I very often sing sacred music, sir, and am ready to do so now, if you wish it.'

'A thousand thanks,' said he, 'for this amiable compliance! I hail it as the harbinger of harmony that shall rise from all our hearts in sweet accord to heaven.'

Rosalind coloured, and her heart whispered, 'I will not be a hypocrite.' But she had agreed to sing, and she prepared to do so, seeking among her volumes for one of the easiest and shortest of Handel's songs, and determined when she had finished to make her escape.

While she was thus employed, however, Mr Cartwright was equally active in turning over the leaves of his pocket companion; and before Miss Torrington had made her selection, he placed the tiny manuscript volume open upon the instrument, saying, 'There, my dear young lady! this is an air and these are words which we may all listen to with equal innocence and delight.'

Rosalind was provoked; but every one in the room had already crowded round the piano, and having no inclination to enter upon any discussion, she sat down prepared to sing whatever was placed before her.

The air was undeniably a popular one, being no other than 'Fly not yet!' which, as all the world knows, has been performed to millions of delighted listeners, in lofty halls and tiny drawing-rooms, and, moreover, ground upon every hand-organ in Great Britain for many years past. Rosalind ran her eyes over the words, which, in fair feminine characters, were written beneath the notes as follows:

> Fly not yet! 'Tis just the hour
> When prayerful Christians own the power
> That, inly beaming with new light,
> Begins to sanctify the night
> For maids who love the moon.
> Oh, pray! – oh, pray!

> 'Tis but to bless these hours of shade
> That pious songs and hymns are made;
> For now, their holy ardour glowing,
> Sets the soul's emotion flowing.
> Oh, pray! – oh, pray!

Prayer so seldom breathes a strain
So sweet as this, that, oh! 'tis pain
To check its voice too soon.
Oh, pray! – oh, pray!

An expression of almost awful indignation rose to the eyes of Rosalind. 'Do you give me this, sir,' she said, 'as a jest? – or do you propose that I should sing it as an act of devotion towards God?'

Mr Cartwright withdrew the little book and immediately returned it to his pocket.

'I am sorry, Miss Torrington, that you should have asked me such a question,' he replied with a kind of gentle severity which might have led almost any hearer to think him in the right. 'I had hoped that my ministry at Wrexhill, short as it has been, could not have left it a matter of doubt whether, in speaking of singing or prayer, I was in jest?'

'Nevertheless, sir,' rejoined Rosalind, 'it does to me appear like a jest, and a very indecent one too, thus to imagine that an air long familiar to all as the vehicle of words as full of levity as of poetry can be on the sudden converted into an accompaniment to a solemn invocation to prayer – uttered, too, in the form of a vile parody.'

'I think that a very few words may be able to prove to you the sophistry of such an argument,' returned the vicar. 'You will allow, I believe, that this air is very generally known to all classes. – Is it not so?'

Rosalind bowed her assent.

'Well, then, let me go a step farther, and ask whether the words originally set to this air are not likely to be recalled by hearing it.'

'Beyond all doubt.'

'Now, observe, Miss Torrington, that what you have been pleased to call levity and poetry, I, in my clerical capacity, denounce as indecent and obscene.'

'Is that your reason for setting me to play it?' said Rosalind in a tone of anger.

'That question, again, does not, I fear, argue an amiable and pious state of mind,' replied Mr Cartwright, appealing meekly with his eyes to the right and left. 'It is to substitute other thoughts for those which the air has hitherto suggested that I conceive the singing this song, as it now stands, desirable.'

'Might it not be as well to leave the air alone altogether?' said Rosalind.

'Decidedly not,' replied the vicar. 'The notes, as you have allowed, are already familiar to all men, and it is therefore a duty to endeavour to make that familiarity familiarly suggest thoughts of heaven.'

'Thoughts of heaven,' said Rosalind, 'should never be suggested familiarly.'

'Dreadful – very dreadful doctrine that, Miss Torrington! and I must tell you, in devout assurance of the truth I speak, that it is in order to combat and overthrow such notions as you now express, that God hath vouchsafed, by an act of his special providence, to send upon earth in these later days my humble self, and some others who think like me.'

'And permit me, sir, in the name of the earthly father I have lost,' replied Rosalind, while her eyes *almost* overflowed with the glistening moisture her earnestness brought into them, – 'permit me in his reverenced name to say, that constant prayer to God can in no way be identified with familiarity of address; and that of many lamentable evils which the class of preachers to whom you allude have brought upon blundering Christians, that of teaching them to believe that there is righteousness in mixing the awful and majestic name of God with all the hourly, petty occurrences of this mortal life, is one of the most deplorable.'

'May your unthinking youth, my dear young lady, plead before the God of mercy in mitigation of the wrath which such sentiments are calculated to draw down!'

'Oh!' sobbed Miss Richards.

'Alas!' sighed Mrs Simpson.

'How can you, Rosalind, speak so to the pastor and master of our souls?' said Fanny, while tears of sympathy for the outraged vicar fell from her beautiful eyes.

'My dear children! – my dear friends!' said Mr Cartwright in a voice that seemed to tremble with affectionate emotion, 'think not of me! – Remember the words "Blessed are they which are persecuted for righteousness' sake!" I turn not from the harsh rebuke of this young lady, albeit I am not insensible to its injustice, – nor, indeed, blind to its indecency. But blessed – oh! most blessed shall I hold this trial, if it lead to the awakening holy thoughts in you! – My dear young lady,' he continued, rising from his seat and approaching Rosalind with an extended hand, 'it may be as well, perhaps, that I withdraw myself at this moment. Haply, reflection may soften your young heart. – But let us part in peace, as Christians should do.'

Rosalind did not take his offered hand. 'In peace, sir,' she said, – 'decidedly I desire you to depart in peace. I have no wish to molest you in any way. But you must excuse my not accepting your proffered hand. It is but an idle and unmeaning ceremony perhaps, as things go; but the manner in which you now stretch forth your hand gives a sort of importance to it which would make it a species of falsehood in me to accept it. When it means anything, it means cordial liking; and this, sir, I do not feel for you.'

So saying, Rosalind arose and left the room.

Fanny clasped her hands in a perfect agony, and raising her tearful eyes to Heaven as if to deprecate its wrath upon the roof that covered so great wickedness, exclaimed, 'Oh, Mr Cartwright! what can I say to you?'

Mrs Simpson showed symptoms of being likely to faint; and as Mr Cartwright and Fanny approached her, Miss Richards, with a vehemence of feeling that seemed to set language at defiance, seized the hand of the persecuted vicar and pressed it to her lips.

Several minutes were given to the interchange of emotions too strong to be described in words. Female tears were blended with holy blessings; and, as Jacob afterwards assured his sister, who had contrived unobserved to escape, he at one time saw no fewer than eight human hands, great and small, all mixed together in a sort of chance-medley heap upon the chair round which they at length kneeled down to 'speak the Lord' upon the scene that had just passed.

It will be easily believed that Miss Torrington appeared no more that night; and after an hour passed in conversation on the persecutions and revilings to which the godly are exposed, Mrs Simpson, who declared herself dreadfully overcome, proposed to Miss Richards that they should use such strength as was left them to walk home. A very tender leave was taken of Fanny, in which Mr Jacob zealously joined, and the party set out for a star-lit walk to Wrexhill, its vicar supporting on each arm a very nervous and trembling hand.

Mr Cartwright soon after passing the Park-lodge, desired his son to step foward and order the clerk to come to him on some urgent parish business before he went to bed. The young man darted forward nothing loth, and the trio walked at a leisurely pace under the dark shadows of the oak-trees that lined the road to the village.

They passed behind the Vicarage; when the two ladies simultaneously uttered a sigh, and breathed in a whisper, 'Sweet spot!' Can it be doubted that both were thanked by a gentle pressure of the arm?

The house of Mrs Simpson lay on the road to that of Mrs Richards, and Miss Louisa made a decided halt before the door, distinctly pronouncing at the same time,

'Good night, my dear Mrs Simpson!'

But this lady knew the duties of a chaperon too well to think of leaving her young companion till she saw her safely restored to her mother's roof.

'Oh! no, my dear!' she exclaimed: 'if your house were a mile off, Louisa, I should take you home.'

'But you have been so poorly!' persisted the young lady, 'and it is so unnecessary!'

'IT IS RIGHT,' returned Mrs Simpson with an emphasis that marked too conscientious a feeling to be further resisted. So Miss Richards was taken home, and the fair widow languidly and slowly retraced her steps to her own door, with no other companion than the Vicar of Wrexhill.

CHAPTER XVI

CHARLES MOWBRAY'S ARRIVAL AT THE PARK

Never had Rosalind Torrington so strongly felt the want of some one to advise her what to do, as the morning after this disagreeable scene. Had she consulted her inclination only, she would have remained in her own apartments till the return of Mrs Mowbray and Helen. But more than one reason prevented her doing so. In the first place, she was not without hope that her letter would immediately bring young Mowbray home; and it would be equally disagreeable to miss seeing him, by remaining in her dressing-room, or to leave it expressly for the purpose of doing so: and secondly, however far her feelings might be from perfect confidence and esteem towards Miss Cartwright, she felt that she owed her something, and that it would be ungrateful and almost cruel to leave her tête-à-tête with the bewildered Fanny, or en tiers with her and the vicar.

She therefore determined to run the risk of encountering Mr Cartwright as usual, but felt greatly at a loss how to treat him. Their last démêlé had been too serious to be forgotten by either; and her opinion of him was such, that far from wishing to conciliate him, or in any way to efface the impression of what she had said on leaving him, her inclination and her principles both led her to wish that it should be indelible, and that nothing should ever lessen the distance that was now placed between them. But Rosalind felt all the difficulty of maintaining this tone towards a person not only on terms of intimate friendship with the family, but considered by part of it as a man whose word ought to be law. She began to fear, as she meditated on the position in which she was placed, that Mowbray Park could not long continue to be her home. The idea of Helen, and what she would feel at losing her, drew tears from her eyes; and then the remembrance of her Irish home, of her lost parents, and the terrible contrast between what she had heard last night, and the lessons and opinions of her dear father, made them flow abundantly.

The day passed heavily. Miss Cartwright appeared to think she had done enough, and devoted herself almost wholly to the perusal of a French metaphysical work which she had found in the library. Fanny was silent and sad, and seemed carefully to avoid being left for a moment alone with Rosalind. Mr Cartwright made no visit to the house during the morning; but Judy informed her mistress, when she came to arrange her dress for dinner, that the reverend gentleman had been walking in the shrubberies with Miss Fanny; and in the evening he made his entrance, as usual, through the drawing-room window.

It was the result of a strong effect produced by very excellent feeling, that kept Rosalind in the room when she saw him approach; but she had little doubt that if she went, Miss Cartwright would follow her, and she resolved that his pernicious tête-à-tête with Fanny should not be rendered more frequent by any selfishness of hers.

It was evident to her from Mr Cartwright's manner through the whole evening, that it was his intention to overload her with gentle kindness, in order to set off in strong relief her harsh and persecuting spirit towards him. But not even her wish to defeat this plan could enable her to do more than answer by civil monosyllables when he spoke to her.

Miss Cartwright laid aside her book and resumed her netting as soon as she saw him approach; but, as usual, she sat silent and abstracted, and the conversation was wholly carried on by the vicar and his pretty proselyte. No man, perhaps, had a greater facility in making conversation than the Vicar of Wrexhill: his habit of extempore preaching, in which he was thought by many to excel, probably contributed to give him this power. But not only had he an endless flow of words wherewith to clothe whatever thoughts suggested themselves, but moreover a most happy faculty of turning everything around him to account. Every object, animate or inanimate, furnished him a theme; and let him begin from what point he would, (unless in the presence of noble or influential personages to whom he believed it would be distasteful,) he never failed to bring the conversation round to the subject of regeneration and grace, the blessed hopes of himself and his sect, and the assured damnation of all the rest of the world.

Fanny Mowbray listened to him with an earnestness that amounted to nervous anxiety, lest she should lose a word. His awful dogmas had taken fearful hold of her ardent and ill-regulated imagination; while his bland and affectionate manner, his fine features and graceful person, rendered him altogether an object of the most unbounded admiration and interest to her.

As an additional proof, probably, that he did not shrink from persecution, Mr Cartwright again opened the piano-forte as soon as the tea equipage was removed, and asked Fanny if she would sing with him.

'With you, Mr Cartwright!' she exclaimed in an accent of glad surprise: 'I did not know that you sang. Oh! how I wish that I were a greater proficient, that I might sing with you as I would wish to do!'

'Sing with me, my dear child, with that sweet and pious feeling which

I rejoice to see hourly increasing in your heart. Sing thus, my dearest child, and you will need no greater skill than Heaven is sure to give to all who raise their voice to the glory of God. This little book, my dear Miss Fanny,' he continued, drawing once more the manuscript volume from his pocket, 'contains much that your pure and innocent heart will approve. Do you know this air?' and he pointed to the notes of 'Là ci darem' la mano.'

'Oh yes!' said Fanny; 'I know it very well.'

'Then play it, my good child. This too we have taken as spoil from the enemy, and instead of profane Italian words, you will here find in your own language thoughts that may be spoken without fear.'

Fanny instantly complied; and though her power of singing was greatly inferior to that of Rosalind, the performance, aided by the fine bass voice of Mr Cartwright, and an accompaniment very correctly played, was very agreeable. Fanny herself thought she had never sung so well before, and required only to be told by the vicar what she was to do next, to prolong the performance till considerably past Mr Cartwright's usual hour of retiring.

About an hour after the singing began, Henrietta approached Miss Torrington, and said in a whisper too low to be heard at the instrument, 'My head aches dreadfully. Can you spare me?'

As she had not spoken a single syllable since the trio entered the drawing-room after dinner, Rosalind could not wholly refrain from a smile as she replied 'Why, yes; I think I can.'

'I am not jesting; I am suffering, Rosalind. You will not leave that girl alone with him?'

'Dear Henrietta!' cried Rosalind, taking her hand with ready sympathy, 'I will not, should they sing psalms till morning. But is there nothing I can do for you – nothing I can give you that may relieve your head?'

'Nothing, nothing! Good night!' and she glided out of the room unseen by Fanny and unregarded by her father.

It more than once occurred to Miss Torrington during the two tedious hours that followed her departure, that Mr Cartwright, who from time to time stole a glance at her, prolonged his canticles for the purpose of making her sit to hear them; a species of penance for her last night's offence by no means ill imagined.

At length, however, he departed; and after exchanging a formal 'Good night,' the young ladies retired to their separate apartments.

Rosalind rose with a heavy heart the following morning, hardly knowing whether to wish for a letter from Charles Mowbray, which it was just possible the post might bring her, or not. If a letter arrived, there would certainly be no hope of seeing him; but if it did not, she should fancy every sound she heard foretold his approach, and she almost dreaded the having to answer all the questions he would come prepared to ask.

This state of suspense, however, did not last long; for, at least one hour before it was possible that a letter could arrive, Charles Mowbray in a chaise and four foaming post-horses rattled up to the door.

Rosalind descried him from her window before he reached the house; and her first feeling was certainly one of embarrassment, as she remembered that it was her summons which had brought him there. But a moment's reflection not only recalled her motives, but the additional reasons she now had for believing she had acted wisely; so, arming herself with the consciousness of being right, she hastened down stairs to meet him, in preference to receiving a message through a servant, requesting to see her.

She found him, as she expected, in a state of considerable agitation and alarm; and feeling most truly anxious to remove whatever portion of this was unnecessary, she greeted him with the most cheerful aspect she could assume, saying, 'I fear my letter has terrified you, Mr Mowbray, more than I wished it to do. But be quite sure that now you are here, everything will go on as it ought to do; and of course, when your mother returns, we can neither of us have any farther cause of anxiety about Fanny.'

'And what is your cause of anxiety about her at present, Miss Torrington? For God's sake explain yourself fully; you know not how I have been tormenting myself by fearing I know not what.'

'I am bound to explain myself fully,' said Rosalind gravely; 'but it is not easy, I assure you.'

'Only tell me at once what it is you fear. Do you imagine Mr Cartwright hopes to persuade Fanny to marry him?'

'I certainly did think so,' said Rosalind; 'but I believe now that I was mistaken.'

'Thank God!' cried the young man fervently. 'This is a great relief, Rosalind, I assure you. I believe now I can pretty well guess what it is you do fear; and though it is provoking enough, it cannot greatly signify. We shall soon cure her of any fit of evangelicalism with which the vicar is likely to infect her.'

'God grant it!' exclaimed Rosalind, uttering a fervent ejaculation in her turn.

'Never doubt it, Miss Torrington. I have heard a great deal about this Cartwright at Oxford. He is a Cambridge man, by the way, and there are lots of men there who think him quite an apostle. But the thing does not take at Oxford, and I assure you, he and his elective grace are famously quizzed. But the best of the joke is, that his son was within an ace of being expelled for performing more outrageous feats in the larking line than any man in the university; and in fact he must have been rusticated, had not his pious father taken him home before the business got wind, *to prepare him privately for his degree.* They say he is the greatest pickle in Oxford; and that, spite of the new light, his father is such an ass as to believe that all this is ordained by Providence only to make his election more glorious.'

'For his election, Mr Mowbray, I certainly do not care much; but for your sister — though I am aware that at her age there may be very reasonable hope that the pernicious opinions she is now imbibing may be hereafter removed, yet I am very strongly persuaded that if you were quite aware of the sort of influence used to convert her to Mr Cartwright's Calvinistic tenets, you would not only disapprove it, but use very effectual measures to put her quite out of his way.'

'Indeed! — I confess this appears to me very unnecessary. Surely the best mode of working upon so pure a mind as Fanny's is to reason with her, and to show her that by listening to those pernicious rhapsodies she is in fact withdrawing herself from the church of her fathers: but I think this may be done without sending her out of Mr Cartwright's way.'

'Well,' replied Rosalind very meekly, 'now you are here, I am quite sure that you will do everything that is right and proper. Mrs Mowbray cannot be much longer absent; and when she returns, you will perhaps have some conversation with her upon the subject.'

'Certainly. — And so Sir Gilbert has absolutely refused to act as executor?'

'He has indeed, and spite of the most earnest entreaties from Helen. Whatever mischief happens, I shall always think he is answerable for it; for his refusal to act threw your mother at once upon seeking counsel from Mr Cartwright, as to what it was necessary for her to do; and from that hour the house has never been free from him for a single day.'

'Provoking obstinacy!' replied Mowbray: 'yet, after all, Rosalind, the worst mischief, as you call it, that can happen, is our not being on such pleasant terms with them as we used to be. And the colonel is at home too; I must and will see him, let the old man be as cross as he will. — But where is your little saint? you don't keep her locked up, I hope, Rosalind? And where is this Miss of the new birth that you told me of?'

Young Mowbray threw a melancholy glance round the empty room as he spoke, and the kind-hearted Rosalind understood his feelings and truly pitied him. How different was this return home from any other he had ever made!

'The room looks desolate — does it not, Mr Mowbray? — Even I feel it so. I will go and let Fanny know you are here; but what reason shall I assign for your return?'

'None at all, Miss Torrington. The whim took me, and I am here. Things are so much better than I expected, that I shall probably be back again in a day or two; but I must contrive to see young Harrington.'

Rosalind left the room, heartily glad that Fanny's brother was near her, but not without some feeling of mortification at the little importance he appeared to attach to the information she had given him.

A few short weeks before, Rosalind would have entered Fanny's room with as much freedom as her own; but the schism which has unhappily entered so many English houses under the semblance of superior piety was rapidly doing its work at Mowbray Park, and the true friend, the familiar companion, the faithful counsellor, stood upon the threshold, and ventured not to enter till she had announced her approach by a knock at the dressing-room door.

'Come in,' was uttered in a gentle and almost plaintive voice by Fanny.

Miss Torrington entered, and, to her great astonishment, saw Mr Cartwright seated beside Fanny, a large Bible lying open on the table before them.

She looked at them for one moment without speaking. The vicar spread his open hand upon the Bible, as if to point out the cause of his being there; and as his other hand covered the lower part of his face, and his eyes rested on the sacred volume, the expression of his countenance was concealed.

Fanny coloured violently, – and the more so, perhaps, because she was conscious that her appearance was considerably changed since she met Miss Torrington at breakfast. All her beautiful curls had been carefully straightened by the application of a wet sponge; and her hair was now entirely removed from her forehead, and plastered down behind her poor little distorted ears as closely as possible.

Never was metamorphosis more complete. Beautiful as her features were, the lovely picture which Fanny's face used to present to the eye, required her bright waving locks to complete its charm; and without them she looked more like a Chinese beauty on a japan screen, than like herself.

Something approaching to a smile passed over Rosalind's features, which the more readily found place there, perhaps, from the belief that Charles's arrival would soon set her ringlets curling again.

'Fanny, your brother is come,' said she, 'and he is waiting for you in the drawing room.'

'Charles?' cried Fanny, forgetting for a moment her new character; and hastily rising, she had almost quitted the room, when she recollected herself, and turning back said,

'You will come too, to see Charles, Mr Cartwright?'

'I will come as usual this evening, my dear child,' said he with the appearance of great composure; 'but I will not break in upon him now. Was his return expected?' he added carelessly as he took up his hat; and as he spoke, Rosalind thought that his eye glanced towards her.

'No indeed!' replied Fanny: 'I never was more surprised. Did he say, Rosalind, what it was brought him home?'

'I asked him to state his reason for it,' replied Miss Torrington, 'and he told me he could assign nothing but whim.'

Rosalind looked in the face of the vicar, as she said this, and she perceived a slight, but to her perfectly perceptible change in its expression. He was evidently relieved from some uneasy feeling or suspicion by what she had said.

'Go to your brother, my dear child; let me not detain you from so happy a meeting for a moment.'

Fanny again prepared to leave the room: but as she did so, her eye chanced to rest upon her own figure reflected from a mirror above the chimney-piece. She raised her hand almost involuntarily to her hair.

'Will not Charles think me looking very strangely?' she said, turning towards Mr Cartwright with a blushing cheek and very bashful eye.

He whispered something in her ear in reply, which heightened her blush, and induced her to answer with great earnestness, 'Oh no!' and without farther doubt or delay, she ran down stairs. Miss Torrington followed her, not thinking it necessary to take any leave of the vicar, who gently found his way down stairs, and out of the house, as he had found his way into it, without troubling any servant whatever.

CHAPTER XVII

CHARLES'S AMUSEMENT AT HIS SISTER'S APPEARANCE – HE DISCUSSES HER CASE
WITH ROSALIND

Rosalind and Fanny entered the drawing-room together, and young Mowbray at the sound of their approach sprang forward to meet them; but the moment he threw his eyes on his sister, he burst forth into a fit of uncontrollable laughter, and though he kissed her again and again, still between every embrace he broke out anew, with every demonstration of vehement mirth.

'I am very glad to see you, Charles,' said Fanny with a little sanctified air that certainly was very amusing; 'but I should like it better if you did not laugh at me.'

'But my dear, dear, dearest child! how can I help it?' replied her brother, again bursting into renewed laughter. 'Oh Fanny, if you could but see yourself just as you look at this moment! Oh! you hideous little quiz! I would not have believed it possible that any plastering or shearing in the world could have made you look so very ugly. Is it not wonderful, Miss Torrington?'

'It certainly alters the expression of her countenance in a very remarkable manner;' replied Rosalind.

'The expression of a countenance may be changed by an alteration from within, as well as from without,' said Fanny, taking courage, and not without some little feeling of that complacency which the persuasion of superior sanctity is generally observed to bestow upon its possessors.

'Why, you most ugly little beauty!' cried Charles, again giving way to merriment; 'you don't mean to tell me that the *impayable* absurdity of that poor little face is owing to anything but your having just washed your hair?'

'It is owing to conviction, Charles,' replied Fanny with great solemnity.

'Owing to conviction? – To conviction of what, my poor little girl?'

'To conviction that it is right, brother.'

'Right, child, to make that object of yourself? What in the world can you mean, Fanny?'

'I mean, brother, that I have an inward conviction of the sin and folly of dressing our mortal clay to attract the eyes and the admiration of the worldly.'

'By worldly, do you mean of all the world?' said Rosalind.

'No, Miss Torrington. By worldly, I mean those whose thoughts and wishes are fixed on the things of the earth.'

'And it is the admiration of such only that you wish to avoid?' rejoined Rosalind.

'Certainly it is. Spiritual-minded persons see all things in the spirit – do all things in the spirit: of such there is nothing to fear.'

Young Mowbray meanwhile stood looking at his sister, and listening to her words with the most earnest attention.

At length he said, more seriously than he had yet spoken, 'To tell you the truth, little puritan, I do not like you at all in your new masquerading suit: though it must be confessed that you play your part well. I don't want to begin lecturing you, Fanny, the moment I come home; but I do hope you will soon get tired of this foolery, and let me see my poor father's daughter look and behave as a Christian young woman ought to do. Rosalind, will you take a walk with me? I want to have a look at my old pony.'

Miss Torrington nodded her assent, and they both left the room together, leaving Fanny more triumphant than mortified.

'He said that my persecutions would begin as soon as my election was made sure! Oh! why is he not here to sustain and comfort me! But I will not fall away in the hour of trial; I will not fear what man can do unto me!'

The poor girl turned her eyes from the window whence she saw her brother and Rosalind walking gaily and happily, as she thought, in search of the old pony, and hastened to take refuge in her dressing-room, now rendered almost sacred in her eyes by the pastoral visit she had that morning received there.

The following hour or two gave Fanny her first taste of martyrdom. She was, or at least had been, devotedly attached to her brother, and the knowing him to be so near, yet so distant from her, was terrible. Yet was she not altogether without consolation. She opened the Bible, – that Bible that *he* had so lately interpreted to her (fearful profanation!) in such a manner as best to suit his own views, and by means of using the process he had taught her, though unconsciously perhaps, she contrived to find a multitude of texts, all proving that she and the vicar were quite right, and all the countless myriads who thought differently, quite wrong. Then followed a thanksgiving which might have been fairly expressed in such words as 'Lord, I thank thee, I am not like other men!' and then, as the sweet summer air waved the acacias to and fro before her windows, and her young spirit, panting for lawns and groves, sunshine and shade, suggested the idea of her brother and Rosalind enjoying it all without her, her poetical vein came to her relief, and she sat down to compose a hymn, in which, after rehearsing prettily enough all the delights of summer rambles through verdant fields, for four stanzas, she completed the composition by a fifth, of which 'sin,' 'begin,' 'within,' formed the rhymes, – and 'Lord' and 'reward,' the crowning couplet.

This having recourse to 'song divine' was a happy thought for her, inasmuch as it not only occupied time which must otherwise have hung with overwhelming weight upon her hands, but the employment soon conjured up, as she proceeded, the image of Mr Cartwright, and the pious smile with which he would receive it from her hands, and the soft approval spoken more by the eyes than the lips, and the holy caress – such, according to his authority, as that with which angel meets angel in the courts of heaven.

All this was very pleasant and consoling to her feelings; and when her hymn was finished, she determined to go down stairs, in order to sing it to some (hitherto) profane air, which she might select from among the songs of her sinful youth.

As she passed the mirror, she again glanced at her disfigured little head; but at that moment she was so strong in 'conviction,' that, far from wishing to accommodate her new birth of *coiffure* to wordly eyes, she employed a minute or two in sedulously smoothing and controlling her rebellious tresses, and even held her head in stiff equilibrium to prevent their escape from behind her ears.

'Good and holy man!' she exclaimed aloud, as she gave a parting glance at the result of all these little pious coquetries. 'How well I know what his kind words would be, if he could see me now! "Of such are the kingdom of heaven, Fanny," he would say. And of such,' she added with a gentle sigh, 'will I strive to be, though all the world should join together to persecute me for it.'

While Mr Cartwright's prettiest convert was thus employed, Miss Torrington and Charles Mowbray, far from being engaged in chasing a pony, or even in looking at the summer luxury of bloom which breathed around them as they pursued their way through the pleasure-grounds, were very gravely discussing the symptoms of her case.

'It is a joke, Rosalind, and nothing more,' said the young man, drawing her arm within his. 'I really can do nothing but laugh at such folly, and I beg and entreat that you will do the same.'

'Then you think, of course, Mr Mowbray, that I have been supremely absurd in sending you the summons I did?'

'Far, very far otherwise,' he replied gravely. 'It has shown me a new feature in your character, Miss Torrington, and one which not to admire would be a sin, worse even than poor Mr Cartwright would consider your wearing these pretty ringlets, Rosalind.'

'*Poor* Mr Cartwright!' repeated Rosalind, drawing away her arm. 'How little do we think alike, Mr Mowbray, concerning that man!'

'The chief difference between us on the subject, I suspect, arises from your thinking of him a great deal, Rosalind, and my thinking of him very little. I should certainly, if I set about reasoning on the matter, feel considerable contempt for a middle-aged clergyman of the Church of England who manifested his care of the souls committed to his charge by making their little bodies comb their hair straight, for the pleasure of saying that it was done upon conviction. But surely there is more room for mirth than sorrow in this.'

'Indeed, indeed, you are mistaken! – and that not only as regards the individual interests of your sister Fanny, – though, God knows, I think that no light matter, – but as a subject that must be interesting to every Christian soul that lives. Do not make a jest of what involves by far the most important question that can be brought before poor mortals: it is unworthy of you, Mr Mowbray.'

'If you take the subject in its general character,' replied Charles, 'I am sure we shall *not* differ. I deplore as sincerely as you can do, Miss Torrington, the grievously schismatic inroad into our national church which these self-chosen apostles have made. But as one objection against them, though perhaps not the heaviest, is the contempt which their absurd puritanical ordinances have often brought upon serious things, I cannot but think that ridicule is a fair weapon to lash them withal.'

'It may be so,' replied Rosalind, 'and in truth it is often impossible to avoid using it; but yet it does not follow that the deeds and doctrines of these *soi-disant* saints give more room for mirth than sorrow.'

'Well, Rosalind, give me your arm again, and I will speak more seriously. The very preposterous and ludicrous manner which Fanny, or her spiritual adviser, has chosen for showing forth her own particular regeneration, has perhaps led me to treat it more slightly than I should have done had the indications of this temporary perversion of judgment been of a more serious character. That is doubtless one reason for the mirth I have shown. Another is, that I conceive it would be more easy to draw poor little Fanny back again into the bosom of Mother Church by laughing at her, rather than by making her believe herself a martyr.'

'Your laughter is a species of martyrdom which she will be taught to glory in enduring. But at present I feel sure that all our discussions on this topic must be in vain. I rejoice that you are here, though it is plain that you do not think her situation requires your presence; and I will ask no further submission of your judgment to mine, than requesting that you will not leave Mowbray till your mother returns.'

'Be assured I will not: and be assured also, that however much it is possible we may differ as to the actual atrocity of this new vicar, or the danger Fanny runs in listening to him, I shall never cease to be grateful, dearest Miss Torrington, for the interest you have shown for her, and indeed for us all.'

'Acquit me of silly interference,' replied Rosalind, colouring, 'and I will acquit you of all obligation.'

'But I don't wish to be acquitted of it,' said Charles rather tenderly: 'you do not know how much pleasure I have in thinking that you already feel interested about us all!'

This was giving exactly the turn to what she had done which poor Rosalind most deprecated. The idea that young Mowbray might imagine she had sent for him from *a general feeling of interest for the family*, had very nearly prevented her writing at all – and nothing but a sense of duty had conquered the repugnance she felt at doing it. It had not been a little vexing to perceive that he thought lightly of what she considered as so important; and now that in addition to this he appeared to conceive it necessary to return thanks for the *interest* she had manifested, Rosalind turned away her head, and not without difficulty restrained the tears which were gathering in her eyes from falling. She was not in general slow in finding words to express what she wished to say; but at this moment, though extremely desirous of answering *suitably*, as she would have herself described the power she wanted, not a syllable would suggest itself which she had courage or inclination to speak: so, hastening her steps towards the house, she murmured, 'You are very kind – it is almost time to dress, I believe,' and left him.

Charles felt that there was something wrong between them, and decided at once very generously that it must be his fault. There is nothing more difficult to trace with a skilful hand than the process by which a young man and maiden often *creep* into love, without either of them being at all aware at what moment they were first seized with the symptoms. When the parties *fall* in love, the thing is easy enough to describe: it is a shot, a thunderbolt, a whirlwind, or a storm; nothing can be more broadly evident than their hopes and their ecstasies, their agonies and their fears. But when affection grows unconsciously, and, like a seed of mignonette thrown at random, unexpectedly shows itself the sweetest and most valued of the heart's treasures, overpowering by its delicious breath all other fragrance, the case is different.

Something very like this creeping process was now going on in the heart of young Mowbray. Rosalind's beauty had appeared to him veiled by a very dark cloud on her first arrival from Ireland: she was weary, heartsick, frightened, and, moreover, dressed in very unbecoming mourning. But as tears gave place to smiles, fears to hopes, and exhausted spirits to light-hearted cheerfulness, he found out that 'she was very pretty indeed' – and then, and then, and then, he could not tell how it happened himself, so neither can I; but certain it is, that her letter gave him almost as much pleasure as alarm; and if, after being convinced that there was no danger of Mr Cartwright's becoming his brother-in-law, he showed a somewhat unbecoming degree of levity in his manner of treating Fanny's case, it must be attributed to the gay happiness he felt at being so unexpectedly called home.

As for the heart of Rosalind, if anything was going on therein at all out of the common way, she certainly was not aware of it. She felt vexed, anxious, out of spirits, as she sought her solitary dressing-room: but it would have been no easy task to persuade her that LOVE had anything to do with it.

CHAPTER XVIII

CHARLES WALKS OVER TO OAKLEY – THE VICAR IMPROVES IN HIS OPINION

At the time Miss Torrington observed to Mr Mowbray that it was near dressing-time, it wanted about four hours of dinner; so, having followed her with his eyes as she mounted the steps and entered the house, he drew out his watch, and perceiving that he had quite enough time for the excursion before 'dressing-time' would be over, set off to walk to Oakley.

How far Rosalind might have been disposed to quarrel with him for the very small proportion of meditation which he bestowed on Fanny during his delightful stroll through the well-known shady lanes, or how far she might have been tempted to forgive him for the much greater portion devoted to herself, it is impossible to say; but he arrived at Sir Gilbert's hall-door in that happy state of mind which is often the result of a delicious day-dream, when Hope lends the support of her anchor to Fancy.

Sir Gilbert and the colonel were out on horseback, the servant said – but 'my lady is in the garden.' And thither Mowbray went to seek her.

He was somewhat startled at his first reception; for the old lady watched his approach for some steps, standing stock-still, and without giving the slightest symptom of recognition. At length she raised her glass to her eye and discovered who the tall stranger was; upon which she sent forth a sound greatly resembling a view 'hollo!' which immediately recalled the servant who had marshalled Mowbray to the garden, and without uttering a word of welcome, gave the following order very distinctly:

'Let Richard take the brown mare and ride her sharp to Ramsden. Sir Gilbert is gone to the post-office, the bank, the saddler's, and the nursery-garden. Let him be told that Mr Mowbray is waiting for him at Oakley and let not a single instant be lost.'

The rapid manner in which 'Very well, my lady,' was uttered in reply, and the man vanished out of sight, showed that the order was likely to be as promptly executed as spoken.

'My dear, dear Charles!' cried the old lady; then stepping forward and placing her hands in his, 'what brings you back to Mowbray? But never mind what it is – nothing very bad, I hope, and then I must rejoice at it. I am most thankful to see you here, my dear boy. How is my sweet Helen? – could you not bring her with you, Charles?'

'She is in London, my dear Lady Harrington, with my mother. Where is the colonel?'

'With his father; – they will return together; no grass will grow under their horses' feet as they ride homeward to meet you, Charles! But how comes it that you are at home? If you have left Oxford, why are you not with your mother and Helen?'

A moment's thought might have told Mowbray that this question would certainly be asked, and must in some manner or other be answered; but the moment's thought had not been given to it, and he now felt considerably embarrassed how to answer. He lamented the estrangement already existing, however, too sincerely, to run any risk of increasing it by ill-timed reserve, and therefore, after a moment's hesitation, very frankly answered – 'I can tell you, my dear lady, why I am here, more easily than I can explain for what purpose. I returned post to Mowbray this morning, because Miss Torrington gave me a private intimation by letter, that she thought the new Vicar of Wrexhill was obtaining an undue influence over the mind of Fanny. She did not express herself very clearly, and I was fool enough to imagine that she supposed he was making love to her: but I find that her fears are only for poor little Fanny's orthodoxy. Mr Cartwright is one of the evangelical, decidedly, I believe, the most mischievous sect that ever attacked the established church; and Miss Torrington, not without good reason, fears that Fanny is in danger of becoming a proselyte to his gloomy and unchristian-like doctrine. But, at her age, such a whim as this is not, I should hope, very likely to be lasting.'

'I don't know that!' replied Lady Harrington sharply. 'Miss Torrington has acted with great propriety, and exactly with the sort of promptitude and decision of character for which I should have given her credit. Beware, Mr Mowbray, how you make light of the appearance of religious schism among you: it is a deadly weapon of discord, and the poison in which it is dipped seldom finds an antidote either in family affection or filial obedience.'

'But Fanny is so nearly a child, Lady Harrington, that I can hardly believe her capable of manifesting any very dangerous religious zeal at present.'

'You don't know what you are talking about, Charles! Of every family into which this insidious and most anti-christian schism has crept, you would find, upon inquiry, that in nine instances out of ten, it has been the young girls who have been selected as the first objects of conversion, and then made the active means of spreading it afterwards. Don't treat this matter lightly, my dear boy! Personally I know nothing of this Mr Cartwright; – we never leave our parish church and our excellent Dr Broughton, to run after brawling extempore preachers; – but I have been told by one or two of our neighbours who do, that he is what is called a *shining light*; which means, being interpreted, a ranting, canting fanatic. Take care, above all things, that your mother does not catch the infection.'

'My mother! – Oh no! Her steady principles and quiet good sense would render such a falling off as that quite impossible.'

'Very well! I am willing to hope so. And yet, Charles, I cannot for the life of me help thinking that she must have had some other adviser than her own heart when she left my good Sir Gilbert's letter without an answer.'

'Of what letter do you speak, Lady Harrington?' said young Mowbray, colouring; – 'of that whereby he refused to execute the trust my father bequeathed him?'

'No, Charles! Of that whereby he rescinded his refusal.'

'Has such a letter been sent?' inquired Mowbray eagerly. 'I never heard of it.'

'Indeed! Then we must presume that Mrs Mowbray did not think it worth mentioning. Such a letter has, however, been sent, Mr Mowbray; and I confess, I hoped, on seeing you arrive, that you were come to give it an amicable, though somewhat tardy answer, in person.'

'I am greatly surprised,' replied Charles, 'to hear that such a letter has been received by my mother, because I had been led to believe that Sir Gilbert had declared himself immovable on the subject; but still more am I surprised that I should not have heard of it. Could Helen know it, and not tell me? It must have been to her a source of the greatest happiness, as the one which preceded had been of the deepest mortification and sorrow.'

'Your sister, then, saw the first letter?'

'She did, Lady Harrington, and wrote me word of it, with expressions of the most sincere regret.'

'But of the second she said nothing? That is not like Helen.'

'So little is it like her, that I feel confident she never heard of the second letter.'

'I believe so too, Charles. But what, then, are we to think of your mother's having shown the first letter, and concealed the second?'

'It cannot be! my mother never conceals anything from us. We have never, from the moment we left the nursery, been kept in ignorance of any circumstance of general interest to the family. My poor father's constant phrase upon all such occasions was – "Let it be discussed in a committee of the whole house."'

'I cannot understand it,' replied the old lady, seating herself upon a bench in the shade; 'but, at any rate, I rejoice that you did not all think Sir Gilbert's recantation – which was not written without an effort, I promise you – so totally unworthy of notice as you have appeared to do.'

Charles Mowbray seated himself beside her, and nearly an hour was passed in conversation on the same subject, or others connected with it. At the end of that time, Sir Gilbert, booted and spurred, appeared at the door of the mansion, followed by his son. There was an angry spot upon his cheek, and though it was sufficiently evident that he was eager to meet young Mowbray, it was equally so that he was displeased with him.

Lady Harrington, however, soon cleared the way to the most frank and cordial communication, rendering all explanation unnecessary by exclaiming, 'He has never seen nor heard of your second letter, Sir Gilbert – nor Helen either.'

The baronet stood still for a moment, looking with doubt and surprise first at his wife, and then at his guest. The doubt, however, vanished in a moment, and he again advanced, and now with an extended hand, towards Charles.

A conversation of some length ensued; but as it consisted wholly of conjectures upon a point that they were all equally unable to explain, it is unnecessary to repeat it. The two young men met each other with expressions of the most cordial regard, and before they parted, Colonel Harrington related the conversation he had held with Helen and Miss Torrington, the result of which was his father's having despatched the letter whose fate appeared involved in so much mystery.

Lady Harrington, notwithstanding those who did not love her, called her masculine, showed some feminine tact in not mentioning, to Sir Gilbert that it was a letter from Miss Torrington which had recalled Charles. It is probable that when her own questionings had forced this avowal from him, she had perceived some shade of embarrassment in his answer; but she failed not to mention the *serious* turn that Fanny Mowbray appeared to have taken, and her suspicions that the new Vicar of Wrexhill must have been rather more assiduous than was desirable in his visits at the Park.

'The case is clear – clear as daylight, my lady: I understand it all. "By their fruits ye shall know them," – and by them shall ye know their fruits. Stop a moment, Charles: if you won't stay dinner, you must stay while I furnish you with a document by means of which you may, I think, make a useful experiment.'

Without waiting for an answer, Sir Gilbert left the party in the garden and hurried into the house, whence he returned in a few minutes with a scrap of paper in his hand.

'Fortunately, Charles, very fortunately, I have kept a copy of my last note to your mother. I am sure I know not what induced me to keep it: had such a thing happened to Mr Cartwright, he would have declared it providential – but I in my modesty only call it lucky. – Take this paper, Charles, and read it if you will: 'tis a d——d shame you have not read it before! You say, I think, that the vicar is expected at Mowbray this evening: just put this scrap of paper into his hand, and ask him if he ever read it before. Let him say what he will, I give you credit for sufficient sharpness to find out the truth. If he has seen it, I shall know whom I have to thank for the insolent contempt it has met with.'

'But my mother!' cried Charles with emotion. 'Is it possible that she could conceal such a note as this from her children, and show it to this man? Sir Gilbert, I cannot believe it.'

'I don't like to believe it myself, Charles; upon my soul I don't. But what can we think? At any rate, make the experiment to-night; it can do no harm; and come here to dinner to-morrow to tell us the result.'

'I will come to you with the greatest pleasure, and bring you all the intelligence I can get. My own opinion is, that the note was lost before it reached my mother's hands. The usual hour, I suppose, Sir Gilbert, – six o'clock?'

'Six o'clock, Charles, – and, as usual, punctual to a moment.'

When Mowbray reached his home, it was in truth rather more than time to dress; but he kept the young ladies waiting as short a time as possible. Fanny presented him in proper style to Miss Cartwright as soon as he appeared in the drawing-room; and he had the honour of giving that silent young lady his arm to the dining-room.

Charles thought her deep-set black eyes very handsome; nevertheless he secretly wished that she were a hundred miles off, for her presence, of course, checked every approach to confidential conversation.

Nothing, indeed, could well be more dull and unprofitable than this dinner. Miss Cartwright spoke not at all; Fanny, no more than was necessary for the performance of her duty at the head of the table; and Rosalind looked pale and languid, and so completely out of spirits that every word she spoke seemed a painful effort to her. She was occupied in recalling to mind the tone and air of the party who dined together in that same room about six months before, when Charles had last returned from Oxford. The contrast these recollections offered to the aspect of the present party was most painful; and as Rosalind turned her eyes round the table with a look of wistful melancholy, as if looking for those who were no longer there, her thoughts were so legibly written on her countenance that Mowbray understood them as plainly as if they had been spoken.

'Rosalind, will you take wine with me? – You look tired and pale.' This was said in a tone of affectionate interest that seemed to excite the attention of Henrietta; and when Miss Torrington raised her eyes to answer it, she observed that young lady's looks fixed on Mr Mowbray's countenance with an expression that denoted curiosity.

The whole party seemed glad to escape from the dinner-table; and the young ladies, with light shawls and parasols, had just wandered out upon the lawn, when they met Mr Cartwright approaching the house.

Fanny coloured, and looked at her brother. Miss Cartwright coloured too; and her eyes followed the direction of Fanny's, as if to see how this familiar mode of approach was approved by Mr Mowbray.

Charles certainly felt a little surprised, and did not take much pains to conceal it. For a moment he looked at the vicar, as if not quite certain who it was, and then, touching his hat with ceremonious politeness, said haughtily enough 'Mr Cartwright, I believe?'

It would have been difficult for any one to find fault with the manner in which this salutation was returned. In a tone admirably modulated between profound respect and friendly kindness, his hat raised gracefully from his head to greet the whole party, and his handsome features wearing an expression of the gentlest benevolence, Mr Cartwright hoped that he had the happiness of seeing Mr Mowbray well.

Charles felt more than half ashamed of the reception he had given him, and stretched out his hand as if to atone for it. The vicar felt his advantage, and pursued it by the most easy, winning, yet respectful style of conversation. His language and manners became completely those of an accomplished man of the world; his topics were drawn from the day's paper and the last review: he ventured a jest upon Don Carlos, and a *bon mot* upon the Duke of Wellington; took little or no notice of Fanny; spoke affectionately to his daughter, and gaily to Miss Torrington; and, in short, appeared to be as little deserving of all Rosalind had said of him as it was well possible for a gentleman to be.

'Fair Rosalind has certainly suffered her imagination to conjure up a bugbear in this man,' thought Charles. 'It is impossible he can be the violent fanatic she describes.'

After wandering about the gardens for some time, Fanny proposed that they should go in to tea; but before they reached the house, Mr Cartwright proposed to take his leave, saying that he had an engagement in Wrexhill, which was to prevent his lengthening his visit.

The adieu had been spoken on all sides, and the vicar turned from them to depart, when Charles recollected the commission he had received from Sir Gilbert, and that he had promised to report the result on the morrow. Hastily following him, therefore, he said, 'I beg your pardon, Mr Cartwright; but, before you go, will you have the kindness to read this note, and tell me if you know whether my mother received such a one before she went to London?'

Mr Cartwright took the note, read it attentively, and then returned it, saying, 'No, Mr Mowbray, I should certainly think not: not because I never saw or heard of it, but because I imagine that if she had, she would not have proceeded to London without Sir Gilbert. Was such a note as that sent, Mr Mowbray?'

Charles had kept his eye very steadily fixed on the vicar, both while he read the note, and while he spoke of it. Not the slightest indication, however, of his knowing anything about it was visible in his countenance, voice, or manner; and, again as he looked at him, young Mowbray felt ashamed of suspicions for which there seemed to be so little cause.

'Such a note as this was sent, Mr Cartwright,' he frankly replied: 'but I suspect that by some unlucky accident it never reached my mother's hands; otherwise, as you well observe, she would not, most assuredly, have set off to London on this business without communicating with Sir Gilbert Harrington.'

'I conceive it must be so, indeed, Mr Mowbray; and it is greatly to be lamented, for the receiving it would have saved poor Mrs Mowbray much anxiety and trouble.'

'She expressed herself to you as being annoyed by Sir Gilbert's refusing to act?'

'Oh yes, repeatedly; so much so, indeed, that nothing but the indispensable duty of my parish prevented my offering to accompany her to London myself. I wished her very much to send for you; but nothing would induce her to interrupt your studies.'

It is not in the nature of a frank-hearted young man to doubt statements thus simply uttered by one having the bearing and appearance of a gentleman; and Charles Mowbray reported accordingly at the dinner-table of Sir Gilbert, assuring him that the *test* had proved Mr Cartwright's innocence on this point most satisfactorily.

CHAPTER XIX

MR STEPHEN CORBOLD

We must now follow Mrs Mowbray and Helen to London, as some of the circumstances which occurred there proved of importance to them afterwards. The journey was a very melancholy one to Helen, and her feelings as unlike as possible to those which usually accompany a young lady of her age, appearance, and station, upon a visit to the metropolis. Mrs Mowbray spoke very little, being greatly occupied by the volume recommended to her notice, at parting, by Mr Cartwright; and more than once Helen felt something like envy at the situation of the two servants, who, perched aloft behind the carriage, were enjoying without restraint the rapid movement, the fresh air, and the beautiful country through which they passed; while she, like a drooping flower on which the sun has ceased to shine, hung her fair head, and languished for the kindly warmth she had lost.

They reached Wimpole Street about eight o'clock in the evening, and found everything prepared for them with the most sedulous attention in their handsome and commodious apartments.

Mrs Mowbray was tired, and, being really in need of the refreshment, blessed the hand, or rather the thought, which had forestalled all her wants and wishes, and spread that dearest of travelling banquets, tea and coffee, ready to greet her as she entered the drawing-room.

'This letter has been left for you, ma'am, by the gentleman who took the apartment,' said the landlady, taking a packet from the chimney-piece; 'and he desired it might be given to you immediately.'

Mrs Mowbray opened it; but perceiving it enclosed another, the address of which she glanced her eye upon, she folded it up again, and begged to be shown to her room while the tea was made.

Her maid followed her, but was dismissed with orders to see if Miss

Mowbray wanted anything. As soon as she was alone, she prepared to examine the packet, the receipt of which certainly startled her, for it was in the handwriting of Mr Cartwright, from whom she had parted but a few hours before.

The envelope contained only these words:

'Mr Stephen Corbold presents his respectful compliments to Mrs Mowbray, and will do himself the honour of waiting upon her tomorrow morning at eleven o'clock.'

'Gray's Inn, July 13th, 1833.'

Mrs Mowbray ran her eyes very rapidly over these words, and then opened the enclosed letter. It was as follows:–

'Do not let the unexpected sight of a letter from your minister alarm you, my dear and much-valued friend. I have nothing painful to disclose; and my sole object in writing is to make you feel that though you are distant from the sheltered spot wherein the Lord hath caused you to dwell, the shepherd's eye which hath been appointed to watch over you is not withdrawn.

'I am no longer a young man, my dear Mrs Mowbray; and during the years through which I have passed, my profession, my duty, and my inclination have alike led me to examine the souls of my fellow-creatures, and to read them, as it were, athwart the veil of their mortal bodies. Habit and application have given me, I believe, some skill in developing the inward character of those amongst whom I am thrown: nor can I doubt that the hand of God is in this, as in truth it is in all things if we do but diligently set ourselves to trace it; – I cannot, I say, but believe that this faculty which I feel so strong within me, of discerning in whom those spirits abide that the Lord hath chosen for his own, – I cannot but believe that this faculty is given me by his especial will and for his especial glory. I wish well, sincerely well, to the whole human race: I would never lose an opportunity of lifting my voice in warning to them, in the hope that peradventure there may be one among the crowd who may turn and follow me. But, my friend, far different is the feeling with which my soul clings with steadfast care and love to those on whom I see the anointing finger of the Lord. It is such that I would lead, even as a pilot leadeth the vessel intrusted to his skill, into the peaceful waters, where glory, and honour, and joy unspeakable and without end, shall abide with them for ever!

'Repine not, oh! my friend, if all your race are not of these. Rather rejoice with exceeding great joy that it hath pleased the Holy One to set his seal on TWO. To this effect, look round the world, my gentle friend, and see what myriads of roofs arise beneath which not one can be found to show forth the saving power of Christ. Mark them! how they thread the giddy maze, and dance onward down the slippery path that leads to everlasting damnation! Mark this, sweet spirit! and rejoice that you and your Fanny are snatched from the burning! My soul revels in an ecstasy of rapture unspeakable, as I gaze upon you both, and know that is I, even I, whom the Lord hath chosen to lead you to his pastures. What are all the victories and glories of the world to this? Think you, my gentle friend, that if all the worldly state and station of Lambeth were offered me on one side, and the task of leading thy meek steps into the way of life called me to the other, that I should hesitate for one single instant which to choose?

'Oh no! Trust me, I would meet the scorn and revilings of all men – ay, and the bitterest persecutions that ever the saints of old were called upon to bear, rather than turn mine eyes from thee and the dear work of thy salvation, though princedoms, principalities, and powers might be gained thereby!

'Be strong then in faith, be strong in hope; for thou art well loved of the Lord, and of him whom it hath been His will to place near thee as his minister on earth!

'Be strong in faith! Kneel down, sweet friend! – even now, as thine eye reads these characters traced by the hand of one who would give his life to guard thy soul from harm, kneel down, and ask that the Holy Ghost may be with thee, – well assured that he who bids thee do so will at the same moment be kneeling, likewise, to invoke blessings on thy fair and virtuous head!

'At the moment when the heart is drawn heavenward, as mine is now, how hateful – I may say, how profane, seem those worldly appellations and distinctions with which the silly vanity of man has sought to decorate our individual nothingness! How much more befitting a serious Christian is it, in such a moment as this, to use that name which was bestowed by the authority of Christ! You have three such, my sweet friend. The two first are now appropriated, as it were, to your daughters; but the third is more especially your own. – Clara! On Clara may the dew of Heaven descend like healing balm! On Clara may the Saviour and the Lamb set his seal! On Clara may the Holy Ghost descend to keep and overshadow her from all danger! – Kneel then, sweet Clara! – thou chosen handmaid of the Lord! kneel down, and think that William Cartwright kneels beside thee!

'Written on my knees in the secret recesses
of my own chamber. – W.C.'

No sooner did Mrs Mowbray's eye reach the words 'kneel down,' than she obeyed them, and in this attitude read to the end of the epistle. Mrs

Mowbray's feelings, whenever strongly excited, either by joy, sorrow, or any other emotion, always showed themselves in tears, and she now wept profusely – vehemently; though it is probable she would have been greatly puzzled to explain why, even to herself. She would certainly, however, have declared, had she spoken on the subject to any one, that those tears were a joy, a blessing, and a comfort to her. But as she had nobody to whom she could thus open her heart, she washed her eyes with cold water, and descended with all the composure she could assume to Helen and the tea-table.

Notwithstanding this precaution, Helen's watchful eye perceived that her mother had been weeping, and, forgetting the unnatural coldness which a breath more fatal than pestilence had placed between them, she exclaimed with all her wonted tenderness,

'What is the matter, dear mamma? – I trust that no bad news has met you?'

If all other circumstances left it a matter of doubt whether evangelical influence (as it is impiously called) were productive of good or evil, the terrible power which it is so constantly seen to have of destroying family union must be quite sufficient to settle the question. Any person who will take the trouble to inquire into the fact, will find that family affection has been more blighted and destroyed by the workings of this fearful superstition than by any other cause of which the history of man bears record.

The tone of Helen's voice seemed for a moment to recall former feelings, and her mother looked at her kindly: but before she could give utterance to any word of affection, the recollection of all Mr Cartwright had said to prove that Helen deserved not the affection of her mother, and that the only chance left to save her soul alive was to be found in the most austere estrangement, till such time as her hard heart should be softened: the recollection of all this came across the terrified mind of Mrs Mowbray, and she resumed the solemn and distant bearing she had of late assumed, with a nervous sensation of alarm at the great crime she had been on the point of committing.

Poor Helen saw the look, and listened with her whole soul in her eyes for the kind words which had so nearly followed it; but when they came not, her heart sank within her, and pleading fatigue, she begged to be shown to her room, where she spent half the night in weeping.

Most punctually at eleven o'clock on the following morning, Mr Stephen Corbold was announced, and a stiff priggish-looking figure entered the drawing-room, who, though in truth a 'special attorney,' looked much more like a thorough-bred methodistical preacher than his friend and cousin Mr Cartwright. In age he was a few years that gentleman's junior, but in all outward gifts most lamentably his inferior; being, in truth, as ill-looking and ungentlemanlike a person as any congregation attached to the 'Philo-Calvin Frybabe' principles could furnish.

The footman might have announced him in the same words as Lépine did Vadius:

> 'Madame, un homme est là, qui veut parler à vous.
> Il est vêtu de noir, et parle d'un ton doux.'

For, excepting his little tight cravat, he appeared to have nothing white about him, and he seldom raised his cautious voice above a whisper.

'I am here, madam,' he began, addressing himself to Mrs Mowbray, who felt rather at a loss what to say to him, 'at the request of my cousin, the Reverend William Jacob Cartwright, Vicar of Wrexhill. He hath given me to understand that you have business to transact at Doctors' Commons, relative to the last will and testament of your late husband. Am I correct, madam?'

'Quite so, Mr Corbold. I wish to despatch this business as quickly as possible, as I am anxious to return again to my family.'

'No delay shall intervene that I can prevent,' replied the attorney. 'Is there any other business, madam, in which my services can be available?'

'You are very kind, sir. I believe there are several things on which I shall have to trouble you. Mr Mowbray generally transacted his own business, which in London consisted, I believe, solely in receiving dividends and paying tradesmen's bills: the only lawyer he employed, therefore, was a gentleman who resides in our county, and who has hitherto had the care of the estates. But my excellent minister and friend Mr Cartwright has written upon this sheet of paper, I believe, what it will be necessary for me to do in order to arrange things for the future.'

Mrs Mowbray put the paper into the lawyer's hands, who read it over with great attention, nodding his head slightly from time to time as any item struck him as particularly interesting and important.

'Three per Cents – very good. Bank Stock – very good. Power of attorney. – All right, madam, all right. It hath pleased the Lord to give my cousin, his servant, a clear and comprehending intellect. All shall be done even as it is here set down.'

'How long, sir, do you think it will be necessary for me to remain in town?'

'Why, madam, there are many men would run this business out to great length. Here is indeed sufficient to occupy a very active professional man many weeks: but, by the blessing of God, which is often providentially granted to me in time of need, I question not but I may be able to release you in a few days, madam, provided always that you are prepared to meet such expenses as are indispensable upon all occasions when great haste is required.'

'Expense will be no object with me, Mr Corbold; but a prolonged absence from home would be extremely inconvenient. Pray remember that I shall be most happy to pay any additional sum which hastening through the business may require.'

'Very good, madam, very good. That the Lord will be good unto me in this business, I cannot presume to doubt; for it hath been consigned unto me by one of God's saints on earth, and it is for the service of a lady who, I am assured by him, is likely to become one of the most favoured agents that the Lord ever selected to do his work on earth.'

Mrs Mowbray coloured from a mixed feeling of modesty and pleasure. That Mr Cartwright should have thus described her, was most soothing to her heart; but when she recollected how far advanced he was in the favour of God, and how very near the threshold of grace she as yet stood, her diffidence made her shrink from hearing herself named in language so flattering.

'Is that fair young person who left the room soon after I entered it your daughter, madam?'

'Yes, sir.'

'Very good. I rejoice to hear it: that is, I would be understood to say, that I rejoice with an exceeding great joy that the child of a lady who stands in such estimation as you do with a chosen minister of God's elected church, should wear an aspect so suitable to one who, by the especial providence of God, will be led to follow her example.'

Mrs Mowbray sighed.

'I lament, madam,' resumed Mr Corbold, 'I may say with great and bitter lamentation, both for your sake, and that of the young person who has left the room, that the London season should be so completely over.'

'Sir!' said Mrs Mowbray in an accent of almost indignant surprise, 'is it possible that any friend and relation of Mr Cartwright's can imagine that I, in my unhappy situation – or indeed, without that, as a Christian woman hoping with fear and trembling to become one of those set apart from worldly things, – is it possible, sir, that you can think I should partake, or let my daughter partake, in the corrupt sinfulness and profane rioting of a London season!'

'May the Lord forgive you for so unjust a suspicion, most respected madam!' cried Mr Corbold, clasping his hands and raising his eyes to heaven. 'The language of the saints on earth is yet new to you, most excellent and highly-to-be-respected convert of my cousin! The London season of which I speak, and which you will hear alluded to by such of the Lord's sinful creatures as, like me, have reason to believe by an especial manifestation of grace that they are set apart for the service of the Lord, – the London season of which I and they speak, is that when, during about six blessed weeks in the spring, the chosen vessels resort in countless numbers to London, for the purpose of being present at all the meetings which take place during that time, with as much ardour and holy zeal as the worldly-minded show in arranging their fêtes and their fooleries at the instigation of Satan – in anticipation, at it should seem, poor deluded souls! of the crowds that they shall hereafter meet amidst fire and brimstone in his realms below. The season of which I speak, and of which you will hear all the elect speak with rapture and thanksgiving, consists of a quick succession of splendid and soul-stirring meetings, at which all the saints on whom the favour of the Lord has descended in the gift of speech hold forth in his glory, some for one, some for two, some for three, some for four, – ay, some for five hours at a time, sustained, as you may suppose, by a visible resting of the Holy Ghost upon them through the Lord's will. This, madam, is the season that, for your sake, and the sake of the fair young person your daughter, I wished was not yet over.'

Mrs Mowbray made a very penitent and full apology for the blunder she had committed, and very meekly confessed her ignorance, declaring that she had never before heard the epithet of 'London season' given to anything so heavenly-minded and sublime as the meetings he described.

The discovery of this species of ignorance on the part of Mrs Mowbray, which was by no means confined to the instance above mentioned, was a very favourable circumstance for Mr Corbold. There was, perhaps, no other subject in the world upon which he was competent to give information (except in the technicalities of his own profession); but in everything relating to missionary meetings, branch-missionary meetings' reports, child's missionary branch committees, London Lord's-day's societies, and the like, he was quite perfect. All this gave him a value in Mrs Mowbray's eyes as a companion which he might have wanted without it. At all conversations of this kind, Mrs Mowbray took great care that Helen should be present, persuaded that nothing could be so likely to give her that savour of righteousness in which, as yet, she was so greatly deficient.

The consequence of this arrangement was twofold. On Helen's side, it generated a feeling compounded of contempt and loathing towards the regenerated attorney, which in most others would have led to the passion called hatred; but in her it seemed rather a passive than an active sentiment, which would never have sought either nourishment or relief in doing injury to its object, but which rendered her so ill at ease in his presence that her life became pefectly wretched from the frequency of it.

On the part of the gentleman, the effect of these frequent interviews was different. From thinking Mrs Mowbray's daughter a very fair young person, he grew by gradual, but pretty rapid degrees, to perceive that she was the very loveliest tabernacle in which the Lord had ever enshrined the spirit of a woman; and by the time Mrs Mowbray had learned by rote the names, titles, connexions, separations, unions, deputations, and endowments of all the missionary societies, root and branch, and of all the central and eccentric evangelical establishments for the instruction of ignorance in infants of four months to adults of four-score, Mr Stephen Corbold had made up his mind to believe that, by fair means or foul, it was his bounden duty, as a pious man and serious Christian, to appropriate the fair Helen to himself in this life, and thereby ensure her everlasting glory in the life to come.

It must not be supposed that while these things passed in London the Vicar of Wrexhill was forgotten. Mrs Mowbray's heart and conscience both told her that such a letter as she had received from him must not remain unanswered: she therefore placed Helen in the drawing-room, with a small but very closely-printed volume on 'Free Grace,' recommended by Mr Corbold, and having desired her, in the voice of command, to study it attentively till dinner-time, she retired to her own room, where, having knelt, wept, prayed, written, and erased, for about three hours, she finally signed and sealed an epistle, of which it is unnecessary to say more than that it conveyed a very animated feeling of satisfaction to the heart of the holy man to whom it was addressed.

CHAPTER XX

MR STEPHEN CORBOLD RETURNS WITH MRS MOWBRAY AND HELEN TO WREXHILL

Mrs Mowbray's business in London, simple and straightforward as it was, might probably under existing circumstances have occupied many weeks, had not a lucky thought which visited the restless couch of Mr Stephen Corbold been the means of bringing it to a speedy conclusion.

'*Soyez amant, et vous serez inventif,*' is a pithy proverb, and has held good in many an illustrious instance, but in none, perhaps, more conspicuously than in that of Mr Stephen Corbold's passion for Miss Mowbray. One of the earliest proofs he gave of this, was the persuading Mrs Mowbray that the only way in which he could, consistently with his other engagements, devote to her as much time as her affairs required, would be, by passing every evening with her. And he did pass every evening with her: and poor Helen was given to understand, in good set terms, that if she presumed to retire before that excellent man Mr Stephen Corbold had finished his last tumbler of soda-water and Madeira, not only would she incur her mother's serious displeasure, but be confided (during their absence from Mowbray) to the spiritual instruction of some *earnest* minister, who would teach her in what the duty of a daughter consisted.

And so Helen Mowbray sat till twelve o'clock every night, listening to the works of the saints of the nineteenth century, and exposed to the unmitigated stare of Mr Stephen Corbold's grey eyes.

The constituting himself the guide and protector of the ladies through a series of extemporary preachings and lecturings on Sunday, was perhaps too obvious a duty to be classed as one of love's invention; but the ingenuity shown in persuading Mrs Mowbray that it would be necessary for the completion of her business that he should attend her home, most certainly deserves this honour.

Though no way wanting in that quality of mind which the invidious denominate 'impudence,' and the judicious 'proper confidence' – a quality as necessary to the fitting out of Mr Stephen Corbold as parchment and red tape, – he nevertheless felt some slight approach to hesitation and shame-facedness when he first hinted the expediency of this measure. But his embarrassment was instantly relieved by Mrs Mowbray's cordial assurance that she rejoiced to hear such a manner of concluding the business was possible, as she knew it would give their 'excellent minister' pleasure to see his cousin.

There is no Christian virtue, perhaps, to which a serious widow lady is so often called (unless she belong to that class invited by the 'exemplary' in bevies, by way of charity, when a little teapot is set between every two of them,) – there is no Christian virtue more constantly inculcated on the minds of *rich* serious widows than that of hospitality; nor is there a text that has been quoted oftener to such, or with greater variety of accent, as admonitory, encouragingly, beseechingly, approvingly, jeremiadingly in reproach, and hallelujahingly in gratitude and admiration, than those three impressive and laudatory words of Saint Paul,

'GIVEN TO HOSPITALITY!'

During a snug little morning visit at the Park, at which only Mrs Mowbray and Fanny were present, Mr Cartwright accidentally turned to these words; and nothing could be more touchingly eloquent than the manner in which he dwelt upon and explained them.

From that hour good Mrs Mowbray had been secretly lamenting the want of sufficient opportunity to show how fully she understood and valued this Christian virtue, and how willing she was to put it in practice toward all such as her 'excellent minister' should approve: it was, therefore, positively with an outpouring of fervent zeal that she welcomed the prospect of a visit from *such a man* as Mr Stephen Corbold.

'It is indeed a blessing and a happiness, Mr Corbold,' said she, 'that what I feared would detain me many days from my home and my family should, by God's providence, be converted into such a merciful dispensation as I must consider your coming to be. When shall you be able to set out, my dear sir?'

'I could set out to-morrow, or, at the very latest, the day after, if I could obtain a conveyance that I should deem perfectly safe for the papers I have to carry.'

Helen shuddered, for she saw his meaning lurking in the corner of his eye as he turned towards her one of his detested glances.

'Perhaps,' said Mrs Mowbray, hesitatingly, and fearful that she might be taxing his great good-nature too far, – 'perhaps, upon such an urgent occasion, you might have the great goodness, Mr Corbold, to submit to making a third in my travelling-carriage?'

'My gratitude would indeed be very great for such a permission,' he replied, endeavouring to betray as little pleasure as possible. 'I do assure you, my dear lady, such precautions are far from unnecessary. The Lord, for his own especial purposes, which are to us inscrutable, ordains that his tender care to usward shall be shown rather by giving us prudence and forethought to avoid contact with the wicked, than by any removal of them, by his holy intervention, from our path: wherefore I hold myself bound in righteousness to confess that the papers concerning your affairs – even yours, my honoured lady, – might run a very fearful risk of being abducted, and purloined, by some of the many ungodly persons with whom no dispensation of Providence hath yet interfered to prevent their jostling his own people when they travel, as sometimes unhappily they must do, in stage-coaches.'

'Ah, Mr Corbold!' replied the widow, (mentally alluding to a conversation which she had held with Mr Cartwright on the separation to be desired between the chosen and the not-chosen even in this world; such being, as he said, a sort of type or foreshowing of that eternal separation promised in the world to come;) – 'Ah, Mr Corbold! if I had the power to prevent it, no chosen servants of the Lord should ever again find themselves obliged to submit to such promiscuous mixture with the ungodly as this unsanctified mode of travelling must lead to. Had I power and influence sufficient to carry such an undertaking into effect, I would certainly endeavour to institute a society of Christians, who, by liberal subscriptions among themselves, might collect a fund for defraying the travelling expenses of those who are set apart for salvation. It must be an abomination in the eyes of the Lord, Mr Corbold, that such should be seen travelling on earth by the same vehicles as those which convey the wretched beings who are on their sure and certain road to eternal destruction!'

'Ah, dearest madam!' replied the attorney, with a profound sigh, 'such thoughts as those are buds of holiness that shall burst forth into full-blown flowers of eternal glory round your head in heaven! But alas! no such society is yet formed, and the sufferings of the righteous, for the want of it, are truly great!'

'I am sure they must be, Mr Corbold,' replied the kind Mrs Mowbray in an accent of sincere compassion; 'but, at least in the present instance, you may be spared such unseemly mixture, if you will be good enough not to object to travelling three in the carriage. Helen is very slight, and I trust you will not be greatly incommoded.'

Mr Corbold's gratitude was too great to be expressed in a sitting attitude; he therefore rose from his chair, and pressing his extended hands together as if invoking a blessing on the meek lady's holy head, he uttered, 'God reward you, madam, for not forgetting those whom the Lord hath remembered!' and as he spoke, he bowed his head low, long, and reverently. As he recovered the erect position on ordinary occasions permitted to man, he turned a little round to give a glance of very lover-like timidity towards Helen, who when he began his reverence to her mother was in the room; but as he now turned his disappointed eyes all round it, he discovered that she was there no longer.

After this, the business which could, as Mr Corbold said, be conveniently transacted in London, was quickly despatched, and the day fixed for their return to Mowbray, exactly one week after they left it.

Mr Stephen Corbold was invited to breakfast previous to the departure; and he came accompanied by so huge a green bag, as promised a long stay among those to whose affairs the voluminous contents related.

When all things in and about the carriage were ready, Mr Stephen Corbold presented his arm to the widow, and placed her in it. He then turned to Helen, who on this occasion found it not so easy as at setting off to avoid the hand extended towards her; that is to say, she could not spring by it unheeded: but as she would greatly have preferred the touch of any other reptile, she contrived to be very awkward, and actually caught hold of the handle beside the carriage-door, instead of the obsequious ungloved fingers which made her shudder as she glanced her eyes towards them.

'You will sit in the middle, Helen,' said Mrs Mowbray.

'I wish, mamma, you would be so kind as to let me sit in the dickey,' replied the young lady, looking up as she spoke to the very comfortable and unoccupied seat in front of the carriage, which, but for Mrs Mowbray's respectful religious scruples, might certainly have accommodated Mr Corbold and his bag perfectly well. 'I should like it so much better, mamma!'

'Let me sit in the middle, I entreat!' cried Mr Corbold, entering the carriage in haste, to prevent further discussion. 'My dear young lady,' he continued, placing his person in the least graceful of all imaginable attitudes, – 'my dear young lady, I beseech you——'

'Go into the corner, Helen!' said Mrs Mowbray hastily, wishing to put so exemplary a Christian more at his ease, and without thinking it necessary to answer the insidious petition of her daughter, which, as she thought, plainly pointed at the exclusion of the righteous attorney.

Helen ventured not to repeat it, and the carriage drove off. For the first mile Mr Stephen Corbold sat, or rather perched himself, at the extremest edge of the seat, his hat between his knees, and every muscle that ought to have been at rest in active exercise, to prevent his falling foward on his nose; every feature, meanwhile, seeming to say, 'This is not my carriage.' But by gentle degrees he slid farther and farther backwards, till his spare person was not only in the enjoyment of ease, but of great happiness also.

Helen, as her mother observed, was 'very slight,' and Mr Corbold began almost to fancy that she would at last vanish into thin air, for, as he quietly advanced, so did she quietly retreat, till she certainly did appear to shrink into a very small compass indeed.

'I fear I crowd you, my dearest lady!' he said, addressing Mrs Mowbray, at least ten times during as many miles; and every time this fear came over him he gave her a little more room, dreadfully to the annoyance of the slight young lady on the other side of him. Poor Helen had need to remember that she was going home – going to Rosalind, to enable her to endure the disgust of her position; but for several hours she did bear it heroically. She thought of Mowbray, – of her flower-garden, – of the beautiful Park, – of Rosalind's snug dressing-room, and the contrast of all this to the life she had led in London. She thought too of Oakley, and of the possibility that some of the family might, by some accident or other, be met in some of the walks which Rosalind and she would be sure to take. In short, with her eyes incessantly turned through the open window towards the hedges and ditches, the fields and the flowers by the road-side, she contrived to keep herself, body and soul, as far as possible from the hated being who sat beside her.

On the journey to London, Mrs Mowbray had not thought it necessary to stop for dinner on the road, both she and Helen preferring to take a sandwich in the carriage; but the fear of infringing any of the duties of that hospitality which she now held in such high veneration, she arranged matters differently, and learning, upon consulting her footman, that an excellent house was situated about half-way between London and Wrexhill, she not only determined upon stopping there, but directed the man to send forward a note, ordering an early dinner to be ready for them.

This halt was an agreeable surprise to Mr Stephen Corbold. It was indeed an arrangement such as those of his peculiar sect are generally found to approve; for it is a remarkable fact, easily ascertained by any who will give themselves the trouble of inquiry, that the serious Christians of the present age indulge themselves bodily, whenever the power of doing so falls in their way, exactly in proportion to the mortifications and privations with which they torment their spirits: so that while a young sinner would fly from an untasted glass of claret that he might not lose the prologue to a new play, a young saint would sip up half-a-dozen (if he could get them) while descanting on the grievous pains of hell which the pursuit of pleasure must for ever bring.

The repast, and even the wine, did honour to the recommendation of the careful and experienced Thomas: and Mrs Mowbray had the sincere satisfaction of seeing Mr Corbold ('*le pauvre homme!*') eat half a pound of salmon, one-third of a leg of lamb, and three-quarters of a large pigeon-pie, with a degree of relish that proved to her that she was 'very right to stop for dinner.'

Nothing can show gratitude for such little attentions as these so pleasantly and so effectually as taking full advantage of them. Mr Corbold indeed carried this feeling so far, that even after the two ladies had left the room, he stepped back and pretty nearly emptied the two decanters of wine before he rejoined them.

The latter part of the journey produced a very disagreeable scene, which, though it ended, as Helen thought at the time, most delightfully for her, was productive in its consequences of many a bitter heart-ache.

It is probable that the good cheer at D——, together with the final libation that washed it down, conveyed more than ordinary animation to the animal spirits of the attorney, and for some miles he discoursed with more than his usual unction on the sins of the sinful, and the holiness of the holy, till poor dear Mrs Mowbray, despite her vehement struggles to keep her eyes open, fell fast asleep.

No sooner was Mr Stephen Corbold fully aware of this fact, than he began making some very tender speeches to Helen. For some time her only reply was expressed by thrusting her head still farther out of the side window. But this did not avail her long. As if to intimate to her that a person whose attention could not be obtained through the medium of the ears must be roused from their apathy by the touch, he took her hand.

Upon this she turned as suddenly as if an adder had stung her, and fixing her eyes, beaming with rage and indignation, upon him, said,

'If you venture, sir, to repeat this insult, I will call to the postilions to stop, and order the footman instantly to take you out of the carriage.'

He returned her glance, however, rather with passion than repentance, and audaciously putting his arm round her waist, drew her towards him, while he whispered in her ear, 'What would your dear good mamma say to that?'

Had he possessed the cunning of Mephistophiles, he could not have uttered words more calculated to unnerve her. The terrible conviction that it was indeed possible her mother might justify, excuse, or, at any rate pardon the action, came upon her heart like ice, and burying her face in her hands, she burst into tears.

Had Mr Stephen Corbold been a wise man, he would have here ceased his persecution: he saw that she was humbled to the dust by the reference he had so skilfully made to her mother, and perhaps, had he emptied only one decanter, he might have decided that it would be desirable to leave her in that state of mind. But, as it was, he had the very exceeding audacity once more to put his arm round her, and by a sudden and most unexpected movement, impressed a kiss upon her cheek.

Helen uttered a piercing scream; and Mrs Mowbray, opening her eyes, demanded in a voice of alarm, 'What is the matter?'

Mr Corbold sat profoundly silent; but Helen answered in great agitation, 'I can remain in the carriage no longer, mamma, unless you turn out this man!'

'Oh, Helen! Helen! what can you mean by using such language?' answered her mother. 'It is pride, I know, abominable pride, – I have seen it from the very first, – which leads you to treat this excellent man as you do. Do you forget that he is the relation as well as the friend of our minister? Fie upon it, Helen! you must bring down this haughty spirit to something more approaching meek Christian humility, or you and I shall never be able to live together.'

It seems almost like a paradox, and yet it is perfectly true, that had not Mrs Mowbray from *the very first*, as she said, perceived the utter vulgarity, in person, language, and demeanour, of the vicar's cousin, she would have been greatly less observant and punctilious in her civilities towards him; nor would she have been so fatally ready to quarrel with her daughter for testifying her dislike of a man who, her own taste told her, would be detestable, were not the holiness of his principles such as to redeem every defect with which nature, education, and habit had afflicted him.

The more Mrs Mowbray felt disposed to shrink from an intimate association with the serious attorney, the more strenuously did she force her nature to endure him; and feeling, almost unconsciously perhaps, that it was impossible Helen should not detest him, she put all her power and authority in action, not only to prevent her showing it, but to prevent also so very sinful and worldly-minded a sentiment from taking hold upon her young mind.

Helen, however, was too much irritated at this moment to submit, as she had been ever used to do, to the commands of her mother; and still feeling the pressure of the serious attorney's person against her own, she let down the front glass, and very resolutely called to the postilions to stop.

The boy who rode the wheeler immediately heard and obeyed her.

'Tell the servant to open the door,' said she with a firmness and decision which she afterwards recalled to herself with astonishment.

Thomas, who the moment the carriage stopped had got down, obeyed the call she now addressed to him, – opened the door, gave her his arm; and before either Mrs Mowbray, or the serious attorney either, had fully recovered from their astonishment, Helen was comfortably seated on the dickey, enjoying the cool breeze of a delicious afternoon upon her flushed cheek.

The turn which was given to this transaction by Mr Stephen Corbold during the tête-à-tête conversation he enjoyed for the rest of the journey with the young lady's mother, was such as to do credit to his acuteness; and that good lady's part in it showed plainly that the new doctrines she had so rapidly imbibed, while pretending to purify her heart, had most lamentably perverted her judgment.

CHAPTER XXI

THE RETURN

On reaching Mowbray, the first figure which greeted the eyes of the travellers was that of Charles, stationed on the portico steps waiting to receive them. A line from Helen to Rosalind, written only the day before, announced their intended return; but the appearance of Charles was a surprise to them, and to Helen certainly the most delightful that she could have experienced.

Mr Cartwright had written a long and very edifying letter to Mrs Mowbray, informing her of the unexpected arrival of her son from the scene of his studies, and making such comments upon it as in his wisdom seemed good. But though this too was written in the secret recesses of his own chamber, with many affecting little circumstances demonstrative of his holy and gentle emotions while so employed, it was nevertheless, under the influence of still riper wisdom, subsequently destroyed, because he thought that the first surprise occasioned by the young man's unwonted appearance would be more likely to produce the effect he desired than even his statement.

Neither Rosalind nor Charles himself had written, because they were both unwilling to state the real cause of his coming, and thought the plea of *whim* would pass off better in conversation than on paper. That Fanny should write nothing which good Mr Cartwright did not wish known, can be matter of surprise to no one.

Helen, who had descried Charles before the carriage stopped, descended from her lofty position with dangerous rapidity, and sprang into his arms with a degree of delight greater, perhaps, than she had ever before felt at seeing him.

The exclamation of Mrs Mowbray certainly had in it, as the wise vicar predicted, a tone that indicated displeasure as well as surprise; and the embrace, which she could not refuse, was so much less cordial than it was wont to be, that he turned again to Helen, and once more pressed her to his heart, as if to console him for the want of tenderness in his mother's kiss.

Meanwhile, Mr Stephen Corbold stood under the lofty portico, lost in admiration at the splendid appearance of the house and grounds. Mrs Mowbray, with a sort of instinctive feeling that this excellent person might not altogether find himself at his ease with her family, hastened towards him, determined that her own Christian humility should at least set them a good example, and putting out both her hands towards him, exclaimed with an earnestness that sounded almost like the voice of prayer,

'Welcome, *dear*, DEAR, Mr Corbold, to my house and home! and may you find in it the comfort and hospitality your exemplary character deserves!' Then turning to her son, she added, 'I know not how long you are likely to stay away from college, Charles; but while you are here, I beg that you will exert yourself to the very utmost to make Mowbray agreeable to this gentleman; and remember, if you please, that his religious principles, and truly edifying Christian sentiments, are exactly such as I would wish to place before you as an example.'

Charles turned round towards the serious attorney, intending to welcome him with an extended hand; but the thing was impossible. There was that in his aspect with which he felt that he could never hold fellowship, and his salutation was turned into a ceremonious bow; a change which it was the less difficult to make, from the respectful distance at which the stranger guest placed himself, while preparing to receive the young man's welcome.

Though Rosalind had purposely remained in her own apartment till the first meeting with Charles was over, Helen was already in her arms;

having exchanged a hasty kiss with Fanny, whom she met in the hall, hastening to receive her mother.

'Oh! my dearest Rosalind! How thankful am I to be once more with you again! I never, I think, shall be able to endure the sight of London again as long as I live. I have been so very, very wretched there!'

'Upon my word, Helen, I have not lived upon roses since you went. You can hardly be so glad to come back, as I am to have you. What did your mother say on seeing Charles?'

'I hardly know. She did not, I think, seem pleased to see him; but I am more delighted at the chance that has brought him, let it be what it will, than I have words to express. Oh! it is such a blessing to me! – dear, dear, Charles! he knows not what a treasure he is. The very sight of him has cured all my sorrows – and yet I was dreadfully miserable just now.'

'Then, thank God! he is here, my own Helen! But tell me, dearest, what is it has made you miserable? Though you tell me it is over, the tears seemed ready to start when you said so.'

'Oh! my woes will make a long story, Rosalind; and some of them must be for your ear only; but this shall be at night, when nobody is near to hear us: – but, by the way, you must have a great deal to tell me. How comes it that Charles is here? And, what seems stranger still, how comes it that, as he *is* here, you have not been living upon roses?'

'My woes may make a story as well as yours, Helen; and a long one too, if I tell all: but it must come out by degrees, – a series of sketches, rather than an history.'

'Have you seen anybody from Oakley, Rosalind?'

'Ah, Helen!' said Rosalind smiling, as she watched the bright colour mounting even to the brows of her friend; 'your history, then, has had nothing in it to prevent your remembering Oakley?'

'My history, as you call it, Rosalind, has been made up of a series of mortifications: some of them have almost broken my heart, and my spirit too; but others have irritated me into a degree of courage and daring that might perhaps have surprised you; and everything that has happened to me, has sent my thoughts back to my home and to my friends, – all my friends, Rosalind, – with a degree of clinging and dependent affection such as I never felt before.'

'My poor Helen! But look up, dearest! and shed no tears if you can help it. We all seem to be placed in a very singular and unexpected position, my dear friend; but it is not tears that will help us out of it. This new man, this vicar, seems inclined to go such lengths with his fanatical hypocrisy, that I have good hopes your mother and Fanny will ere long get sick of him and his new lights, and then all will go right again. Depend upon it, all that has hitherto gone wrong, has been wholly owing to him. I certainly do not think that your poor father's will was made in the spirit of wisdom: but even *that* would have produced none of the effects it has done, had not this hateful man instilled, within ten minutes after the will was read, the poison of doubt and suspicion against Charles, into the mind of your mother. Do you not remember his voice and his look, Helen, when he entered the room where we were all three sitting with your mother? I am sure I shall never forget him! I saw, in an instant, that he intended to make your mother believe that Charles resented the will; and that, instead of coming himself, he had sent him to your mother to tell her of it. I hated him then; and every hour that has passed since, has made me hate him more. But let us take hope, Helen, even from the excess of the evil. Your mother cannot long remain blind to his real character; and, when she once sees him as he is, she will again become the dear kind mother you have all so fondly loved.'

'Could I hope this, Rosalind, for the future, there is nothing I could not endure patiently for the present, – at least, nothing that could possibly happen while Charles is here; but I do not hope it.'

There was a melancholy earnestness in Helen's voice, as she pronounced the last words, that sounded like a heavy prophecy of evil to come, in the ears of Rosalind. 'God help us, then!' she exclaimed. 'If we are really to live under the influence and authority of the Vicar of Wrexhill, our fate will be dreadful. If your dear father had but been spared to us a few years longer, – if you and I were but one-and-twenty, Helen, – how different would be the light in which I should view all that now alarms us; my fortune would be plenty for both of us, and I would take you with me to Ireland, and we would live with——'

'Oh Rosalind! how can you talk so idly? Do you think that anything would make me leave my poor dear mother?'

'If you were to marry, for instance?'

'I should never do that without her consent; and that, you know, would hardly be leaving her.'

'Well! "God and our innocency defend and guard us!" for I do think, Helen, we are in a position that threatens vexation, to say the least of it. I wonder if Miss Cartwright's visit is to end with your absence? She is the very oddest personage! sometimes I pity her; sometimes I almost admire her; sometimes I feel afraid of her, but never by any chance can I continue even to fancy that I understand her character.'

'Indeed! Yet in general you set about that rather rapidly, Rosalind. But must we not go down? I have hardly seen Fanny, and I long to talk a little to my own dear Charles.'

'And you will like to have some tea after your journey. Mrs Mowbray, I think, never stops *en route*?'

'In general she does not; but today ——' a shudder ran through

Helen's limbs as she remembered the travelling adventures of the day, and she stopped.

'You look tired and pale, Helen! Come down, take some tea, and then go to bed directly. If we do not act with promptitude and decision in this matter, we shall sit up talking all night.'

As they passed Miss Cartwright's door, Rosalind knocked, and that young lady immediately opened it.

'Oh! you *are* come back then? I fancied, by Mr Cartwright's not coming this evening, that something might have occurred to prevent you?'

'If it had,' said Helen, smiling, 'it must have been announced by express, for you can only have had my letter this morning.'

'True!' replied Miss Cartwright.

When the three young ladies entered the drawing-room, they found nobody in it but Mr Stephen Corbold; Mrs Mowbray having gone with Fanny to her own room, and Charles ensconced himself in the library, to avoid a tête-à-tête with the unpromising looking stranger.

Rosalind gave him a glance, and then looked at Helen with an eye that seemed to say, 'Who in the world have you brought us?' Helen, however, gave no glance of intelligence in return; but, walking to a table which stood in that part of the room which was at the greatest distance from the place occupied by Mr Corbold, she sat down, and began earnestly reading an old newspaper that she found upon it.

Miss Cartwright started on recognising her cousin, and though she condescended to pronounce, 'How do you do, Mr Corbold?' there was but a cold welcome to him expressed either by her voice or manner. No one presented him to Rosalind, and altogether he felt as little at his ease as it was well possible for a gentleman to do, when the door opened, and Mrs Mowbray and Fanny appeared. From that moment he became as much distinguished as he was before overlooked. Fanny, who knew that it was Mr Cartwright's cousin who stood bowing to her, delighted at the honour of being told that she was 'Miss Fanny Mowbray,' received him with a kindness and condescension which soothed her own feelings as much as his, for she felt that every word she spoke to him was a proof of her devotion to her dear, good Mr Cartwright! and that, when he heard of it, he could not fail to understand that it was for his sake.

The party retired early, ostensibly for the sake of the travellers; but perhaps the real cause of this general haste to separate, was, that they all felt themselves singularly embarrassed in each other's company. Before Mrs Mowbray had been five minutes in her house, she had ordered a splendid sleeping apartment to be made ready for Mr Corbold; and the first half-hour after retiring to it, was spent by him in taking an accurate survey of its furniture, fittings-up, and dimensions: after which, he very nearly stifled himself (forgetful of the dog-days) by striving to enjoy the full luxury of the abounding pillows with which his magnificent couch was furnished.

Mrs Mowbray and Fanny separated after a short but confidential colloquy. Miss Cartwright took her solitary way to her chamber, where, as the housemaids asserted, she certainly spent half the night in reading, or writing, or something or other, before she put out her light: and Rosalind and Helen, spite of their good resolutions, not only sat up talking in the library themselves, but permitted Charles to share their watch with them; so that, before they separated, every fact, thought, or opinion, treasured in the minds of each, were most unreservedly communicated to the others, – excepting that Helen did not disclose at full length *all* the reasons she had for detesting Mr Corbold, and Charles did not think it necessary to mention, that Rosalind grew fairer to his eyes, and dearer to his heart, every hour.

CHAPTER XXII

THE VICAR AND HIS COUSIN

None of the Mowbray family were present at the meeting between the Vicar of Wrexhill and his cousin. The latter, indeed, set out from the Park at a very early hour on the morning after his arrival, in order to breakfast with his much esteemed relation, and to enjoy in the privacy of his Vicarage a little friendly and confidential conversation as to the projects and intentions concerning him, which had been hinted at in his letters.

He was welcomed by Mr Cartwright with very obliging civility; not but that the vicar felt and showed, upon this, as well as all other occasions, a very proper consciousness of his own superiority in all ways. However, the Corbold connexion had been very essentially useful to him in days past; and Mr Stephen, the present representative of the family, might *possibly* be extremely useful to him in days to come. Several fresh-laid eggs were therefore placed on the table, – coffee was added to tea, – and his reception in all ways such as to make Mr Stephen feel himself extremely comfortable.

When the repast was ended, Mr Jacob received a hint to withdraw; and, as soon as the door was closed behind him, the serious vicar approached his chair to that of the serious attorney, with the air of one who had much to hear, and much to communicate.

'You seem hereunto, cousin Stephen, to have managed this excellent business, which by God's providence I have been enabled to put into your hands, with great ability; and, by a continuation of mercy, I am not without hope, that you will, as I heretofore hinted, bring the same to good effect.'

'There is hope, great and exceeding merciful hope, cousin William, that all you have anticipated, and peradventure more too, may come to pass. A blessing and a providence seem already to have lighted upon you, cousin, in your new ministry; for into this vessel which the Lord and your cousinly kindness have set within my sight, you have poured grace and abounding righteousness. Surely there never was a lady endowed with such goodly gifts, who was more disposed to make a free-will offering of them to the Lord and to his saints, than this pious and in all ways exemplary widow.'

'Your remarks, cousin, are those of a man on whom the light shines. May the mercy of the Lord strengthen unto you, for his glory, the talent he has bestowed! And now, with the freedom of kinsmen who speak together, tell to me what are the hopes and expectations to which your conversation with this excellent, and already very serious lady, have given birth?'

'I have no wish or intention, cousin William, of hiding from you any portion of the thoughts which it has pleased the Lord to send into my heart; the which are in fact, for the most part, founded upon the suggestions which, by the light of truth, and the aid of the Holy Spirit, that suffereth not his own to stumble in darkness, I discerned in the first letter upon the widow Mowbray's affairs which you addressed unto me.'

'Respecting the agency of her own business, and peradventure that of her ward's also?'

'Even so. I have, in truth, well-founded faith and hope that by the continuation of your friendship and good report, cousin William, I may at no distant period attain unto both.'

'And if you do, cousin Stephen,' returned the vicar, with a smile, 'your *benefice* in the parish of Wrexhill will be worth considerably more than mine.'

A serious, waggish, holy, cunning smile now illuminated the red, dry features of the attorney, and, shaking his head with a Burleigh-like pregnancy of meaning, he said, 'Ah, cousin!'

The vicar smiled again, and, rising from his chair, put his head and shoulders out of the open window, looking carefully, as it seemed, in all directions; then, drawing them in again, he proceeded to open the door of the room, and examined the passage leading to it in the same cautious manner.

'My son Jacob is one of the finest young men in Europe, cousin Stephen,' said the vicar reseating himself; 'but he is young, and as full of little childish innocent fooleries as any baby: so it is as well not to speak all we may have to say, without knowing that we are alone; for many an excellent plan, in which Providence seemed to have taken a great share, has been impiously spoiled, frustrated, and destroyed, by the want of caution in those to whom the Lord intrusted it. Let not such sin lie at our door! Now tell me then, cousin Stephen, and tell me frankly, why did you smile and say, "Ah, cousin?"'

'Because, while speaking of what, by God's mercy, I may get at Wrexhill, it seemed to me like a misdoubting of Providence not to speak a little hint of what God's chosen minister there may get too——'

'I get my vicar's dues, cousin Stephen; and it may be, by the blessing of God upon my humble endeavours, I may, when next Easter falls, obtain some trifle both from high and low in the way of Easter offering.'

'Ah, cousin!' repeated the attorney, renewing his intelligent smile.

'Well then,' said the well-pleased vicar, 'speak out.'

'I am but a plodding man of business,' replied Mr Corbold, 'with such illumination of the spirit upon matters of faith as the Holy Ghost hath been pleased to bestow; but my sense, such as it is, tells me that the excellent and pious widow of Mowbray Park will not always be permitted by the Lord to remain desolate.'

'She does, in truth, deserve a better fate,' rejoined the vicar.

'And what better fate can befall her, cousin William, than being bound together in holy matrimony with one of the most shining lights to be found among God's saints on earth?'

'Yes!' responded the vicar with a sigh; 'that is the fate she merits, and that is the fate she ought to meet!'

'And shall we doubt the Lord? – shall we doubt that a mate shall be found for her? No, cousin William; doubt not, for I say unto thee, "Thou art the man!"'

The vicar endeavoured to look solemn; but, though his handsome features were in general under excellent control, he could not at this moment repress a pleasant sort of simpering smile that puckered round his mouth. Mr Stephen Corbold, perceiving that his cousin was in nowise displeased by the prophecy he had taken the liberty to utter, returned to the subject again, saying,

'I wish you had seen her face, – she must have been very like her daughter, – I wish you could have seen her, cousin William, every time I named you!'

'Indeed! Did she really testify some emotion? I trust you are not jesting, cousin Stephen; this is no subject for pleasantry.'

'Most assuredly it is not! and I think that you must altogether have forgotten my temper and character, if you suppose that I should think it such. To tell you the truth, cousin, I look upon the time present as a period marked and settled by the providence of the Lord, for the calling you, his anointed, up to the high places. Will it not be a glory for his name, to have his minister and servant placed in such a palace as Mowbray? and will it not be converting what hitherto has doubtless been the abode of sinners, into a temple for the people of the Lord?'

'I will not deny,' replied the vicar, 'that such thoughts have occasionally found place in my own mind. There have already been some very singular and remarkable manifestations of the Lord's will in this matter; and it is the perceiving this, which has led me to believe, and indeed feel certain, that my duty calls upon me so to act, that this wealthy relict of a man too much addicted to the things of this world, may finally, by becoming part and parcel of myself, lose not the things eternal.'

'I greatly rejoice,' rejoined Mr Corbold, 'that such is your decision in this matter; and if it should so fall out that the Lord in his wisdom and goodness shall ordain you to become the master of Mowbray Park, (at these words the vicar cast his eyes upon the ground and meekly bowed his head,) and I have a persuasion that he will so ordain, borne strongly in upon my mind, then and in that case, cousin William, I trust that your patronage and support will not be withdrawn from me.'

'Cousin Stephen,' replied the vicar, 'you are a man that on many occasions I shall covet and desire to have by me and near me, both for your profit and advantage and my own; but in the case which you have put, and which the Lord seems to have whispered to your soul – in the case, Stephen, that I should ever become the master and owner of Mowbray, and all the sundry properties thereunto belonging, I think – no offence to you, cousin – that I should prefer managing the estates myself.'

The serious attorney looked somewhat crestfallen, and perhaps some such questionings were borne in upon his mind as – 'What is it to me if he marries the widow, if I do not get the management of the estates?'

When the vicar raised his eyes to the face of his cousin, he probably perceived the impression his words had produced, and kindly anxious to restore him to more comfortable feelings, he added, – 'The fine property of Miss Torrington, cousin Stephen, might certainly be placed entirely in your hands – the management of it I mean – till she comes of age; but then, if she marries my son, which I think not unlikely, it is probable that Jacob may follow my example, and prefer taking care of the property himself.'

'Then, at the very best,' replied Mr Corbold, 'I can only hope to obtain an agency for a year or two?'

'I beg your pardon, cousin; my hopes for you go much farther than that. In the first place, I would recommend it to you, immediately to settle yourself at Wrexhill: I am told that there is a good deal of business up and down the country hereabouts; and, if I obtain the influence that I hope to do in more ways than one, I shall take care that no attorney is employed but yourself, cousin Stephen. Besides this, I know that there may happen to be settlements or wills wanting amongst us, my good friend, which may make your being at hand very convenient; and, in all such cases, you would do your work, you know, pretty much at your own price. All this, however, is only contingent, I am quite aware of that; and therefore, in order that you may in some sort share my good fortune, – if such indeed should fall upon me, – I have been thinking, cousin Stephen, that when I shall be married to this lady, whom it has pleased Providence to place in my path, you, being then the near relative of a person of consequence and high consideration in the county, may also aspire to increase your means by the same holy ordinance; and, if such a measure should seem good to your judgment, I have a lady in my eye, – also a widow, and a very charming one, my dear friend, – who lives in a style that shows her to be favoured by Providence with the goods of fortune. What say you to this, cousin Stephen?'

'Why, it is borne in upon me to say, cousin William, that, in such a case as this, I should be inclined to follow your good example and choose for myself. And, truth to speak, I believe the choice is in some sort made already; and I don't see but your marriage may be as likely to help me in this case as in the other; and as to fortune, it is probable that you may be able to lend me a helping hand there, too; for the young lady, I fancy, is no other than your own daughter-in-law that is to be, – the pretty Miss Helen, cousin William?'

The vicar, as he listened to these words, very nearly uttered a whistle. He was, however, as he whispered to himself, mercifully saved from such an indecorum by the timely remembrance that his cousin, though an attorney, was a very serious man; but, though he did not whistle, he deemed it necessary to express in a more solemn and proper manner his doubts of the success to be hoped from the scheme proposed by Mr Corbold.

'As to the fortune of the young person who may, as you observe, some day by the blessing of Providence become my daughter-in-law, I must tell you as a friend and kinsman, cousin Stephen, that I hold it to be very doubtful if she ever have any fortune at all. Are you aware that she is not regenerate?'

'I partly guess as much,' replied the attorney. 'But,' he added with a smile, 'I can't say I should have any objection to marrying her first, and leading her into the way of salvation afterwards. And when I can testify to her having forsaken the errors of her ways, and that I have made her a light to lighten the Gentiles; I suppose you won't object *then* to her coming in for a share of her mother's inheritance?'

'That would certainly make a difference; but I won't disguise from you, cousin, that I consider this young person's as a hopeless case. She was foredoomed from the beginning of the world: I see the mark upon her. However, that might not perhaps make such difference in your determination, for I know you to be a man very steadfast in hope, cousin Stephen. But there is, moreover, I think, another obstacle. You must not take my frankness amiss; but I have an inward misgiving as to her being willing to accept you.'

'As the young lady is a minor, cousin William, I should count upon its being in your power to make her marry pretty well whom you please. And this you may rely upon, that, in case you favour me heartily in this matter, there is no work of any kind that you could put me to, that I should not think it my bounden duty to perform.'

'You speak like a just and conscientious man, cousin Corbold; and, by the blessing of the Lord upon us, I trust that we shall be so able to work together for righteousness' sake, that in the end we may compass that which we desire. Nevertheless, I confess that it is still borne in upon me that the fair and excellent widow Simpson would be the wisest choice for you.'

'Should it please the Lord that such should be my own opinion hereafter, cousin Cartwright, I will not fail to make it known unto you.'

'I will rest my faith on your wisdom therein,' replied the vicar: 'but it is now time that I should go to speak the blessing of a minister, and the welcome of a friend, to the excellent lady at the Park. And remember two things, cousin Stephen: the first is, never to remain in the room with the widow Mowbray and myself, when no other persons are present; and the next is in importance like unto it, – remember that the lady is even yet new in widowhood, and that any imprudent and premature allusion to my possibly taking her in marriage might ruin all. There are those near her, cousin Stephen, who I question not will fight against me; albeit, I shall approach her in the name of the Lord.'

The attorney promised to be awake and watchful, and never to permit his tongue to betray the counsels of his heart.

The cousins and friends (who, notwithstanding the difference of their callings, considered themselves, as Mr Corbold observed, fellow-labourers in the vineyard of the Lord,) then walked forth together towards Mowbray Park, well pleased with themselves and all things around them at the present, and with pious confidence in the reward of their labours for the future.

CHAPTER XXIII

CHARLES'S SORROW – MRS SIMPSON IN HER NEW CHARACTER – THE VICAR'S
PROCEEDINGS DISCUSSED

The two gentlemen found the family at the Park very sociably seated round a late breakfast table. Helen, Rosalind, and Charles, before they broke up their conclave in the library the night before, or rather that morning, had all decided that in the present thorny and difficult position of affairs, it was equally their duty and interest to propitiate the kind feelings of Mrs Mowbray by every means in their power, and draw her thereby, if possible, from the mischievous and insidious influence of her new associates.

'It is hardly possible to believe,' said Charles, 'that my mother can really prefer the society of such an animal as this methodistical attorney, to that of her own family, or of those neighbours and friends from whom, since my father's death, she has so completely withdrawn herself. It is very natural she should be out of spirits, poor dear soul! and Mr Cartwright is just the sort of person to obtain influence at such a time; but I trust this will wear off again. She will soon get sick of the solemn attorney, and we shall all be as happy again as ever.'

'God grant it!' said Helen with a sigh.

'God grant it!' echoed Rosalind with another.

It was in consequence of this resolution, that the trio continued to sit at the table much longer than usual; exerting themselves to amuse Mrs Mowbray, to win from Fanny one of her former bright smiles, and even to make Miss Cartwright sociable.

Their efforts were not wholly unsuccessful. There was a genuine animation and vivacity about Charles that seemed irresistible: Mrs Mowbray looked at him with a mother's eye; Miss Cartwright forsook her monosyllables, and almost conversed; and Fanny, while listening first to Helen, and then to her brother, forgot her duty as a professing Christian so far as to let a whole ringlet of her sunny hair get loose from behind her ear, and not notice it.

In the midst of this gleam of sunshine, the door opened, and Mr Cartwright and Mr Corbold were announced. Ambitious of producing effect as both these serious gentlemen certainly were, they could hardly have hoped, when their spirits were most exalted within them, to have caused a more remarkable revolution in the state of things than their appearance now produced.

Mrs Mowbray coloured, half rose from her chair, sat down again, and finally exclaimed, 'Oh! Mr Cartwright!' in a tone of voice that manifested almost every feeling he could wish to inspire.

Fanny, who was in the very act of smiling when the door opened, immediately became conscious that her hair was out of order, and that her whole attitude and manner were wanting in that Christian grace and sobriety which had been of late her chiefest glory. Such Christian grace and sobriety, however, as she had lately learned, poor child! are not difficult to assume, or long in putting on; so that before 'her minister' had completed his little prayer and thanksgiving in the ear of her mother, for her eternal happiness and her safe return, Fanny was quite in proper trim to meet his eye, and receive his blessing.

Henrietta at once fell back into her wonted heavy silent gloom, like a leaden statue upon which the sun, shining for a moment, had thrown the hue of silver.

Charles stood up, and saluted the vicar civilly but coldly; while to his companion's low bow he returned a slight and stiff inclination of the head.

It should be observed that, during the few days which intervened beween the arrival of Charles and the return of his mother, the vicar had greatly relaxed in his attentions to Fanny, and indeed altogether in the frequency of his pastoral visitations at the Park. He had explained this in the ear of his pretty proselyte, by telling her that he was much engaged in pushing forward the work of regeneration in his parish, to the which holy labour he was the more urgently incited by perceiving that the seed was not thown upon barren ground. Nor indeed was this statement wholly untrue. He had taken advantage of the leisure which the present posture of affairs at the Park left upon his hands, in seeking to inflame the imaginations of as many of his parishioners as he could get to listen to him.

Among the females he had been particularly successful; and, indeed, the proportion of the fair sex who are found to embrace the tenets which this gentleman and his sect have introduced in place of those of the Church of England, is so great, that, as their faith is an exclusive one, it might be conjectured that the chief object of the doctrine was to act as a balance-weight against that of Mahomet, who, atrocious tyrant as he was, shut the gates of heaven against all woman-kind whatsoever; were it not that an occasional nest of he-saints may here and there be found, – sometimes in a drum-profaned barrack, and sometimes in a cloistered college, which show that election is not wholly confined to the fair. There are, however, some very active and inquiring persons who assert, that upon a fair and accurate survey throughout England and Wales, Ireland, Scotland, and the town of Berwick-upon-Tweed, no greater number of this sect can be found of the masculine gender than may suffice to perform the duties of ministers, deputy ministers, missionaries, assistant missionaries, speech-makers both in and out of parliament, committee-men, and such serious footmen, coachmen, butchers, and bakers, as the fair inhabitants of the Calvinistic heaven require to perform the unfeminine drudgery of earth.

It was in consequence of this remission in the vicar's labours for the regeneration of Fanny, that Charles Mowbray still treated him with the respect due to the clergyman of his parish. Rosalind felt it quite impossible to describe to him all she had seen, and her promise to Henrietta forbad her to repeat what she had heard; so that young Mowbray, though he disapproved of the puritanic innovations of Fanny's toilet, and so much disliked Mr Cartwright's extempore preaching as to have decided upon attending divine service at Oakley church for the future, to avoid hearing what he considered as so very indecent an innovation, he was still quite unaware of Rosalind's real motives for recalling him, though extremely well inclined to think her right in having done so.

Miss Torrington and Helen left the room very soon after the two gentlemen entered it. Henrietta, with the stealthy step of a cat, followed them, and young Mowbray felt strongly tempted to do the like; but was prevented, not so much by politeness perhaps, as by curiosity to ascertain, if possible, the terms on which both these gentlemen stood with his mother.

But it was not possible. As long as he remained with them, the very scanty conversation which took place was wholly on uninteresting subjects; and Charles at length left the room, from feeling that it was not his mother's pleasure to talk to the attorney of the business that he presumed must have brought him there, as long as he remained in it.

There is in the domestic history of human life no cause productive of effects so terrible as the habit of acting according to the impulse, or the convenience, of the moment, without fully considering the effect what we are doing may produce on others.

Mrs Mowbray, in waiting till Charles left the room before she spake to Mr Corbold of the title-deeds and other papers which she was to put into his hands, was almost wholly actuated by the consciousness that the attorney she was employing (though a serious) was a very vulgar man. She knew that her son was rather fastidious on such points; and she disliked the idea that a man, whose distinguished piety rendered him so peculiarly eligible as a man of business, should, at his first introduction to the confidential situation she intended he should hold, lay himself open to the ridicule of a youth, who, she sighed to think, was as yet quite incapable of appreciating his merit in any way.

If any secondary motive mixed with this, it arose from the averseness she felt, of which she was not herself above half conscious, that any one should hear advice given by Mr Cartwright, who might think themselves at liberty to question it; but, with all this, she never dreamed of the pain she was giving to Charles's heart. She dreamed not that her son, – her only son, – with a heart as warm, as generous, as devoted in its filial love, as ever beat in the breast of a man, felt all his ardent affection for her, – his proud fond wish of being her protector, her aid, her confidential friend – now checked and chilled at once, and for ever!

This consequence of her cold, restrained manner in his presence, was so natural, – in fact, so inevitable, – that had she turned her eyes from herself and her own little unimportant feelings, to what might be their effect upon his, it is hardly possible that she could have avoided catching some glimpse of the danger she ran, – and much after misery might have been spared; as it was, she felt a movement of unequivocal satisfaction when he departed; and, having told Fanny to join the other young ladies while she transacted business, she was left alone with the two gentlemen, and, in a few minutes afterwards, the contents of her late husband's strong-box, consisting of parchments, memoranda, and deeds almost innumerable, overspread the large table, as well as every sofa and chair within convenient reach.

The two serious gentlemen smiled, but it was inwardly. Their eyes ran over the inscriptions of every precious packet; and if those of the professional man caught more rapidly at a glance the respective importance of each, the vicar had the advantage of him in that prophetic feeling of their future importance to himself, which rendered the present hour one of the happiest of his life.

Meanwhile, Charles sought Helen and her friend. Far, however, from wishing to impart to them the painful impression he had received, his principal object in immediately seeking them was, if possible, to forget it. He found the four girls together in the conservatory, and, affecting more gaiety than he felt, exclaimed, 'How many recruits shall I get among you to join me in a walk to Wrexhill? One, two, three, four! That's delightful! Make haste; bonnet and veil yourselves without delay: and if we skirt round the plantations to the lodge, we shall escape being broiled, for the lanes are always shady.'

When he had got his convoy fairly under way, they began to make inquiries as to what he was going to do at Wrexhill. 'I will tell you,' he replied, 'if you will promise not to run away and forsake me.'

They pledged themselves to be faithful to their escort, and he then informed them that it was his very particular wish and desire to pay sundry visits to the *beau monde* of Wrexhill.

'It is treason to the milliner not to have told us so before, Charles,' said Helen; 'only look at poor Fanny's little straw-bonnet, without even a bow to set it off. What will Mrs Simpson think of us?'

'I assure you, Helen,' said Fanny, 'that if I had known we were going to visit all the fine people in the county, I should have put on no other bonnet; and as for Mrs Simpson, I believe you are quite mistaken in supposing she would object to it. I hope she has seen the error of her ways, as well as I have, Charles; and that we shall never more see her dressed like a heathenish woman, as she used to do.'

'Oh Fanny! Fanny!' exclaimed Charles, laughing. 'How long will this spirit vex you.'

Fortunately however, for the harmony of the excursion, none of the party appeared at this moment inclined to controversy, and the subject dropped. Instead, therefore, of talking of different modes of faith, and of the bonnets thereunto belonging, the conversation turned upon the peculiar beauty of the woodland scenery around Wrexhill; and Miss Cartwright, as almost a stranger, was applied to for her opinion of it.

'I believe I am a very indifferent judge of scenery,' she replied. 'The fact is, I never see it.'

'Do you not see it now?' said Rosalind. 'Do you not see that beautiful stretch of park-like common, with its tufts of holly, its rich groups of forest-trees, with their dark heavy drapery of leaves, relieved by the light and wavy gracefulness of the delicate and silvery birch? and, loveliest of all, do you not see that stately avenue of oaks, the turf under them green in eternal shade, and the long perspective, looking like the nave of some gigantic church?'

Rosalind stood still as she spoke, and Henrietta remained beside her. They were descending the bit of steep road, which, passing behind the church and the Vicarage, led into the village street of Wrexhill, and the scene described by Miss Torrington was at this point completely given to their view.

Henrietta put her arm within that of Rosalind with a degree of familiarity very unusual with her, and, having gazed on the fair expanse before her for several minutes, she replied,

'Yes, Rosalind, I do see it now, and I thank you for making it visible to me. Perhaps in future, when I may perchance be thinking of you, I may see it again.'

Rosalind turned to seek her meaning in her face, and saw that her dark deep-set eyes were full of tears. This was so unexpected, so unprecedented, so totally unlike any feeling she had ever remarked in her before, that Rosalind was deeply touched by it, and, pressing the arm that rested on hers, she said:

'Dear Henrietta! Why are you so averse to letting one understand what passes in your heart? It is only by an accidental breath, which now and then lifts the veil you hang before it, that one can even find out you have any heart at all.'

'Did you know all the darkness that dwells there, you would not thank me for showing it to you.'

Having said this, she stepped hastily forward, and drawing on Rosalind, who would have lingered, with her, till they had overtaken the others, they all turned from the lane into the village street together.

They had not proceeded a hundred yards, before they were met by a dozen rosy and riotous children returning from dinner to school. At sight of the Mowbray party, every boy uncapped, and every little girl made her best courtesy; but one unlucky wag, whose eyes unfortunately fixed themselves on Fanny, being struck by the precision of her little bonnet, straight hair, and the total absence of frill, furbelow, or any other indication of worldly-mindedness, restrained his bounding steps for a moment, and, pursing up his little features into a look of sanctity, exclaimed – 'Amen!' – and then, terrified at what he had done, galloped away and hid himself among his fellows.

Fanny coloured; but immediately assumed the resigned look that announceth martyrdom. Charles laughed, though he turned round and shook his switch at the saucy offender. Helen looked vexed, Rosalind amused, and Henrietta very nearly delighted.

A few minutes more brought them to the door of Mrs Simpson's. Their inquiry for the lady was answered by the information that she 'was schooling miss; but if they would be pleased to walk in, she would come down directly.' They accordingly entered the drawing-room, where they were kept waiting for some time, which was indeed pretty generally the fate of morning visitors to Mrs Simpson.

The interval was employed as the collectors of albums and annuals intend all intervals should be, namely, in the examination of all the morrocco-bound volumes deposited on the grand round table in the middle of the room, and on all the square, oblong, octagon, and oval mirror tables, in the various nooks and corners of it.

On the present occasion they seemed to promise more amusement than usual to the party, who had most of them been frequently there before, – for they were nearly all new. Poor little Fanny, though she knew that not one of those with her were capable of enjoying the intellectual and edifying feast that almost the first glance of her eye showed her was set before them, could not restrain an exclamation of – 'Oh! How heavenly-minded!'

The whole collection indeed, which though recently and hastily formed, had evidently been brought together by the hand of a master of such matters, was not only most strictly evangelical, but most evangelically ingenious.

Helen, however, appeared to find food neither for pleasantry nor edification there; for having opened one or two slender volumes, and as many heavy pamphlets, she abandoned the occupation with a sigh, that spoke sadness and vexation. Miss Cartwright, who had seated herself on the same sofa, finished her examination still more quickly, saying in a low voice as she settled herself in a well-pillowed corner –

'Surfeit is the father of much fast.'

Miss Torrington and young Mowbray got hold of by far the finest volume of all, whose gilt leaves and silken linings showed that it was intended as the repository of the most precious gifts, that, according to the frontispiece, Genius could offer to Friendship. Having given a glance at its contents, Charles drew out his pencil, and on the blank side of a letter wrote the following catalogue of them, which, though imperfect as not naming them all, was most scrupulously correct as far as it went:

'Saint Paul's head, sketched in pen and ink;
  "Here's the bower," to words of grace;
The death-bed talk of Master Blink;
  Lines on a fallen maiden's case.
Sonnet upon heavenly love;
  A pencil drawing of Saint Peter,
Emblem's – the pigeon and the dove.
  Gray's Odes, turned to psalm-tune metre.
A Christian ode in praise of tea,
  Freely translated from Redi.'

He had just presented the scrap to Rosalind when Mrs Simpson entered, leading her little girl in her hand; but the young lady had leisure to convey it unnoticed to her pocket, as the mistress of the house had for the first few minutes eyes only for Fanny. In fact, she literally ran to her the instant she perceived her little bonnet, and, folding her arms round her, exclaimed –

'My dear, dear child! My dear, dear sister! This is providential! It is a blessing I shall remember alway! Our minister told me that I should read at a glance the blessed change wrought upon you: I do read it, and I will praise the Lord therefore! I beg your pardon, ladies. Mr Mowbray, pray sit down – I beg your pardon: I rejoice to see you, though as yet——'

Her eyes fixed themselves on the bonnet of Helen, which, besides being large, had the abomination of sundry bows, not to mention a bunch of laburnum blossoms.

'Ah! my dear Miss Helen! The time will come – I will supplicate the Lord alway that it may – when you too, like your precious sister, shall become a sign and ensample to all men. How the seed grows, my sweet Miss Fanny!' she continued, turning to the only one of her guests whom, strictly speaking, she considered it right to converse with. 'How it grows and spreads under the dew of faith and the sunshine of righteousness. It is just three months, three little blessed months, since the beam first fell upon my heart, Miss Fanny; and look at me, look at my child, look at my albums, look at my books, look at my card-racks, look at my missionary's box on one side, and my London Lord-days' society box on the other. Is not this a ripening and preparing for the harvest, Miss Fanny?'

Fanny coloured, partly perhaps from pride and pleasure; but partly, certainly, from shyness at being so distinguished, and only murmured the word 'Beautiful!' in reply.

Miss Mowbray felt equally provoked and disgusted; but, while inwardly resolving that she would never again put herself in the way of witnessing what she so greatly condemned, she deemed it best to stay, if possible, the torrent of nonsense which was thus overwhelming her sister, by giving another turn to the conversation.

'Have you seen Mrs Richards lately, Mrs Simpson?' she said.

'Mrs Richards and I very rarely meet now, Miss Mowbray,' was the reply. 'The three young ladies indeed, I am happy to say, have wholly separated themselves from their mother in spirit, and are all of them becoming shining lights. Oh, Miss Fanny! how sweetly pious are those lines written between you and little Mary!'

Fanny suddenly became as red as scarlet.

'The alternate verses, I mean, in praise and glory of our excellent minister. He brought them to me himself, and we read them together, and we almost shed tears of tender blessing on you both, dear children!'

Charles, who thought, and with great satisfaction, that whatever stuff his poor little sister might have written, she was now very heartily ashamed of it, wishing to relieve her from the embarrassment, which nevertheless he rejoiced to see, rose from his chair and approaching a window, said,

'What a very pleasant room you have here, Mrs Simpson; it is almost due east, is it not? If the room over it be your apartment, I should think the sun must pay you too early a visit there, unless your windows are well curtained.'

'Oh, Mr Mowbray! Sunrise is such a time of praise and blessing, that, even though the curtains are drawn, I always try, if I am awake, to think how heavenly it is looking outside.'

'Are you an early riser, Mrs Simpson?' said Helen.

'Not very, − at least not always; but since my election I have been endeavouring to get down to prayers by about half-past eight. It is so delightful to think how many people are coming down stairs to prayers just at half-past eight!'

'Your little girl is very much grown, Mrs Simpson,' said Miss Torrington, willing to try another opening by which to escape from under the heels of the lady's hobby; but it did not answer.

'Hold up your head, Minima dear!' said the mamma; 'and tell these ladies what you have been learning lately. She is still rather shy; but it is going off, I hope. Precious child! she is grown such a prayerful thing, Miss Fanny, you can't imagine. Minima, why did you not eat up all your currant-pudding yesterday? tell Miss Fanny Mowbray!'

'Because it is wicked to love currant-pudding,' answered the child, folding her little hands one over the other upon the bosom of her plain frock, no longer protruding in all directions its sumptuous chevaux-de-frise of lace and embroidery.

'Darling angel! And why, my precious! is it wicked?'

'Because it is a sin to care for our vile bodies, and because we ought to love nothing but the Lord.'

'Is not that a blessing?' said Mrs Simpson, again turning to Fanny. 'And how can I be grateful enough to the angelic man who has put me and my little one in the right way?'

It was really generous in good Mrs Simpson to give all the praise due for the instruction and religious awakening of her little girl to the vicar, for it was in truth entirely her own work; as it generally happened, that when Mr Cartwright paid her a visit, fearing probably that the movements of a child might disturb his nerves, she dismissed her little Minima to her nursery.

One or two more attempts on the part of Helen to bring the conversation to a tone that she should consider as more befitting the neighbourly chit-chat of a morning visit, and, in plain English, less tinctured with blasphemy, having been made and failed, she rose and took her leave, the rest of her party following; but not without Fanny's receiving another embrace, and this fervent farewell uttered in her ear:

'The saints and angels bless and keep you, dear sister in the Lord!'

After quitting the house of this regenerated lady, the party proposed to make a visit to that of Mrs Richards; but Miss Cartwright expressed a wish to go to the Vicarage instead, and begged they would call at the door for her as they passed. Miss Torrington offered to accompany her, but this was declined, though not quite in her usual cynical manner upon such occasions; and, could Rosalind have followed her with her eye up the Vicarage hill, she would have seen that she stopped and turned to look down upon the common and its trees, just at the spot where they had stood together before.

On entering Mrs Richard's pretty flower-scented little saloon, they were startled and somewhat embarrassed at finding that lady in tears, and Major Dalrymple walking about the room with very evident symptoms of discomposure. Helen, who, like everybody else in the neighbourhood, was perfectly aware of the major's unrequited attachment, or, at any rate, his unsuccessful suit, really thought that the present moment was probably intended by him to decide his fate for ever; and felt exceedingly distressed at having intruded, though doubtful whether to retreat now would not make matters worse. Those who followed her shared both her fears and her doubts: but not so the widow and the major; who both, after the interval of a moment, during which Mrs Richards wiped her eyes, and Major Dalrymple recovered his composure, declared with very evident sincerity that they were heartily glad to see them.

'We are in the midst of a dispute, Mowbray,' said the major, addressing Charles; 'and I will bet a thousand to one that you will be on my side, whatever the ladies may be. Shall I refer the question to Charles Mowbray, Mrs Richards?'

'Oh yes! I shall like to have it referred to the whole party!' she replied.

'Well then, this it is: – I need not tell you, good people, that the present Vicar of Wrexhill is – but *halte là!*' he exclaimed, suddenly stopping himself and fixing his eyes on Fanny; 'I am terribly afraid by the trim cut of that little bonnet, that there's one amongst us that will be taking notes. Is it so, Miss Fanny? Are you as completely over head and ears in love with the vicar, as your friend little Mary? and, for that matter, Louisa, Charlotte, Mrs Simpson, Miss Minima Simpson, Dame Rogers the miller's wife, black-eyed Betsy the tailor's daughter, Molly Tomkins, Sally Finden, Jenny Curtis, Susan Smith, and about three-score and ten more of our parish, have all put on the armour of righteousness, being buckled, belted and spurred by the vicar himself. Are you really and truly become one of his babes of grace, Fanny?'

'If it is your intention to say anything disrespectful of Mr Cartwright,' replied Fanny, 'I had much rather not hear it. I will go and look at your roses, Mrs Richards;' and, as Mrs Richards did not wish her to remain, she quietly opened the glass-door which led into the garden, let her pass through it, and then closed it after her.

'Pretty creature!' exclaimed Major Dalrymple; 'what a pity!'

'It will not last, major,' said Charles. 'He has scared her conscience, which is actually too pure and innocent to know the sound of its own voice; and then he seized upon her fanciful and poetic imagination, and set it in arms against her silly self, till she really seems to see the seven mortal sins, turn which way she will; and I am sure she would stand for seven years together on one leg, like an Hindoo, to avoid them. She is a dear good little soul, and she will get the better of all this trash, depend upon it.'

'I trust she will, Mowbray; but tell me, while the mischief is still at work, shall you not think it right to banish the causer of it from your house? For you must know this brings us exactly to the point at issue between Mrs Richards and me. She is breaking her heart because her three girls – ay, little Mary and all – have been bit by this black tarantula; and because she (thank God!) has escaped, her daughters have thought proper to raise the standard of rebellion, and to tell her very coolly, upon all occasions, that she is doomed to everlasting perdition, and that their only chance of escape is never more to give obedience or even attention to any word she can utter.'

The major stopped, overcome by his own vehemence; and Charles would have fancied that he saw tears in his eyes, if he had dared to look at him for another moment.

Rosalind, who had more love and liking for Mrs Richards than is usually the growth of six months' acquaintance, had placed herself close beside her, and taken her hand; but, when Major Dalrymple ceased speaking, she rose up, and with a degree of energy that probably surprised all her hearers, but most especially Charles and Helen, she said:

'If, Major Dalrymple, you should be the first in this unfortunate parish of Wrexhill to raise your voice against this invader of the station, rights, and duties of a set of men in whose avocations he has neither part nor lot, you will deserve more honour than even the field of Waterloo could give you! Yes! turn him from your house, dear friend, as you would one who brought poison to you in the guise of wholesome food or healing medicine. Let him never enter your doors again; let him preach (if preach he must) in a church as empty as his own pretensions to holiness; and if proper authority should at length be awaked to chase him from a pulpit that belongs of right to a true and real member of the English church, then let him buy a sixpenny licence, if he can get it, to preach in a tub, the only fitting theatre for his doctrines.'

'Bravo!' cried the major in a perfect ecstasy; 'do you hear her, Mrs Richards? Charles Mowbray, do you hear her? and will either of you ever suffer Cartwright to enter your doors again?'

'I believe in my soul that she is quite right,' said Charles: 'the idiot folly I have witnessed at Mrs Simpson's this morning; and the much more grievous effects which his ministry, as he calls it, has produced here, have quite convinced me that such *ministry* is no jesting matter. But I have no doors, Dalrymple, to shut against him; all I can do is to endeavour to open my mother's eyes to the mischief he is doing.'

Helen sighed, and shook her head.

'Is, then, your good mother too far gone in this maudlin delirium to listen to him?' said the major in an accent of deep concern.

'Indeed, major, I fear so,' replied Helen.

'I told you so, Major Dalrymple,' said Mrs Richards; 'I told you that in such a line of conduct as you advise I should be supported by no one of any consequence, and I really do not feel courage to stand alone in it.'

'And it is that very want of courage that I deplore more than all the rest,' replied the major. 'You, that have done and suffered so much, with all the quiet courage of a real hero, – that you should now sink before such an enemy as this, is what I really cannot see with patience.'

'And whence comes this new-born cowardice, my dear Mrs Richards?' said Rosalind.

'I will tell you, Miss Torrington,' replied the black-eyed widow, her voice trembling with emotion as she spoke, – 'I will tell you: all the courage of which I have ever given proof, has been inspired, strengthened, and set in action by my children, – by my love for them, and their love for me. This is over: I have lost their love, I have lost their confidence. They look upon me, – even my Mary, who once shared every feeling of my heart, – they all look upon me as one accursed of God, separated from them through all eternity, and doomed by a decree of my Maker, decided on thousands of years before I was born, to live for countless ages in torments unspeakable. They repeat all this, and hug the faith that teaches it. Is not this enough to sap the courage of the stoutest heart that ever woman boasted?'

'It is dreadful!' cried Helen; 'oh! most dreadful! Such then will be, and already are, the feelings of my mother respecting me, – respecting Charles. Yet, how she loved us! A few short months ago, how dearly she loved us both!'

'Come, come, Miss Mowbray; I did not mean to pain you in this manner,' said the major. 'Do not fancy things worse than they really are: depend upon it, your brother will take care to prevent this man's impious profanation of religion from doing such mischief at Mowbray as it has done here. Had there been any master of the house at Meadow Cottage, this gentleman, so miscalled *reverend*, would never, never, never, have got a footing there.'

'Then I heartily wish there were,' said Charles, 'if only for the sake of setting a good example to the parish in general; but, for the Park in particular, it is as masterless as the cottage.'

'I believe,' said Mrs Richards, 'that amongst you I shall gain courage to be mistress here; and this, if effectually done, may answer as well. You really advise me, then, all of you, to forbid the clergyman of the parish from entering my doors?'

'Yes,' replied the major firmly; and he was echoed zealously by the rest of the party.

'So be it then,' said Mrs Richards. 'But I would my enemy, for such indeed he is, held any other station among us. I could shut my doors against all the lords and ladies in the country with less pain than against the clergyman.'

'I can fully enter into that feeling,' said Helen: 'but surely, in proportion as the station is venerable, the abuse of it is unpardonable. Let this strengthen your resolution; and your children will recover their wits again, depend upon it. I would the same remedy could be applied with us! but you are so much respected, my dear Mrs Richards, that I am not without hope from your example. Adieu! We shall be anxious to hear how you go on; and you must not fail to let us see you soon.'

The Mowbray party, having recalled the self-banished Fanny, then took leave, not without the satisfaction of believing that their visit had been well-timed and useful.

CHAPTER XXIV

DISCUSSION ON TRUTH – MR CORBOLD INSTALLED

Having called at the Vicarage for Miss Cartwright, they proceeded homeward along the pleasant paths they had so often trod with light-hearted gaiety; but now there was a look of care and anxious thoughtfulness on each young brow, that seemed to say their happiness was blighted by the fear of sorrow to come.

Though not at all able to understand Henrietta, and not above half liking her, there was yet more feeling of intimacy between Miss Torrington and her than had been attained by any other of the family. It was she, therefore, who, after preceding the others by a few rapid steps up the hill, rang the bell of the Vicarage, and waited in the porch for Miss Cartwright.

During these few moments the trio had passed on, and Miss Torrington, finding herself tête-à-tête with the vicar's daughter, ventured to relate to her pretty nearly all that occurred at the house of Mrs Richards; by no means omitting the resolution that lady had come to respecting Mr Cartwright.

'I am very sorry for it,' said Henrietta.

'You regret the loss of their society? Then for your sake, Henrietta, I am sorry too.'

'For my sake? *I* regret the loss of their society! Are you not mocking me?'

'You know I am not,' replied Rosalind in a tone of vexation; 'why should you not regret the loss of Mrs Richards's society?'

'Only because there is no society in the world that I could either wish for, – or regret.'

'It is hardly fair in you, Miss Cartwright,' said Rosalind, 'to excite my interest so often as you do, and yet to leave it for ever pining, for want of a more full and generous confidence.'

'I have no such feeling as generosity in me; and as to exciting your interest, I do assure you it is quite involuntarily; and, indeed, I should think that no human being could be less likely to trouble their fellow-creatures in that way than myself.'

'But is there not at least a little wilfulness, Henrietta, in the manner in which from time to time you throw out a bait to my curiosity?'

'It is weakness, not wilfulness, Rosalind. I am ashamed to confess, even to myself, that there are moments when I fancy I should like to love you; and then I would give more than my worthless life, if I had it, that you should love me. When this contemptible folly seizes me, I may, perhaps, as you say, throw out a bait to catch your curiosity, and then it is I utter the words of which you complain. But you must allow that this childishness never holds me long, and that the moment it is past I become as reasonable and as wretched again as ever.'

'Will you tell me whether this feeling of profound contempt for yourself, whenever you are conscious of a kindly sentiment towards me, arises from your conviction of my individual despicability, or from believing that all human affections are degrading?'

'Not exactly from either. As for you, Rosalind, – is it not the weak and wavering Hamlet who says, in one of those flashes of fine philosophy that burst athwart the gloom of his poor troubled spirit,

"Give me that man that is not passion's slave?"

My wits are often as much diseased as his, I believe; but I too have my intervals; and, when the moon is not at the full, I sometimes sketch the portrait of a being that one might venture to love. I, however, have no quarrel against passion, – it is not from thence my sorrows have come: – but I would say,

"Give me that friend
That is not *falsehood's* slave, and I will wear him
(or her, Rosalind,)
In my heart's core, – ay, in my heart of heart."

And if after all my hard schooling I could be simple enough to believe that anything in human form could be true, I should be more likely to commit the folly about you than about any one I ever saw in my life.'

'But still you believe me false?'

'I do.'

'And why, Henrietta?'

'Because you are a woman: – no, no, because you are a human being.'

'And you really, without meaning to season your speech with pungent crystals of satire, – you really do not believe that truth can be found in any human being?'

'I really do not.'

'God help you, then! I would rather pass my life in a roofless cabin, and feed on potato-parings, than live in such a persuasion.'

'And so would I, Rosalind.'

'Then why do you nourish such hateful theories? I shall begin to think your jesting words too true, Henrietta; and believe, indeed, that your wits are not quite healthy.'

'Would I could believe it! I would submit to a strait-waistcoat and shaven crown to-morrow if I could but persuade myself that I was mad, and that all I have fancied going on around me were but so many vapours from a moon-sick brain.'

'And so they have been, if you construe every word you hear, and every act you see, into falsehood and delusion.'

'Rosalind! Rosalind! – how can I do otherwise? Come, come, enough of this: do not force me against my will, against my resolution, to tell you what has brought me to the wretched, hopeless state of apathy in which you found me. Were I to do this, you would only have to follow the weakness of your nature, and believe, in order to become as moody and as miserable as myself.'

'But you do not mean to tell me that I should be proving my weakness in believing *you?*'

'Indeed I do. You surely cannot be altogether so credulous as to suppose that all you see in me is true, sincere, candid, open, honest?'

'Are you honest now in telling me that you are false?'

'Why, partly yes, and partly no, Rosalind; and it is just such a question as that which sets one upon discovering how contrary to our very essence it is, to be purely and altogether true. But were I one of those who fancy that pincushions are often made by the merciful decrees of an all-wise Providence, I should say that we were ordained to be false, in order to prevent our being straightforward, undisguised demons. Why, I, – look you, – who sit netting a purse that I hope will never be finished, as diligently as if my life would be saved by completing the last stitch by a given time, and as quietly as if I had no nails upon my fingers, and no pointed scissors in my netting-case, – even I, all harmless as I seem, would be likely, were it not for my consummate hypocrisy, to be stabbing and scratching half a dozen times a day.'

'And, were you freed from this restraint, would your maiming propensities betray themselves promiscuously, or be confined to one or more particular objects?'

'Not quite promiscuously, I think. But hypocrisy apart for a moment, do you not perceive that Mr Charles Mowbray has been looking round at us, – at both of us, observe, – about once in every second minute? Do you know that I think he would like us, – both of us, observe, – to walk on and join the party.'

'Well, then, let us do so,' said Rosalind.

* * *

As they drew near the house, they perceived Mr Stephen Corbold wandering round it, his hands behind his back and under his coat, and his eyes now raised to the stately portico, now lowered to the long range of windows belonging to the conservatory; at one moment sent afield over the spacious park, and in the next brought back again to contemplate anew the noble mansion to which it belonged. During one of the wanderings of those speculating orbs, he spied the advancing party; and immediately settling himself in his attire, and assuming the more graceful attitude obtained by thrusting a hand in each side-pocket of his nether garments, he resolutely walked forward to meet them.

Fanny, his friends and kinsfolk being ever in her memory, made an effort which seemed to combat instinct, and put out her little hand to welcome him; but before he was fully aware of the honour, for indeed his eyes were fixed upon her elder sister, she coloured, and withdrew it again, satisfying her hospitable feelings by pronouncing simply his name, but with a sort of indistinctness in the accent which seemed to signify that something more had either preceeded or followed it.

This word, the only one which greeted him, brought him instantly to her side, and even gave him the prodigious audacity to offer his arm, which, however, she did not accept; for at that moment the hook of her parasol became entangled in the fringe of her shawl, and it seemed to require vast patience and perseverence to extricate it. Still, notwithstanding this little disappointment, he kept close to her side, for Helen leaned upon the arm of her brother; and, though still persuaded that by the aid of his reverend cousin he should be able to obtain her, and pretty nearly everything else he wished for, he had no particular inclination to renew the courtship he had begun on the journey in the presence of Charles.

Fanny, therefore, and her attendant entered the house together; while the rest wheeled off in order to avail themselves of a postern entrance, by which the ladies might reach their rooms without any risk of again encountering Mr Corbold, who by a sort of tacit consent seemed equally avoided by all.

The survey which this person was taking of the premises when the walking party returned, was neither the first, second, third, nor fourth which he had had the opportunity of making since their setting out; for, in obedience to Mr Cartwright's hint, he had no sooner received from Mrs Mowbray, under the instructions from that reverend person, the orders necessary for the new arrangements about to be made, than he retired, – the vicar remaining with the widow and the keys of her title-deeds, which perhaps he had reason for thinking would be as safe anywhere else as in his cousin Stephen's pocket.

The tête-à-tête which followed the attorney's departure was long, interesting, and very confidential. On the part of the gentleman great skill was displayed by the manner in which the following subjects were made to mix and mingle together, till, like to a skilfully composed ragout, no flavour of any kind was left distinctly perceptible, but the effect of the whole was just what the artist intended it should be. The subjects leading to, and composing this general effect, were: first, the deep interest raised in the breast of every good man by the sight of a gentle and heavenly-minded woman in want of assistance to carry her through the wearying and unspiritual cares incident to our passage through this world of sin; secondly, the exceeding out-pouring of mercy to be traced in such dispensations as led the unawakened to look for such aid and assistance from those who have been called and elected by the Lord; thirdly, the blessed assurance of everlasting joy that never failed to visit those who left husband or child for the Lord's sake; fourthly, the unerring wisdom of the Lord in the placing the tender consciences of the newly-chosen in the keeping of those who best know how to lead them aright; fifthly, the damnable and never-to-be-atoned-for wickedness of struggling against the Lord for the sake of any worldly feelings or affections whatever: and sixthly, the saving merit, surpassing all the works that our sinful nature could ever permit us to perform, which the Lord finds in such as cling to his spoken word, and hold fast to the persecuted and oppressed who preach it. On these themes, blended and harmonised together so as completely to mystify the mind of the weak and nervous Mrs Mowbray, and accompanied with just so much gentle demonstration of affectionate tenderness as might soften, without alarming her, did the Vicar of Wrexhill discourse for the three hours that they were left alone.

* * *

It would lead my narrative into too great length were every step recorded by which all Mrs Mowbray's other feelings were made to merge in the one overwhelming influence of Calvinistic terror on one side, and Calvinistic pride at presumed election on the other. The wily vicar contrived in the course of a few months so completely to rule the heart and head of this poor lady, that she looked upon her son Charles as a reprobate, who, unless speedily changed in spirit by severe discipline and the constant prayers of Mr Cartwright, must inevitably pass from this mortal life to a state of endless torture in the life to come. For Helen she was bade to hope that the time of election, after much wrestling with the Lord, would come; in Fanny she was told to glory and rejoice; and for Miss Torrington, quietly to wait the appointed time, till the Lord should make his voice heard, when it would be borne in upon his mind, or upon that of some one of the elect, whether she must be given over to eternal destruction, or saved with the remnant of the true flock which he and his brother shepherds were bringing together into one fold.

But with all this, though eternally talking of mystical and heavenly love, which was ever blended with insidious demonstrations of holy, brotherly, and Christian tenderness, Mr Cartwright had never yet spoken to the widow Mowbray of marriage.

She had been six months a widow, and her deep mourning weeds were exchanged for a dress elegantly becoming, but still marking her as belonging to what Mr Cartwright constantly called, in the midst of all his prosperous intrigues, the 'persecuted church of Christ.' Mr Stephen Corbold was comfortably settled in a snug little mansion in the village, and though he had never yet got hold of the title-deeds, he had begun to receive the rents of the Mowbray estates. He too was waiting the appointed time, – namely, the installing of his cousin at the Park, – for the fruition of all his hopes in the possession of Helen, and in such a fortune with her as his report of her progress towards regeneration might entitle her to. Mrs Richards had been refused bread by a converted baker; beer, by an elected brewer; and soap and candles, by that pious, painstaking, prayerful servant of the Lord, Richard White, the tallow-chandler. Her daughters, however, still held fast to the faith; though their poor mother grew thinner and paler every day, and continued to meet the vicar sometimes in the highways, sometimes in the byeways, and sometimes in the exemplary Mrs Simpson's drawing-room. Colonel Harrington had returned to his regiment without ever again seeing Helen, who had been forbidden with such awful denunciations in case of disobedience from ever holding any intercourse direct or indirect with the family at Oakley, that though she pined in thought, she obeyed, and was daily denounced by Sir Gilbert and his lady, though happily she knew it not, as the most ungrateful and heartless of girls. Fanny was growing tall, thin, sour-looking, and miserable; for having a sort of stubborn feeling within her which resisted the assurances she almost hourly received of having been elected to eternal grace, she was secretly torturing her distempered conscience with the belief that she was deluding every one but God, – that he alone read her heart and knew her to be reprobate, hardened and unregenerate, and that she must finally and inevitably come to be the prey of the worm that dyeth not and the fire that is never quenched. The sufferings of this innocent young creature under this terrible persuasion were dreadful, and the more so because she communicated them to none. Had she displayed the secret terrors of her soul to Mr Cartwright or her mother, she knew she should be told with praises and caresses that she was only the more blessed and sure of immortal glory for feeling them. Had she opened her heart to her sister, her brother, or Rosalind, her sufferings would probably have soon ceased; but from this she shrank as from degradation unbearable.

Poor Rosalind, meanwhile, was as profoundly unhappy as it was well possible for a girl to be who was young, beautiful, rich, talented, well-born, sweet-tempered, high-principled, not crossed in love, and moreover in perfect health.

Young Mowbray had just taken a distinguished degree at Oxford, and having given a farewell banquet to his college friends, returned home with the hope of speedily obtaining the commission in a regiment of horse for which his name had been long ago put down by his father.

It was at this time that several circumstances occurred at Wrexhill sufficiently important to the principal personages of my narrative to be recorded at some length.

CHAPTER XXV

FANNY'S RELIGION – A VISIT TO OAKLEY

It was towards the end of November that young Mowbray returned from Oxford to his mother's house in Hampshire. As usual, the first three or four hours' chat with Helen and Rosalind put him *au fait* of all that had taken place during his absence. The retrospect was not a cheering one; yet most of the circumstances which tended to annoy him were of that minor kind which none but a very gossipping correspondent would detail – and Helen was not such. Besides, since the mysterious letter which had recalled Charles to keep watch over Fanny, (the full and true purpose of which letter he had never yet discovered,) Miss Torrington had not written to him; and as she was now the chief historian, her round and unvarnished tale made him acquainted with many particulars to which Helen had scarcely alluded in her correspondence with him.

Helen Mowbray's was not a spirit to exhaust itself and its sorrows by breathing unavailing complaints; and though her brother had pretty clearly understood from her letters that she was not happy or comfortable at home, it was from Rosalind he first learned how many circumstances were daily occurring to make her otherwise.

The only point on which he blamed her, or in which, according to Rosalind's account, she had shown more yielding, and, as he called it, weakness than her helpless and most unhappy position rendered unavoidable, was in the never having attempted to see Lady Harrington.

This he declared was in itself wrong, and rendered doubly so by her situation, which would have rendered the society and counsel of such a friend invaluable. But he did not know – even Rosalind did not know – that this forbearance for which he blamed her was the result of those qualities for which they most loved her. But Helen knew, though they did not, that if she had gone to Oakley, she should have thought more of hearing news of Colonel Harrington than of any advice her godmother could have given her, and have been infinitely more anxious to learn if he ever mentioned her in his letters, than to know whether Lady Harrington thought it best that she should be civil, or that she should be rude, in her demeanour towards the Vicar of Wrexhill.

It was this conscious weakness which lent strength to the unreasonable violence of her mother on this point. Had Helen been quite fancy-free and altogether heart-whole, she would have had courage to discover that a passionate prohibition, originating, as she could not doubt it did, with a man for whom she entertained no species of esteem, ought not to make her abandon one of the kindest friends she had ever known. But there is a feeling stronger than reason in a young girl's breast; and again and again this feeling had whispered to Helen,

"'It is not maidenly——"

to go to the house of a man that I fear I love, and that I hope loves me, for the chance of hearing his name mentioned – and that too when my mother forbids me to enter his father's doors.'

But there was an authority in Charles's voice when he said, 'You have been wrong, Helen,' which seemed to have power even over this, and she promised that if after he paid the visit to Oakley, which he was fully determined to do on the morrow, he should report that her friends there were not too angry to receive her, she would consent to volunteer a visit to them, assigning as her reason for doing so, to her mother, that it was Charles's wish.

This conversation took place on the night of his arrival, and lasted for some hours after every individual of the household, excepting those engaged in it, were in bed. Poor Fanny was among those who had the earliest retired, but she was not among the sleepers. She too had once loved Charles most dearly, and most dearly had she been loved in return. But now she felt that they were separated for ever in this world, and that if they were doomed to meet in the world to come, it could only be amidst torturing and devouring flames. As she knelt for long hours beside her bed before she dared to lay her aching head on the pillow, her thoughts reverted to her early youth, and to all the innocent delights she had enjoyed with him and the now avoided Helen; and as she

remembered the ecstasy with which she once enjoyed the bloom of
flowers, the songs of birds, the breath of early morning, and all the poetry
of nature, tears of silent, unacknowledged, but most bitter regret,
streamed from her eyes. But then again came the ague fit of visionary
remorse and genuine Calvinistic terror, and she groaned aloud in agony
of spirit for having suffered these natural tears to fall.

This dreadful vigil left such traces on the pale cheek and heavy eye of
the suffering girl, that her brother's heart ached as he looked at her; and
though with little hope, after what he had heard, of doing any good, he
determined to seek half an hour's conversation with her before he went
out.

When she rose to leave the breakfast-table therefore, Charles rose too,
and following her out of the room, stopped her as she was in the act of
ascending the stairs by putting his arm round her waist and saying,
'Fanny, will you take a walk with me in the shrubbery?'

Fanny started, and coloured, and hesitated, as if some deed of very
doubtful tendency had been proposed to her. But he persevered. 'Come,
dear! put your bonnet on – I will wait for you here – make haste, Fanny!
Think how long it is since you and I took a walk together.'

'Is Helen going?' The question was asked in a voice that trembled: for
the idea that Charles meant during this walk to question her concerning
her faith occurred to her, and she would have given much to avoid it.
But before she could invent an excuse for doing so, her conscience,
always ready to enforce the doing whatever was most disagreeable to her,
suggested that this shrinking looked like being ashamed of her principles;
and no sooner had this idea suggested itself, than she said readily, 'Very
well, Charles; I will come to you in a moment.'

But the moment was rather a long one; for Fanny, before she rejoined
him, knelt down and made an extempore prayer for courage and strength
to resist and render of no effect whatever he might say to her. Thus
prepared, she set forth ready to listen with the most determined obstinacy
to any argument which might tend to overthrow any part of the creed
that was poisoning the very sources of her life.

'You are not looking well, my Fanny,' said her brother, fondly pressing
her arm as they turned into the most sheltered part of the garden. 'Do
you think the morning too cold for walking, my love? You used to be
such a hardy little thing, Fanny, that you cared for nothing; but I am
afraid the case is different now.'

This was not exactly the opening that Fanny expected, and there was a
tenderness in the tone of his voice that almost softened her heart towards
him; but she answered not a word, – perhaps she feared to trust her
voice.

'I wish you would tell me, dearest, if any sorrow or vexation has chased away the bloom and the gladness that we all so loved to look upon. Tell me, Fanny, what is it that has changed you so sadly? You will not? – Then you do not love me as I love you; for I am sure if I had a sorrow I should open my heart to you.'

'When a Christian has a sorrow, brother Charles, he should open his heart to the Lord, and not to a poor sinful mortal as wicked and as weak himself.'

'But surely, my dear Fanny, that need not prevent a brother and sister from conversing with the greatest confidence together. How many texts I could quote you in which family unity and affection are inculcated in the Bible!'

'Pray do not quote the Bible,' said Fanny in a voice of alarm, 'till the right spirit has come upon you. It is a grievous sin to do it, or to hear it.'

'Be assured, Fanny, that I feel quite as averse to quoting the Bible irreverently as you can do. But tell me why it is you think that the right spirit, as you call it, is not come upon me?'

'As I call it!' repeated Fanny, shuddering. 'It is not I, Charles, – it is one of the Lord's saints who says it; and it is a sin for me to listen to you.'

'It is doubtless Mr Cartwright who says it, Fanny. Is it not so?'

'And who has so good a right to say it as the minister of your parish, and the friend and protector that the Lord has sent to your widowed mother?'

Poor Mowbray felt his heart swell. It was difficult to hear the man who had come between him and all his best duties and affections named in this manner as his own maligner, and restrain his just and natural indignation; – yet he did restrain it, and said in a voice of the utmost gentleness,

'Do you think, my beloved Fanny, that Mr Cartwright's influence in this house has been for our happiness?'

'May the Lord forgive me for listening to such words!' exclaimed Fanny, with that look of nervous terror which her beautiful face now so often expressed. 'But he can't! he can't! – I know it, I know it! It is my doom to sin, and you are only an agent of that enemy who is for ever seeking my soul to destroy it. – Leave me! leave me!'

'Fanny, this is dreadful! Can you really believe that the God of love and mercy will hold you guilty for listening to the voice of your brother? What have I ever done, my Fanny, to deserve to be thus driven from your presence?'

The unhappy girl looked bewildered. 'Done!' she exclaimed. 'What have you done? – Is not that works? – Is not that of works you speak, Charles? – Oh! he knew, he foretold, he prophesied unto me that I should be spoken to of works, and that I should listen thereunto, to my everlasting destruction, if I confessed not my soul to him upon the instant. I must seek him out: he said IF, – oh, that dear blessed IF! Let go my arm, brother Charles! – let me seek my salvation!'

'Fanny, this is madness!'

She looked at him, poor girl, as he said this, with an expression that brought tears to his eyes. That look seemed to speak a dreadful doubt whether the words he had spoken were not true. She pressed her hand against her forehead for a moment, and then said in a voice of the most touching sadness,

'God help me!'

'Oh, Fanny! – darling Fanny!' cried the terrified brother, throwing his arms round her: 'save us from the anguish of seeing you destroyed body and mind by this frightful, this impious doctrine! Listen to me, my own sweet girl! Think that from me you hear the voice of your father – of the good and pious Wallace – of your excellent and exemplary governess, and drive this maddening terror from you. Did you live without God in the world, Fanny, when you lived under their virtuous rule? How often have you heard your dear father say, when he came forth and looked upon the beauty of the groves and lawns, bright in the morning sunshine, "Praise the Lord, my children, for his goodness, for his mercy endureth for ever!" Did not these words raise your young heart to heaven more than all the frightful denunciations which have almost shaken your reason?'

'Works! works! – Oh, Charles, let me go from you! Your voice is like the voice of the serpent: – it creeps dreadfully near my heart, and I shall perish, everlastingly perish, if I listen to you. IF: – is there yet an IF for me now? Let me go, Charles: let me seek him; – if you love me, let me seek my salvation.'

'Do you mean that you would seek Mr Cartwright, Fanny? You do not mean to go to his house, do you?'

'His house? How little you know him, Charles! Think you that he would leave me and my poor mother to perish? Poor, poor Charles! You do not even know that this shepherd and guardian of our souls prays with us daily?'

'Prays with you? Where does he pray with you?'

'In mamma's dressing-room.'

'And who are present at these prayers?'

'Mamma, and I, and Curtis, and Jem.'

'Jem? Who is Jem, Fanny?'

'The new stable-boy that our minister recommended, Charles, when that poor deluded Dick Bragg was found walking in the fields with his sister Patty on the Sabbath.'

'You don't mean that Dick Bragg is turned away? He was, without exception, the steadiest lad in the parish.'

'Works! works!' exclaimed Fanny, wringing her hands. 'Oh, Charles! how your poor soul clings to the perdition of works!'

'Gracious Heaven!' exclaimed Mowbray, with great emotion, 'where will all this end? What an existence for Helen, for Rosalind! Is there no cure for this folly, – this madness on one side, and this infernal craft and hypocrisy on the other?'

On hearing these words, Fanny uttered a cry which very nearly amounted to a scream, and running off towards the house with the fleetness of a startled fawn, left her brother in a state of irritation and misery such as he had never suffered before.

The idea of seeing Sir Gilbert Harrington immediately had perhaps more comfort and consolation in it than any other which could have suggested itself, and the lanes and the fields which divided Oakley from Mowbray were traversed at a pace that soon brought the agitated young man to the baronet's door.

'Is Sir Gilbert at home, John?' he demanded of an old servant who had known him from childhood; but instead of the widely-opened door, and ready smile which used to greet him, he received a grave and hesitating 'I don't know, sir,' from the changed domestic.

'Is Lady Harrington at home?' said Charles, vexed and colouring.

'It is likely she may be, Mr Mowbray,' said the old man relentingly. 'Will you please to wait one moment, Master Charles? I think my lady can't refuse——'

Charles's heart was full; but he did wait, and John speedily returned, saying almost in a whisper, 'Please to walk in, sir; but you must go into my lady's closet, – that's the only safe place, she says.'

'Safe?' repeated Charles; but he made no objection to the taking refuge in my lady's closet, and in another moment he found himself not only in the closet, but in the arms of the good old lady.

'Oh, Lord! – if Sir Gilbert could see me!' she exclaimed after very heartily hugging the young man. 'He's a greater tiger than ever, Charles, and I really don't know which of us would be torn to pieces first; – but only tell me one thing before I abuse him any more: – how long have you been at home?'

'The coach broke down at Newberry,' replied Charles, 'and I did not get to Mowbray till nine o'clock last night.'

'Thank God!' ejaculated Lady Harrington very fervently. 'Then there's hope in Israel at least for you. – But what on earth can you say to me of my beautiful Helen? Three months, Charles, three whole months since she has been near me – and she knows I dote upon her, and that Sir Gilbert himself, untamable hyena as he is, has always been loving and gentle to her, as far as his nature would permit. Then why has she treated us thus? You can't wonder, can you, that he swears lustily every morning that ingratitude is worse than all the mortal sins put together?'

'I dare not throw the charge back upon you, my dear lady; and yet it *is* being ungrateful for poor Helen's true affection to believe it possible that she should so long have remained absent from you by her own free will. You know not, dearest Lady Harrington, what my poor Helen has to endure.'

'Endure? What do you mean, Charles? Surely there is nobody living who dares to be unkind to her? My poor boy, – I am almost ashamed to ask the question, but you will forgive an old friend: is there any truth, Charles, in that damnable report? (God forgive me!) that horrid report, you know, about your mother?'

'What report, Lady Harrington?' said Mowbray, colouring like scarlet. 'I have heard no report, excepting that which is indeed too sure and certain to be called a report; – namely, that she has become a violent Calvinistic Methodist.'

'That's bad enough, my dear Charles, – bad enough of all conscience; and yet I have heard of what would be worse still; I have heard, Charles, that she is going to be weak and wicked enough to marry that odious hypocritical Tartuffe, the Vicar of Wrexhill.'

Mowbray put his hand before his eyes, as if he had been blasted by lightning, and then replied, as steadily as he could, 'I have never heard this, Lady Harrington.'

'Then I trust – I trust it is not true, Charles. Helen, surely, and that bright-eyed creature Miss Torrington, who have both, I believe, (for, God help me, I don't know!) – both, I believe, been staying all the time at Mowbray; – and surely – and surely, if this most atrocious deed were contemplated, they must have some knowledge of it.'

'And that they certainly have not,' returned Charles with recovered courage; 'for I sat with them both for two or three hours last night, listening to their miserable account of this man's detestable influence over my mother and Fanny; and certainly they would not have concealed from me such a suspicion as this, had any such existed in the breast of either.'

'Quite true, my dear boy, and I can hardly tell you how welcome this assurance is to me – not for your mother's sake, Charles; if you cannot bear the truth, you must not come to me, – and on this point the truth is, that I don't care one single straw about your mother. I never shall forgive her for not answering Sir Gilbert's note. I know what the writing it cost him – dear, proud, generous-hearted old fellow! And not to answer it! not to tell her children about it! No, I never shall forgive her, and I should not care the value of a rat's tail if she were to marry every tub preacher throughout England, and all their clerks in succession – that is, not for her own sake. I dare say she'll preach in a tub herself before she has done with it; but for your sakes, my dear souls, I do rejoice that it is not true.'

'That would indeed complete our misery: and it is already quite bad enough, I assure you. The house, Helen says, is a perfect conventicle. The girls are ordered to sing nothing but psalms and hymns; some of the latter so offensively ludicrous, too, as to be perfectly indecent and profane. A long extempore sermon, or lecture as he calls it, is delivered to the whole family in the great drawing-room every night; missionary boxes are not only hung up beside every door, but actually carried round by the butler whenever any one calls; and a hundred and fifty other absurdities, at which we should laugh were we in a gayer mood: but this farce has produced the saddest tragedy I ever witnessed, in the effect it has had upon our poor Fanny. I have had some conversation with her this morning, and I do assure you that I greatly fear her reason is unsettled, or like to be so.'

'God forbid, Charles! Pretty innocent young thing! that would be too horrible to think of.'

The old lady's eyes were full of tears, a circumstance very unusual with her, but the idea suggested struck her to the heart; and she had not yet removed the traces of this most unwonted proof of sensibility, when a heavy thump was heard at the door of the closet.

'Who's there?' said her ladyship in a voice rather raised than lowered by the emotion which dimmed her eyes.

'Let me in, my lady!' responded the voice of Sir Gilbert.

'What do you want, Sir Gilbert? I am busy.'

'So I understand, my lady, and I'm come to help you.'

'Will you promise, if I let you in, not to hinder me, instead?'

'I'll promise nothing, except to quarrel with you if you do not.'

'Was there ever such a tyrant! Come in, then; see, hear, and understand.'

The door was opened, and Sir Gilbert Harrington and Charles Mowbray stood face to face.

Charles smiled, and held out his hand.

The baronet knit his brows, but the expression of his mouth told her experienced ladyship plainly enough that he was well enough pleased at the sight of his unexpected guest.

'He only got to Mowbray at nine o'clock last night,' said Lady Harrington.

Sir Gilbert held out his hand. 'Charles, I am glad to see you,' said he.

'Thank God!' ejaculated the old lady.

'My dear Sir Gilbert,' said Charles, 'I have learnt your kind and friendly anger at the prolonged absence of my poor sister. The fault is not hers, Sir Gilbert; she has been most strictly forbidden to visit you.'

'By her mother?'

'By her mother, Sir Gilbert.'

'And pray, Charles, do you think it her duty to obey?'

'I really know not how to answer you. For a girl just nineteen to act in declared defiance of the commands of her mother, and that mother her sole surviving parent, is a line of conduct almost too bold to advise. And yet, such is the lamentable state of infatuation to which my mother's mind appears to be reduced by the pernicious influence of this Cartwright, that I think it would be more dangerous still to recommend obedience.'

'Upon my soul I think so,' replied Sir Gilbert, in an accent that showed he thought the proposition too self-evident to be discussed. 'I have been devilish angry with the girls, – with Helen, I mean, – for I understand that little idiot, Fanny, is just as mad as her mother; but that Helen, and that fine girl, Rosalind Torrington, should shut themselves up with an hypocritical fanatic and a canting mad woman, is enough to put any man out of patience.'

'The situation has been almost enough to put Helen in her grave; she looks wretchedly; and Miss Torrington is no longer the same creature. It would wring your heart to see these poor girls, Sir Gilbert; and what are they to do?'

'Come to us, Charles. Let them both come here instantly, and remain here till your mother's mad fit is over. If it lasts, I shall advise you to take out a commission of lunacy.'

'The madness is not such as a physician would recognise, Sir Gilbert; and yet I give you my honour that, from many things which my sister and Miss Torrington told me last night, I really do think my mother's reason must be in some degree deranged. And for my poor little Fanny, six months ago the pride and darling of us all, she is, I am quite persuaded, on the verge of insanity.'

'And you mean to leave her in the power of that distracted driveler, her mother, that the work may be finished?'

'What can I do, Sir Gilbert?'

'Remove them all. Take them instantly away from her, I tell you.'

The blood rushed painfully to poor Mowbray's face. 'You forget, Sir Gilbert,' he said, 'that I have not the means: you forget my father's will.'

'No, sir; I do not forget it. Nor do I forget either that, had I not in a fit of contemptible passion refused to act as executor, I might, I think it possible, – I might have plagued her heart out, and so done some good. I shall never forgive myself!'

'But you could have given us no power over the property, Sir Gilbert. We are beggars.'

'I know it, I know it!' replied the old gentleman, clenching his fists. 'I told you so from the first: and now mark my words, – she'll marry her saint before she's six months older.'

'I trust that in this you are mistaken. The girls have certainly no suspicions of the sort.'

'The girls are fools, as girls always are. But let them come here, I tell you, and we may save their lives at any rate.'

'Tell them both from me, Charles, that they shall find a home, and a happy one, here; but don't let them chill that old man's heart again by taking no notice of this, and keeping out of his sight for another three months. He'll have the gout in his stomach as sure as they're born; just tell Helen that from me.'

Mowbray warmly expressed his gratitude for their kindness; and though he would not undertake to promise that either Helen or Miss Torrington would immediately decide upon leaving his mother's house, in open defiance of her commands, he promised that they should both come over on the morrow, to be cheered and supported by the assurance of their continued friendship. He was then preparing to take his leave when Lady Harrington laid her hand upon his arm, saying,

'Listen to me, Charles, for a moment. Those dear girls, and you too, my dear boy, you are all surrounded with great difficulties, and some consideration is necessary as to how you shall meet them best. It won't do, Sir Gilbert; it will be neither right nor proper in any way for Helen to set off at once in utter and open defiance of Mrs Mowbray. What I advise is, that Charles should go home, take his mother apart, and, like Hamlet in the closet scene, "speak daggers, but use none." It does not appear, from all we have yet heard, that any one has hitherto attempted to point out to her the deplorable folly, ay, and wickedness too, which she is committing. I do not believe she would admit Sir Gilbert; and, to say the truth, I don't think it would be very safe to trust him with the job.'

'D——n it! I wish you would,' interrupted Sir Gilbert. 'I should like to have the talking to her only just for an hour, and I'd consent to have the gout for a month afterwards; I would, upon my soul!'

'Do be tame for a moment, you wild man of the woods,' said her ladyship, laying her hand upon his mouth, 'and let me finish what I was saying. No, no, Sir Gilbert is not the proper person; but you are, Charles. Speak to her with gentleness, with kindness, but tell her *the truth*. If you find her contrite and yielding, use your victory with moderation; and let her down easily from her giddy elevation of saintship to the sober, quiet, even path of rational religion, and domestic duty. But if she be restive – if she still persist in forbidding Helen to visit her father's oldest friends, while making her own once happy home a prison, and a wretched one, –

then, Charles Mowbray, I would tell her roundly that she must choose between her children and her Tartuffe, and that if she keeps him she must lose you.'

'Bravo! capital! old lady; if Charles will just say all that, we shall be able to guess by the result as to how things are between them, and we must act accordingly. You have your allowance paid regularly, Charles? I think she doubled it, didn't she, after your father died?'

Charles looked embarrassed, but answered, 'Yes, Sir Gilbert, my allowance was doubled.'

'D——n it, boy, don't answer like a jesuit. – Is it regularly paid? – That was my question, my main question.'

'The first quarter was paid, Sir Gilbert; but before I left the University, instead of the remittance, I received a letter from my mother, desiring me to transmit a statement of all my debts to Stephen Corbold, Esq. solicitor, Wrexhill; and that they should be attended to; which would, she added, be more satisfactory to her than sending my allowance without knowing how I stood with my tradesmen.'

'And have you done this, my fine sir?' said Sir Gilbert, becoming almost purple with anger.

'No, Sir Gilbert, I have not.'

The baronet threw his arms round him, and gave him a tremendous hug.

'I see you are worth caring for, my boy; I should never have forgiven you if you had. Audacious rascal! Why, Charles, that Corbold has been poking his snuffling, hypocritical nose, into every house, not only in your parish but in mine, and in at least a dozen others, and has positively beat poor old Gaspar Brown out of the field. The old man called to take leave of me not a week ago, and told me that one after another very nearly every client he had in this part of the world had come or sent to him for their papers, in order to deposit them with this canting Corbold; and, as I hear, all the little farmers for miles round are diligently going to law in the name of the Lord. But what did you do, my dear boy, for money?'

'Oh! I have managed pretty well. It was a disappointment certainly, and at first I felt a little awkward, for the letter did not reach me till I had ordered my farewell supper; and as in truth I had no tradesman's bills to pay, I gave my orders pretty liberally, and of course have been obliged to leave the account unpaid, – an arrangement which to many others would have had nothing awkward in it at all; but as my allowance has been always too liberal to permit my being in debt during my part of the time I have been at the college, the not paying my last bill there was disagreeable. However the people were abundantly civil, and I flatter myself that, without the assistance of Mr Corbold, I shall be able to settle this matter before long.'

'What is the sum you have left unpaid, Charles?' inquired the baronet bluntly.

'Seventy-five pounds, Sir Gilbert.'

'Then just sit down for half a moment, and write a line enclosing the money; you may cut the notes in half if you think there is any danger.'

And as he spoke he laid bank-notes to the amount of seventy-five pounds on her ladyship's botanical dresser.

Young Mowbray, who had not the slightest doubt of receiving his allowance from his mother as soon as he should ask her for it, would rather not have been under a pecuniary obligation even for a day; but he caught the eye of Lady Harrington, who was standing behind her impetuous husband, and received thence a perfectly intelligible hint that he must not refuse the offer. Most anxious to avoid renewing the coldness so recently removed, he readily and graciously accepted the offered loan, and thereby most perfectly re-established the harmony which had existed throughout his life between himself and the warm-hearted but impetuous Sir Gilbert.

'Now, then,' said the old gentleman with the most cordial and happy good-humour, 'be off, my dear boy; follow my dame's advice to the letter, and come back as soon as you conveniently can, to let us know what comes of it.'

Cheered in spirit by this warm renewal of the friendship he so truly valued, young Mowbray set off on his homeward walk, pondering, as he went, on the best mode of opening such a conversation with his mother as Lady Harrington recommended; a task both difficult and disagreeable, but one which he believed it his duty not to shrink from.

CHAPTER XXVI

CHARLES'S CONFERENCE WITH MRS MOWBRAY

Strolling in the shrubbery near the house, where for some time they had been anxiously awaiting his return, he met his eldest sister and Miss Torrington. Helen's first words were, 'Are they angry with me?' and the reply, and subsequent history of the visit, filled her heart with gladness. 'And now, my privy counsellors,' continued Charles, 'tell me at what hour you should deem it most prudent for me to ask my mother for an audience.'

'Instantly!' said Rosalind.

'Had he not better wait till to-morrow?' said Helen, turning very pale.

'If my advisers disagree among themselves, I am lost,' said Charles; 'for

I give you my word that I never in my whole life entered upon an undertaking which made me feel so anxious and undecided. Let me hear your reasons for thus differing in opinion? Why, Rosalind, do you recommend such prodigious promptitude?'

'Because I hate suspense, – and because I know the scene will be disagreeable to you, – wherefore I opine that the sooner you get over it the better.'

'And you, Helen, why do you wish me to delay it till to-morrow?'

'Because, – oh! Charles, – because I dread the result. You have no idea as yet how completely her temper is changed. She is very stern, Charles, when she is contradicted; and, if you should make her angry, depend upon it that it would be Mr Cartwright who would dictate your punishment.'

'My punishment! Nonsense, Helen! I shall make Miss Torrington both my Chancellor and Archbishop, for her advice has infinitely more wisdom in it than yours. Where is she? in her own dressing-room?'

'I believe so,' faltered Helen.

'Well, then, – adieu for half an hour, – perhaps for a whole one. Where shall I find you when it is over?'

'In my dressing-room,' said Helen.

'No, no,' cried Rosalind; 'I would not have to sit with you there for an hour, watching you quiver and quake every time a door opened, for my heiressship. Let us walk to the great lime-tree, and stay there till you come.'

'And so envelop yourselves in a November woodland fog, wherein to sit waiting till about four o'clock! The wisdom lies with Helen this time, Miss Torrington; I think you have both of you been pelted long enough with falling leaves for to-day, and therefore I strongly recommend that you come in and wait for my communication beside a blazing fire. Have you no new book, no lively novel or fancy-stirring romance, wherewith to beguile the time?'

'Novels and romances! Oh! Mr Mowbray, – what a desperate sinner you must be! The subscription at Hookham's has been out these three months; and the same dear box that used to be brought in amidst the eager rejoicings of the whole family, is now become the monthly vehicle of Evangelical Magazines, Christian Observers, Missionary Reports, and Religious Tracts, of all imaginable sorts and sizes. We have no other modern literature allowed us.'

'Poor girls!' said Charles, laughing; 'what do you do for books?'

'Why, the old library supplies us indifferently well, I must confess; and as Fanny has changed her morning quarters from thence to the print-room, which is now converted into a chapel of ease for the vicar, we contrive to abduct from thence such volumes as we wish for without difficulty. But we were once very near getting a book, which, I have been told, is of the most exquisite interest and pathos of any in the language, by a pleasant blunder of Mrs Mowbray's. I chanced to be in the room with her one day when she read aloud an old advertisement which she happened to glance her eye upon, stitched up in a Review of some dozen years standing, I believe, "Some passages in the life of Mr Adam Blair, Minister of the Gospel." "That's a book we ought to have," said she, very solemnly; "Rosalind, give me that list for Hatchard's, I will add this." I took up the advertisement as she laid it down, and, not having it before her eyes, I suspect that she made some blunder about the title; for, when the box came down, I took care to be present at the opening of it, and to my great amusement, instead of the little volume that I was hoping to see, I beheld all Blair's works, with a scrap of paper from one of the shopmen, on which was written, "Mrs Mowbray is respectfully informed that the whole of Blair's works are herewith forwarded, but that J.P. is not aware of any other life of Adam than that written by Moses." This was a terrible disappointment to me, I assure you.'

They had now reached the house; the two girls withdrew their arms, and, having watched Charles mount the stairs, they turned into the drawing-room, – and from thence to the conservatory, – and then back again, – and then up stairs to lay aside their bonnets and cloaks, – and then down again; first one and then the other looking at their watches, till they began to suspect that they must both of them stand still, or something very like it, so creepingly did the time pass during which they waited for his return.

On reaching the dressing-room door, Charles knocked, and it was opened to him by Fanny.

The fair brow of his mother contracted at his approach; and he immediately suspected, what was indeed the fact, that Fanny had been relating to her the conversation which had passed between them in the morning.

He rather rejoiced at this than the contrary, as he thought the conversation could not be better opened than by his expressing his opinions and feelings upon what had fallen from her during this interview. He did not, however, wish that she should be present, and therefore said,

'Will you let me, dear mother, say a few words to you tête-à-tête. Come, Fanny; run away, will you, for a little while?'

Fanny instantly left the room, and Mrs Mowbray, without answering his request, sat silently waiting for what he was about to say.

'I want to speak to you, mother, about our dear Fanny. I assure you I am very uneasy about her; I do not think she is in good health, either of body or mind.'

'Your ignorance of medicine is, I believe, total, Charles,' she replied dryly, 'and therefore your opinion concerning her bodily health does not greatly alarm me; and you must pardon me if I say that I conceive your ignorance respecting all things relating to a human soul, is more profound still.'

'I am sorry you should think so, dearest mother; but I assure you that neither physic nor divinity have been neglected in my education.'

'And by whom have you been taught? Blind guides have been your teachers, who have led you, I fear, to the very brink of destruction. When light is turned into darkness, how great is that darkness!'

'My teachers have been those that my dear father appointed me, and I have never seen any cause to mistrust either their wisdom or their virtue, mother.'

'And know you not that your poor unhappy father was benighted, led astray, and lost by having himself listened to such teaching as he caused to be given to you? But you, Charles, if you did not harden your heart, even as the nether millstone, might even yet be saved among the remnant. Put yourself into the hands and under the training of the pious, blessed minister whom the Lord hath sent us. Open your sinful heart to Mr Cartwright, Charles, and you may save your soul alive!'

'Mother!' said Charles with solemn earnestness, 'Mr Cartwright's doctrines are dreadful and sinful in my eyes. My excellent and most beloved father was a Protestant Christian, born, educated, and abiding to his last hour in the faith and hope taught by the established church of his country. In that faith and hope, mother, I also have been reared by him and by you; and rather than change it for the impious and frightful doctrines of the sectarian minister you name, who most dishonestly has crept within the pale of an establishment whose dogmas and discipline he profanes, – rather, mother, than adopt this Mr Cartwright's unholy belief, and obey his unauthorised and unscriptural decrees, I would kneel down upon the steps of God's altar and implore him to lay my bones beside my father's.'

'Leave the room, Charles Mowbray!' exclaimed his mother almost in a scream; 'let not the walls that shelter me be witness to such fearful blasphemy!'

'I cannot, and I will not leave you, mother, till I have told you how very wretched you are making me and my poor sister Helen by thus forsaking that form of religion in which from our earliest childhood we have been accustomed to see you worship God. Why, – why, dearest mother, should you bring this dreadful schism upon your family? Can you believe this to be your duty?'

'By what right, human or divine, do you thus question me, lost, unhappy boy? But I will answer you; and I trust the mercy of the Lord will visit me with forgiveness for intercommuning with one who lives in open rebellion to his saints! Yes, sir; I do believe it is my duty to hold fast the conviction which the Lord, in his heavenly goodness, has sent me by the hand of his anointed. I do believe it is my duty to testify by my voice, and by every act of my life during the remaining time for which the Lord shall spare me for the showing forth of his glory, that I consider the years that are past as an abomination in the sight of the Lord; that my living in peace and happiness with your unawakened and unregenerate father was an abomination in the sight of the Lord; and that now, at the eleventh hour, my only hope of being received by Christ rests in my hating and abhorring, and forsaking and turning away from, all that is, and has been, nearest and dearest to my sinful heart!'

Charles listened to this rant with earnest and painful attention, and, when she ceased, looked at her through tears that presently overflowed his eyes.

'Have I then lost my only remaining parent?' said he. 'And can you thus close your heart against me, and your poor Helen, my mother?'

'By the blessing of the Lord I am strong,' replied the deluded lady, struggling to overcome God's best gift of pure affection in her heart. 'By the blessing of Jesus, and by the earnest prayers of his holiest saint, I am able, wretched boy, to look at thee and say, Satan, avaunt! But the Lord tries me sorely,' she continued, turning her eyes from the manly countenance of her son, now wet with tears. 'Sorely, sorely, doomed and devoted boy, does he try me! But he, the Lord's vicar upon earth, the darling of the holy Jesus, the chosen shepherd, the anointed saint, – he, even he tells me to be of good cheer, for whom the Lord loveth he chasteneth.'

'Can you then believe, mother, that the merciful God of heaven and of earth approves your forsaking your children, solely because they worship him as they have been taught to do? Can you believe that he approves your turning your eyes and heart from them to devote yourself to a stranger to your blood, a preacher of strange doctrine, and one who loves them not?'

'I have already told you, impious maligner of the holiest of men, that I know where my duty lies. I know, I tell you, that I not only know it, but will do it. Torment me no more! Leave me, leave me, unhappy boy! leave me, that I may pray to the Lord for pardon for having listened to thee so long.'

She rose from her seat, and approached him, as if to thrust him from the chamber; but he suffered her to advance without moving, and when she was close to him, he threw his arms round her, and held her for a moment in a close embrace. She struggled violently to disengage herself, and he relaxed his hold; but, dropping on his knees before her, at the same moment he exclaimed with passionate tenderness, 'My dear, dear mother! have I then received your last embrace? Shall I never again feel your beloved lips upon my cheeks, my lips, my forehead? Mother! what can Helen and I do to win back your precious love?'

'Surely the Lord will reward me for this!' said the infatuated woman almost wildly. 'Surely he will visit me with an exceeding great reward! and will he not visit thee too, unnatural son, for art thou not plotting against my soul to destroy it?'

'There is, then, no hope for us from the voice of nature, no hope from the voice of reason and of truth? Then hear me, mother, for I too must act according to the voice of conscience. Helen and I must leave you; we can no longer endure to be so near you in appearance, while in reality we are so fearfully estranged. You have been very generous to me in the sum which you named for my allowance at my father's death; and as soon as my commission is obtained, that allowance will suffice to support me, for my habits have never been extravagant. May I ask you to assign a similar sum to Helen? This will enable her to command such a home with respectable people as may befit your daughter; and you will not doubt, I think, notwithstanding the unhappy difference in our opinions on points of doctrine, that I shall watch over her as carefully as our dear father himself could have done.'

'He is a prophet! yea, a prophet!' exclaimed Mrs Mowbray; 'and shall I be blind even as the ungodly, and doubt his word into whose mouth the Lord hath put the gift of prophecy and the words of wisdom? He hath spoken, and very terrible things are come to pass. Can your heart resist such proof as this, Charles?' she continued, raising her eyes and hands to heaven: – 'even what you have now spoken, that did he predict and foretell you should speak!'

'He guessed the point, then, at which we could bear no more,' replied Charles with bitterness: 'and did he predict too what answer our petition should receive?'

'He did,' returned Mrs Mowbray either with real or with feigned simplicity; 'and even that too shall be verified. Now, then, hear his blessed voice through my lips; and as I say, so must thou do. Go to your benighted sister, and tell her that for her sake I will wrestle with the Lord in prayer. With great and exceeding anguish of spirit have I already wrestled for her; but she is strong and wilful, and resisteth always. – Nevertheless, I will not give her over to her own heart's desire; nor will I turn mine eyes from her. For a while longer I will endure, for so hath the Lord commanded by the lips of his anointed: and for you, unhappy son, I must take counsel of the Lord from the same holy well-spring of righteousness, and what he shall speak, look that it come to pass.'

'You have denounced a terrible sentence against Helen, mother! For nearly two years, then, she must look forward to a very wretched life; but, without your consent, I cannot till she is of age remove her. Dear girl! she has a sweet and gentle spirit, and will, I trust, be enabled to bear patiently her most painful situation. But as for myself, it may be as well to inform Mr Cartwright at once, through you, that any interference with me or my concerns will not be endured; and that I advise him, for his own sake, to let me hear and see as little of him as possible.'

Mrs Mowbray seemed to listen to these words in perfect terror, as if she feared a thunderbolt must fall and crush at once the speaker and the hearer of such daring impiety. But the spirit of Charles was chafed; and conscious perhaps that he was in danger of saying what he might wish to recall on the influence which his mother avowed that the vicar had obtained over her, he hastened to conclude the interview, and added: 'I will beg you, ma'am, immediately to give me a draft for my quarter's allowance, due on the first of this month. I want immediately to send money to Oxford.'

'Did I not tell you, Charles, to inform my man of business, – that serious and exemplary man, Mr Corbold, – what money you owed in Oxford, and to whom? And did I not inform you at the same time that he should have instructions to acquit the same forthwith?'

'Yes, mother, you certainly did send me a letter to that effect; but as my father permitted me, before I came of age to pay my own bills, and to dispose of my allowance as I thought fit, I did not choose to change my usual manner of proceeding, and therefore left what I owed unpaid, preferring to remit the money myself. Will you please to give me the means of doing this now?'

'May the Lord be gracious to me and mine, as I steadily now, and for ever, refuse to do so great iniquity! Think you, Charles, that I, guided and governed, as I glory to say I am, by one sent near me by the providence of the Lord to watch over me now in my time of need, – think you that I will hire and pay your wicked will to defy the Lord and his anointed?'

'Do you mean, then, mother, to withdraw my allowance?' said Charles.

'I thank my Lord and Saviour that I do!' she replied, casting her eyes to heaven: 'and humbly on my knees will I thank the blessed Jesus for giving me that strength, even in the midst of weakness!'

As she spoke, she dropped upon her knees on the floor, with her back towards her unhappy son. He remained standing for a few moments, intending to utter some nearly hopeless words of remonstrance upon the cruel resolution she had just announced; but as she did not rise, he left the room, and with a heavy heart proceeded to look for Helen and her friend; though he would gladly have prepared himself by an hour of solitude for communicating tidings which had very nearly overthrown his philosophy. But he had promised to see them and to tell them all that passed; and he prepared to perform this promise with a heavier heart than had ever before troubled his bosom. He shrank from the idea of appearing before Rosalind in a situation so miserably humiliating, for at this moment fears that the report mentioned by Lady Harrington might be true pressed upon him; and though his better judgment told him that such feelings were contemptible, when about to meet the eye of a friend he could not subdue them, and as he opened the drawing-room door, the youthful fire of his eye was quenched and his pale lip trembled.

'Oh! Charles, how dreadfully ill you look!' exclaimed Helen.

'What can have passed?' said Miss Torrington looking almost as pale as himself.

'Much that has been very painful,' he replied; 'but I am ashamed at being thus overpowered by it. Tell me, both of you, without any reserve, have you ever thought – has the idea ever entered your heads, that my unfortunate mother was likely to marry Cartwright?'

'No, – never,' replied Helen firmly.

'Yes,' said Rosalind falteringly; – but less with the hesitation of doubt, than from fear of giving pain.

'Lady Harrington told me it was spoken of,' said Mowbray with a deep sigh.

'It is impossible!' said Helen, 'I cannot: – I will not believe it. Rosalind! if you have had such an idea, how comes it that you have kept it secret from me?'

'If, instead of darkly fearing it,' replied Rosalind, 'I had positively known it to be true, I doubt if I should have named it, Helen; – I could not have borne that words so hateful should have first reached the family from me.'

'Has she told you it is so?' inquired Helen, her lips so parched with agitation that she pronounced the words with difficulty.

'No, dearest, she has not; and perhaps I am wrong both in conceiving such an idea, and in naming it. But her mind is so violently, so strangely wrought upon by this detestable man, that I can only account for it by believing that he is——'

There was much filial piety in the feeling that prevented his finishing the sentence.

'It is so that I have reasoned,' said Rosalind. 'Heaven grant that we be both mistaken! – But will you not tell us, Charles, what it is that has suggested the idea to you? For Heaven's sake relate, if you can, what has passed between you?'

'If I can! – Indeed I doubt my power. She spoke of me as of one condemned of God.'

Rosalind started from her seat. – 'Do not go on, Mr Mowbray!' she exclaimed with great agitation; 'I cannot bear this, and meet her with such external observance and civility as my situation demands. It can do us no good to discuss this wicked folly, – this most sinful madness. I, at least, for one, feel a degree of indignation – a vehemence of irritation on the subject, that will not, I am sure, produce good to any of us. She must go on in the dreadful path in which she has lost herself, till she meet something that shall shock and turn her back again. But all that can be done or said by others will but drive her on the faster, adding the fervour of a martyr to that of a convert.'

'You speak like an oracle, dear Rosalind,' said poor Mowbray, endeavouring to smile, and more relieved than he would have avowed to himself at being spared the task of narrating his downfall from supposed wealth to actual penury before her.

'She speaks like an oracle, but a very sad one,' said Helen. 'Nevertheless, we will listen and obey. – You have spoken to my mother, and what you have said has produced no good effect: to me, therefore, it is quite evident that nothing can. Were it not that the fearful use which we hear made of the sacred name of God makes me tremble lest I too should use it irreverently, I would express the confidence I feel, that if we bear this heavy sorrow well, his care will be with us: and whether we say it or not, let us feel it. And now, Rosalind, we must redeem our lost time, and read for an hour or so upstairs. See! we have positively let the fire go out; – a proof how extremely injurious it is to permit our thoughts to fix themselves too intensely on anything: – it renders one incapable of attending to the necessary affairs of life. – There, Charles, is a sermon for you. But don't look so miserable, my dear brother; or my courage will melt into thin air.'

'I will do my best to master it, Helen,' he replied; 'but I shall not be able to make a display of my stoicism before you this evening, for I must return to Oakley.'

'Are you going to dine there? Why did you not tell me so?'

'If my conversation with my mother had ended differently, Helen, I should have postponed my visit till to-morrow; but as it is, it will be better for me to go now. I will drive myself over in the cab. I suppose I can have Joseph?' He rang the bell as he spoke.

'Let the cab be got ready for me in half an hour: and tell Joseph I shall want him to go out with me to dinner.'

'The cab is not at home, sir,' replied the servant.

'Is it gone to the coach-maker's? – What is the matter with it?'

'There is nothing the matter with it, sir; but Mr Cartwright has got it.'

'Then let my mare be saddled. She is in the stable, I suppose?'

'Mr Corbold has had the use of your mare, Mr Charles, for more than a month, sir: and terribly worked she has been, Dick says.'

'Very well – it's no matter: I shall walk, William.'

The servant retired, with an expression of more sympathy than etiquette could warrant. Helen looked at her brother in very mournful silence; but tears of indignant passion started to the bright eyes of Rosalind. 'Is there no remedy for all this?' she exclaimed. 'Helen, let us run away together. They cannot rob me of my money, I suppose. Do ask Sir Gilbert, Charles, if I am obliged to stay here and witness these hateful goings-on.'

'I will – I will, Miss Torrington. It would indeed, be best for you to leave us. But my poor Helen, – she must stay and bear it.'

'Then I shall stay too: and that I think you might guess, Mr Mowbray.'

Rosalind's tears overflowed as she spoke; and Charles Mowbray looked at her with that wringing of the heart which arises from thinking that all things conspire to make us wretched. When he was the reputed heir of fourteen thousand a year, he had passed whole weeks in the society of Rosalind, and never dreamed he loved her; – but now, now that he was a beggar, and a beggar too, as it seemed, not very likely to be treated with much charity by his own mother, – now that it would be infamy to turn his thoughts towards the heiress with any hope or wish that she should ever be his, he felt that he adored her – that every hour added strength to a passion that he would rather die than reveal, and that without a guinea in the world to take him or to keep him elsewhere, his remaining where he was would expose him to sufferings that he felt he had no strength to bear.

CHAPTER XXVII

THE VICAR'S PROGRESS, AND HIS COUNSEL TO FANNY AS TO THE BEST MEANS OF ASSISTING THE POOR

When the family assembled at dinner, and Mrs Mowbray perceived the place of her son vacant, she changed colour, and appeared discomposed and absent during the whole time she remained at table. This, however, was not long; for, a very few minutes after the cloth was removed, she rose, and saying, 'I want you, Fanny,' left the room with her youngest daughter without making either observation or apology to those she left. The result of this conference between the mother and daughter was the despatching a note to the Vicarage, which brought the vicar to join them with extraordinary speed.

Mrs Mowbray then related with a good deal of emotion the scene which had taken place between herself and her son in the morning;

concluding it with mentioning his absence at dinner, and her fears that, in his unregenerate state of mind, he might be led to withdraw himself altogether from a home where godliness had begun to reign, and where, by the blessing of the Lord Jesus, it would multiply and increase every day that they were spared to live.

When she had concluded, Mr Cartwright remained for several minutes silent, his eyes fixed upon the carpet, his arms folded upon his breast, and his head from time to time moved gently and sadly to and fro, as if the subject on which he was meditating were both important and discouraging. At length he raised his eyes, and fixed them upon Fanny,

'My dear child,' he said, 'withdraw yourself, and pray, while your mother and I remain together. Pray for us, Fanny! – pray for both of us, that we may so do the duty appointed unto us by the Lord, as what we may decide to execute shall redound to his glory, and to our everlasting salvation, world without end, amen!'

Fanny rose instantly, and clasping her innocent hands together, fervently exclaimed 'I will! – I will!'

Having opened the door, and laid his delicate white hand upon her head, whispering an ardent blessing as she passed through it, he watched her as she retreated with a rapid step to her chamber anxious to perform the duty assigned her; and then closing and bolting it after her, he returned to the sofa near the fire, and seated himself beside Mrs Mowbray.

'My friend!' said Mr Cartwright, taking her hand; 'my dear, dear friend! you are tried, you are very sorely tried. But it is the will of the Lord, and we must not repine at it: rather let us praise his name alway!'

'I do!' ejaculated the widow with very pious emotion; 'I do praise and bless his holy name for all the salvation he hath vouchsafed to me, a sinner – and to my precious Fanny with me. Oh, Mr Cartwright, it is very dear to my soul to think that I shall have that little holy angel with me in paradise! But be my guide and helper' – and here the good and serious lady very nearly returned the pressure with which her hand was held, – 'oh! be my guide and helper with my other misguided children! Tell me, dear Mr Cartwright, what must I do with Charles!'

'It is borne in upon my mind, my dear and gentle friend, that there is but one chance left to save that deeply-perilled soul from the everlasting gulf of gnawing worms and of eternal flame.'

'Is there one chance?' exclaimed the poor woman in a real ecstasy. 'Oh! tell me what it is, and there is nothing in the wide world that I would not bear and suffer to obtain it.'

'He must abandon the profession of arms, and become a minister of the gospel.'

'Oh! Mr Cartwright, he never will consent to this. From his earliest childhood, his unhappy and unawakened father taught him to glory in the thought of fighting the battles of his country; and with the large fortune he must one day have, is it not probable that he might be tempted to neglect the cure of souls? And then, you know, Mr Cartwright, that the last state of that man would be worse than the first.'

Mr Cartwright dropped the lady's hand and rose from his seat. 'I must leave you, then,' he said, his rich voice sinking into a tone of the saddest melancholy. 'I must not – I may not give any other counsel; for in doing so, I should betray my duty to the Lord, and betray the confidence you have placed in me. Adieu, then, beloved friend! adieu for ever! My heart – the weak and throbbing heart of a man is even now heaving in my breast. That heart will for ever forbid my speaking with harshness and austerity to you. Therefore, beloved but too feeble friend, adieu! Should I stay longer with you, that look might betray me into forgetfulness of everything on earth – and heaven too!'

The three last words were uttered in a low and mournful whisper. He then walked towards the door, turned to give one last look, and having unfastened the lock and shot back the bolt, was in the very act of departing, when Mrs Mowbray rushed towards him, exclaiming 'Oh, do not leave us all to everlasting damnation! Save us! save us! Tell me only what to do, and I will do it.'

In the extremity of her eagerness, terror, and emotion, she fell on her knees before him, and raising her tearful eyes to his, seemed silently to reiterate the petition she had uttered.

Mr Cartwright looked down upon her, turned away for one short instant to rebolt the door, and then, raising his eyes to heaven, and dropping on his knees beside her, he threw his arms around her, impressed a holy kiss upon her brow, exclaiming in a voice rendered tremulous, as it should seem, by uncontrollable agitation, 'Oh, never! never!'

After a few moments unavoidably lost by both in efforts to recover their equanimity, they rose and reseated themselves on the sofa.

The handkerchief of Mrs Mowbray was at her eyes. She appeared greatly agitated, and totally unable to speak herself, sat in trembling expectation of what her reverend friend should say next.

It was not immediately, however, that Mr Cartwright could recover his voice; but at length he said, 'It is impossible, my too lovely friend, that we can either of us any longer mistake the nature of the sentiment which we feel for each other. But we have the comfort of knowing that this sweet and blessed sentiment is implanted in us by the will of the Lord – holy and reverend be his name! And if it be sanctified to his honour and glory, it becometh the means of raising us to glory everlasting in the life to come. Wherefore, let us not weep and lament, but rather be joyful and give thanks that so it hath seemed good in his sight?'

Mrs Mowbray answered only by a deep sigh, which partook indeed of the nature of a sob; and by the continued application of her handkerchief, it appeared that she wept freely. Mr Cartwright once more ventured to take her hand; and that she did not withdraw it, seemed to evince such a degree of Christian humility, and such a heavenly-minded forgiveness of his presumption, that the pious feelings of his heart broke forth in thanksgiving.

'Praise and glory to the Lord alway!' he exclaimed, 'your suffering sweetness, dearest Clara, loveliest of women, most dearly-beloved in the Lord, – your suffering sweetness shall be bruised no more! Let me henceforward be as the shield and buckler that shall guard thee, so that thou shalt not be afraid for any terror by night, nor for the arrow that flieth by day. And tell me, most beloved! does not thy spirit rejoice, and is not thy heart glad, even as my heart, that the Lord hath been pleased to lay his holy law upon us – even upon thee and me?'

'Oh, Mr Cartwright!' replied the agitated Mrs Mowbray, 'I know not what I can – I know not what I ought to do. May the Lord guide me! – for, alas! I know not how to guide myself!'

'And fear not, Clara, but he will guide thee! for he hath made thee but a little lower than the angels, and hath crowned thee with glory and honour. And tell me, thou highly-favoured of the Lord, doth not thy own heart teach thee, that heart being taught of him, that I am he to whom thou shouldst look for comfort now in the time of this mortal life? Speak to me, sweet and holy Clara. Tell me, am I deceived in thee? Or art thou indeed, and wilt thou indeed be mine?'

'If I shall sin not by doing so, I will, Mr Cartwright; for my spirit is too weak to combat all the difficulties I see before me. My soul trusts itself to thee – be thou to me a strong tower, for I am afraid.'

'Think you, Clara, that he who has led you out of darkness into the way of life would now, for the gratification of his own earthly love, become a stumbling-block in thy path? My beloved friend! how are you to wrestle and fight for and with that misguided young man, who hath now, even now, caused you such bitter sufferings? He is thine; therefore he is dear to me. Let me lead him, even as I have led thee, and his spirit too, as well as thine and Fanny's, shall rejoice in the Lord his Saviour!'

'Then be it so!' exclaimed Mrs Mowbray. 'Promise me only to lead Helen also into life everlasting, and not to leave the poor benighted Rosalind for ever in darkness, and I will consent, Mr Cartwright, to be your wife!'

Nothing could be more satisfactory than the vicar's answer to this appeal, and had not the good Mrs Mowbray been too generous to exact a penalty in case of failure, there can be little doubt but that he would willingly have bound himself under any forfeiture she could have named, to have ensured a place in heaven, not only to all those she mentioned, but to every individual of her household, the scullion and stable-boys included.

The great question answered of 'To be or not to be the husband of Mrs Mowbray?' the vicar began to point out to her in a more composed and business-like manner the great advantages both temporal and spiritual which must of necessity result to her family from this arrangement; and so skilfully did he manage her feelings and bend her mind to his purpose, that when at length he gave her lips the farewell kiss of affianced love, and departed, he left her in the most comfortable and prayerful state of composure imaginable. In about ten minutes after he was gone, she rang her bell, and desired that Miss Fanny might come to her; when, without exactly telling her the important business which had been settled during the time she passed upon her knees, she gave her to understand that Mr Cartwright had probably thought of the only means by which all the unhappy disagreements in the family could be settled.

'Indeed, mamma, I prayed for him,' said Fanny, lifting her eyes to Heaven; 'I prayed most earnestly, that the Holy Spirit might bring him wisdom to succour you according to your wish, and therein to heal all our troubles.'

'And your prayers have been heard, my dear child; and the Lord hath sent him the wisdom that we all so greatly needed. – Have they had tea in the drawing-room, Fanny?'

'I don't know, mamma. I have been kneeling and praying all the time.'

'Then, my dear, you must want refreshment. Go down and tell them that I am not quite well this evening, and shall therefore not come down again; but they may send me some tea by Curtis.'

'I hope you are not very ill, my dearest mother?' said Fanny, looking anxiously at her.

'No, dear, – not very ill – only a little nervous.'

* * *

While these scenes passed at Mowbray Park, poor Charles was relieving his heart by relating, without reserve, what had passed between him and his mother. His first words on entering the library, where Sir Gilbert and Lady Harrington were seated, were, 'Have you sent that letter to Oxford, Sir Gilbert?'

'Yes, I have,' was the reply. 'But why do you inquire, Charles?'

'Because, if you had not, I would have begged you to delay it.'

'And why so?'

In reply to this question, young Mowbray told all that had passed; observing, when his painful tale was ended, that such being his mother's decision, he intended to apply immediately to Corbold for the money he wanted.

'Not you, by Jove, Charles! You shall do no such thing, I tell you! What! knuckle and truckle to this infernal gang of hypocrites? You shall do no such thing. Just let me know all that is going on in the garrison, and if I don't counter-plot them, I am a Dutchman.'

'Puff not up your heart, Sir Knight, with such vain conceits,' said Lady Harrington. 'You will plot like an honest man, and the Tartuffe will plot like a rogue. I leave you to guess which will do the most work in the shortest time. Nevertheless, you are right to keep him out of the way of these people as long as you can.'

Notwithstanding the heavy load at his heart, which Mowbray brought with him to Oakley, before he had passed an hour with his old friends his sorrows appeared lighter, and his hopes from the future brighter and stronger. Sir Gilbert, though exceedingly angry with Mrs Mowbray, still retained some respect for her; and, spite of all his threatening hints to the contrary, he no more believed that the widow of his old friend would marry herself to the Reverend William Jacob Cartwright, than that he, when left a widower by my lady, should marry the drunken landlady of the Three Tankards at Ramsden. He therefore spoke to Charles of his present vexatious embarrassments as of all evils that must naturally clear away, requiring only a little temporary good management to render them of very small importance to him. Of Helen's situation, however, Lady Harrington spoke with great concern, and proposed that she and Miss Torrington should transfer themselves from the Park to Oakley as soon as Charles joined his regiment, and there remain till Mrs Mowbray had sufficiently recovered her senses to make them comfortable at home.

Before the young man left them, it was settled that Colonel Harrington should immediately exert himself to obtain the commission so long promised; a service in the performance of which no difficulty was anticipated, as the last inquiries made on the subject at the Horse-Guards were satisfactorily answered.

'Meanwhile,' said the baronet as he wrung his hand at parting, 'give not way for one single inch before the insolent interference of these canters and ranters: remember who and what you are, and that you have a friend who will make the county too hot to hold any one, male or female, who shall attempt to shake or shackle you in your natural rights. Treat your mother with the most perfect respect and politeness; but make her understand that you are your father's son, and that there is such a thing as public opinion, which, on more occasions than one, has been found as powerful as any other law of the land. Cheer the spirits of the poor woe-begone girls as much as you can; and tell Helen that her duty to her father's memory requires that she should not neglect her father's friends. And now, good night, Charles! Come to us as often as you can; and God bless you, my dear boy!'

By this advice young Mowbray determined to act; and wishing to escape any discussion upon lesser points, he avoided all tête-à-tête conversations with his mother, kept as much out of Mr Cartwright's way as possible, turned his back upon the serious attorney whenever he met him, and devoted his time to walking, reading, and singing, with Miss Torrington and his sister Helen, while waiting to receive the news of his appointment. When this should arrive, he determined once more to see his mother in private, and settle with her, on the best footing he could, the amount and manner of his future supplies.

This interval, which lasted nearly a month, was by no means an unhappy one to Charles. He had great confidence in the judgment of Sir Gilbert Harrington, and being much more inclined to believe in his mother's affection than to doubt it, he resolutely shut his eyes upon whatever was likely to annoy him, and gave himself up to that occupation which beyond all others enables a man or a woman either to overlook and forget every other, – namely, the making love from morning to night.

The manner in which this undeclared but very intelligible devotion of the heart was received by the fair object of it was such, perhaps, as to justify hope, though it by no means afforded any certainty that the feeling was returned. Even Helen, who fully possessed her brother's confidence, and had hitherto, as she believed, fully possessed the confidence of Rosalind also, – even Helen knew not very well what to make of the varying symptoms which her friend's heart betrayed. That Miss Torrington took great pleasure in the society of Mr Mowbray, it was impossible to doubt; and that she wished him to find pleasure in hers, was equally clear. His favourite songs only were those which she practised in his absence and sang in his presence; he rarely praised a passage in their daily readings which she might not, by means of a little watching, be found to have read again within the next twenty-four hours. The feeble winter-blossoms from the conservatory, of which he made her a daily offering, might be seen preserved on her toilet in a succession of glasses, and only removed at length by a remonstrance from her maid, who assured her that 'stale flowers were unwholesome; though, to be sure, coming out of that elegant conservatory did make a difference, no doubt.' Yet even then, the bouquet of a week old was not permitted to make its exit till some aromatic leaf or still green sprig of myrtle had been drawn from it, and deposited somewhere or other, where its pretty mistress, perhaps, never saw it more, but which nevertheless prevented her feeling that she had thrown the flowers he had given her on Sunday in the breakfast-room, or on Monday in the drawing-room, &c. &c. &c., quite away.

Yet, with all this, it was quite impossible that Charles, or even Helen, who knew more of these little symptomatic whims than he did, could feel at all sure what Rosalind's answer would be if Mr Mowbray made her a proposal of marriage.

From time to time words dropped from Rosalind indicative of her extreme disapprobation of early marriages both for women and men, and declaring that there was nothing she should dread so much as forming a union for life with a man too young to know his own mind. When asked by Charles at what age she conceived it likely that a man might attain this very necessary self-knowledge, she answered with a very marked emphasis,

'Decidedly not till they are many years older than you are, Mr Mowbray.'

Even to her own heart Rosalind would at this time have positively denied, not only that she loved Charles Mowbray, but that Charles Mowbray loved her. She was neither insensible nor indifferent to his admiration, or to the pleasure he took in her society; but she had heard Charles's judgment of her on her arrival more than once repeated in jest. He had said, that she was neither so amiable as Helen, nor so handsome as Fanny. To both of these opinions she most sincerely subscribed, and with such simple and undoubting acquiescence, that it was only when she began to read in his eyes the legible 'I love you,' that she remembered his having said it. Then her woman's heart told her, that inferior though she might be, it was not her husband that must be the first to discover it, and superior as he was, – which she certainly was not disposed to deny, – it was not with such disproportionate excellence that she should be most likely to form a happy union.

Had Mowbray guessed how grave and deeply-seated in Rosalind's mind were the reasons which would have led her decidedly to refuse him, this flowery portion of his existence would have lost all its sweetness. It was therefore favourable to his present enjoyment that, confident as he felt of ultimately possessing the fortune to which he was born, he determined not to propose to Rosalind till his mother had consented to assure to him an independence as undoubted as her own. The sweet vapour of hope, therefore, – the incense with which young hearts salute the morning of life, – enveloped him on all sides: and pity is it that the rainbow-tinted mist should ever be blown away from those who, like him, are better, as well as happier, for the halo that so surrounds them!

Many a storm is preceded by a calm, – many a gay and happy hour only gives the frightful force of contrast to the misery that follows it.

Mr Cartwright having once and again received the plighted faith of Mrs Mowbray, for the present confined his operations solely to the gentle task of urging her to hasten his happiness, and the assurance of eternal salvation to all her family.

But here, though the obstacles he had to encounter were of a soft and malleable nature, easily yielding to the touch, and giving way at one point, they were yet difficult to get rid of altogether; for they were sure to swell up like dough, and meet him again in another place.

Thus, when he proved to the pious widow that the Lord could never wish her to delay her marriage till her year of mourning was out, seeing that his honour and glory, his worship and service, would be so greatly benefited and increased thereby, she first agreed perfectly in his view of the case as so put, but immediately placed before him the violent odium which they should have to endure from the opinion of the world. And then, when his eloquence had convinced her, that it was sinful for those who set not their faith in princes, nor in any child of man, to regulate their conduct by such worldly considerations, – though she confessed to him that as their future associations would of course be wholly and only among the elect, she might perhaps overcome her fear of what her neighbours and unregenerate acquaintance might say, yet nevertheless she doubted if she could find courage to send orders to her milliner and dress-maker for coloured suits, even of a sober and religious tint, as it was so very short a time since she had ordered her half-mourning.

It was more difficult perhaps to push this last difficulty aside than any other; for Mr Cartwright could not immediately see how to bring the great doctrine of salvation to bear upon it.

However, though the lady had not yet been prevailed upon to fix the day, and even at intervals still spoke of the eligibility of waiting till the year of mourning was ended, yet on the whole he had no cause to complain of the terms on which he stood with her, and very wisely permitted the peace of mind which he himself enjoyed to diffuse itself benignly over all the inhabitants of the Park and the Vicarage.

Henrietta, who throughout the winter had been in too delicate a state of health to venture out of the house, was permitted to read what books she liked at the corner of the parlour-fire; while Mr Jacob, far from being annoyed by any particular strictness of domestic discipline, became extremely like the wind which bloweth where it listeth, wandering from farm-house to farm-house – nay, even from village to village, without restriction of any kind from his much-engaged father.

Fanny, however, was neither overlooked nor neglected; though to have now led her about to little tête-à-tête prayer-meetings in the woods was impossible. First, the wintry season forbad it; and secondly, the very particular and important discussions which business rendered necessary in Mrs Mowbray's dressing-room – or, as it had lately been designated, Mrs Mowbray's morning-parlour – must have made such an occupation as difficult as dangerous.

At these discussions Fanny was never invited to appear. She prayed in company with her mother and Mr Cartwright, and some of the most promising of the domestics, for an hour in the morning and an hour in the evening; but the manner in which the interval between these two prayings was spent showed very considerable tact and discrimination of character in the Vicar of Wrexhill.

Soon after the important interview which has been stated to have taken place between the lady of the manor and the vicar had occurred, Mr Cartwright having met Fanny on the stairs in his way to her mamma's morning parlour, asked her, with even more than his usual tender kindness, whether he might not be admitted for a few minutes into her 'study;' for it was thus that *her* dressing-room was now called by as many of the household as made a point of doing everything that Mr Cartwright recommended.

'Oh yes,' she replied with all the zealous piety which distinguishes the sect to which she belonged, whenever their consent is asked to do or suffer anything that nobody else would think it proper to do or suffer, – 'Oh, yes! – will you come now, Mr Cartwright?'

'Yes, my dear child, it is now that I wish to come;' – and in another moment the Vicar of Wrexhill and his beautiful young parishioner were sitting tête-à-tête on the sofa of the young lady's dressing-room.

As usual with him on all such occasions, he took her hand. 'Fanny!' he began, – 'dear, precious Fanny! you know not how much of my attention – how many of my thoughts are devoted to you!'

'Oh! Mr Cartwright, how very, very kind you are to think of me at all!'

'You must listen to me, Fanny,' (he still retained her hand,) 'you must now listen to me with very great attention. You know I think highly of your abilities – indeed I have not scrupled to tell you it was my opinion that the Lord had endowed you with great powers for his own especial service and glory. That last hymn, Fanny, confirms and strengthens me in this blessed belief, and I look upon you as a chosen vessel of the Lord. But, my child, we must be careful that we use, and not abuse, this exceeding great mercy and honour. Your verses, Fanny, are sweet to my ear, as the songs of the children of Israel to those who were carried away captive. But not for me – not for me alone, or for those who, like me, can taste the ecstasy inspired by holy song, has the Lord given unto you that power which is to advance his kingdom upon earth. The poor, the needy, those of no account in the reckoning of the proud – they have all, my dearest Fanny, a right to share in the precious gift bestowed on you by the Lord. Wherefore, I am now about to propose to you a work to which the best and holiest devote their lives, but on which you have never yet tried your young strength: – I mean, my dearest child, the writing of tracts for the poor.'

'Oh! Mr Cartwright! Do you really think it possible that I can be useful in such a blessed way?'

'I am sure you may, my dear Fanny; and you know this will be the means of doing good both to the souls and bodies of the Lord's saints. For what you shall write, will not only be read to the edification and salvation of many Christian souls, but will be printed and sold for the benefit either of the poor and needy, or for the furthering such works and undertakings as it may be deemed most fit to patronise and assist.'

'Oh! Mr Cartwright! If I could be useful in such a way as that, I should be very thankful to the Lord; – only – I have a doubt.'

Here the bright countenance of Fanny became suddenly overclouded; she even trembled and turned pale.

'What is it, my dear child, that affects you thus?' said the vicar with real surprise; 'tell me, my sweet Fanny, what I have said to alarm you?'

'If I do this,' said Fanny, her voice faltering with timidity, 'shall I not seem to be trusting to works?'

'Do you mean because the writings of authors are called their works?' said Mr Cartwright very gravely.

'No! Mr Cartwright!' she replied, colouring from the feeling that if so good and holy a man could quiz, she should imagine that he was now quizzing her, – 'No! Mr Cartwright! – but if I do this, and trust to get saving grace as a reward for the good I may do, will not this be trusting to works?'

'My dear child,' he said, gently kissing her forehead, 'such tenderness of conscience is the best assurance that what you will do will be done in a right spirit. Then fear not, dear Fanny, that those things which prove a snare to the unbeliever should in like manner prove a snare to the elect.'

Again Fanny Mowbray trembled. 'Alas! then I may still risk the danger of eternal fire by this thing, – for am I of the elect?'

The vicar knew that Mrs Mowbray was waiting for him, and fearing that this long delay might have a strange appearance, he hastily concluded the conversation by exclaiming with as much vehemence as brevity, 'You are! You are!'

CHAPTER XXVIII

MRS SIMPSON'S CHARITABLE VISIT – CHARLES'S TROUBLES CONTINUE

From this time most of Fanny Mowbray's hours were spent in writing tracts; which, as soon as completed, were delivered to Mr Cartwright. He received them ever with expressions of mingled admiration and gratitude, constantly assuring her the next time they met, that nothing could be more admirably calculated to answer the effect intended, and that the last was incomparably superior to all which had preceded it.

This occupation of writing tracts, first hit upon for the convenient occupation of Fanny Mowbray, was soon converted by the ready wit of Mr Cartwright into an occupation in one way or another for all the professing Christians in his parish who happened to have nothing to do.

Those who are at all acquainted with the manner in which the 'Church Methodists,' as they are called, obtain the unbounded influence which they are known to possess in their different parishes, particularly over the female part of their congregations, must be aware, that great and violent as the effect of their passionate extempore preaching often is, it is not to that alone that they trust for obtaining it. From the time Mr Cartwright became Vicar of Wrexhill, he had been unremitting in his exertions of every kind to obtain power, influence, and dominion throughout the parish, and, on the whole, had been pretty generally successful. How far his handsome person and pleasing address contributed to this, it is not here necessary to inquire; but it is certain that he drew upon these advantages largely in his intercourse with the females in general, and with the ladies in particular. But though at first this particular species of devotion was exceedingly agreeable to him, both in its exercise and its success, he now found very considerable inconvenience from the difficulty of keeping up the frequency of his pastoral visits to his fair converts without giving more time to them than was consistent with his infinitely more important avocations at the Park.

As soon, however, as he perceived how completely the writing of tracts occupied Fanny Mowbray during the time that was formerly bestowed upon listening to his sentimental divinity, he determined that several others of his female parishioners should dispose of their superfluous time in the same manner.

Within twenty-four hours after he came to this decision, the three Misses Richards had, each and every of them, purchased a quire of foolscap paper, a quarter of a hundred of goose-quills, with a bottle of ink, and a Concordance to the Bible, in common between them. Miss Stokes too, the little blue-eyed milliner, and Mrs Knighton, the late post-master's widow, and Mrs Watkins, the haberdasher's wife, were all furnished with abundant materials of the same value; and all of them determined to give up every earthly thing, if it were necessary, rather than disappoint the dear, blessed Mr Cartwright of the comfort of receiving anything he expected from them.

The widow Simpson, and even her little holy Minima, had also employment found for them: which though it could but ill supply to that regenerate lady the loss of Mr Cartwright's society, which at this particular time she was in a great degree deprived of, served nevertheless to soothe her by the conviction, that though not seen, she was remembered.

The part of the business consigned to Mrs Simpson was the selling the tracts. It was not without surprise that the people of the neighbourhood, particularly the unawaked, saw the parlour-windows of 'the principal person in the village' disfigured by a large square paper, looking very much as if it announced lodgings to let, but which upon closer examination proved to be inscribed as follows: 'Religious tracts, hymns, and meditations sold here, at one penny each, or ninepence halfpenny for the dozen.'

Miss Minima's duty was to hold in her hand a square box, with a slit cut in the lid thereof, in which all who purchased the tracts were requested to deposit their money for the same; and when the customer's appearance betokened the possession of more pennies than their purchase required, the little girl was instructed to say,

'One more penny, please ma'am, (or sir,) for the love of the Lord.'

Thus, for the pleasant interval of a few weeks, everything went on smoothly. Helen, at the earnest request of her brother, and convinced by his arguments, as well as those of Lady Harrington and Rosalind, that under existing circumstances it was right to do so, made several morning visits to Oakley.

Had she been questioned concerning this, she would most frankly have avowed both the act and the motives for it. But no such questionings came. Charles himself dined there repeatedly, but was never asked why he absented himself, nor where he had been.

During this period, Mrs Mowbray seemed to encourage rather more than usual the intercourse of the family with their Wrexhill neighbours. The season being no longer favourable for walking, the Mowbray carriage was to be seen two or three times in a week at Mrs Simpson's, Mrs Richards's, and the Vicarage; but it often happened, that though Mrs Mowbray proposed a visit to Wrexhill while they were at the breakfast-table, and that the coachman immediately received orders to be at the door accordingly, when the time arrived her inclination for the excursion was found to have evaporated, and the young people went thither alone.

Upon one occasion of this kind, when, Fanny being deeply engaged in the composition of a tract, and Charles gone to Oakley, Miss Torrington and Helen had the carriage to themselves, they agreed that instead of making the proposed visit to Mrs Simpson, they should go to inquire for a little patient of Helen's, the child of a poor hard-working woman, who had long been one of her pensioners at Wrexhill.

The entrance to the house was by a side door from a lane too narrow to permit the carriage to turn; the two young ladies therefore were put down at the corner of it, and their approach was unheard by those who occupied the room upon which the door of the house opened, although it stood ajar. But as they were in the very act of entering, they were stopped by words so loud and angry, that they felt disposed to turn back and abandon their charitable intention altogether.

But Rosalind's ear caught a sound that made her curious to hear more: and laying her hand on Helen's arm, and at the same time making a sign that she should be silent, they stood for a moment on the threshold, that they might decide whether to retreat or advance.

'You nasty abominable woman, you!' these were the first words which indistinctly reached them; 'you nasty untidy creature! look at the soap-suds, do, all splashed out upon the ground! How can you expect a Christian lady, who is the principal person in the parish, to come and look after your nasty dirty soul, you untidy pig, you?'

'Lord love you, my lady! 'tis downright unpossible to keep one little room neat, and fit for the like of you, when I have the washing of three families to do in it, – the Lord be praised for it! – and to cook my husband's bit of dinner, and let three little ones crawl about in it, besides.'

'Stuff and nonsense!' responded the principal person in the village; 'whoever heard of washing making people dirty? Look here, – put out your hand, can't you? I am sure I shall come no nearer to you and your tub. Take these three tracts, and take care you expound them to your husband; and remember that you are to bring them back again in one month without a single speck of dirt upon them.'

'You be sent by the new vicar, beant you, Madam Simpson?' inquired the woman.

'Sent, woman? I don't know what you mean by "sent." As a friend and joint labourer with Mr Cartwright in the vineyard of the Lord, I am come to take your soul out of the nethermost pit: but if you will persist in going on soaping and rubbing at that rate instead of listening to me, I don't see that you have any more chance of salvation than your black kettle there. Mercy on me! I shall catch my death of cold here! Tell me at once, do you undertake to expound these tracts to your husband?'

'Dear me! no, my lady; I was brought up altogether to the washing line.'

'What has that to do with it, you stupid sinner? I can't stay any longer in this horrid, damp, windy hole: but take care that you expound, for I insist upon it; and if you don't, you may depend upon it Mr Cartwright won't give you one penny of the sacrament money.'

So saying, the pious lady turned away and opened the door upon Miss Torrington and Helen.

Conscious, perhaps, that her *Christian duty* had not been performed in so lady-like a manner as it might have been, had she known that any portion of the Park family were within hearing, the principal person in the village started and coloured at seeing them: but, aware how greatly she had outrun the two young ladies in the heavenly race, she immediately recovered herself and said,

'I am afraid, young ladies, that your errand here is not the same as mine. Betty Thomas is a poor sinful creature, and I hope you are not going to give her money till she is reported elect, Miss Mowbray? It will really be no less than a sin against the Holy Ghost if you do.'

'She has a sick child, Mrs Simpson,' replied Helen, 'and I am going to give her money to buy what will make broth for it.'

Helen then entered the room, made her inquiries for the little sufferer, and putting her donation into sinful Betty Thomas's soapy hand, returned to Mrs Simpson and Rosalind, who remained conversing at the door.

It was raining hard, and Miss Mowbray asked Mrs Simpson if she should take her home.

'That is an offer that I won't refuse, Miss Mowbray, though I am within, and you are without, the pale. But I am terribly subject to catching cold; and I do assure you that this winter weather makes a serious Christian's duty very difficult to do. I have got rid of seventy tracts since the first of December.'

'You sell the tracts, do you not, Mrs Simpson?' said Rosalind.

'Yes, Miss Torrington, – I sell them and lend them, and now and then give them, when I think it is a great object to have them seen in any particular house.'

'Have you collected much, ma'am, by the sale?'

'Not a very large sum as yet, Miss Torrington; but I am getting on in many different ways for the furtherance of the Lord's work. Perhaps, ladies, though you have not as yet put your own hands to the plough that shall open the way for you to a place among the heavenly host, you may like to see my account?'

'I should like it very much, Mrs Simpson,' said Rosalind.

The lady then drew from her reticule a small pocket-book, from which she read several items, which from various sources contributed, as she said, 'to fill a bag for the Lord,' to be expended upon his saints by the hands of their pious vicar.

By the time this interesting lecture was finished, the carriage had reached Mrs Simpson's door, and having set her down, was ordered home.

'Now will I give Charles a *pendant* to the exquisite poetical effusion which he bestowed on me some time since,' said Rosalind, drawing forth a pencil and paper from a pocket of the carriage, in which Mrs Mowbray was accustomed of late to deposit what the vicar called 'sacred memoranda;' by which were signified all the scraps of gossip respecting the poor people among whom she distributed tracts, that she could collect for his private ear.

Having invoked the Sisters Nine for the space of five minutes, she read aloud the result to Helen, who declared herself willing to give testimony, if called upon, to the faithful rendering (save and except the rhymes) of the financial document to which they had just listened.

> Sixpence a week paid by each serious pew
> In Mr Cartwright's church, makes – one pound two;
> From Wrexhill workhouse, by a farthing rate
> Collected by myself, just one pound eight;
> Crumbs for the Lord, gather'd from door to door
> Through Hampshire, makes exactly two pound four;
> From twelve old ladies, offerings from the hive
> In various sums, amount to three pound five;
> From our new Sunday school, as the Lord's fee,
> By pennies from each child, we've shillings three;
> And last of all, and more deserving praise
> Than all the sums raised by all other ways,
> 'The desperate Sinner's certain Road to Heaven,'
> Sold at the gallows foot, – thirteen pound seven.

'This is a new accomplishment,' said Helen, laughing; 'and I declare to you, Rosalind, I think it very unnecessary, Catholic-like, and unkind, to perform any more works of supererogation in that fascinating style upon the heart of poor Charles. I am afraid he has had more than is good for him already.'

'I do not think the beauty of my verses will at all tend to injure Mr Mowbray's peace of mind,' replied Rosalind rather coldly. 'However, we can watch their effects, you know, and if we see any alarming symptoms coming on, we can withdraw them.'

Just before they reached the lodge-gates, they perceived Charles on foot before them; and stopping the carriage, Helen made him get in, just to tell them, as she said, how her dear godmother was, what kind messages she had sent her, and though last, not least, whether any tidings had been heard of the commission.

Charles appeared to be in excellent spirits; repeated many pleasant observations uttered by Sir Gilbert on the effervescent nature of his mother's malady; told them that a commission in the Horse-Guards was declared to be at his service as soon as the money for it was forthcoming, for which, if needs must, even Sir Gilbert had permitted him to draw on Mr Corbold; and finally, that he believed they had all alarmed themselves about Mr Cartwright and his pernicious influences in a very young and unreasonable manner.

On reaching the house, they entered the library, which was the usual winter sitting-room; but it was quite deserted. They drew round the fire for a few minutes' further discussion of the news and the gossip which Charles had brought; and, apropos of some of the Oakley anecdotes of the evangelical proceedings at Wrexhill, Helen requested Rosalind to produce her version of Mrs Simpson's deeds of grace.

'Willingly,' replied Miss Torrington, drawing the paper, from her pocket. 'You dedicated a poem to me, Mr Mowbray, some weeks ago; and I now beg to testify my gratitude by presenting you with this.'

Charles took the paper, and while fixing his eyes with a good deal of meaning upon the beautiful giver, kissed it, and said, 'Do you make it a principle, Miss Torrington, to return in kind every offering that is made you?'

'That is *selon*,' she replied, colouring, and turning round to say something to Helen: but she was gone.

'Rosalind!' said Charles, thrusting her paper unread into his bosom. 'This commission, though we hail it as good fortune, will yet put an end to by far the happiest period of my existence, unless – I may hope, Rosalind, that – if ever the time should come – and I now think it will come – when I may again consider myself as the heir to a large property, I may hope that you will some day suffer me to lay this property at your feet.'

'Never lay your property at the feet of any one, Mr Mowbray,' she replied carelessly.

Charles coloured and looked grievously offended. 'You teach me at least, Miss Torrington, to beware how I venture again to hope that you would accept anything I could lay at yours.'

'Nay, do not say so, Mr Mowbray: I accept daily from you most willingly and gratefully unnumbered testimonies of friendship and good will; and if their being kindly welcomed will ensure their continuance, you will not let them cease.'

'I am a coxcomb for having ever hoped for more,' said Charles, leaving the room with cheeks painfully glowing and a heart indignantly throbbing. He had not looked for this repulse, and his disappointment was abundantly painful. Over and over again had he decided, while holding counsel with himself on the subject, that he would not propose to Rosalind till his mother had made him independent; but these resolutions were the result rather of a feeling of generosity than of timidity. Yet Charles Mowbray was no coxcomb. Miss Torrington was not herself aware how many trifling but fondly-treasured symptoms of partial liking she had betrayed towards him during the last few weeks; and as it never entered his imagination to believe that she could doubt the reality of his strong attachment, he attributed the repulse he had received, as well as all the encouragement which led him to risk it, as the result of the most cruel and cold-hearted coquetry.

It is probable that he left Rosalind little better satisfied with herself than he was with her; but unfortunately there is no medium by which thoughts carefully hid in one bosom can be made to pour their light and warmth into another, and much misery was in this instance, as well as in ten thousand others, endured by each party, only for want of understanding what was going on in the heart of the other.

Mowbray determined not to waste another hour in uncertainty as to the manner in which his commission was to be paid for, and his future expenses supplied. But in his way to his mother, he delayed long enough to say to Helen,

'I have proposed, and been most scornfully rejected, Helen. How could we either of us ever dream that Miss Torrington showed any more favour to me than she would have done to any brother of yours, had he been a hunchbacked idiot?'

Without waiting to receive any expression either of surprise or sympathy, he left his sister with the same hurried abruptness with which he sought her, and hastened on to find his mother.

She was sitting alone, with a bible on one side of her, and two tracts on the other. In her hand was a little curiously-folded note, such as she now very constantly received at least once a day, even though the writer might have left her presence in health and perfect contentment one short hour before.

She started at the sudden entrance of her son, and her delicately pale face became as red as a milkmaid's as she hastily placed the note she was reading between the leaves of her bible. But Charles saw it not; every pulse within him was beating with such violence, that it required all the power left him to speak that which he had to say. Had his mother been weighing out a poison, and packets before her labelled for himself and his sisters, he would not have seen it.

'Mother,' he said, 'I have received notice that the commission in the

Horse-Guards which my father applied for some time before he died is now ready for me. Will you have the kindness to furnish me with the means of paying for it? and will you also inform me on what sum I may reckon for my yearly expenses? I mean to join immediately.'

Mrs Mowbray's little agitation had entirely subsided, and she answered with much solemnity, 'You come to me, Charles, in a very abrupt manner, and apparently in a very thoughtless frame of mind, to speak on subjects which to my humble capacity seem fraught with consequences most awfully important. – The Horse-Guards! Oh! Charles! is it possible you can have lived for many weeks in such a regenerated family as mine, and yet turn your thoughts towards a life so profane as that of an officer in the Horse-Guards?'

'Let my life pass where it may, mother, I trust it will not be a profane one. I should ill repay my father's teaching if it were. This is the profession which he chose for me; it is the one to which I have always directed my hopes, and it is that which I decidedly prefer. I trust, therefore, that you will not object to my following the course which my most excellent father pointed out to me.'

'I shall object to it, sir: and pray understand at once, that I will never suffer the intemperate pleadings of a hot-headed young man to overpower the voice of conscience in my heart.'

Poor Mowbray felt inclined to exclaim,

> 'When sorrows come, they come not single spies,
> But in battalions.'

For a moment he remained perfectly silent, and then said, 'This is very terrible news for me, mother. You shall hear, I trust, no intemperate pleadings, but I hope you will let me reason with you on the subject. Surely you will not blame me for wishing in this, and in all things, to adhere as closely as may be to my dear father's wishes?'

'If your poor father, Charles, groped through life surrounded on all sides with outer darkness, is that any reason that I should suffer the son he left under my care and control to do so likewise? When he left the whole of my property at my whole and sole disposal, it was plain that he felt there was more hope of wisdom abiding in me than in you. It is herein, and herein only, that I must labour to do according to his wishes and his will, and endeavour so to act that all may see his confidence in me was not misplaced.'

'For God's sake, mother! think well before you determine upon disappointing all my hopes in this most cruel manner; and believe me, that no lookers-on between you and me – except perhaps the mischievous fanatic who has lately chosen to meddle so impertinently in our affairs – but will feel and say that I have been ill-treated.'

Had Mowbray not been stung and irritated as he was before this conversation, it is probable he would not have remonstrated thus warmly with a mother, whom he had ever been accustomed to treat with the most tender observance and respect.

She looked at him with equal anger and astonishment, and remained for some time without speaking a word, or withdrawing her eyes from his face. If her son felt inclined to quote Shakespeare at the beginning of the conversation, she might have done so at the end of it; for all she wished to say was comprised in these words:

'Nay, then, I'll send those to you that can speak.'

She did not, however, express herself exactly thus, but ended her long examination of his flushed and agitated countenance by pronouncing almost in a whisper,

'This is very terrible! But I thank the Lord I am not left quite alone in the world!'

Having thus spoken, she rose and retired to her bed-room, leaving her very unhappy son in possession of her 'morning parlour,' and of more bitter thoughts than had ever before been his portion.

Having continued for some moments exactly in the position in which she left him, he at length started up, and endeavouring to rouse himself from the heavy trance that seemed to have fallen on him, he hastened to find Helen.

'It is all over with me Helen!' said he. 'You know what I met with in the library; – and now my mother protests against my accepting my commission, because she says that officers lead profane lives. What is to become of me, Helen?'

'Have patience, dearest Charles! All this cannot last. It cannot be supposed that we can submit ourselves to the will of Mr Cartwright: and depend upon it that it is he who has dictated this refusal. Do not look so very miserable, my dear brother! I think you would do very wisely if you returned to Oakley to dinner, – for many reasons.'

'God bless you, love, for the suggestion! It will indeed be a relief to me. I know not at this moment which I most desire to avoid – my mother, or Miss Torrington. Have you seen her – Rosalind, I mean?'

'No, Charles, – not since you parted from her. I heard her enter her room and lock the door. The answer you have received from her surprises me more, and vexes me more, than even my mother's.'

'God bless you, Helen! you are a true sister and a true friend. I will go to Sir Gilbert; – but it rains hard – I wish I had the cab, or my own dear mare to ride. But that's a minor trouble; – it irks me though, for it comes from the same quarter.'

'It does indeed; – and it irks me too, believe me. But patience, Charles! – courage and patience will do much.'

'Will it give me the heart of the woman I love, Helen? – or rather, will it give her a heart? It is that which galls me. I have been deceived – trifled with, and have loved with my whole heart and soul a most heartless fair-seeming coquette.'

'That you have not, Charles!' replied Helen warmly; 'that you have not! I too have mistaken Rosalind's feelings towards you. Perhaps she has mistaken them herself: but she is not heartless; and above all, there is no seeming about her.'

'How I love you for contradicting me, Helen! – and for that bright flush that so eloquently expresses anger and indignation at my injustice! But if she be not a coquette, then must I be a most consummate puppy; for as I live, Helen, I thought she loved me.'

'I cannot understand it. But I know that Rosalind Torrington is warm-hearted, generous, and sincere; and whatever it is which has led us to misunderstand her, either now or heretofore, it cannot be coquetry, or false-seeming of any kind.'

'Well – be it so: I would rather the fault were mine than hers. But I will not see her again to-day if I can help it. So good-b'ye, Helen: my lady must excuse my toilet; – I cannot dress and then walk through Oakley lane.'

CHAPTER XXIX

THE ENTRY

It was very nearly midnight when Mowbray returned from his visit to Sir Gilbert Harrington's. To his great surprise, he found Helen waiting for him, even in the hall; for the moment she heard the door-bell she ran out to meet him.

'Why are you up so late, Helen?' he exclaimed: 'and for God's sake tell me what makes you look so pale. – Where is Rosalind?'

'She is in bed; – she has been in tears all day; I made her go to bed. But, oh Charles! my mother! – she has left the house.'

'Gracious Heaven! what do you mean? Did she leave the house in anger? Did she ask for me?'

'No, Charles: nor for me either!'

'And where on earth is she gone?'

'No one in the house has the remotest idea: it is impossible even to guess. But she has taken Fanny and Curtis with her.'

'When did she set out?'

'While Rosalind and I were eating our miserable, melancholy dinner. Mr Cartwright, I find, called after you went, and was shown, as usual, to her dressing-room; but he did not stay, Thomas says, above half an hour, for he both let him in and out. Soon after he went away, Fanny was sent for; and she and Curtis remained with her till a few minutes before dinner-time. Curtis then went into the kitchen, it seems, and ordered a tray to be taken for my mother and Fanny into the dressing-room, and the only message sent to Rosalind and me was, that mamma was not well, and begged not to be disturbed. Curtis must have seen the coachman and settled everything with him very secretly; for not one of the servants, except the new stable-boy, knew that the carriage was ordered.'

'How are we to interpret this, Helen? – Such a night too! – as dark as pitch. Had I not known the way blindfold, I should never have got home. I left Sir Gilbert in a rage because I would not sleep there; – but my heart was heavy; I felt restless and anxious at the idea of remaining from you during the night: I think it was a presentiment of this dreadful news. – Oh! what a day has this been to me! So gay, so happy in the morning! so supremely wretched before night! – I can remember nothing that I said which could possibly have driven her to leave her home. What can it mean, Helen?'

'Alas! Charles, I have no power to answer you. If asking questions could avail, might I not ask what I have done? And yet, at the moment of her leaving home for the night, she sent me word that I was *not to disturb her!*'

'The roads too are so bad! Had she lamps, Helen?'

'Oh yes. Some of the maids, while shutting up the rooms upstairs, saw the lights moving very rapidly towards the lodges.'

'It is an inexplicable and very painful mystery. But go to bed, my dearest Helen! you look most wretchedly ill and miserable.'

'Ill? – No, I am not ill, Charles, but miserable; yes, more miserable than I have ever felt since my poor father's death was first made known to me.'

The following morning brought no relief to the anxiety which this strange absence occasioned. Rosalind joined the brother and sister at breakfast, and her jaded looks more than confirmed Helen's report of the preceding night. Charles, however, hardly saw her sufficiently to know how she looked, for he carefully avoided her eyes; but if the gentlest and most soothing tone of voice, and the expression of her almost tender sympathy in the uneasiness he was enduring, could have consoled the young man for all he had suffered and was suffering, he would have been consoled.

The day passed heavily; but Helen looked so very ill and so very unhappy, that Charles could not bear to leave her; and though a mutual feeling of embarrassment between himself and Rosalind made his remaining with them a very doubtful advantage, he never quitted them.

But it was quite in vain that he attempted to renew the occupations which had made the last six weeks pass so delightfully. He began to read; but Helen stopped him before the end of the page by saying, 'I cannot think what is the reason of it, Charles, but I cannot comprehend a single syllable of what you are reading.'

Rosalind, blushing to the ears, and actually trembling from head to foot, invited him to play at chess with her. Without replying a word, he brought the table and set up the men before her; but the result of the game was, that Charles gave Rosalind checkmate, and it was Helen only who discovered it.

At an early hour they separated for the night; for the idea of waiting for Mrs Mowbray seemed equally painful to them all, and the morrow's sun rose upon them only to bring a repetition of the sad and restless hours of the day that was past. Truly might they have said they were weary of conjecture; for so completely had they exhausted every supposition to which the imagination of either of the party could reach, without finding one on which common sense would permit them to repose, that, by what seemed common consent, they ceased to hazard a single 'maybe' more.

They were sitting with their coffee-cups before them, and Rosalind was once more trying to fix the attention of Charles, as well as her own, to the chess-board, when a lusty pull at the door-bell produced an alarm which caused all the servants in the house to jump from their seats, and one half the chessmen to be overturned by the violent start of Rosalind.

A few moments of breathless expectation followed. The house door was opened, and the steps of several persons were heard in the hall, but no voice accompanied them. Helen rose, but trembled so violently, that her brother threw his arms round her and almost carried her to a sofa. Rosalind stood beside her, looking very nearly as pale as herself; while Charles made three steps forward and one back again, and then stood with his hands clasped and his eyes fixed on the door in a manner which showed that, in spite of his manhood, he was very nearly as much agitated as his companions.

The next sound they heard was the voice of the lady of the mansion, and she spoke loud and clear, as she laid her hand on the lock, and partly opening the door, said, addressing the butler, who with half a dozen other serving-men had hurried to answer the bell,

'Chivers! order all the servants to meet me in this room immediately; and fail not to come yourself.'

Mowbray had again stepped forward upon hearing his mother's voice, but stopped short to listen to her words; and having heard them, he turned back again, and placing himself behind the sofa on which Helen sat, leaned over it to whisper in her ear – 'Let me not see you overcome, Helen! and then I shall be able to bear anything.'

As he spoke, the door was thrown widely open, and a lady entered dressed entirely in white and very deeply veiled, followed by Fanny Mowbray and Mr Cartwright.

A heavy sense of faintness seized on the heart of Helen, but she stood up and endeavoured to advance; Rosalind, on the contrary, stepped back and seated herself in the darkest corner of the room; while Charles hastily walked towards the veiled lady, and in a voice thick from emotion, exclaimed, 'My mother!'

'Yes, Charles!' she replied; 'your mother; but no longer a widowed, desolate mother, shrinking before the unnatural rebuke of her son. I would willingly have acted with greater appearance of deliberation, but your conduct rendered this impossible. Mr Cartwright! permit me to present you to this hot-headed young man and his sister, as my husband and their father.'

This terrible but expected annunciation was received in total silence. Mowbray seemed to think only of his sister; for without looking towards the person thus solemnly presented to him, he turned to her, and taking her by the arm, said, 'Helen! – you had better sit down.'

Fanny, who had entered the room immediately after her mother, looked pale and frightened; but though she fixed a tearful eye on Helen, she attempted not to approach her.

Mr Cartwright himself stood beside his bride, or rather a little in advance of her; his tall person drawn up to its greatest height. Meekness, gentleness, and humility appeared to have his lips in their keeping; but unquenchable triumph was running riot in his eyes, and flashed upon every individual before him with a very unequivocal and somewhat scornful air of authority.

This tableau endured till the door was again thrown open, and one by one the servants entered, forming at last a long line completely across the room. When all were in their marshalled places, which here, as elsewhere, were in as exact conformity to the received order of precedence as if they had been nobles at a coronation, the lady bride again lifted her voice and addressed them thus:

'I have called you all together on the present occasion in order to inform you that Mr Cartwright is my husband and your master. I hope it is unnecessary for me to say that everything in the family must henceforward be submitted solely to his pleasure, and that his commands must on all occasions supersede those of every other person. I trust you will all show yourselves sensible of the inestimable blessing I have bestowed upon you in thus giving you a master who can lead you unto everlasting life; and as I have married for the glory of God, so I trust to receive his blessing upon the same, and to see every member of my family advancing daily under the guidance of their earthly master's hand to that state which shall ensure them favour from their heavenly one in the life to come. Amen! Repeat, I beg you – all of you repeat with me Amen!'

Though there were some throats there in which Amen would have stuck, there were enough present besides these to get up a tolerably articulate Amen.

Mr Cartwright then stepped forward, and laying his hat and gloves on the table, said aloud, 'Let us pray!'

The obedient menials knelt before him, – all save one. This bold exception was the housekeeper; a staid and sober person of fifty years of age, who during the dozen years she had presided over the household, had constantly evinced a strict and conscientious adherence to her religious duties, and was, moreover, distinguished for her uniformly respectful, quiet, and unobtrusive demeanour. But she now stepped forward from her place at the head of the line, and said in a low voice, but very slowly and distinctly,

'I cannot, sir, on this occasion kneel down to pray at your bidding. This is not a holy business at all, Mr Cartwright; and if you were to give me for salary the half of what you are about to wring from the orphan children of my late master, (deceased just eight calendar months ago,) I would not take it, sir, to live here and witness what I cannot but look upon as great sin.'

The good woman then gave a sad look at Helen and her brother who were standing together, dropped a respectful curtsey as her eyes rested on them, and then left the room.

'Her sin be on her own head!' said Mr Cartwright as he himself knelt down upon a footstool whch stood near the table. He drew a cambric handkerchief from his pocket, gave a preparatory 'hem,' and apparently unconscious that Miss Torrington had darted from the remote corner in which she had been ensconced and followed the housekeeper out of the room, remained for a moment with his eyes fixed on Mowbray and Helen, who remained standing.

'It would be a frightful mockery for us to kneel!' said Charles, drawing his sister back to the sofa she had quitted. 'Sit down with me, Helen; and when we are alone, we will pray to God for strength to endure as we ought to do whatever calamity it is his will to try us with.'

The bride was kneeling beside her husband; but she rose up and said, 'You are of age, Charles Mowbray, and too stiff-necked and wilful to obey your mother: but you, Helen, I command to kneel.'

She then replaced herself with much solemnity; and Helen knelt too, while breathing a silent prayer to be forgiven for what she felt to be profanation.

Charles stood for a moment irresolute, and then said, dropping on his knees beside her, 'God will pardon me for your sake, dear Helen, – even for kneeling at a service that my heart disclaims.'

Mr Cartwright hemmed again, and began:

'I thank thee, O Lord! that by thy especial calling and election I am placed where so many sinful souls are found, who through and by me may be shown the path by which to escape the eternal pains of hell. But let thy flames blaze and burn, O Lord! for those who neglect so great salvation! Pour down upon them visibly thy avenging judgments, and let the earth see it and be afraid. To me, O Lord! grant power, strength, and courage to do the work that is set before me. Let me be a rod and a scourge to the ungodly; and let no sinful weakness on the part of the wife whom thou hast given me come across or overshadow the light received from thee through the Holy Ghost for the leading of the rebellious back unto thy paths. Bless, O Lord! my virtuous wife; teach her to be meekly obedient to my word, and to thine through me; and make her so to value the inestimable mercy of being placed in the guiding hands of thy elected servant, that the miserable earthly dross which she maketh over to me in exchange for the same may seem but as dirt and filthiness in her sight! May such children as are already born unto her be brought to a due sense of thy exceeding mercy in thus putting it into their mother's heart to choose thine elected servant to lead them through the dangerous paths of youth; – make them rejoice and be exceeding glad for the same, for so shall it be good in thy sight!'

This terrible thanksgiving, with all its minute rehearsing of people and of things, went on for a considerable time longer; but enough has been given to show the spirit of it. As soon as it was ended, the new master of the mansion rose from his knees, and waiting with an appearance of some little impatience till his audience had all recovered their feet, he turned to his bride with a smile of much complacency, and said,

'Mrs Cartwright, my love, where shall I order Chivers to bring us some refreshments? Probably the dining-room fire is out. Shall we sup here?'

'Wherever you please,' answered the lady meekly, and blushing a little at the sound of her new name pronounced for the first time before her children.

This address and the answer to it were too much for Helen to endure with any appearance of composure. She hid her face in her handkerchief as she passed her mother, and giving Fanny, who was seated near the door, a hasty kiss, left the room, followed by her brother.

Helen ran to the apartment of Rosalind; and Mowbray ran with her, forgetful, as it seemed, of the indecorum of such an unauthorised intrusion at any time, and more forgetful still of the icy barrier which had seemed to exist between him and its fair inhabitant since the first expression of his love and of his hope had been so cruelly chilled by her light answer to it. But in this moment of new misery everything was forgotten but the common sorrow: they found Rosalind passionately sobbing, and Mrs Williams, the housekeeper, weeping very heartily, beside her.

'Oh, my Helen!' exclaimed the young heiress, springing forward to meet her; 'Williams says they cannot take my money from me. Will you let us divide my fortune and live together?'

'Williams forgets your age, Rosalind,' replied Helen: but though there was pain in recalling this disqualifying truth, there was a glance of pleasure too in the look with which Helen thanked her; and Charles, as he gazed on her swollen eyes and working features, felt that, cruel as she had been to him, she must ever be the dearest, as she was the best and the loveliest, being in the world.

And there was assuredly comfort, even at such a moment, in the devoted friendship of Rosalind, and in the respectful but earnest expressions of affection from the good housekeeper; but the future prospects of Charles and his sisters was one upon which it was impossible to look without dismay.

'What ought we to do?' said Helen, appealing as much to her old servant as her young friend. 'Can it be our duty to live with this hypocritical and designing wretch, and call him *father*?'

'No!' replied Rosalind vehemently. 'To do so would be shame and sin.'

'But where can the poor girls take refuge? You forget, Miss Torrington, that they are penniless,' said Charles.

'But I am not penniless, sir,' replied Rosalind, looking at him with an expression of anger that proceeded wholly from his formal mode of address, but which he interpreted as the result of a manner assumed to keep him at a distance.

'May I venture to say one word, my dear children, before I take my leave of you?' said Mrs Williams.

'Oh yes!' said Helen, taking her by the hand, 'I wish you would give us your advice, Williams: we are too young to decide for ourselves at such a dreadful moment as this.'

'And for that very reason, my dear Miss Helen, I would have you wait a little before you decide at all. Master Charles, – I beg his pardon – Mr Mowbray, – is altogether a different consideration: and if so be it is any

way possible for him, I think he should leave, and wait for the end
elsewhere; but for you and poor Miss Fanny, my dear young lady, I do
think you must learn to bear and forbear till such time as you may leave
your misguided mamma, and perhaps accept this noble young lady's offer,
and share her great fortune with her, – for a time I mean, Miss Helen, –
for it can't be but my mistress will come to her senses sooner or later, and
then she will remember she is a mother; and she will remember too, take
my word for it, the noble-hearted but too confiding gentleman, who was
your father.'

Tears flowed from every eye, for poor Mowbray was no exception, at
this allusion to the beloved father, the gentle master, and the friendly
guardian; but this did not prevent the good woman's words from having
their full weight, – it rather added to it, for it brought back the vivid
remembrance of one in whose temper there was no gall.

'It will be hard to bear, Williams,' replied Helen; 'but I do indeed
believe that you are right, and that, for a time at least, this cruelly
changed house must be our home. But do you know that in the midst of
all our misery, I have one comfort, – I think poor Fanny will be restored
to us. Did you see the expression of her lovely face as she looked at us,
Charles? Even you did not look more miserable.'

'And if that be so, Miss Helen, it may atone for much; for it was a
grievous sight to see the poor innocent child taking all Mr Cartwright's
brass for gold. If she has got a peep at his cloven foot, I shall leave you
almost with a light heart – for I have grieved over her.'

'I will take all the comfort I can, Williams, from your words, and will
follow your counsel too, upon one condition; and that is, nobody must
prevent my setting off betimes to-morrow morning, as you and I did,
Rosalind, once before, for Oakley. If my dear godmother advises me as
you do, Williams, I will return and quietly put my neck into this hateful
yoke, and so remain till Heaven shall see fit to release me.'

'Heaven knows, I shall not oppose that plan,' said Rosalind, eagerly;
'for, to my judgment, it is the very best you can pursue.'

'Indeed I think so,' added Charles; 'and, dark and dismal as the
mornings are, I would advise you, Helen, to set out before the time
arrives for either accepting or refusing the general summons to join the
family breakfast-table.'

'And may I go too?' said Rosalind with a glance half reproachful at
Charles for the manner in which he seemed to avoid speaking to her.

'May you, Rosalind?' cried Helen. 'For pity's sake, do not fancy it
possible that I can do anything without you now: I should feel that you
were forsaking me.'

'I never forsake any one that I have ever loved,' said Rosalind with
emotion, 'whatever you or any one else may think to the contrary.'

'Well, then, we will all three go together. But you little thought, Rosalind, when you first came here, that you would have to trudge through muddy lanes and under wintry skies for want of a carriage: but on this occasion, at least, we will not ask Mr Cartwright to permit us the use of one of his.'

'Then go to bed, my dear young ladies,' said Mrs Williams, 'that you may be early up to-morrow: and let me hear from you, Miss Helen. I shall not go from Wrexhill, at least not till I know a little how you will settle everything. I will take Mrs Freeman's pretty little rooms, that you always admire so much, Master Charles; and there I will stay for the present.'

'Oh! that beautiful little cottage that they call the Mowbray Arms!' said Rosalind. 'How we shall envy her, Helen!'

The party then separated; for the good housekeeper most strenuously opposed Rosalind's proposition of passing the night with her friend.

'You would neither of you sleep a wink, ladies, if you bide together. And now, though there is more sorrow with you than such young hearts ought to have, yet you will sleep when you have nobody to talk to about it; for what makes old folks wake and watch, will often make young folks sleep.'

And the good woman's prediction proved true: though the sleep that followed the tremendous blow they had received was too feverish and full of dreams to make the waking feel like the delightful return to new life and new joy which the waking of the young should ever be.

CHAPTER XXX

WALK TO OAKLEY – DOMESTIC ARRANGEMENTS – THE VILLAGE INN

Fortunately for their proposed expedition, the morning broke more brightly than a December morning could reasonably be expected to do, and the trio set off on their walk to Oakley almost as soon as it was light. The expedition, notwithstanding the unhappy cause of it, would have been less silent and less sad, had not Charles thought Rosalind capricious and cruel, and had not Rosalind thought Charles unkind and cold.

Nothing could appear more likely to perpetuate the unfortunate misunderstanding between them than the heavy misfortune that had fallen upon Mowbray. His total dependence, contrasted with Miss Torrington's wealth, was perpetually recurring to him, producing a degree of restraint in his manner that cut Rosalind to the heart, and roused all her womanly pride to prevent the long-combated feeling of attachment to which his present sorrows gave tenfold strength from betraying itself.

The tripping lightly through summer paths, and the picking one's way through wintry lanes, are two very different operations; and notwithstanding their early rising, they found the baronet and his lady already at the breakfast-table.

The astonishment occasioned by their appearance was great, but yet it was a joyous astonishment, and it was some time before Sir Gilbert's noisy welcome subsided sufficiently for her ladyship's more quiet and more anxious inquiries to be either answered or heard.

At length there was something in the tone of Helen's voice, the glance of Rosalind's eye, and the silent pressure of Mowbray's hand, which awakened his attention.

'Why, you have walked over to see us, my dear girls, and it was behaving like a pair of little angels to do so; but you're not one half as well pleased to see me as I am to see you. Come here, Helen; sit down in my own chair here and get warm, and then the words will thaw and come forth like the notes from the horn of Munchausen's post-boy. And your black eyes, Miss Rose, don't look half as saucy as they used to do: and as for Charles, – What, in God's name, is the matter with ye all?'

Helen burst into tears and buried her face in Lady Harrington's bosom.

'Sir Gilbert,' said Mowbray, colouring to the temples, 'my mother is married!'

'The devil she is!' thundered the old man, clenching his fists. 'Married, is she? – Jesabel! – May your poor father's ghost haunt her to her dying hour! – Married! To that canting cur the Vicar of Wrexhill? Is it not so?'

'Even so, Sir Gilbert.'

'God help you, my poor children!' said Lady Harrington in accents of the deepest sorrow; 'this is a grief that it will indeed be hard to bear!'

'And we come to you for counsel how to bear it, my dear lady,' said Mowbray, 'though little choice is left us. Yet, Helen says, if you tell her that she must submit to call this man her father, it will be easier for her to do it.'

'God bless her, darling child!' said the old lady, fondly caressing her; 'how shall I ever find the heart to bid her do what it must break her heart to think of?'

'Bid her call that rascal father?' cried Sir Gilbert. 'My Lady Harrington must be strangely altered, Mowbray, before she will do that: she is a very rebellious old lady, and a most prodigious shrew; but you do her no justice, Charles, in believing she would utter such atrocious words.'

'But what is to become of Helen, my dear Sir Gilbert, if she quarrel with this man?'

'Come to us, to be sure, – what's the man to her? Has your precious mother made any settlement upon you all?'

'I imagine not; indeed I may say that I am sure she has not.'

'Am I a prophet, my lady? how did I tell you Mowbray's sentimental will would answer? And has this meek and gentle lady proved herself deserving of all the pretty things I said of her?'

'There is but small comfort in remembering truly, how very truly, your predictions foretold what has happened, Gilbert: and he has predicted that you must come here, my sweet Helen; let this come true likewise.'

'I cannot leave poor Fanny, Lady Harrington,' replied Helen: 'I cannot leave my dear and generous friend Rosalind: and yet your offered kindness cheers my heart, and I shall think of it with pleasure and gratitude as long as I live.'

'But I thought Fanny was a disciple of this Calvinistic gentleman's? If so, it were better she remained with him till she has learned to distinguish hypocrisy from virtue, and cant from true religion. And for Miss Torrington, I shall rejoice to have her for my guest for as long a time as she can find our old-fashioned mansion agreeable to her.'

'You are very, very kind!' replied the two friends in the same breath.

'Then so let it be. Charles, these good girls will stay here for the present; so let us eat our breakfast, – sufficient to the day is the evil thereof. Let me save them from the odious spectacle of the Vicar of Wrexhill establishing himself at Mowbray Park, and the future must take care of itself.'

'But, Fanny,' said Helen doubtingly, 'she looked so unhappy as she followed my mother in last night, that I feel almost certain her fit of enthusiasm is already over.'

'So much the better, my dear,' said Sir Gilbert; 'but it will do her a vast deal of good to watch the reverend gentleman's proceedings in his new character. That scratch upon her intellect must be cauterised before I shall believe it cured; and when the operation is complete, she may join the party here. As for you, my dear boy, when your breakfast is finished I have something for your ear in private.'

This *something* was the proposal of a loan sufficient for the purchase of the commission, and for the supply of the expenses consequent upon joining his corps. But this Mowbray could not be prevailed upon to accept; and his reasons for refusing it were such, that when he could prevail on the friendly old gentleman to listen to him, he could not deny that there was much weight in them.

'If I withdraw myself altogether from my mother at this moment,' said Charles, 'I shall give her husband an excellent and very plausible excuse for persuading her to banish me from her house and her heart for ever.

Whereas if I remain near her, it can hardly, I think, be doubted that some reaction will take place in her feelings, and that she will at last be induced to treat me as a son. At any rate, Sir Gilbert, not even your generous kindness shall induce me to abandon this hope till I feel persuaded that it is a vain one. In my opinion, my duty and my interest equally dictate this line of conduct; and if so, you are the last man in the world to dissuade me from pursuing it.'

Whether there were too much of firm decision in Mowbray's manner to leave any hope of overcoming it, or that Sir Gilbert was really convinced by his arguments, was difficult to decide; but he yielded the point on condition that the two girls should be left at Oakley, at least for the present, and be regulated as to their future conduct by the manner in which affairs went on at the Park.

This being settled much to the satisfaction of all parties, Lady Harrington made Miss Torrington describe the entrée of this most undesired interloper; a task which the fair Rosalind performed with great spirit, though she confessed that the impatient feeling to which she yielded in leaving the room was now a cause of regret, as she had lost thereby some notable traits in the history of that eventful hour.

Lady Harrington was greatly delighted at the conduct of Mrs Williams; and when Charles left them to inform Mrs Cartwright that her daughter and her ward had accepted an invitation to remain at Oakley for a few days, she proposed that they should pay her a visit at the Mowbray Arms, both to give her the satisfaction of knowing that her conduct was approved, and likewise to give her the comfort of knowing that Helen and Miss Torrington were for the present removed from such scenes as they had witnessed the night before.

It was about two o'clock in the afternoon when Lady Harrington's carriage drove across the common to the little public-house already described as the Mowbray Arms. As they approached, they perceived several persons who appeared to be occupied in very eager and deep discussion before the door.

'What are they doing there?' said Lady Harrington.

Rosalind put forward her head to ascertain this, but in an instant drew it back again, exclaiming, 'Mr Cartwright is there!'

'Mr Cartwright!' exclaimed Helen, turning very pale. 'Oh, Lady Harrington, do not let me see him!'

Lady Harrington let down the glass behind the coachman, and said aloud, 'Turn round instantly and drive home.'

This order being immediately obeyed, the party escaped the sight of the vicar; but in gaining this advantage they lost that of beholding a scene which must have drawn forth a smile, even from Helen herself.

The parties engaged in it were Mrs Freeman, her daughter Sally, Jem the horse-boy, an elderly traveller called forth by the clamour from the warm comforts of Mrs Freeman's fire-side, and Mr Cartwright himself. A short retrospect will be necessary to explain his business there.

As soon as the prayer of that morning had reached its final Amen – for as the subject matter of it consisted chiefly in vehement implorings of the divine favour on such of his new family and household as should show unto him the most perfect submission and obedience, the Amen, to make assurance doubly sure, was three several times repeated; – as soon however as it was finally pronounced, the vicar, his lady, and the pale Fanny sat down to breakfast. It would be tedious to tell how many glances of furtive but deep-felt delight the newly-made master of the house cast on each and every of the minute yet not unimportant differences between this breakfast-table and any others at which he had occupied a place of equal authority: suffice it to say that there were many. The meal, indeed, altogether lasted much longer than usual; but as soon as it was ended, and that Mr Cartwright had watched with feelings of great complacency the exit of its component parts by the hands of two footmen, and a butler, he told his wife that he should be obliged, though most unwillingly, to leave her for some hours, as there were many things to which his personal attention was required.

'Will the rooms be ready to-day for Jacob and Henrietta, my love?'

'They are quite ready now, my dear Mr Cartwright. When may we hope to see them?'

'To call and give them their orders about coming here, is one part of the business that takes me from you, my sweet Clara. There are some small bills in the village, too, with which your happy husband must not be dunned, sweet love. What ready-money have you, dearest, in the house?'

'Of money I have very little indeed,' said Mrs Cartwright, unlocking her desk and drawing thence a purse with ten or twelve sovereigns in it. 'I pay everything by drafts.'

'By far the best way, my love. But your drafts, dear, are no longer worth anything; and I must therefore see Corbold, to give orders that everything is put right about that at the banker's, and so forth: and this must really be done without delay.'

'Certainly it must,' said the lady. 'Shall I . . . I mean, will you send one of the men to Wrexhill to bring him here?'

Mr Cartwright laid his hand on the bell, but ere he pulled it, checked his hand and said, 'No! I must walk to the village, and therefore I will call on him myself.'

'Shall you prefer walking, my dear Mr Cartwright?'

'Why, no: I had forgot: perhaps it would be as well to take the carriage.'

'Oh, certainly! And you can bring Henrietta back with you.'

'True, dear, – she will certainly want the carriage: I will go, and send her and her band-boxes back in it – and then perhaps drive myself back in the cab. It is at the Vicarage, you know.'

'Is it? I did not remember that. Then how are they gone this morning? – those undutiful children, I mean, who have chosen to set off this morning without even leaving a message for us. I imagined that Charles had packed them both into the cab, as he has often done his sisters.'

'Do not waste a thought on them, my beloved Clara! It is evident that they have neither of them ever felt the slightest affection for you; and would it not be worse than folly for you, beloved and adored as you are, to let any thought of them come to blight our happiness?'

After this and many more tender and affectionate passages had passed between them, Mr Cartwright set off for the Vicarage *in his own coach*, as he told himself more than once as he drove along; and having informed his son and daughter, not greatly to the surprise of either, that Mowbray Park was to be their future home, he left them to prepare for their removal, telling Henrietta that he would send his carriage back from Mr Corbold's, where it should set him down, and that she might fill it, if she chose, with her own luggage, as he should drive Jacob *home* in his cab.

At Mr Corbold's the conversation was rather religious, and moreover extremely satisfactory to both parties. One or two of his most prayerful parishioners among the tradespeople were next called upon, and permitted to offer their congratulations and thanksgivings, and then told to send their bills to the Park. After this, the reverend bridegroom walked down the village street to the common, returning the humble bowings and curtsyings that crossed his path with a benignant sweetness of countenance that spoke much of the placid contentment that dwelt within.

It was not, however, solely to enjoy this pleasing interchange of heavenly-minded civility that he directed his steps along this well-frequented path – though that was something, – but for the purpose also of transacting a little business with Freeman, the prosperous landlord of the Mowbray Arms.

This good man and his family, it may be observed, had been great favourites with the family of Mr Wallace, the late vicar, but stood not so high by many degrees in the estimation of the present. They were honest, industrious, regular church-going people, who had never, during the twenty years they had kept the village inn, been accused or even suspected of having neglected a Sabbath, or of having ever permitted any indecorum either on that or any other day, to be practised under their roof. But they had steadily refused to attend Mr Cartwright's Tuesday evening's expounding, and his Thursday evening's lecture; the good woman, who was no bad scholar, alleging as the reason for this, that they knew of no such religious service being enjoined by the church of which they were members, and that not considering themselves in any way called upon to amend the ordinances of the religion in which they were born and bred, they thought it more according to their condition to remain at home and endeavour to do their duty in that state of life to which it had pleased God to call them.

This explanation having been very clearly and distinctly given to the vicar in the presence of several witnesses, before whom he had intended to make a rather marked display of pastoral piety and eloquence, though uttered with very becoming modesty and respect, had produced an impression against the painstaking Dorothy and all her household never to be forgotten or forgiven.

Mr Cartwright had even taken the trouble of waiting upon the magistrates of the neighbourhood, requesting them to refuse to continue Freeman's licence, assuring them that he was a man whose character was likely to produce a very demoralising influence on his parish. But as these gentlemen had happened to know the good man for many years, they begged to consider of it; and the Vicar of Wrexhill was thus left to discover other ways and means by which to dislodge his obnoxious parishioner.

A very favourable occasion for this now seemed to offer itself, and he accordingly proceeded with an elastic step and dignified gait towards the Mowbray Arms.

At the moment he appeared in sight, the ex-housekeeper of the Park was describing to Mrs Freeman and her daughter Sally the return of its mistress and most unwelcome master on the preceding evening.

'Why, here he comes, as sure as I live!' exclaimed Dorothy. 'What in the wide world can bring him here? It must be to preachify you, Mrs Williams.'

'And that's what he shall never do again: – so step out and speak to him outside – there's a dear good woman; and if I see you can't get rid of him, I'll make my way out of the back door, and so go round and slip in again and up to my own room before he can catch me.'

To facilitate this escape, Mrs Freeman walked forth and met the reverend bridegroom just as he had reached the foot of the post from whence depended the Mowbray Arms.

'Good morning, Mrs Freeman,' he said, in the peculiar accent in which he always addressed those who were not (to use his own phrase) of his father's house, – a tone in which cold outward civility was struggling with hot internal hatred; 'Good morning, Mrs Freeman.'

'Good morning, sir,' responded Mrs Freeman with a very proper and ceremonious curtsy.

'I have called to mention to you a necessary alteration that must immediately take place on your premises. You must forthwith take down the Mowbray Arms, which have no longer any connexion with the neighbourhood; and it may be, if you conduct yourselves properly, I may permit you to substitute the Cartwright Arms.'

'I believe, sir,' said Mrs Freeman in a tone rather too much approaching to indifference, 'that a publican may exhibit what sign he likes, provided it be not offensive to common decency: and I think there may be a many,' she added, turning away to re-enter her house, 'who might object to the sign you propose, as not coming within that line.'

She had made a step or two towards the door, when she turned again upon hearing the voice of the vicar raised to a very unusual pitch. He was not addressing her, however, but the boy Jem, who chanced at that moment to be entering the little rickyard with a ladder upon his shoulder.

'Bring here that ladder, boy!' vociferated the imperious great man.

The boy obeyed, saying, as he drew near, 'What's your pleasure, sir?'

'Fix your ladder against this post, d'ye hear? and mount – steady, mind, – and take the sign off the hooks. When you have got it loose, you may let it drop. If it breaks, it's no matter, – it is of no farther value.'

'Take down master's sign, your honour?' said Jem, opening his mouth and eyes to their greatest dimensions, but not approaching an inch nearer to the signpost.

'Do you dispute my orders, you little ruffian?' cried the holy vicar, his eyes flashing, and his cane raised in a very threatening attitude.

'You be the parson of the parish, I know,' said the boy, looking steadily in his face; 'and they do say you be something else besides, now; but I don't see that's a reason for my lugging master's sign down.'

At this moment the feelings of the man overcame those of the saint, and Mr Cartwright seizing upon the ladder, succeeded in disengaging it from the boy's hands, and himself placing it against the post, had already got one foot upon it, when Mrs Freeman stepped back, and taking a quiet but firm hold of his arm, said,

'It is a trespass and a damage you are committing, sir, and I warn you to desist; and I wish with all my heart that there was no worser trespass and damage upon your conscience – or at least that there was still as good time to stop it. But, married or not to the lady, we won't have nothing to do with your arms, Mr Cartwright, nor your legs neither, if you please, sir; so don't be after climbing that fashion to disturb our property, for it don't look clerical nohow.'

Mr Cartwright raised his voice much beyond its usual pitch, to answer; and at this moment Sally and the traveller, moved by a very natural feeling of curiosity, joined the group.

'Why, what's the gentleman after?' said the wayfaring man, deliberately taking out a pair of huge near-sighted spectacles to examine into the mystery. 'I should take un to be a parson by his cloth; only I never did hear of a reverend climbing a ladder, save and except the famous Dr Dodd, as I've read of in the Newgate Calendar.'

This harangue, short as it was, saved the Mowbray Arms from farther molestation for the present; for the vicar withdrew his foot. But the glance with which he greeted the speaker was very nearly awful. Dorothy Freeman, however, turned on her heel, nothing heeding it: her guest and daughter followed her into the house; Jem quietly took up his ladder and proceeded on his business; and the Vicar of Wrexhill, with feelings which the hope of future vengeance alone enabled him to endure with decent philosophy, was fain to turn on his heel also and walk off.

CHAPTER XXXI

MR AND MRS CARTWRIGHT'S LETTER

The very elegant cab, with its beautiful horse and accoutrements, led round to the door of the Vicarage as his own – the agreeable vivacity, as he always thought it, of his remarkably clever son – the multitude of low bows and lower curtsies which greeted him as he drove along – and above all, perhaps, the merry peal from the church tower, which had been ordered by himself to ring him into Mowbray Park, produced altogether so favourable an effect upon the nerves of the vicar, that when he stopped at the portico of his mansion, his spirits and his temper appeared altogether to have recovered the shock they had received at the foot of the sign-post.

The family party which met at dinner consisted of Mr and Mrs Cartwright, Miss Cartwright, Mr Jacob Cartwright, and poor Charles Mowbray and his sister Fanny.

Mowbray thought the genial hour of dinner might probably be the most favourable for mentioning the invitation of Sir Gilbert and Lady Harrington to his sister and Miss Torrington; an idea which probably occurred to him in consequence of the remarkably well-pleased and complaisant air visible on his stepfather's countenance as he took his place at the bottom of the table. Poor Charles! he made this observation, and he determined to profit by it; though it was not without a pang that he saw himself thus pushed from the stool that nature and fortune seemed to have assigned to him.

'I am glad,' thought he, 'that the proud Rosalind, who advised me to lay my fortune at the feet of no one, is not here to witness the moment at which I take my place at my father's board, "Lord of my presence and no land beside!"'

But his young spirit soon o'ermastered the sensation which seemed threatening to choke him, when Mr Cartwright said in the most obliging voice in the world, 'Charles, let me give you some soup.'

This over, he said with the easiest accent he could assume, and addressing his mother, 'I am the bearer, ma'am of a message from Lady Harrington. She hopes that you will spare her the society of Miss Torrington and Helen for a short time.'

Mrs Cartwright looked at her husband to ascertain his sentiments, before she ventured to have any of her own.

'It is very considerate of the old lady,' said the vicar, with a soft smile, of which his daughter only knew the full value. 'I dare say she thought we should be a good deal engaged just at first. . . . Chivers! don't you see Mr Jacob Cartwright is waiting for sauce? . . . I think, my love, we shall make no objection to the arrangement; however, we will talk together on the subject before we decide.'

As this amiable speech will not be found to accord exactly with his subsequent conduct, it may be well to remark that the servants were waiting at table, who doubtless would report his answer, and speculate on the temper of it.

The family party seemed expected to sit at table rather longer than usual. The master of the banquet was evidently enjoying himself; and though Charles sickened alike at his dignity and his condescension, and Henrietta looked more pale and Fanny more melancholy every moment, still Mr Jacob appeared in ecstasies; and as Mrs Cartwright continued to smile upon her handsome husband with every symptom of satisfaction, he continued to perform his new and delightful task at the bottom of the table till long past the usual hour of withdrawing.

At length, however, the watchful bride received the little nod which her husband had that morning informed her must always precede her moving from table. The ladies retired, and Charles followed them as far as the hall, where, impatiently seizing upon his hat, and wrapping himself in his cloak, he set off, despite the heavy darkness of the night, to relieve his heart from the load that oppressed it, by passing an hour at Oakley.

Mr Cartwright and Jacob remained in the dining-room for another very delightful half-hour; and then followed coffee and tea, and Fanny's own hymns sung to Irish melodies, and a few conjugal kindnesses exchanged on the sofa; and Henrietta pleaded illness and went to bed;

and then another very appropriate extempore prayer was uttered, and the family separated.

'Will you not take a little wine and water, and a biscuit, my dear Mr Cartwright?' said his attentive wife. 'You always used to do it.'

'I had rather the tray were taken to your dressing-room, my love.'

There was something so affectionately comfortable in the proposition, that the lady added a tender smile to her nodded assent, and in a few minutes the newly-married pair found themselves in robes de chambre, luxuriously seated in two soft arm-chairs before a blazing fire, in the very room that a few short weeks before had witnessed the first full disclosure of the vicar's love.

Madeira, sugar, nutmeg, hot water, and dainty biscuits, tempted to negus and to chat; and thus the conversation ran:

'Only second to my service to the Lord, my Clara, is my adoration of you!' began the fond husband: 'and in nothing perhaps shall I be more likely to show this, than in the pains I shall almost involuntarily take to guard you from every spiteful and envious observation which our union, sweetest, is likely to excite. It was in this spirit, my beauteous Clara, that I replied in the manner I did to the message from those very infamous people the Harringtons. Had I, my love, at once proclaimed my feelings on the subject, I well knew what the result would be. You would have been abused throughout the country for having married a tyrant, whose first act of power was to vex and thwart your children. Therefore, when your sweet eyes looked towards mine, for the purpose of consulting me, I at once decided upon the line of conduct most certain of securing you from any invidious remark.'

'How very kind! My dearest husband, I must pray to the Lord for power to prove my gratitude for such kindness as I ought!'

'Sweet love! Together will we pray to the Lord! – together learn from his holy Spirit how best to prove the virtuous tenderness of our souls! But do not, my Clara, suspect me guilty of the contemptible weakness of really intending that your daughter and your ward should remain inmates in a family that has so cruelly insulted you. Oh! do not believe it! No! I would rather submit to insult myself in the most painful form, than permit you, my best beloved, to encounter it unresisted. You must write, my Clara – you must write a letter to Helen, and send it with the carriage early to-morrow morning to Oakley. It must be such a letter, dearest, as shall bring her home without an hour's delay.'

'But, my dearest Mr Cartwright, Charles is gone there to-night, you may depend upon it, and probably for the express purpose of telling the girls how graciously you received the invitation.'

'You think so, my Clara? I own I hoped it was the case. This, you see, is exactly what we could most wish to happen. My answer was spoken precisely in the spirit which I thought could be repeated most favourably for you. Now therefore your asserting a mother's rights and a mother's feelings must do you honour even in the eyes of those you disoblige, and no sort of reflection fall upon the blessed choice which has made me the happiest of men.'

'That was so thoughtful of you!' replied Mrs Cartwright, kissing the hand that clasped hers. 'But what shall I say to Helen, dearest?'

'Give me your desk, my Clara, and I will write a line or two, that you shall copy. It must be expressed with strength and firmness, my best love, and it may prevent a repetition of this very improper request for the future.'

The desk was brought; and while Mrs Cartwright prepared a second glass of negus for the vicar, who declared that the night was unusually chilly, he composed the following epistle:

'Helen!

'That it should have entered into your heart, into the heart of my own dear child, to wish for permission to become the guest of a family who from the hour of your late father's death has ever treated me with the most cruel and unmerited unkindness, is a mystery that I cannot understand. It was this unkindness that drove me, sooner than I could have wished to do it, to find a friend and adviser in Mr Cartwright; and my only fear now is, that his indulgent gentleness towards my children may prevent his being so firm a support to me in the guiding them as I may sometimes require. But in the present instance I want no strength beyond my own to declare to you, that I will not permit you to remain an hour longer at Sir Gilbert Harrington's; that I command you instantly to put yourself into the carriage I send for you, and return to Cartwright Park; (for so, of course, will my residence be called for the future;) and moreover, I beg you to inform the unprincipled pair who would seduce you from your mother's roof, that if on the present or any future occasion they should persuade you to commit so great a sin, I shall take legal measures to recover the possession of your person till such time as you shall be of age; when, if unhappily evil counsellors should still have influence over you, I shall give you up to them, to penniless obscurity, to your own heart's remorse, and to that sentence of everlasting condemnation which will in such case infallibly doom you to the region where there is howling and gnashing of teeth.

'As for my ward Miss Torrington, I must of course take the same summary mode of getting her again under my protection, for such time as I shall continue to be her legal guardian.

'CLARA HELENA FRANCES CARTWRIGHT.'

'Cartwright Park, Wednesday.'

When this composition was completed, Mr Cartwright turned the desk to his lady, laid a fair sheet of blank paper before her, put a pen into her hand, drew the wax-lights near her, and then set about sipping the negus she had so kindly prepared for him, without appearing to think it at all necessary to ask her opinion of the document she was about to copy.

Being, however, rather new to the yoke into which it had pleased her to thrust her head, she took the liberty of reading it. A slight augmentation of colour was perceived on her delicate cheek as she proceeded, by the watchful eye of her husband, as he turned it towards her, over the top of the beautifully cut goblet he held in his hand. But he nibbled a biscuit, and said nothing.

When the perusal of it was completed, Mrs Cartwright dipped the pen she still held between her fingers, in the ink; but before she began to use it, she paused, the colour mounted a little higher still, and she ventured to say in the very gentlest accent in the world,

'My dear friend, – do you not think this might be a little softened?'

'As how, my sweetest?'

Mrs Cartwright's eye again ran over it, but she seemed unwilling to speak: at length she said,

'If you, dear Cartwright, agree with me about it, you would make the alteration so much better yourself!'

'Perhaps I might, my lovely Clara; but as the fact is that I do not agree with you at all on the subject, I suspect your epistle would be rather the worse than the better for anything further that I could do to it.'

He rose as he spoke, and going behind her, appeared to read the paper over her shoulder, and having satisfied himself with the examination, kissed her fair throat as he bent over it, adding, as he took a light from the table,

'I am going to the library to look for a book, my love: write it exactly as you like, and I will seal it for you when I return.'

No one who knew Mrs Cartwright could have the slightest doubt that the letter would be very fairly copied by the time her obliging husband returned: and so it was, every word of it excepting the date. She appeared to be in the very act of writing this when he came back, and stopping short as he entered, she said in a voice that certainly faltered a little,

'My dear Cartwright, – don't you think it would be better to let those odious Harringtons hear from some other quarter of this change in the name of our place? Not but that I approve it, I assure you perfectly; but I know Lady Harrington so well! and I can guess so exactly the sort of style in which she will observe upon it!'

'Then, perhaps, dearest,' said he, again coming behind her and caressing her neck, – 'perhaps you may think it would please her ladyship better if your own name, as you have accepted it from me, were to be suppressed? – Is it so, my fairest?'

'Good Heaven, no! – May the Lord forgive me for using such an expression, Cartwright! How could you say such cruel words?'

'Nay! – my own Clara! – what could I think of your wishing that the house we dwell in should retain the name of your former husband? Ah, dearest! you know not all the jealousy of affection so ardent as mine! What is the importance of the name of the place, Clara, compared to your own? Are you not mine?' he continued, throwing his arms round her; 'and if you are – why should you torment me with the remembrance that another has called you his? – that another's name has been your signature, your date, your history? Oh, Clara, spare me such thoughts as these! – they unman me!'

'My dearest Cartwright!' returned the lady, only disengaging herself from his arms sufficiently to write with firm though hurried characters the name of CARTWRIGHT PARK, – 'how deeply you have touched me!'

CHAPTER XXXII

THE WIDOW SIMPSON'S DISAPPOINTMENT

This letter was certainly commented upon pretty freely in all its parts by the knight and lady of Oakley; but not the less did it produce the effect intended: for not even could Sir Gilbert, after the first hot fit of rage was over, advise poor Helen to expose herself to be recalled by force. In the case of Miss Torrington, the hated authority of Mr Cartwright, though not necessarily so lasting, was for the present equally imperative, and he therefore advised her peaceably to accompany her friend to her unhappy home, and then to set about applying to Chancery in order to emancipate herself from it.

The parting was a very sad one. Poor Helen wept bitterly. She had felt more consolation perhaps than she was aware in having been received with such very *parental* kindness at Oakley; and her present departure from it was, she thought, exceedingly like being driven, or rather dragged, out of paradise. But there was no help for it. The carriage was waiting at the door, and even the rebellious Sir Gilbert himself said she must go, – not without adding, however, that it should go hard with him if he did not find some means or other, before she were twenty-one, of releasing her from such hateful thraldom.

Helen had given, as she thought, her last kiss to her warm-hearted godmother, and was in the very act of stepping aside that Miss Torrington might take her place in the carriage, when that young lady, blushing most celestial rosy red, said abruptly, as if prompted thereto by a sudden and desperate effort of courage,

'Sir Gilbert Harrington! – may I speak to you for one single minute alone?'

'For a double century, fair Rose, if we can but make the tête-à-tête last so long. – You may give poor god-mamma another hug, Helen: and don't hurry yourself about it. – Miss Rose and I shall find a great deal to say to each other.'

As soon as the old baronet had completed the flourish with which he led her into his library, Miss Torrington turned to him, and with a voice and manner that betrayed great agitation, she said,

'I believe, Sir Gilbert, I may change my present guardian, by applying to the Court of Chancery. If I make myself a ward of the court, it will be necessary, I believe, for me to obtain the Lord Chancellor's consent if I should wish to marry before I am of age?'

'Certainly, my dear.'

'And what is necessary for the obtaining such consent, Sir Gilbert?'

'That the person who proposes to marry you should be able to offer settlements in proportion to your own fortune.'

'And if I should choose a person unable to do so?'

'To guard against such imprudence, Miss Torrington, the Chancellor has the power of preventing such a marriage.'

Rosalind's colour came, and went and came again, before she could utter another word; but at length she said,

'Have I not the power of choosing another guardian, Sir Gilbert?'

'I believe you have, my dear.'

'If I have, – then will you let me choose you?'

These words burst so eagerly from her, and she clasped her hands, and fixed her eyes upon him with a look so supplicating, that no man would have found it an easy task to refuse her. Sir Gilbert probably felt little inclination to do so, though he had, in the course of his life, repeatedly refused to take the office now offered him in so singular a manner.

'This request, my dear Miss Rose,' said he, smiling, 'looks very much as if you thought I should prove such an old fool of a guardian, as to let you have your own way in all things. I hardly know whether I ought to thank you for the compliment, or not. However, I am very willing to accept the office; for I think, somehow or other, that you will not plague me much. – What is your fortune, my dear? – and is it English or Irish property?'

'Entirely English, Sir Gilbert: and produces, I believe, between three and four thousand a year.'

'A very pretty provision, my dear young lady. Would you wish to proceed in this immediately.'

'Immediately, – without a day's delay, if I could help it.'

Sir Gilbert patted her cheek, and smiled again with a look of very great contentment and satisfaction. 'Very well, my dear, – I think you are quite right – quite right to get rid of such a guardian as the Reverend Mistress Cartwright with as little delay as possible. I imagine you would not find it very easy to negotiate the business yourself, and I will therefore recommend my lawyer to you. Shall I put the business into his hands forthwith?'

So bright a flash of pleasure darted from the eyes of Rosalind, as made the old gentleman wink his own – and, in truth, he appeared very nearly as well pleased as herself. 'Now then,' she said, holding her hand towards him that he might lead her out again, 'I will keep Mr Cartwright's carriage waiting no longer. – God bless you, Sir Gilbert! Do not talk to anybody about this till it is done. Oh! how very kind you are!'

Sir Gilbert gallantly and gaily kissed the tips of her fingers, and led her again into the drawing-room. Helen, who was still weeping, and seemed as much determined to persevere in it as ever Beatrice did, looked with astonishment in the face of her friend, which, though still covered with blushes, was radiant with joy. It was in vain she looked at her, however – it was a mystery she could not solve; so, once more uttering a mournful farewell, Helen gave a last melancholy gaze at her old friends, and followed Rosalind into the carriage.

'May I ask you, Rosalind,' she said as soon as it drove off, 'what it is that you have been saying to Sir Gilbert, or Sir Gilbert to you, which can have caused you to look so particularly happy at the moment that you are about to take up your residence at Cartwright Park, under the guardianship of its master the Vicar of Wrexhill?'

'I will explain the mystery in a moment, Helen. I have asked Sir Gilbert Harrington to let me name him as my guardian, and he has consented.'

'Have you such power?' replied Helen. 'Oh, happy, happy Rosalind!'

'Yes, Helen, there may be happiness in that; – but I may find difficulties, perhaps, – and if I do!——'

'I trust you will not. – I trust that ere long you will be able to withdraw yourself from a house so disgraced and afflicted as ours!'

'And leave you behind, Helen? You think that is part of my scheme?'

'How can you help it, Rosalind? You have just read my mother's letter: – you see the style and tone in which she announces her right over *my person*; – and this from the mother I so doted on! I do assure you,

Rosalind, that I often seem to doubt the reality of the misery that surrounds me, and fancy that I must be dreaming. Throw back your thoughts to the period of your first coming to us, and then say if such a letter as this can really come to me from my mother.'

'The letter is a queer letter – a very queer letter indeed. And yet I am under infinite obligations to it; for had she not used that pretty phrase, – "for such time as I shall continue to be her legal guardian," – it might never have entered my head to inquire for how long a time that must of necessity be.'

'I rejoice for you, Rosalind, that the odious necessity of remaining with us is likely to be shortened: and will mix no malice with my envy, even when I see you turn your back for ever upon Cartwright Park.'

'There would be little cause to envy me, Helen, should I go without taking you with me.'

A tear stood in Rosalind's bright eye as she said this, and Helen felt very heartily ashamed of the petulance with which she had spoken. As a penance for it, she would not utter the sad prognostic that rose to her lips, as to the impossibility that anything could give her power to bestow the freedom she might herself obtain.

Their return seemed to be unnoticed by every individual of the family except Henrietta. She saw the carriage approach from her own room, and contrived to waylay Rosalind as she passed to hers.

'I know the sight of me must be hateful to you, Miss Torrington,' she said, 'and I have been looking out for you in order that the shock of first seeing me might be over at once. Poor, pretty Helen Mowbray! – notwithstanding the hardness of heart on which I pique myself, I cannot help feeling for her. How does she bear it, Miss Torrington?'

'She is very unhappy, Henrietta: and I think it is your duty, as well as mine, to make her feel her altered home as little miserable as possible.'

'I should think so too, if I believed I had any power to make it better or worse, – except, indeed, that of meeting her eyes, or avoiding them. The sight of any of us must be dreadful to her.'

'You have such a remarkable way of shutting yourself up – your intellectual self I mean, from every one, that it is not very easy to say how great or how little your power might be. From the slight and transient glances which you have sometimes permitted me to take through your icy casing, I am rather inclined to believe that you ought to reckon for something in the family of which you make a part.'

Henrietta shook her head. 'Your glances have not penetrated to the centre yet, Miss Torrington. Should you ever do so, you, and your friend Helen too, would hate me, – even if my name were not Cartwright.'

'I would not hear your enemy say so,' replied Rosalind. 'However, we are now likely to be enough together to judge each other by the severest of all tests, daily experience.'

'An excellent test for the temper, – but not for the heart,' replied Henrietta.

'You seem determined to make me afraid of you, Miss Cartwright. I have no great experience of human nature as yet; but I should think a corrupt heart would rather seek to conceal than proclaim itself.'

'I think you are right; but I have no idea that my heart is corrupt: – it is diseased.'

'I wish I could heal it,' said Rosalind kindly, 'for I suspect its illness, be it what it may, causes your cheek to grow pale. You do not look well, Miss Cartwright.'

'Well? – Oh, no! I have long known I am dying.'

'Good Heaven! – what do you mean? Why do you not take advice?'

'Because no advice could save me: – and because if it could, I would not take it.'

'I hope you are not in earnest. Perhaps this strange marriage, if it do no other good, may benefit your health by placing you in a larger family. I cannot think you are happy at the Vicarage.'

'Indeed!' replied Henrietta with a melancholy smile.

'And I cannot but hope that you will be more happy here.'

'Well! – we shall see. But I should take it very kind of you if you would make the three young Mowbrays understand, that if I could have prevented this iniquitous marriage, I would have done it.'

'Would it be safe to say so much to Fanny?'

'Yes. Mr Cartwright will never hear her bosom secrets more.'

* * *

In the midst of the tide of triumph and of joy which seemed at this time to bear the Vicar of Wrexhill far above the reach of any earthly sorrow, there was a little private annoyance that beset him, – very trifling indeed, but which required a touch of his able diplomatic adroitness to settle satisfactorily.

The widow Simpson was as thorough a coquette as ever decorated the street of a country village; and often had it happened, since her weeds were laid aside, that Mr This, or Mr That, had been congratulated as likely to succeed to her vacant heart and hand. But hitherto Mrs Simpson had preferred the reputation of having many adorers, to the humdrum reality of a second husband. But when Mr Cartwright appeared, her hopes, her wishes, her feelings underwent a sudden and violent change. At first, indeed, she only looked at him as a very handsome man, who must, by some means or other, be brought to think her a very handsome woman: but more serious thoughts quickly followed, and the idea of a home at the Vicarage, and the advantage of having all her bills made out to the Revd Mr Cartwright, became one of daily and hourly recurrence. Mrs Simpson was not a person to let such a notion lie idle; nor was Mr Cartwright a man to permit the gentle advances to intimacy of a Mrs Simpson to stop short or lead to nothing. But from any idea of her becoming mistress of the Vicarage, or of her bills being made out to him, he was as pure as the angels in heaven.

Nevertheless, the intimacy did advance. One by one, every personal decoration that marks the worldling was laid aside, and the livery of holiness adopted in its stead. False ringlets were exchanged for false bands; gauze bonnets covered with bows gave place to straw bonnets having no bows at all: lilac faded into grey, and the colour of the rose was exchanged for that of its leaf. These important and very heavenly-minded reforms were soon followed by others, not more essential, for that is hardly possible: but they went the length of turning her little girl into a methodist monkey; her card-boxes, into branch missionary fund contribution cases; her footstools, into praying cushions; and her sofa, into a pulpit and a pew, whence and where she very often listened to 'the word,' when pretty nearly all the parish of Wrexhill were fast asleep.

In all former affairs of the heart in which Mrs Simpson had engaged since the demise of her husband, she had uniformly come off the conqueror; for she had never failed to obtain exactly as much flirtation as she required to keep her on good terms with herself, and on bad terms with all coquettish young ladies for five miles round, and had never granted any favour in return that she did not consider as a fair price for the distinction she received.

But poor Mrs Simpson's example should be a warning to all widow ladies to be careful how they enter into holy dalliance and sanctified trifling with the regenerated and elect. They should remember, that 'once called, there is no falling off;' that 'the merit of good works is a stink and abomination;' and that 'faith can make sin seem as white as wool.' Common prudence, in short, is no fair match for uncommon holiness, and the principal person in the village of Wrexhill was at the time of Mrs Mowbray's marriage with its vicar really very much to be pitied.

It is probably no very agreeable task for a bridegroom to pay a visit to a lady under such circumstances; but Mr Cartwright felt that it must be done, and with nerves braced to the task by the remembrance of the splendid silver urn, tea and coffee pots, the exquisite French china, and all the pretty elaborate finishing of his breakfast equipage, – in a word, at about eleven o'clock on the next morning but one after his installation (as Jacob called it), he set off on foot, like an humble and penitent pilgrim, to call on the widow Simpson.

He was, as usual, shown into the quiet parlour, overlooked by no village eye, that opened upon the garden. Here he found everything much as it used to be – sofas, footstools, albums, missionary boxes and all, but no Mrs Simpson.

'Let missis know, sir,' said the boy-servant; and he closed the door, leaving the vicar to his meditations.

At length the door re-opened, and the pale and languid Mrs Simpson, her eyes red with weeping, and her rouge (not partially, as during the process of election, but really and altogether) laid aside, entered. The air and manner with which the vicar met her was something of a mixed breed between audacity and confusion. He was in circumstances, however, highly favourable to the growth of the former, and equally so to the stifling of the latter feeling.

He took the widow's hand, kissed it, and led her to the sofa.

Her handkerchief was at her eyes, and though she made no resistance, she manifested no inclination to return the tender pressure bestowed upon her fingers.

'You weep, my dear friend!' said the vicar in an accent of surprise. 'Is it thus you congratulate me on the great change that has taken place in my circumstances?'

'Congratulate you! Oh, Mr Cartwright! is it possible that you can be so coldly cruel? – Congratulate you! Gracious Heaven! have you no thought, no pity for all the anguish that you have made me suffer?'

'I know not why you should talk of suffering, my dear friend. I had hoped that the sweet friendship which for several months past has united us, was to you, as to me, a source of the tenderest satisfaction. But our feelings for each other must indeed be widely different. There is no circumstance that could befall you, productive of even worldly convenience and advantage, but I should rejoice at it as if the Lord had sent it to myself: but you, my friend, appear to mourn because from a poor man I am become a rich one.'

'Alas! – Cruel! – Is it for that I mourn? Think you that my heart can forget what I have been to you, or what I hoped to be? Can you forget the hours that you have devoted to me? And is this the end of it?'

'I neither can nor will forget the happy period of our tender friendship. Nor is there any reason, my excellent Mrs Simpson, that it should not continue, even as the Lord hath permitted that it should begin. Believe me, that were a similar circumstance to happen to you: – I mean, were you accidentally to connect yourself by means of marriage with great wealth and extended influence; – instead of complaining of it, I should rejoice with an exceeding great joy. It could, as I should imagine, make no possible difference in our friendly and affectionate feelings for each other; and I should know that your piety and heavenly-minded zeal in the cause of grace and faith would be rendered greatly more profitable and efficient thereby.'

'You do not, then, understand a woman's heart, Mr Cartwright! What is there, short of the torments of the bottomless pit, that can compare to the suffering of seeing the heart one believed to be one's own, given to another.'

'I dare say it must be very disagreeable indeed, my dear friend. But no such idea, I do assure you, would occur to me were you to marry. Indeed, my own view of the case is, that as an ordinance of the Lord, it should be entered into with as little attention as possible to mere pleasure. To a man like myself, whose soul is altogether given to things above, the idea of making a marriage of love, as it is called, would be equally absurd and profane. My object in the connexion I have just formed, was to increase my sphere of influence and utility; and nothing, I assure you, can be more opportune and fortunate than my having found this very worthy and richly-endowed person. It would give me unfeigned satisfaction, my dear friend, to hear that you had been equally fortunate, and, permit me to say, equally wise.'

'Oh, Mr Cartwright! I am sure I had no idea when – when I attached myself to you, that you disapproved of marriage among those who love, as I thought you and I did; for most surely I thought, Mr Cartwright, that I should have been your wife.'

'No? – Is it possible, my dear friend, that such an idea as that, so perfectly unauthorised by the evident intention of the Lord in the ordinance, could have occurred to you? I really am greatly surprised, for I thought that we understood one another perfectly.'

'Indeed, indeed, Mr Cartwright, I never was more mistaken in any one in my whole life; and I am sure that if poor Mrs Mowbray is as much deceived in you as I was, she will be a very unhappy woman when she finds it out, poor thing.'

'My dear friend, allow me to assure you that you altogether mistake the nature of the friendship I have been so happy as to form with you, as well as that of the connexion I have just ratified with her. I trust the Lord will give me grace so to conduct myself, as that I may never be suspected of confounding the two together, which, by the nature of the Lord's ordinances, ought to be kept as separate and distinct as possible. I will not now enter more fully with you into this interesting question, for much business presses upon me: but when we shall happen to find ourselves more at leisure, my dear friend, which I trust will be often the case, I will explain to you, in a manner that will, I think, be satisfactory, my opinions on the subject. Meanwhile, dear Mrs Simpson, let me entreat you not to spoil your charming eyes by weeping, nor let anything lead you for an instant to doubt that my sentiments for you are exactly the same as they have ever been; and above all, cease not to work out your eternal salvation with fear and trembling. Mrs Cartwright is by no means, I believe, a very active minded person; and I think it probable that I shall often feel it borne in upon my mind, that by applying to you I shall be able to forward the great work of grace and redemption that I have in hand more effectually than by any personal assistance that she is likely to render me. Her wealth indeed is great, as I hope some little keepsakes from me may prove to you ere long; but as to energy and fervour of character, there is but one Mrs Simpson.'

The reverend gentleman here saluted the fair lady's lips, and departed, leaving her exactly in the state he wished; that is to say, puzzled, confounded, mystified, and not knowing the least in the world what she should say to him next.

CHAPTER XXXIII

CHARLES'S INTERVIEW WITH HIS STEP-FATHER – HIS SUDDEN DEPARTURE FROM WREXHILL

There were moreover other ladies to be encountered, most of whom, as the vicar well knew, would not hear of his brilliant nuptials with pleasure; but this was a matter of small moment. The benevolent attentions he had bestowed upon them were chiefly for the purpose of insuring popularity and acquiring influence, – and these were now too much at his command for him to experience the slightest anxiety from the fear of losing them.

The remembrance of the three Misses Richards was indeed rather heavy upon him; especially from the circumstance of Miss Mary's having accidentally seen him kiss Miss Louisa, which he happened to do, in the little shrubbery behind their cottage, upon occasion of a serious discourse which they had been holding together upon the nature and influence of especial grace. Little Mary, who was purity and simplicity personified, firmly believed, in her very innocent heart, that this caress could only be given by such a gentleman as Mr Cartwright as the ratification of a treaty of marriage; and had accordingly not only alluded to Louisa's happy prospects herself, but had fully persuaded her sister Charlotte likewise to

believe that this blessed union would be the result of the vicar's soft
attentions to them all. So that upon a smart discussion with their mother
upon the sin of works, when matters had gone so far as to induce the
young lady to declare that she considered the door of her mother's house
as nothing less than a type of the gates of hell, she had, in relating the
scene of this praiseworthy combat of the apostle, ventured these
remarkable words:

'There is sorrow and sin in dwelling under the roof of the scorner; but
when dear Louisa has quite consented to all your wishes, Mr Cartwright,
her bowels will yearn towards her sisters, and you will both of you draw
us out of the way of temptation under the shelter and the shadow of your
wing.'

The only reply which the vicar made to this speech was the utterance
of a fervent blessing.

'May the Lord have you in his holy keeping, my beloved friends!' said
he, 'now and for ever, world everlasting. Amen!'

He now remembered with considerable satisfaction the cautious
tendency of this reply, and, upon the whole, thought that there was no
occasion to fatigue his spirits by making these young ladies a private visit
to announce his change of condition, as in the case of Mrs Simpson. He
therefore turned from the widow's door, after the pause of a moment on
her threshold, during which these thoughts were rapidly but healthily
digested, leaving him, that is to say, neither loaded with remorse, nor
fevered by anxiety.

Upon this occasion, for some reason or other, connected perhaps with
that tranquillity of mind in his lady which it was so unquestionably his
duty to guard, the Vicar of Wrexhill had not made use of his carriage and
servants. He walked therefore back to the Park, and met Charles
Mowbray coming through the lodge gates, as he entered them.

The young man touched his hat, and was walking on; but the vicar
stopped him.

'Where are you going, my dear Charles?' said he. 'It is getting quite
late; you will not have time for a walk before dinner – it is almost dark.
You know my habits are those of great punctuality.'

'I shall never interfere with those habits, sir. It is probable that I may
not return to dinner.'

'Indeed! – we shall be very sorry to lose you. Where are you going,
then, my dear boy?'

Charles hesitated. His heart seemed to swell in his bosom at this
questioning; and though, in fact, he had strolled out without any idea of
absenting himself at dinner, something like a spirit of rebellion induced
him to answer,

'To Sir Gilbert Harrington's, sir.'

'Good evening, then. Let me bespeak your ear for half an hour in my library to-morrow morning, between the hours of eleven and twelve.'

Charles bowed, but uttered not a word, and proceeded towards Oakley, inwardly muttering '*his library!*'

He entered the mansion of his old friends without an apology, but stated the cause of his visit as it really was.

'I could not bear to be examined by him as to where I was going, and when I was coming; and rather to prove my independence, than for any other reason, I am come to you. Can you forgive this?'

'Ay, truly can we,' replied the old lady; 'and be sure to do the same next time, Charles. It makes me sick to think of this species of paternal admonishing.'

'I am to be lectured for my impatience under it, as I suspect; for he bade me meet him in *his library* to-morrow morning.'

'HIS library! Scoundrel!' exclaimed Sir Gilbert through his closed teeth.

'Shall I obey the mandate, Sir Gilbert?' said Charles. 'Or shall I take no notice of it?'

'The question seems an easy one to answer Charles,' replied the baronet; 'and had I been to answer yesterday morning, I should have said without hesitation, – set fire to the library, and stifle him in it like a weazel as he is, rather than come at his call. But I have taken it into my head since, that our best game will be to keep things soft and smooth for a while. So wait upon him, Master Charles, in your father's library, and hear all he has got to say; and don't turn yourself out of the house; and don't spit upon him if you can help it. – But, d——n it! I hope he won't sit in poor Mowbray's chair!'

* * *

In consequence of this counsel, Charles did wait upon the vicar in his father's library at the appointed hour, and took what comfort he could from perceiving that he was not seated in that lamented father's chair, but had ensconced himself in a newly-invented fauteuil of surpassing softness, which he had caused to be brought from the drawing-room for his especial comfort.

'You have not kept me waiting, and I commend you for it, my son. May the Lord, in whom I trust, lead you in his own good time to be all that your pious mother can wish to see you. Sit down, Charles – pray sit down.'

Poor Charles! – the whole scene was purgatory to him; but his courage did not forsake him: and instead of running out of the room, as he felt terribly tempted to do, he sat down opposite to his step-father, determined to hear everything he had to say.

'I think, Charles, that the pious nature of your mother, awakened as it has of late been by the immediate operation of grace upon her, must by this time be so sufficiently known to you all, as to prevent the possibility of your mistaking her motives for marrying the second father, in whose presence you are now placed. Her motives have been of the holiest kind, and never, probably, did any person perform a more acceptable service to the Lord than she did when, placing her hand within mine before His altar, she resigned that power over her children, which maternal weakness rendered almost nugatory, to one who is too strong in the Lord to permit any human feelings or motives ever to make him swerve from that course which the Holy Spirit has taught him to believe the best. It would be a very shining pleasure to me if your thankfulness for this most merciful dispensation were at this very moment to impel you to kneel down on one of these cushions; – of such there are always sufficient, and to spare, in the dwellings of the chosen: – I wish, I say, that even now I could see you fall down before me to give thanks to the Lord for having sent to you and to your sisters one of His own, as your guide and protector through the pitfalls of this life, and to usher you with favour into His presence in the life to come. I would willingly see you thus grateful for manifest mercies, – but I shall not insist upon it at this moment, for I know, Charles, how far from the Lord have been the paths in which your teachers have hitherto led you.'

The vicar here paused; but as there was no point in his harangue to which Mowbray could have replied in the spirit which his friend had recommended to him, he resolutely kept silence.

'The time will come,' resumed the vicar, 'the time *shall* come, when your knees, young man, shall be less stubborn. But it is time that I unfold to you the business upon which I wished to speak when I permitted your attendance in this apartment. You have been led, doubtless by the active machinations of the devil, to turn your sinful thoughts towards that profession which, beyond all others, has made Satan its patron and its Saint. In one word, you have thought of going into the army; and it is to inform you that I shall not permit this dreadful sin against the Holy Ghost to be committed by one of my family, that you are now before me. Open not your mouth, young man, in defence of the God-abandoned set to whom you would wish to belong: my ears must not be profaned by any words of such abhorrent tendency. Instead of speaking yourself, hear me. My will is, that you return to College, there to prepare yourself for ordination. I utter this command with a conscience void of offence; for though your awful deficiency in religion is well known to me, I have confidence in the Lord, and in the power he will give me to work a change: and moreover, I know to what bishop I shall lead you for ordination; thereby securing to myself the consolation of knowing that no human learning will enable you to be received within the pale that we are strengthening around us, and within which none shall be admitted (if we can help it) but the regenerate and adopted, or such as we of the evangelical church may choose to pledge ourselves shall become so. As to the manner and amount of your future income, I shall take the arrangement of it entirely into my own hands, reserving to myself the power of varying your allowance from time to time, as shall seem good in the sight of the Lord and in mine. You may have a few days' holidays here if you wish it, in honour of your mother's marriage; after which I will give you ten pounds for your journey and other contingent expenses, and permit you to employ such tradesmen at Oxford as I shall point out, for such necessaries as it is proper I should furnish you with. Their bills must be forwarded to Mr Corbold, who, for the present, I shall probably continue as my agent; and when I have duly examined them, they shall be paid. Your College expenses I shall also order to be transmitted to him, and through him to me. – I must now dismiss you, for I have letters to write. – Be careful in passing these windows, if you please, not to approach them too closely. This room is a favourite apartment of mine, and I must not be interrupted or annoyed in it in any way. Remember this, if you please. Good morning.'

During the whole of this very trying interview, Mowbray had not uttered a single word. He knew that if he opened his lips, the indignation that burned at his heart would burst forth with a vehemence he should no longer be able to control. He felt his heart throb, and every pulse so fiercely keeping time to it, that he was terrified at himself, and fearful lest the tide of passion that worked thus fearfully within him should drive him to do, or even to say what he might repent, he hastened from the room, leaving Mr Cartwright very comfortably persuaded that the eloquence which the Lord had bestowed on him, if it sometimes failed in converting those who heard him to his doctrine, was of a nature well calculated to enforce his authority; a species of success which perhaps satisfied him better still.

The unfortunate Charles took refuge in Helen's dressing-room from the storm that raged in his bosom. He longed to hear the gentle voice of his sister with as much eagerness as one panting in fever longs for a cool breeze or a refreshing stream; and when he entered the room and found it unoccupied, he felt as if that misfortune were greater than all which had fallen upon him before.

In a state of the most pitiable depression of spirits he seated himself most forlornly on a *chaise longue* that stood in a recess as far as possible from the windows, and there, resting his head on the side of it, and covering his face with his hands, he remained for a considerable time perfectly immovable, and quite as miserable as his worst enemy could wish.

At length the door opened, and a female entered. Charles sprang forward to meet her, and very narrowly escaped encircling Miss Torrington in his arms. She drew back, certainly, but hardly with so sudden a movement as that of Mowbray, who, colouring and stammering in extreme confusion, said as he retreated to his former place, 'I beg your pardon: I came here to look for Helen.'

'And so did I, Mr Mowbray: I cannot think where she has hid herself. – But you do not look like yourself, Charles. Has Mr Cartwright been speaking to you? I heard him tell his wife that he had desired you to meet him in the library.'

'In his library, Miss Torrington; pray call it as he does, *his* library. – But what a fool am I to care thus for a word! It is his library; the man says right. But what then is poor Helen? what is Fanny? what am I?'

His features expressed such terrible agony of mind, that Rosalind almost felt afraid to leave him, and stood at some distance from him as he sat, with her looks riveted upon his face and her eyes overflowing with tears.

'Tell me, dear Charles,' she said, 'what is it that has happened to you? I will go and seek Helen, and bring her to you in a moment. Only tell me before I go if any new thing has happened to make us all more miserable than we were. Is it not common cause, Mr Mowbray? For God's sake tell me what has befallen you?'

'It is not common cause, Miss Torrington,' he replied with bitterness. 'My situation is, I heartily hope, without a parallel; and as none can share my wretchedness, as none can relieve it, it were better, I believe, that none should know it.'

'That is not the language of friendship, Mr Mowbray. Were poor Helen here, I trust you would not answer her inquiries so harshly.'

'Harshly? If so, I have been very wrong. Forgive me. – Could you have heard the language this man held to me, – could you have seen him enthroned in my poor father's library, and heard him tell me that when I passed before the windows I must take care not to approach too nearly, – oh, Rosalind! could you have heard all this, you would not wonder if I answered even madly to any questions asked.'

Rosalind stood silently before him when he had ceased to speak, her hands tightly clasped, and her eyes riveted on the ground. 'I will ask you but one question more,' said she after a long pause.

'And what is that, Miss Torrington?'

'*Miss Torrington!*' said she, muttering between her teeth. 'Alas! – how madly have I acted! and how difficult is it to retrace a wrong step once taken!'

She trembled violently; so violently, that she was obliged to support herself by leaning on the back of a chair which stood near her. Charles Mowbray's head again rested on the sofa, and his eyes were hid from her. She felt that he saw her not, and this perhaps it was which gave her courage to proceed in the task she had determined to perform; but her breast heaved almost convulsively, and her mouth became so parched that it was with difficulty she could articulate these words:

'I learn from Sir Gilbert Harrington, Mr Mowbray, that – I have the power – of making him my guardian——'

'Thank God!' exclaimed Charles, interrupting her; 'I thank God for it, Miss Torrington. – You may then escape, and immediately, from this place of torment. This will indeed help me to bear it better.'

He spoke the last words more composedly, and again buried his face on the sofa.

'But, think you, Mr Mowbray, I would leave Helen here?'

'I fear you will have no power to take her,' he replied.

'Not I – but you. Oh! Mr Mowbray! – Charles! Charles! – will you not understand me? Will you spare me this agony? No? you will not. But I have deserved it all, and I will bear it. Charles Mowbray! – it is I who would now lay my fortune at your feet. Oh! do not answer me as I once answered you! Charles Mowbray, will you take me for your wife?'

'No, by Heaven!' he exclaimed, falling on his knees before her. 'Poor Rosalind! dear, generous, devoted friend! And for her sake, then – for my dear Helen's sake, you would submit to be my wife – *my wife!* – an outcast, penniless, insulted beggar? – No, Rosalind: by Heaven, no! I would rather perish in the lowest state of human wretchedness than so abuse your noble nature. But do me justice, noble Rosalind; let there on one point at least be some equality between us. Believe that I love you, – and that with a strength of passion of which, as I think, your unawakened heart has yet no power to judge. But should you, Rosalind, ever learn what it is to love, then do me justice, and know how dear was honour to my soul when I adored but could refuse you.'

He seized her dress and pressed it to his lips; and then, rising from his knees, he darted out of the room, without daring to trust his eyes to look at her.

* * *

Had Mowbray's state of mind been somewhat less miserable – had the buoyant spirit given to him by nature been less completely crushed by the galling interview of the morning, it is probable that his memory might have suggested to him some circumstances in the hours passed heretofore with Rosalind, which might have raised some blessed hope upon his mind as to the motive and feelings that had led her to act as she had done. But, as it was, no such light from heaven fell upon him. In simplest sincerity he believed that she had rejected his suit because she did not love him, and that she had now offered to become his wife solely for Helen's sake, and in the generous hope of saving her by giving to him the power of offering her a home.

With this conviction, he determined to spare her the embarrassment and himself the torture of meeting again. With all the feverish hurry of impatient suffering, he instantly sought his mother; informed her of Mr Cartwright's wish that he should return to Oxford, and of his own desire to comply with this immediately.

There was something in the suddenness of this unresisting obedience that seemed to startle her. She applauded his resolution, but seemed to wish that for some short time, at least, he should delay the execution of it. But on this point he was immovable; and as Mr Cartwright appeared well pleased that so it should be, he succeeded in so hastening the arrangements for his departure that within twenty-four hours he had left the house, and that without having again seen Rosalind. The greater part of this interval, indeed, was passed at Oakley, where his reiterated assurances that he should be much, very much happier at Oxford than at home, were accepted in excuse for the suddenness of his departure. Sir Gilbert, indeed, had so well read Rosalind's heart, and so confidently did he anticipate his speedy and even triumphant return, that both himself and his lady, who as usual was wholly in his confidence, saw him depart without regret, and uttered their farewells with a cheerfulness that grated sadly on the feelings of the poor exile.

CHAPTER XXXIV

THE VICAR'S PROSPERITY – HE SETS ABOUT MAKING SOME IMPORTANT REFORMS
IN THE VILLAGE

The departure of Charles, so immediate and so unrepining, seemed to the vicar a most satisfactory proof that the talent and firmness which he had himself displayed in their final interview had produced exactly the effect which he hoped and intended. 'He will, I think, trouble me no more:' such was the comfortable little mental soliloquy with which, as he sat in his noble library, the Vicar of Wrexhill listened to the wheels of the cab, lent to convey Mowbray to the nearest town through which the coach passed.

This good work achieved, which was of that species permitted by the peculiar doctrine of his sect, Mr Cartwright, of Cartwright Park, began to look around him among his neighbours and dependents for opportunities of displaying both his sanctity and his magnificence.

Everything seemed to prosper with him; and the satisfaction produced by this success was very greatly enhanced by the consciousness that he owed it all, from the humble courtesy of the village maidens up to the crowning glory of his lady's love, and all the wealth it brought, wholly and solely to himself. Ungrateful would he have been for such unnumbered blessings had he neglected to reward that self by every kind observance and by every thoughtful care which his active fancy, his fastidious taste, and his luxurious nature could suggest. But he did it all so '*doucely*,' that no voice was raised to censure the dainty appetite of the high-fed priest; no lip was curled in scorn as every week brought forth some new indulgence, some exquisite refinement of elaborate luxury.

Everything seemed to prosper with him. The wines he ordered could hardly be accounted dear even at the unheard-of prices he gave for them. The beautiful creature he bought for his own riding, with just action enough to show off his handsome figure, and not sufficient to occasion him the least fatigue, appeared to be so born and bred on purpose for his use, that every eye was fixed in admiration as he paced along, and no tongue wagged to tell that while young Mowbray departed from his father's house with ten pounds in his pocket, his step-father's ambling hack cost two hundred.

Everything seemed to prosper with him. Mrs Simpson, instead of spoiling her fine eyes, and reducing by her secession his fair congregation of elected saints, which he had certainly good reason to fear, listened to his doctrine now with the same yielding obedience that she did before; and so far was the tongue of slander from finding anything amiss in the frequent pastoral visits he continued to pay her, that her credit, particularly with her tradespeople, stood higher than ever, and her begging-boxes, and her tract-selling, and her albums, flourished quite as well as when she believed that she and they would ere long be translated to the Vicarage.

Of Mrs Richards's converted daughters, little Mary was the only one who ventured openly to declare that she thought the vicar had behaved extremely ill; and after what she saw pass between him and sister Louisa, it was a sin before God and man not to marry her; and that she did not think poor Mrs Mowbray would ever be happy with a man who was so very much in love with another person.

But it was only little Mary who said all this, and nobody paid much attention to it. The pious Louisa herself declared, indeed, that there never had been anything but the purest evangelical love between them; and that the kiss about which silly Mary made such a fuss, was nothing in the world but a kiss of holy peace and brotherly love.

The same eloquence which persuaded the young lady so to think, or, at any rate, so to say, persuaded her likewise, and her sister Charlotte with her, to persevere in their evangelical avocations. They continued to compose tracts, to get them printed and sold when they could, and to read them aloud and give them away in manuscript when they could not. They also continued most perseveringly to expound both tracts and Scriptures for the edification of their very unhappy mother; who having passed the last twenty years of her life in exerting every faculty to render them happy around her, could not now so change her plan as to give them that portion of her house for the display of their inspired eloquence which she herself did not occupy – and thus she passed by far the greater portion of every day in listening to their ceaseless assurances that the pit of hell was yawning to receive her.

Major Dalrymple being present on one occasion when this was going on with peculiar fervour, waited very patiently till there was a pause in the eloquence of Miss Charlotte, who was holding forth, and then said Scotchly and quietly, 'Well, well, I see not but it is all very fair between you and your mother, my bonny lasses: she has been always forgetting herself for your sakes, and you are now forgetting yourselves for hers.'

It was not very long, however, after the marriage of the vicar, that a welcome and much-needed ray of hope once more gleamed upon her. It rose from the fair forehead of little Mary. From the time of her conversion, all her very pretty curls had been straightened and pushed behind her ears, and the little straw bonnet which covered them was the rival, or rather, the model of Fanny Mowbray's. But, by degrees, a few of these curls began to reappear round her face; her sad-coloured ribbons were exchanged for the bright tints that suited so well with her clear brown skin: her laughing eyes began to recover their brightness, and at last she whispered in her mother's ear,

'Forgive me, dearest mamma, for all my folly, my presumption. Forgive me, dearest mother; and pray God to forgive me too!'

From that moment, Mrs Richards felt restored to happiness. She had too early learnt that, at the best, life is but like a changeable web of silk, in which the dark tints predominate, to poison the enjoyment which Mary's return to reason brought her, by remembering at any moment when it was possible to forget it, that she had still two daughters who declared their persuasion that they could never meet her in the life to come. She wisely and with true piety turned all her thoughts to Mary, soothed her remorse, and reconciled her to herself. In addition to this great joy, she thought she saw the promise of another, that for years had formed her favourite castle in the air. She thought she saw that Major Dalrymple looked at the recovered Mary with eyes expressive of love as well as of joy; and with this hope before her, and the delightful occupation of watching Mary sometimes blush, and always smile when the major entered, her life once more ceased to be a burden, and Rosalind again found that she sang the very sweetest second in the world.

As soon as the occupation of receiving and returning the wedding visits was pretty well over, Mr Cartwright set about making some important alterations and reforms in the village of Wrexhill.

His attentive wife suggested to him, that he would find the fatigues of a large landed proprietor who so actively inquires into everything as he did, too much for his health and spirits, if he continued Vicar of Wrexhill. But to this he answered,

'God forbid, my lovely Clara, that I should ever suffer my cares for my earthly possessions to interfere with those especially relating to my heavenly ones! The cure of souls, my love, has ever been a favourite occupation with me. It greatly assists in giving one that sort of influence over the minds of one's fellow-creatures which every wise and holy man would wish to possess. But I have already secured the services of a very serious and exemplary curate, my dear love, who will relieve me from that part of the duty which, as you justly fear, might prove injurious to my health. This arrangement will, I trust, answer all your wishes for the present, sweet love; and in future I intend that our son Charles shall be my curate. He will, I have no doubt, like the Vicarage as a residence: it is really very pretty, and sufficiently near us to permit of easy, and, I should hope, frequent intercourse. But it must be a year or two before this can be put in practice; and, in the mean time, I trust that we shall find Mr Samuel Hetherington a pious and prayerful young man. I am not without hopes that he will arrive at the Vicarage to-night. I forget, dear, if I mentioned to you anything about him? – I certainly, as you observe, am very much occupied! – However, don't let me forget to say, that if he comes to-night, he must be invited to dine here to-morrow.'

Another of Mr Cartwright's new arrangements arose from a scene that passed between Mr Marsh, the quiet, peaceable, pains-taking village schoolmaster, and himself. This poor man, who had a wife and some half-dozen children, contrived to maintain them all by keeping school. He had a good house and extensive play-ground, which tempted many a tradesman in the county town, and some even in London, to send their sons to Wrexhill to improve at once their lungs and their learning. He had also a considerable number of day-boarders from all the farmers round, besides many of the most decent and well-born of the village children as day-scholars.

To keep up this flourishing concern certainly took up every hour of Mr Marsh's waking existence, and weary enough was he at night, poor man when he laid his head on his pillow. But no one had ever heard him complain. His wife and children were comfortably clothed, fed, and lodged; his '*parents*' were all well contented with the learning and the health of their children, and all his neighbours esteemed and spoke well of him.

Before Mr Cartwright had been many weeks at Wrexhill, he took an opportunity of making a very kind and condescending call upon the worthy schoolmaster. Mr Marsh happened at that moment to be superintending the afternoon writing-lessons; but he instantly obeyed the summons, and received the vicar in his best parlour with every demonstration of reverence.

'You have good premises here, Mr Marsh,' said the newly-installed clergyman of the parish; 'really a very decent and respectable-looking domain. How many boys have you, sir?'

'Twenty-seven boarders, twelve day-boarders, and sixteen day-scholars.'

'Indeed! – that makes a considerable number of Christian souls. And what, sir, may be the method and the principle of your religious instruction?'

'I take all my boarders, sir, to church twice every Sunday; and they read from the Bible twice a week. In addition to which, we have family prayer night and morning.'

'Then it is as I feared, Mr Marsh,' replied the vicar: 'you altogether neglect, both for your pupils and yourself, sir, my nine o'clock Sabbath evening lecture in the church, together with the Tuesday evening's expounding and the Thursday evening's church lecture. This is awful negligence, sir; it is a terrible tempting of the Lord!'

'I think, Mr Cartwright,' replied the poor schoolmaster, colouring, 'that I shall be able to explain to your satisfaction my reasons for not attending your evening lectures. Some of my boys, sir, are almost grown-up lads: I have two hard upon seventeen, and I need not tell a gentleman like you that there is a deal of caution necessary at that age to keep lads out of harm's way. I have had the character of sending home very good, sober, decent lads; and this, I think, has done me more service in getting scholars than even my writing and book-keeping. But perhaps you don't know, sir, and I am sure I don't wish to put myself forward to tell you – but the truth is, Mr Cartwright, that these late meetings, which break up quite in the dark, do bring together a great many disorderly people. 'Tis an excuse, sir, for every boy and girl that is in service to get out just when they ought to be at home, and altogether it is not quite the sort of thing I approve for my boys.'

'But when I tell you, Mr Marsh,' replied the vicar with much dignity, 'that it *is* the sort of thing which I approve, for all the girls and boys too who live under my ministry, I presume that you do not intend to persevere in your very futile, and I must call it, impious objection. If you, sir, paid the attention that you ought to do to the religous object of the meeting, your impure imagination would not be quite so busy about its moral consequences. I am sorry to tell you, Mr Marsh, that you are splitting on the rock which sends more wrecked and wretched souls to hell than any other peril of this mortal life, let it be what it may.'

'Well, sir,' replied the schoolmaster, mildly, 'I must make up my account between God and my own conscience, and trust to his mercy to overlook my deficiencies.'

'Overlook your deficiencies? – Poor deluded man! – Do you really hope that the Lord will pardon the clinging to works, and neglecting to hear His word? – Do you really doubt that Satan stands ready at the door to seize your soul, and bear it in his poisoned claws to everlasting torture? – Do you really doubt this, Mr Marsh?'

'Indeed, I do, sir!'

'This is terrible!' cried the vicar, starting up and attempting to stop his ears. 'Such blasphemy cannot be listened to without sin. I leave you, sir, and I will shake the dust of this your carpet from off my feet. But remember this, – I am your pastor and master, appointed to be the minister and guide of all the souls in my parish unto the presence of the Lord. As for your soul – I have no hope left for it: it must, and it will have its portion among the condemned of the Lord and of His saints, and will exist only to burn in unspeakable tortures for ever. – I have spoken, and you know your doom. But not so is it with the young persons committed to your charge; though, alas! the peril in which they now abide is sore to think of. Nevertheless, I will neither leave them nor forsake them as long as hope is left that a single brand can be snatched from the burning. Wherefore hear me! – This day is Thursday; let me this night see yourself, and every boy abiding in your house, in the gallery which you occupy in the church, or I will set to work to weed the vineyard of the Lord. Yea! I will cleanse it root and branch from the corruption and abomination of you and your boys. Poor wretches, that you are labouring and striving to prepare for the kingdom of hell! But I speak sinfully in joining you and them together! and may the Lord forgive me, as I will strive to atone for it. I will clear my vineyard – the Lord's vineyard, of you – but not till I have separated your boys from you. They shall be saved, – by my hand shall they be saved; and when I shall have effected this, you may perchance, while enjoying the leisure that will be your portion, remember this day, and value at its worth the wisdom which made you brave a minister of the evangelical church. Have I softened your hard heart, Mr Marsh? Will you bring your school to my lecture this evening? Say "Yes!" and you are forgiven of God and of me.'

'No, sir, I will not!' was the quiet but firm reply of the good man.

Not another syllable was spoken on either side; but well did the Vicar of Wrexhill keep his word. Public estimation and private good-will appeared for a time to resist all the efforts he could make to persuade the villagers, and the farmers round about, that Mr Marsh was a very impious and dangerous man, and one whom it was dangerous to trust with their children. They knew better; they knew that he was honest, pains-taking, intelligent, patient, and strictly attentive to his religious duties. But constant dropping will wear away a stone; and constant malevolence, kept in constant action, by one who was not very scrupulous as to the truth or falsehood of any statement that tended to produce the effect he wished, at length began, like rust upon steel, to cover and hide its true colour and its real brightness. One by one his daily scholars fell away from him, – one by one the neighbouring farmers came with some civil reason for not finding the sending their boys so likely to answer as formerly; and one by one his distant patrons found out the same thing: so that soon after the vicar's marriage, he had the great delight of hearing that Mr Marsh was sent to prison because he could not pay his rent, that his furniture was seized for taxes, and his tidy little wife lying ill of a brain fever at a small public-house near the prison, with her children starving round her.

The sort of inward chuckle with which the prosperous vicar received this bit of village gossip from his valet has no letters by which it can be spelt; – it was the hosannah of a fiend.

The supplying Mr Marsh's place in Wrexhill was one of the things that now demanded Mr Cartwright's immediate attention; and notwithstanding the many delicious temptations to idleness which surrounded him, his love of power, stronger even than his love of luxury, led him to hunt for and to find an individual to fill the situation, whose perfect obedience to his will made the dominion of the village school worth counting among the gratifying rights and immunities of his enviable position.

Many of the country families, partly from curiosity, and partly from respect for the owner of the Park, let him be who he would, paid their visits, and sent their invitations with an appearance of consideration very dear to his heart, particularly when it chanced that this consideration proceeded from persons blessed by bearing a title. As to his domestic circle, it went on rather better than he expected: if not a happy, it was a very quiet one. Helen drooped, it is true, and looked wofully pale; but she seldom complained at all, and if she did, he heard her not. Rosalind was very wretched; but a host of womanly feelings were at work within her to prevent its being guessed by any. Even Helen thought that she had a wondrous portion of philosophy so speedily to forget poor Charles, and so very soon to reconcile herself to the hateful dominion of the usurper who had seized his place. But Helen knew not how she passed the hours when no eye saw and no ear heard her. Neither did Helen know the terrible effort she had made to redeem the folly and the pride shown in her answer to Charles, the first and only time that he had ever ventured to disclose his love. Had Helen known this, and the manner in which this offer of herself had been refused, she would have loved, and not blamed the resolution with which the heart-stricken Rosalind hid her wound from every eye.

Fanny was gloomy, silent, and abstracted; but Mr Cartwright only thought that the poor girl, having been passionately in love with him, was suffering a few natural pangs while teaching herself to consider him as her father. But all this was so natural, so inevitable indeed, that he permitted it not to trouble him: and, in truth, he was so accustomed in the course of his ministry to win young ladies, and sometimes old ones too, from the ordinary ways of this wicked world, to his own particular path of righteousness, by means of a little propitiatory love-making, that the moans and groans which usually terminated this part of the process towards perfect holiness among the ladies had become to him a matter of great indifference. Notwithstanding his long practice in the study of the female heart, however, he did not quite interpret that of Fanny Mowbray rightly. He knew nothing of the depths and reality of fanatic enthusiasm into which he had plunged her young mind; nor could he guess how that pure, but now fettered spirit, would labour and struggle to reach some vantage-ground of assurance on which to rest itself, and thence offer its unmixed adoration to the throne of grace. He had no idea how constantly Fanny was thinking of heaven, when he was talking of it.

Of Henrietta he never thought much. She had given him some trouble, and he had used somewhat violent measures to bring her into such outward training as might not violently shock his adherents and disciples. But all this was now settled much to his satisfaction. She combed her hair quite straight, never wore pink ribands, and sat in church exactly as many hours as he commanded.

Mr Jacob was, as usual, his joy and his pride; and nothing he could do or say sufficed to raise a doubt in the mind of his admiring father of his being the most talented young man in Europe. That Jacob was not yet quite a saint, he was ready to allow; but so prodigiously brilliant an intellect could not be expected to fold its wings and settle itself at once in the temperate beatitude of saintship. He would come to it in time. It offered such inestimable advantages both in this world and the next, that Jacob, who had even now no objection to an easy chair, would be sure to discover the advantages of the calling.

The wife of his bosom was really everything he could wish a wife to be. She seemed to forget that there could be any other use for her ample revenue, than that of ministering to his convenience; and so complete was the devotion with which she seemed to lay herself and all that was hers at his feet, that no shadowy doubts or fears tormented him respecting that now first object of his life, the making her will.

But though thus assured of becoming her heir whenever it should please the Lord to recall her, he took care to omit nothing to render assurance doubly sure. Not a caress, not a look, not a tender word, but had this for its object; and when his 'dearest life' repaid him with a smile, and his 'loveliest Clara' rewarded him with a kiss, he saw in his mind's eye visions of exquisite engrossings, forming themselves day by day more clearly into – 'all my estates, real and personal, to my beloved husband.'

Thus, beyond contradiction, everything seemed to prosper with him; and few perhaps of those who gratified his vanity by becoming his guests, guessed how many aching hearts sat around his daily banquet.

CHAPTER XXXV

THE VICAR AT HOME

Spring succeeded to winter, and summer to spring, without producing any important change at Cartwright Park. Charles Mowbray requested and obtained permission to continue his studies without interruption, and for five months Helen and Rosalind lived upon his letters, which, spite of all his efforts to prevent it, showed a spirit so utterly depressed as to render them both miserable.

They seemed both of them to be converted into parts of that stately and sumptuous machine which Mr Cartwright had constructed around him, and of which he was himself the main spring. The number of servants was greatly increased, the equipages were much more splendid, and from an establishment remarkably simple and unostentatious for the income of its owners, the Park became one of the most magnificent in the country.

Among the periodical hospitalities with which the vicar, – for Mr Cartwright was still Vicar of Wrexhill, – among his periodical hospitalities was a weekly morning party, which opened by prayers read by his curate, and ended by a blessing pronounced by himself.

At about two o'clock a déjeûner à la fourchette was laid in the dining-room, around which were discussed all the serious and serio-political, and serio-literary subjects of the day. On this occasion the selection of company, though always pious, was not so aristocratical as at the pompous dinners occasionally given at the Park. But what was lost to vanity on one side by the unconspicuous rank of some of the guests, was gained to it on the other by the profound veneration for their host expressed in every word and in every look. Not only Mr Corbold, the lawyer, – who was indeed in some sort ennobled by his relationship to the great man himself, – but the new curate, and the new apothecary, and even the new schoolmaster, were admitted.

The company were always received by Mr Cartwright and his lady in the drawing-room, where all the family were expected (that is, commanded on pain of very heavy displeasure) to assemble round them. The tables were covered with bibles, tracts, Evangelical Magazines, sanctified drawings, and missionary begging machines.

Hardly could Chivers, who was become an example to all serious butlers in voice, in look, and in step, produce a more delightful sensation on his master's organs by announcing my Lord This, or my Lady That, than that master received from watching the reverential bows of the sycophants who hung upon his patronage. A sort of frozen blandishment on these occasions smoothed his proud face as he stood, with his lady beside him, to receive them. The tall, obsequious curate, who hardly dared to say his soul was his own, though he freely took upon himself to pronounce the destiny of other people's, bent before him, lower than mortal ever need bend to mortal; and he was rewarded for it by being permitted to aspire to the hand of the only daughter of Mr Cartwright, of Cartwright Park. The little round apothecary, who by evangelical aid withal had pushed out his predecessor as effortlessly as ever pellet did pellet in a pop-gun, sighed, whined, bought tracts, expounded them, kneeled down, though almost too fat to get up again, and would have done aught else that to a canting doctor's art belongs so that it were not physically impossible, for one sole object, which for some months past had hardly quitted his thoughts by day or night. This lofty object of ambition and of hope was the attending the lady of Mr Cartwright, of Cartwright Park, at her approaching accouchement.

The new schoolmaster, who was already making hundreds where his unprofessing predecessor made tens of pounds, was a huge, gaunt man, who had already buried three wives, and who had besides, as he hoped and believed, the advantage of being childless; – for he had always made it a custom to quarrel early with his sons and daughters, and send them to seek their fortune where they could find it; – this prosperous gentleman actually and bona fide fell in love with Miss Torrington; and having very tolerably good reasons for believing that there were few things at Cartwright Park which might not be won by slavish obedience and canting hypocrisy, he failed not to divide the hours during which he was weekly permitted an entrée there, between ogling the young lady, and worshipping the master of the mansion.

Poor Rosalind had found means, after her dreadful scene with Mowbray, secretly to convey a note to Sir Gilbert, informing him that she no longer wished to change her guardian; as her doing so would not, she feared, enable her to free Helen from her thraldom: she was still therefore Mrs Cartwright's ward, and the vicar had not yet quite abandoned the hope that his talented son might obtain her and her fortune; but hitherto Mr Jacob had declined making proposals, avowing that he did not think he was sufficiently advanced in the fair lady's good graces to be quite sure of success. So, as no avowed claim had been hitherto made to her hand, the schoolmaster went on ogling every Wednesday morning, and dreaming every Wednesday night, unchecked by any; for the fair object of his passion was perfectly unconscious of having inspired it.

Mrs Simpson, of course, never failed to embellish these morning meetings with her presence when she happened to be in the country; but she had lately left it, for the purpose, as it was understood, of making a visit of a month or two to a distant friend, during which she had intended to place her charming little Minima at a boarding-school in a neighbouring town; but Mr Cartwright so greatly admired that sweet child's early piety, that he recommended his lady to invite her to pass the period of her mamma's absence at Cartwright Park.

Then there were the Richards' family, who for various reasons were among the most constant Wednesday visitors. Mrs Richards came to see Rosalind, little Mary to whisper good counsel to her friend Fanny, and the two elder sisters to meet all the serious young men that the pompous vicar could collect round him from every village or town in the vicinity.

Besides these, there were many others, too numerous indeed to be permitted a place in these pages, who came from far and near to pray and to gossip, to eat and to drink, at Cartwright Park.

It happened at one of these meetings, about the middle of the month of June, when the beauty of the weather had brought together rather a larger party than usual, that a subject of great interest to the majority of the company was brought under discussion by Mr Cartwright.

No sooner had Mr Samuel Hetherington, his curate, finished his prayer, and such of the company risen from their knees as chose to come early enough to take part in that portion of the morning's arrangements, than the vicar opened the subject.

'My dear friends and neighbours,' he said, 'I have to communicate what I am sure will give you all pleasure: for are we not a society united in the Lord? Notwithstanding the little differences of station that may perhaps exist among us, have we not all one common object in view; namely, the glory of the Lord Jesus? It is for the furtherance of this divine object that I have now to mention to you a circumstance at which my soul and the soul of Mrs Cartwright rejoice, and at which I am fully persuaded that your souls will rejoice likewise.'

This preface produced a movement of lively interest throughout the whole room, and there was hardly a person present who did not eagerly undertake to answer for the sympathy of his or her soul with those of the vicar and his lady.

'Since we had the pleasure of seeing you last,' resumed the vicar, 'I have received a despatch from the secretary of the South Central African Bible Association, by which I learn that it is in contemplation to send out to Fababo a remarkably serious young Jew, recently converted, as missionary, and minister plenipotentiary in all spiritual affairs relative to the church about to be established for Fababo and its dependencies. But as you all well know that such a glorious enterprise as this cannot be undertaken without funds, and it has been requested of me, in the despatch to which I have alluded, that I should exert such little influence as I have among you, my dear friends and neighbours, for the collecting a sum in aid of it, our good Mrs Simpson's sweet little cherub Minima is furnished with a box, which she will carry round as soon as the collation is ended, to petition your generous contributions.'

A murmur of approbation, admiration, and almost of adoration, burst from the whole company, and the conversation immediately turned upon the conversion of Jews, and the happiness of having found so very desirable a mission for Mr Isaacs. While the enthusiasm was at its height, Mrs Cartwright, having previously received a hint from her husband, proposed that a serious fancy-fair should be held on that day month, on the lawn before the drawing-room windows of Cartwright Park, for assisting the outfit of Mr Isaacs.

'If all the ladies present,' continued Mrs Cartwright, 'and such of their friends as they can prevail upon to join them, will only occupy themselves during the ensuing month in the making of pincushions, the composition of tracts, the sketching some dozens of Saviour's and Apostles' heads, together with a few thousand allumettes and pen-wipers, we should, I have no doubt, collect a sum not only very serviceable to the exemplary Mr Isaacs, but highly honourable to ourselves.'

'Delightful!' cried several ladies at once.

'There is nothing,' said the little girlish wife of a neighbouring curate, 'that I dote upon like a fancy-fair; – a serious fancy-fair, of course I mean, my dear,' she added, colouring, as she caught the eye of her alarmed young husband fixed upon her.

'A serious fancy-fair for *such* an object,' observed Mr Cartwright, 'is indeed a charming spectacle. If the Lord favours us by granting a fine day, the whole of the ceremonies, – I mean, including the opening prayers, the exposition of some chapters in the Old and New Testaments bearing upon the subject, the reading a tract which I will direct my curate to compose for the occasion, and the final blessing: all this, I think, if the weather prove favourable, should be performed out of doors, as well as the sale of the ladies' works. This, I question not, will produce a very imposing effect, and will, I think, be likely to bring many persons who, by the blessing of the Lord upon our labours, may be induced to purchase. The elderly ladies will of course sell the articles; and the younger ones, whose piety will lead them to attend, may conceal themselves as much as possible from the public eye, by walking about in my groves and shrubberies, which shall be open for the occasion. It will be desirable, I imagine, to get handbills printed, to invite the attendance of the whole neighbourhood! Do you not think this will be advisable? I am sure that no one can avoid everything like general display and ostentation more cautiously than I do; but I conceive this public announcement on the present occasion absolutely necessary to the profitable success of our endeavours.'

'Absolutely!' was the word caught by echo for the reply.

'Have the goodness, Mr Hetherington, to sit down at that small table – you will there find all things needful for writing, and indite the handbill that will be necessary for us. There is a warmth of feeling by the Lord's especial providence at this blessed moment generated among us towards this holy work, which it would be sin to neglect. Let it not, like those good feelings and resolutions of which we have been told by the preacher, pass away from us to pave the courts of hell, and be trodden under the feet of the scorners who inhabit there. No, my brethren; let it rather rise like a sweet savour of incense to the nostrils of the Lord, to tell him that not in vain do we pronounce his name on earth!'

Before these words were all spoken, the assiduous curate was already seated, pen in hand, as nearly as possible in the attitude of Dominichino's St John, and looking up to Mr Cartwright for inspiration.

In truth, the vicar, though the dignity of a secretary was in some sort necessary to his happiness, would by no means have entrusted the sketching out of this document to any hand but his own. He felt it to be probable that it demanded his best attention. While Mr Hetherington therefore sat with his pen between his fingers, like a charged gun waiting for the pressure of the finger that should discharge it, Mr Cartwright, with the ready hand of a master, produced the following outline in pencil.

CARTWRIGHT PARK

On Wednesday, the 12th July, 1834,
will be held
a serious
FANCY FAIR,
on the lawn of the Revd Mr Cartwright's
Mansion,
at
Cartwright Park,
For the promotion of an object,
most precious
in the eyes of all
PROFESSING CHRISTIANS:
namely,

The fitting out a mission to Fababo, of which the Revd Isaac Isaacs is to be the head and chief; to him being entrusted the first formation of an organised Christian establishment for

FABABO

and its dependencies, together with the regulation of all adult and infant schools therein, and the superintendence of all the bible societies throughout the district.

LARGE FUNDS

being required for this very promising and useful mission, the ladies and gentlemen in the neighbourhood of CARTWRIGHT PARK are religiously requested to attend the SERIOUS FANCY-FAIR hereby announced, both as contributors and purchasers; whereby they will ensure the especial favour of Providence to themselves, and the blessings of religious and civil freedom, and the purest evangelical instruction, to unnumbered

THOUSANDS
yet unborn
of
the natives
of
FABABO.

N.B. – Collations will be served at three o'clock, in five of the principal saloons of Mr Cartwright's mansion. Prayers to be pronounced at one. Blessing (from the Reverend Mr Cartwright himself), at five.

The whole of the religious ceremonies to be performed in the open air.

This sketch, as the inspired author called it, having been read aloud and approved by acclamation, was delivered to the curate to copy; and as soon as this was completed, Mr Cartwright received it from him, and holding it aloft in his right hand, pronounced aloud, in a very solemn and impressive manner, these words:

'May this service, dedicated to the Lord, be found acceptable in his sight, and bring forth honour and glory to us and to him in the world to come and the life everlasting. Amen.'

This business happily completed, the religious amusements of the morning continued to go on as usual; – Mr Bateman, the anamoured schoolmaster, constantly sitting, standing, and moving, with his eyes fixed on Miss Torrington; and the despairing Corbold, whose six passionate proposals had been six times formally refused by Helen, reposing himself on a sofa in deep meditation on the ways and means by which he might so wheedle or work himself into the secrets of his magnificent cousin as to make it necessary for him to wink at any means by which he could get Helen into his power, and so oblige her to marry him.

At length the elegant banquet drew the company from their tracts and their talk to the dinner-parlour; and iced champagne refreshed the spirits of all, but particularly of those exhausted by the zealous warmth with which they had discussed the sinful adherence to good works so frightfully prevalent among the unregenerated clergy of the Church of England and Ireland. This was a theme upon which the majority of the company at the Cartwright Park meetings never wearied.

At length, the final blessing was pronounced, the party separated, and the tired family left to repose themselves as they best liked till the hour of dinner.

The increasing delicacy of Miss Cartwright's health, and Rosalind's drooping spirits, had prevented the intimacy between them from gaining ground so rapidly as they had, perhaps, both expected, when the families of the Park and Vicarage became blended into one. Yet it was evident that Rosalind was the only person to whom the pale Henrietta ever wished to speak, and equally so that Rosalind always listened to her with interest.

They were mounting the stairs together after the company were dispersed, when Henrietta said,

'Are you not wearied to death by all this, Miss Torrington? Oh, how you are changed since the time I told you that I had pleasure in looking at your face! It was then the brightest looking countenance I ever gazed upon: but now – to use the words of, I know not whom – all the sunshine is out of you.'

'It is a sorry compliment you pay me, my dear Henrietta; but I believe I am not quite the same sort of person I was then.' Tears started in her eyes as she spoke.

'I have overheard painful comparisons, Miss Torrington, between times past and present, and I am sorry for it. I really would not willingly add to the sorrow and suffering my race has brought upon you. Do not go and sit by yourself and weep till you are sick, as I have done many's the time and oft. Let us take a very slow ramble into that very thickest part of the Reverend Mr Cartwright's shrubbery, where the sun never enters – shall we? We are quite fine enough for such godly people, without any more dressing for dinner. So we can sit in the shade till the last bell rings.'

'I should like nothing so well,' replied Rosalind: and hastily skirting the sunny lawn, they took their stations on a seat which the morning sun visited as if on purpose to prevent its being dark and damp, but which for the rest of the twenty-four hours remained almost as cool as if there were no such globe in the heavens.

'We are growing very seriously gay, Rosalind, – are we not?' said Henrietta in a lighter tone than she usually indulged in. 'Fancy-fairs used to be the exclusive property of the worldlings; but it seems that we are now to come in for a share of their fraudulent charity, – and their vain benevolence: – not a bad pun that, Rosalind, if I had but intended to make one? But do tell me if you do not think Mr Cartwright has a magnificent taste?'

'Very – for a person who professes himself so given to the contemplation of things above the world. But, to tell you the truth, Henrietta, I am much less surprised at the vain-glorious manner in which he displays his newly-acquired riches, than at the continuance of his saintly professions. I expected that the Vicarage of Wrexhill would have been resigned, and all the world peaceably permitted to be just as wicked as they liked, without Mr Cartwright of Cartwright Park giving himself the least trouble concerning it.'

'You little know the nature of the clique to which he belongs. That they value pleasure fully as much as other men, is quite certain; that they struggle for riches with anxiety as acute, and hold it with a grasp as tight, as any human beings can do, it were equally impossible to doubt: but that POWER is dearer to them than either, is a truth well known to all who have sat within the conventicle, and watched its professors, as I have done.'

'But how can a man so addicted to self-indulgence, as it is evident Mr Cartwright is, endure the sort of trouble which the charge of a living must inevitably bring with it? – especially in the style so universally practised, I believe, by all serious ministers – that of interfering with the affairs of every individual in their parish.'

'It is that interference that makes the labour a joy. But you are not initiated, and cannot comprehend it. You do not, I am sure, conceive the delight of feeling, that not a man or woman – not a boy or girl in the parish either do, or leave undone, any single act of labour or of relaxation, without thinking whether Mr Cartwright would approve it. And then, the dependence of so many on him for their daily bread! – the curate, the clerk, the sexton, the beadle, – and the schoolmaster, and the schoolmaster's assistant, and the apothecary, and the attorney, and the undertaker, and – dozens of poor dependent simpletons besides, who, if, like poor Seymour's organ-grinder, they "knew the valley of peace and quiet," would run away to batten on the first moor they came to, rather than endure the slavery of living dependant upon the favour of an evangelical divine. Whatever it may be to them, however, depend upon it, that to him, and the like of him, this petty power, this minute tyranny of interference, is dearer than the breath of life; and that, much as Mr Cartwright loves his fair lady and all that belongs to her, he would think that all still dearly purchased, were he thereby to lose the right of entering every house in the parish, and unblushingly to ask them what they have done, are doing, and are about to do.'

The conversation then rambled on to all things connected with the fancy-fair and its object, till they had talked themselves tired; and then they sat silently watching the beautiful checker-work of light and shade which fell on the grass carpet before them, till the languid Henrietta, resting her head against a tree, fell fast asleep. Rosalind sat beside her for some minutes; but, growing weary of the extreme stillness necessary to guard her slumbers, she quietly withdrew herself, and wandered on under the trees.

Having left the sleeper for about half an hour, she turned to walk gently back again; but, fancying as she approached the spot that she heard the sound of a man's voice, she slanted off by another path, which took her close behind the seat occupied by Miss Cartwright, though a thick trimly-cut laurel hedge rendered it impossible for any one to see or be seen from the other.

The hedge, though a good one, had not however the same effect on sound as on sight, and Rosalind was not a little startled, as her soft footfall silently drew near the seat, to hear a very passionate declaration of love in the drawling voice of Mr Hetherington.

She stopped, by no means from any wish to hear more, but greatly embarrassed lest, her step being heard, she might appear to have stolen to this obscure spot for the express purpose of being a listener.

'Make me the happiest of men, adored Miss Cartwright!' reiterated the young man. 'Your father has permitted my addresses; then do not you, most charming Henrietta, refuse to listen to them!'

'It would not be for your happiness, sir,' replied the deep low voice of Henrietta, 'that I should do so.'

'Let me be the judge of that! Oh! if such a fear be all that parts us, we shall not, lovely Miss Cartwright! be long asunder,' replied the ardent Mr Hetherington.

'I know myself, sir' said Henrietta, 'far better than you can know me; and though we have not been long acquainted, your situation as curate of the parish enables me to know your sentiments and opinions better than you can know mine. I hear you preach twice every Sunday, Mr Hetherington, and I do assure you there is not a single question of importance on which we think alike.'

'Name them, sweet Henrietta! generously tell me wherein we differ, and trust me that it shall be the study of my life to bring my opinions into conformity with yours.'

'I heard you, in the middle of your sermon last Sunday, stop short to scold a little boy who had accidentally made a noise by letting his hat fall on the ground. You said to him, "Before next Sunday you may be brought into this church in your coffin." I saw the little fellow turn pale, yet you repeated the words. I really should not like to marry any one who could so terrify little boys, for he might perhaps think it right to terrify me also.'

'Never – oh, never again will I so offend you: and for yourself, beloved Miss Cartwright, what could I say to you but words of hope and joy?'

'Neither your joy nor your hope, Mr Hetherington, would do me much good, I am afraid. In one word, much as it will surprise you to hear it from my father's daughter, I am not evangelical, sir.'

'It is but a reason the more for my wishing to call you mine! If my opinions are unsound, you shall correct them.'

'I wish you would be persuaded, Mr Hetherington, to desist from this suit. I know that if my father has permitted it, I may find it become very troublesome to me, unless you have yourself the generosity to withdraw it; for my father does not brook contradiction.'

'Ask any proof of my obedience but this, and you shall find me a slave, having no will but that of my charming mistress; but to resign you while I enjoy the inestimable privilege of your illustrious father's sanction, it is impossible.'

'Then sir,' said Henrietta, in an altered voice that betokened strong emotion, 'if nothing less will save me from this persecution, I will disclose to you the great secret of my life; make of it what use you will. I am an Atheist.'

'Surely you cannot suppose, my beloved Miss Cartwright, that this confession can produce any effect upon my love, unless indeed it be to augment it. What noble frankness! what confiding trust! Believe me, there can be no difference of opinion between us on any subject sufficiently strong to conquer the tender and powerful passion you have inspired. Yield then to the soft violence which I know will be sanctioned by your respected father – let me thus——'

'Leave me, wretch!' exclaimed Henrietta in a voice that made Rosalind tremble. 'He may lock me up and half-starve me, for he has done it before to make me obey his will, and I have obeyed it, and hated myself for my cowardice; but I will not marry you, Mr Hetherington, even should he treat me worse than he has yet done – which would not be easy. Go, sir, go – I am an Atheist; but horrible as that sounds even to my own ears, it is better than to be what you have proved yourself.'

Rosalind, hardly less agitated than Henrietta appeared to be, stood trembling from head to foot in her retreat, till aware that the unscrupulous Mr Hetherington had retreated in one direction, and the unhappy Henrietta returned to the house by another.

CHAPTER XXXVI

A SECOND VISIT TO THE LIME TREE

Rosalind, as she walked slowly back towards the house, repeated to herself in shuddering the fearful words of Henrietta Cartwright – I AM AN ATHEIST, – and her very soul seemed sick and faint within her. She had sought in some degree the friendship of this unhappy girl, chiefly because it was evident that not even the connexion of father and daughter had sufficed to blind her to the hateful hypocrisy and unholy fanaticism of the vicar. Did, then, hatred and contempt for him lead to the hideous abyss of Atheism? She trembled as she asked herself the question; but the weakness lasted not a moment: the simple and true piety of her spirit awoke within her, and with kindly warmth cheered and revived her heart. That the unhappy Henrietta, when revolted by watching the false religion of her father, should have fled from it with such passionate vehemence as to plunge her into the extreme of scepticism, offered no precedent for what would be likely to befall a person who, like her, loathed the dark sin of hypocrisy, but who, unlike her, had learned the benignant truths of religion with no false and frightful commentaries to disfigure them.

As she remembered this – as she remembered that, probably, the only religious lessons ever given to this most unhappy girl were such as her judgment must revolt from, and the sincerity of her nature detest as false and feigned, pity and compassion took place of terror and repugnance, and a timid, but most earnest wish, that she might herself be the means of sending a ray of divine light to cheer the fearful gloom of poor Henrietta's mind, took possession of her heart.

The delightful glow of feeling that seemed to pervade every nerve of Rosalind as this thought took possession of her cannot be described. Tears again filled her beautiful eyes, but they were no longer the tears of disappointment and despondency; yet a dread of incurring the guilt of presumption, by assuming the office of teacher on a theme so awfully important, so sublimely exalted, mixed fear with her hope, and she determined to restrict her efforts wholly to the selection of such books as might tend to enlighten the dark night of that perverted mind, without producing in it the painful confusion of thought which must ever result from a loose and unlogical arrangement of proofs and arguments, however sound or however unquestionable they may individually be.

When she met Henrietta in the drawing-room, where all the family were assembled before dinner, she was conscious of being so full of thoughts concerning her, that she almost feared to encounter her eyes, lest her own might prematurely disclose her being acquainted with the scene she had gone through.

But the moment she heard Henrietta speak, the sound of her voice, so quiet, so cold, so perfectly composed, convinced her that the conversation which she had supposed must have agitated her so dreadfully, had in truth produced no effect on her whatever; and when, taking courage from this, she ventured to speak to, and look at her, the civil smile, the unaltered eye, the easy allusion to their walk and their separation, led her almost to doubt her senses as to the identity of the being now before her, and the one to whom she had listened in horror a short half-hour ago. This perplexity was, however, in a great measure relieved by an interpretation suggested by her fancy, and immediately and eagerly received by her as truth.

'It was in bitter irony, and shrewdly to test the sincerity of that man's assumed sanctity, that she uttered those terrible words,' thought Rosalind; and inexpressibly relieved by the supposition, she determined to take an early opportunity of confessing to Miss Cartwright her involuntary participation of Mr Hetherington's tender avowal, and of her own temporary credulity in believing for a moment that what was uttered, either to get rid of him or to prove the little worth of his pretended righteousness, was a serious avowal of her secret sentiments.

This opportunity was not long wanting; for, perfectly unconscious that Miss Torrington's motive for hovering near her was to seek a confidential conversation, a species of communication from which she always shrunk, – Henrietta, who really liked and admired her more than any person she had ever met with, readily seconded her wish, by again wandering into the garden-walks, on which the sun had just poured his parting beams, and where the full moon, rising at the same moment to take her turn of rule, shone with a splendour increasing every moment, and rendering the night more than a rival in beauty to the day.

'Let us go to the same seat we occupied this morning,' said Rosalind.

'No, no; go anywhere else, and I shall like it better. Let us go where we can see the moon rise, and watch her till she reaches her highest noon; – of all the toys of creation it is the prettiest.'

'Shall you be afraid to go as far as the lime-tree?' asked Rosalind.

'What! The tree of trees? the bower of paradise? – in short, the tree that you and I have once before visited together?'

'The same. There is no point from whence the rising moon is seen to such advantage.'

'Come along, then; let us each put on the armour of a good shawl, and steal away from this superlatively dull party by the hall-door.'

The two girls walked on together arm-in-arm, both clad in white, both raising a fair young face to the clear heavens, both rejoicing in the sweet breath of evening, heavy with dew-distilling odours. Yet, thus alike, the wide earth is not ample enough to serve as a type whereby to measure the distance that severed them. The adoration, the joy, the hope of Rosalind, as her thoughts rose 'from Nature up to Nature's God,' beamed from her full eye; thankfulness and love swelled her young heart, and every thought and every feeling was a hymn of praise.

Henrietta, as she walked beside her, though sharing Nature's banquet so lavishly prepared for every sense, like a thankless guest, bestowed no thought upon the hand that gave it. Cold, dark, and comfortless was the spirit within her; she saw that all was beautiful, but remembered not that all was good, – and the thankless heart heaved with no throb of worship to the eternal God who made the lovely world, and then made her to use it.

Notwithstanding the interpretation, which Rosalind had put upon the words spoken by Henrietta in the morning, and the consolation she had drawn from it, it was not without considerable agitation that she anticipated the conversation she was meditating. 'If she were mistaken? – if beneath that pure sky, from whence the eye of God seemed to look down upon them, she were again to hear the same terrific words – how should she answer them? How should she find breath, and strength, and thought, and language, to speak on such a theme?'

She trembled at her own temerity as this fear pressed upon her, and inwardly prayed in most true and sweet humility for God's forgiveness for her presumptuous sin. A prayer so offered never fails of leaving in the breast it springs from a cheering glow, that seems like an assurance of its being heard. Like that science-taught air, which blazes as it exhales itself, prayer – simple, sincere, unostentatious prayer, sheds light and warmth upon the soul that breathes it, even by the act of breathing.

They had, however, reached the seat beneath the lime-tree before Rosalind found courage to begin: and then she said, as they seated themselves beneath the spreading canopy,

'Miss Cartwright, – I have a confession to make to you.'

'To me? – Pray what is it? To judge by the place you have chosen for your confessional, it should be something rather solemn and majestical.'

'Do you remember that I left you on the shrubbery seat this morning fast asleep?'

'Oh! perfectly. – You mean, then, to confess that the doing so was unwatchful and unfriendly: and indeed I think it was. How did you know but I might be awakened by some venomous reptile that should come to sting me?'

'Believe me, I thought the place secure from interruption of every kind. But I had reason to think afterwards that it did not prove so.'

'What do you mean, Miss Torrington?' replied Henrietta in an accent of some asperity. 'I presume you did not creep away for the purpose of spying at me from a distance?'

'Oh no! – You cannot, I am sure, suspect me of wishing to spy at you at all. And yet things have so fallen out, that when I tell you all, you must suspect me of it – unless you believe me, as I trust you do, incapable of such an action.'

'Pray do not speak in riddles,' said Henrietta impatiently. 'What is it you have got to confess to me? Tell me at once, Miss Torrington.'

'You really do not encourage me to be very frank with you, for you seem angry already. But the truth is, Miss Cartwright, that I did most unintentionally overhear your conversation with Mr Hetherington.'

'The whole of it? – Did you hear the whole of it, Rosalind?'

'Not quite. The gentleman appeared to be in the midst of his declaration when my unwilling ears became his confidants.'

'And then you listened to the end?'

'I did.'

A deathlike silence followed this avowal, which was at last broken by Henrietta, who said in a low whisper,

'Then at last you know me!'

'Oh! do not say so; – do not say that the fearful words that I heard were spoken in earnest! – Do not say that; – I cannot bear to hear it!'

'Poor girl! – poor Rosalind!' said Henrietta in a voice of the deepest melancholy. 'I have always wished to spare you this – I have always wished to spare myself the pain of reading abhorrence in the eyes of one that I do believe I could have loved, had not my heart been dead.'

'But if you feel thus, Henrietta, – if indeed you know that such words as I heard you utter must raise abhorrence, – it is because that you yourself must hate them. I know you are unhappy – I know that your nature scorns the faults that are but too conspicuous in your father; but is it not beneath a mind of such power as yours to think there is no God in heaven, because one weak and wicked man has worshipped him amiss?'

'He worship! – Trust me, Rosalind, had I been the child of a Persian, and seen him in spirit and in truth worshipping the broad sun as it looked down from heaven upon earth, making its fragrant dews rise up to him in incense, I should not have been the wretched thing I am, – for I should have worshipped too,'

'Henrietta! – If to behold the Maker of the universe, and the Redeemer whom he sent to teach his law – if to see worship offered to their eternal throne could teach you to worship too, then look around you. Look at the poor in heart, the humble, pious Christians who, instead of uttering the horrible doom of eternal damnation upon their fellow-men, live and die in the delightful hope that all shall one day meet in the presence of their God and Father, chastised, purified, and pleading to his everlasting mercy, with the promised aid of his begotten Son, for pardon and for peace. – Look out for this, Henrietta, and you will find it. Find it, and your heart will be softened, and you will share the healing balm that makes all the sorrow and suffering of this life seem but as the too close fitting of a heavy garment that galls but for an hour!'

'Dear, innocent Rosalind! – How pure and beautiful your face looks in the bright moonlight! – But, alas! I know that very sinful faces may look just as fair. There is no truth to rest on. In the whole wide world, Rosalind, there is not honesty enough whereon to set a foot, that one may look around and believe, at least, that what one sees, one sees. But this is a perfection of holiness – a species of palpable and present divinity, that is only granted to mortals in their multiplication tables. – Twice two are four – I feel sure of it, – but my faith goes no farther.'

'I cannot talk to you,' cried Rosalind in great agitation; 'I am not capable of doing justice to this portentous theme, on which hangs the eternal life of all the men that have been, are, and shall be. It is profane in me to speak of it, – a child – a worm. Father of mercy, forgive me!' she cried, suddenly dropping upon her knees.

Henrietta uttered a cry which almost amounted to a shriek. 'I had almost listened to you!' she exclaimed, – 'I had almost believed that your voice was the voice of truth; but now you put yourself in that hateful posture, and what can I think of you, but that you are all alike – all juggling – all! The best of ye juggle yourselves, – the worst do as we saw Mr Cartwright do; – on that very spot, Rosalind, beneath the shelter of that very tree, did he not too knuckle down? and for what? – to lure and cajole a free and innocent spirit to be as false and foul as himself! Yet this is the best trick of which you can bethink you to teach the sceptical Henrietta that there is a God.'

'Truth, Henrietta,' said Rosalind, rising up and speaking in a tone that indicated more contempt than anger, – 'neither truth nor falsehood can be tested by a posture of the body. It is but a childish cavil. The stupendous question, whether this world and all the wonders it contains be the work of chance, or of unlimited power and goodness, conceiving, arranging, and governing the whole, can hardly depend for its solution upon the angle in which the joints are bent. You have read much, Miss Cartwright, – read one little passage more, which I think may have escaped you. Read the short and simple instructions given by Jesus Christ as to the manner in which prayer should be offered unto God – read this passage of some dozen lines, and I think you will allow that in following these instructions, greatly as they have been misconstrued and abused, there is nothing that can justify the vehement indignation which you express.'

Poor Henrietta shrunk more abashed before this simple word of common sense, than she would have done before the revealed word of God. Rosalind saw this, and pointed out the anomaly to her, simply, but strongly.

'Does it not show a mind diseased?' she continued. 'You feel that you were wrong to make an attitude a matter of importance, and you are ashamed of it: but from the question, whether you shall exist in pure and intellectual beatitude through countless ages, or perish to-morrow, you turn with contempt, as too trifling and puerile to merit your attention.'

'If I do turn from it, Rosalind, – if I do think the examination of such a question a puerile occupation, – it is in the same spirit that I should decline to share the employment of a child who would set about counting the stars. Such knowledge is too excellent for me; I cannot attain unto it.'

'Your illustration would be more correct, Henrietta, were you to say that you shut your eyes and would not see the stars, upon the same principle that you declined inquiring into the future hopes of man. It would be quite as reasonable to refuse to look at the stars because you cannot count them, as to close your eyes upon the book of life because it tells of intellectual power beyond your own. – But this is all contrary to my resolution, Henrietta, – contrary to all my hopes for your future happiness. Do not listen to me; do not hang a chance dearer than life upon the crude reasonings of an untaught woman. Will you read, Henrietta? – if I will find you books and put them in your hands, will you read them, and keep your judgment free and clear from any foregone conclusion that every word that speaks of the existence and providence of God must be a falsehood? Will you promise me this?'

'Let us go home, Rosalind; my head is giddy and my heart is sick. I had hoped never again to fever my aching brain in attempting to sift the truth from all the lies that may and must surround it. I have made my choice deliberately, Rosalind. I have never seen sin and wickedness flourish anywhere so rapidly and so vigorously as where it has been decked in the masquerading trappings of religion. I hate sin, Rosalind, and I have thrown aside for ever the hateful garb in which I have been used to see it clothed. If there be a God, can I stand guilty before his eyes for this?'

'Oh yes! most guilty! If you have found hypocrisy and sin, turn from it with all the loathing that you will; and be very sure, let it wear what mask it will, that religion is not there. Look then elsewhere for it. Be not frightened by a bugbear, a phantom, from seeking what it is so precious to find! Dearest Henrietta! will you not listen to me? – will you not promise for a while to turn your thoughts from every lighter thing, till you are able to form a surer judgment upon this?'

'Dearest? – Do you call me dear, and dearest, Rosalind? Know you that I have lived in almost abject terror lest you should discover the condition of my mind? I thought you would hate and shun me. – Rosalind Torrington! you are a beautiful specimen, and a very rare one. To please you, and to approach you if I could, I would read much, and think and reason more, and try to hope again, as I did once until I was stretched upon the torturing rack of fear: but there is no time left me!'

'Do not say that, dear friend,' said Rosalind, gently drawing Henrietta's cold and trembling arm within her own. 'You are still so young, that time is left for harder studies than any I propose to you.'

'I am dying, Rosalind. I have told you so before, but you cannot believe me because I move about and send for no doctor – but I am dying.'

'And if I could believe it, Henrietta, would not that be the greatest cause of all for this healing study that I want to give you?'

'Perhaps so, Rosalind; but my mind, my intellect, is weak and wayward. If there be a possibility that I should ever again turn my eyes to seek for light where I have long believed that all was darkness, it must be even when and where my sickly fancy wills. – Here let the subject drop between us. Perhaps, sweet girl! I dread as much the chance of my perverting you, as you can hope to convert me.'

Rosalind was uttering a protest against this idle fear, when Henrietta stopped her by again saying, and very earnestly, 'Let the subject drop between us; lay the books you speak of in my room, where I can find them, but let us speak no more.'

Satisfied, fully satisfied with this permission, Rosalind determined to obey her injunction scrupulously, and silently pressing her arm in testimony of her acquiescence, they returned to the house without uttering another word.

CHAPTER XXXVII

THE WILL

It was about this time that Mr Cartwright, for reasons which will be sufficiently evident in the sequel, set about convincing his wife that there was a very pressing necessity, from motives both temporal and spiritual, that her son Charles should be immediately ordained. There are many ways of convincing a woman and a wife besides beating – and Mr Cartwright employed them all by turns, till his lady, like a bit of plastic dough, took exactly the impression he chose to give, – as evanescent too as it was deep, for he could make her act on Monday in direct opposition to the principles he had laid down on Saturday, yet leave her persuaded all the while that he was the wisest and best, as well as the most enamoured of men.

But though living with the wife of his bosom in the most delightful harmony, and opening his heart to her with the most engaging frankness on a thousand little trifling concerns that a less tender husband might never have thought it necessary to mention, Mr Cartwright nevertheless did not deem it expedient to trouble her with the perusal of his letter to Charles on the subject of his immediate ordination.

The especial object of this letter was to obtain a decided refusal to the command it contained, and, like most of the Vicar of Wrexhill's plans, it answered completely. Mowbray's reply contained only these words:

'Sir,

'Though all my hopes for this life have been blighted through your agency, I will not risk my happiness in that which is to come by

impiously taking upon me the office of God's minister, for which I am in
no way prepared.

'CHARLES MOWBRAY.'

As soon as this letter was received, read, and committed to the flames,
Mr Cartwright repaired to the dressing-room of his lady, where, as usual,
he found her reposing on the sofa; a little table beside her loaded with
tracts and other evangelical publications, and in her hand a small bit of
very delicate embroidery, which was in time to take the form of a baby's
cap.

'My sweet love! how have you been since breakfast? Oh! my Clara!
how that occupation touches my heart! But take care of your precious
health, my angel! My life is now bound up with yours, sweet! ten-
thousand times more closely than it ever was before: and not mine only, –
the life of the dear unborn being so inexpressibly dear to us both.
Remember this, my lovely wife!'

'Oh, Cartwright! – your tender affection makes me the happiest of
women. Never, surely, was there a husband who continued so completely
a lover! Were my children but one half as sensible of their happiness in
having you for a father as I am in calling you my husband, I should have
nothing left to wish!'

'Turn not your thoughts that way, my Clara! – it is there that it hath
pleased the Lord to visit us with very sore affliction. But our duty is to
remember his mercies alway, and so to meet and wrestle with the
difficulties which he hath for his own glory permitted the Evil One to
scatter in our path, that in the end we may overcome them. Then shall
we by the heel crush the head of the serpent, and so shall his mercy upon
his chosen servants shine out and appear with exceeding splendour and
with lasting joy!'

'God prosper your endeavours, my dear Cartwright, to bring the same
to good effect! How I wish that Helen would make up her mind at once
to marry Mr Corbold! I am sure that, with your remarkably generous
feelings, you would not object to giving her immediately a very
handsome fortune if she would comply with our wishes in this respect.
Mr Corbold told me yesterday that he had every reason to believe she
was passionately attached to him, but that her brother had made her
promise to refuse. This interference of Charles is really unpardonable! I
do not scruple to say, that in my situation it would be infinitely more
agreeable to me if Helen were married, – we could give Miss Torrington
leave to live with her, dear Cartwright, – and I am quite sure the change
would be for the happiness of us all.'

'Unquestionably it would, my love; – but this unfortunate boy! Alas,
my Clara! I have just received fresh proof of the rebellious spirit that

mocks at all authority, and hates the hand that would use it. I have this morning received such a letter from him, in answer to that in which I expressed my wish that he should adopt a profession and prepare to settle himself in life, as wrung my heart. It shall never blast your eyes, my Clara! I watched it consume and burn, and turn to harmless ashes, before I came to cheer and heal my wounded heart by pressing thee to it!'

The action answered to the word, – and it was from the bosom of her fond husband that Mrs Cartwright murmured her inquiries as to what her unworthy son had now done to pain the best of fathers.

'Not only refused, dearest, to adopt the sacred and saving profession we have chosen for him with the most ribald insolence, but addressed me in words of such bitter scorn, that not for worlds would I have suffered thy dear eyes to rest upon them.'

'Is it possible! What then, dear Cartwright, will it be best for us to do? It is terrible to leave him to his own wilful desire, and suffer him to enter the army, when we know it will lead him to inevitable perdition! What can we do to save him?'

'It appears to me, my sweet love, that at the present moment it will be most consonant to the will of the Lord to use towards him the most indulgent gentleness.'

'My dearest Cartwright! After such conduct on his part! Oh! you are too good!'

'Sweetest! he is your son. I can never forget that: though I fear that he himself does not too well remember this. If he did, my Clara! he would hardly utter such bitter jestings on what he is so cruel as to call "my beggarly dependence" on you. This phrase has cut me to the heart's core, I will not deny it, Clara: it has made me feel my position and shudder at it.'

Mr Cartwright here rose from the sofa, and putting his handkerchief to his eyes, walked towards the window: his breast heaved with audible sobs.

'My beloved Cartwright, what mean you?' exclaimed his affectionate wife, following him to the window, and gently attempting to withdraw the cambric that concealed his features: 'what can that undutiful boy mean? Your dependence upon me? Good Heaven! is there anything that was ever mine that is not now your own?'

'Alas! dear love, he has not launched a random shot, – he knows but too well how to take aim, and how to point his dart, – and it has done its work.'

This was spoken in a tone of such profound sadness, that the soul of Mrs Cartwright was moved by it. She threw her arms around her husband's neck, and fondly kissing him, implored that he would tell her if there were anything she could do to prove her love, and place him in a situation *at once* to render the repetition of such a hateful phrase impossible.

'I thought,' she continued, 'that your being my husband, dearest Cartwright, gave you a right to all I possess. – Is it not so, my love?'

'To your income, dearest Clara, during your life; and as you are several years my junior, sweetest! this, as far as my wants and wishes are concerned, is quite enough. But the young man has doubtless found some wily lawyer to inform him, that should you die intestate he would be your heir; as by your late husband's will, my love, though he has left everything to you, should you not make a will every shilling of the property will go to him, whatever other children you have now, or may have hereafter.'

'Oh, Cartwright! why did you not tell me this before! Should any thing happen to me in the hour of danger that is approaching, think what a dreadful injustice would be done to all! Let me not delay another day, – do send for Mr Corbold, – I cannot rest till all this is set right. My dear unborn babe, as well as its beloved father, may reproach me for this cruel carelessness.'

'Compose yourself, sweet Clara! I *will* send for Corbold without delay. But for God's sake do not agitate your dear spirits! – it was the fear of this which has alone prevented me from reminding you of the interest of our dear unborn babe.'

'And your own, my dear generous husband! Do you doubt, dear Cartwright, that the father's interest is as dear to me, as the child's?'

A tender caress answered this question. But delay in matters of business was not the besetting sin of Mr Cartwright; and while the embrace yet lasted, he stretched his arm to the bell. The summons was answered, and the cab despatched for the lawyer with a celerity that did much credit to the establishment.

When Mr Corbold arrived, he was received by his cousin in the library, which, in conformity to the resolution announced long ago to Charles Mowbray, was preserved religiously for his own use and comfort; and a few minutes' short but pithy conversation sufficed to put the serious attorney *au fait* of what was expected of him.

'You know, cousin Stephen,' said the Vicar of Wrexhill, 'that the Lord is about to bless my house with increase; and it is partly on this account, and partly for the purpose of making a suitable provision for me in case of her death, – which may the Lord long delay!'

'I am sure, cousin Cartwright, there is no work that I could set about with greater readiness and pleasure. Shall I receive my instructions from you, cousin, at this present time?' and the zealous Mr Corbold accompanied the question by an action very germain to it, – namely, the pulling forth from a long breast-pocket a technically-arranged portion of draught-paper tied round with red tape.

'By no means, cousin Stephen,' replied the Vicar of Wrexhill; 'it is from my beloved wife herself that I wish you to receive your instructions. Of course, what you do to-day can only be preparatory to the engrossing it on parchment: and though, from delicacy, I will not be present during your interview with her, yet before the document be finally signed, sealed, and delivered, I shall naturally wish to glance my eye over it. There is no longer, therefore, any occasion to delay; come, with me, cousin Stephen, to my dear wife's dressing-room; and may the Lord bless to you and to me the fruits of this day's labour!'

The master of the house then proceeded the serious but admiring attorney through the stately hall, and up the stately staircase, and into the beautiful little apartment where Mrs Cartwright, with a very pensive expression of countenance, sat ready to receive them.

'Oh! Mr Corbold,' she said, kindly extending her hand to him, 'I am very glad to see you. But my joy is dashed with remorse when I remember the thoughtless folly with which I have so long delayed this necessary interview. – My dearest Cartwright,' she continued, turning to her husband, 'can you forgive me for this? – Perhaps, dearest, you can, – for your soul is all generosity. But I shall never forgive myself. My only excuse rests in my ignorance. I believed that the law gave, as I am sure it ought to do, and as in fact it did in the case of my first marriage, everything that belongs to me to my husband. It is true that I only brought my first husband about three hundred thousand pounds in money, and most of it has been since very profitably converted into land. Perhaps, Mr Corbold, it is this which makes the difference.'

Mr Corbold assured her that she was perfectly right, not considering himself as called upon at the present moment to allude to the accident of her having children.

'Now then, my beloved Clara, I leave you,' said Mr Cartwright. 'Not for worlds would I suffer my presence to influence you, even by a look, in the disposition of property so entirely your own!'

'This generous delicacy, my beloved husband, is worthy of you. I shall, I own, prefer being left alone on this occasion with our pious kinsman and friend.'

The vicar kissed his lady's delicate fingers and departed.

'The Lord has been exceeding gracious to me, Mr Corbold. It must be seldom, I fear, that in your profession you meet with so high-minded and exemplary a character as that of your cousin. Ah, my dear sir! how can I be thankful enough for so great mercy!'

'The Lord hath rewarded his handmaiden,' replied the serious attorney. 'You have deserved happiness, excellent lady, – and you have it.'

Corbold now again pulled out his draught-paper, and with an air of much deference, placed himself opposite to Mrs Cartwright.

'I presume you have ink and pens at hand, my honoured lady?'

'Take my keys, Mr Corbold; – in that desk you will find everything you want for writing; and in the drawer of it is the copy of my late husband's will. It is this that I mean to make the model of my own. He set me an example of generous confidence, Mr Corbold, and I cannot, I think, do better than follow it.'

Mrs Cartwright drew the desk towards her, and from the drawer of it took the instrument which had made her mistress, not only of all the property she had originally brought her husband, but also of an estate which had come to him after his marriage.

'This deed, sir,' she said, putting the parchment in Mr Corbold's hands, 'will, I hope, supersede the necessity of instructions from me. I am a very poor lawyer, Mr Corbold, and I think it very probable that were you to write after my dictation, my will might turn out to be something very different from what I wish to make it. But if you take this as your model, it cannot fail to be right, as by this instrument I have been made to stand exactly in the position in which I now wish to place my exemplary husband Mr Cartwright.'

'If such be your wish, dearest lady,' said the attorney, 'I will, with your permission, take this parchment with me; and by so doing I shall not only avoid the necessity of troubling you, but, by the blessing of the Lord upon my humble endeavours, I shall be enabled accurately to prepare precisely such a document as it appears to be your wish to sign. In these matters no instructions can make us such plain sailing, my dear madam, as the having a satisfactory precedent in our hands. – Ah! dearest lady! when I witness the conjugal happiness of yourself and my ever-to-be-respected cousin, my heart sinks within me, as I remember that equal felicity would be my own, were it not for the cruel interference of one to whom I have never done an injury, and for whom I would willingly show, if he let me, all a brother's love.'

'Keep up your spirits, my good cousin!' replied the lady. 'If Helen favours your suit, – and on this point you must be a better judge than I, – Charles's opposition will not long avail to impede your union.'

The lover sighed, raised his eyes to heaven, and probably, not very well knowing what to say, departed without replying a word.

As he reached the bottom of the stairs, he perceived his cousin standing within the door of his library, which he held ajar. He put out his hand and beckoned him in.

'You have made quick work of it, cousin Stephen,' said the anxious vicar. 'I trust you have not hurried away without fully understanding my dear wife's wishes. I ask no questions, cousin Corbold, and do not, I beseech you, imagine that I wish you to betray any trust; – merely tell me if my dear Mrs Cartwright appears to be easier in her mind now that she has disclosed her intentions to you.'

The best and soberest minded men are sometimes assailed by temptation; of which painful fact Mr Stephen Corbold at that moment became proof. Some merry devil prompted him to affect the belief that his reverend cousin was in earnest, and, putting on a sanctified look of decorum, he replied,

'Of course, cousin Cartwright, I know you too well to believe that you would wish to meddle or make with such an instrument as this. When your excellent and, I doubt not, well-intentioned lady shall be defunct, you will in the course of law be made acquainted with her will. I rejoice to tell you that her mind seems now to be perfectly unburdened and clear from all worldly anxieties whatever.'

As the attorney ended these words, he raised his eyes, which were fixed as he spoke upon the roll of parchment which he held in his hand, and caught, fixed full upon him, such a broadside of rage from the large and really very expressive eyes of his cousin, that he actually trembled from top to toe, and heartily repenting him of the temerity which led him to hazard so dangerous a jest, he quietly sat down at a table, and spreading open the parchment upon it, added,

'But although it would be altogether foreign to your noble nature, cousin Cartwright, to express, or indeed to feel anything like curiosity on the subject, it would be equally foreign to mine not to open my heart to you with all the frankness that our near kindred demands. Do not then refuse, dear cousin, to share with me the pleasure I feel in knowing that the Lord has taken care of his own! The only instruction I have received from your pious and exemplary wife, cousin Cartwright, was to draw her will exactly on the model of this, which, as you may perceive, is a copy of the one under which she herself was put into possession of the splendid fortune of which, by the especial providence of the Lord, you have already the control, and of which, should it please the merciful Disposer of all things so to order it that this lady, really fitter for heaven than earth, should be taken to Abraham's bosom before you, you will become the sole owner and possessor, you and your heirs for ever, world without end. Amen.'

Mr Cartwright had in general great command over himself, rarely betraying any feeling which he wished to conceal. Perhaps even the anger which gleamed in his eye a few moments before, and which had now given place to a placidity that would by every serious lady in England have been denominated 'heavenly,' – perhaps even this, though it seemed to dart forth involuntarily, was in truth permitted to appear, as being a more safe and desirable mode of obtaining his object than the collaring his cousin and saying, 'Refuse to let me see that paper, and I murder you!'

But no object was now to be obtained by permitting his looks to express his feelings; and therefore, though he felt his heart spring within him in a spasm of joy and triumph, he looked as quiet and unmoved as if nothing extraordinary had happened.

'It is very well, cousin Stephen,' he said, 'make not any unnecessary delay in the preparing of this deed. Life is very uncertain: the Lord giveth, and the Lord taketh away; and moreover, the time is known to no man. Wherefore, let this thing be done immediately.'

'Could I see Miss Helen for a moment alone, if I got this completed, signed, sealed, and delivered by to-morrow night?' said the attorney.

'Yes, my good cousin, yes; I pledge you my word for it.'

In justice to the character of the unfortunate Mrs Mowbray, it is but fair to remark, that notwithstanding the ceaseless process by which, from the very first hour of their acquaintance, the Vicar of Wrexhill had sought to estrange her from her children, he never ceased to speak of Charles as her undoubted heir, and of Helen and Fanny as young ladies of large fortune. The lamentable infatuation, therefore, which induced her to put everything in his power, went not the length of intending to leave her children destitute; though it led her very sincerely to believe that the power thus weakly given would be properly, – and, as she would have said, poor woman! 'religiously' exercised for their advantage.

CHAPTER XXXVIII

THE LETTER-BAG

Among the many highly-valued comforts and privileges which Mr Cartwright's exclusive possession of the library afforded him, that of receiving in solitary state – and privacy, the family letter-bag, was not the one least valued.

It may, I believe, be laid down as a pretty general rule, that those persons who conceive, or profess it to be their duty, to dive into the hearts and consciences of their fellow-creatures, and to regulate the very thoughts and feelings of all the unfortunate people within their reach, are not very scrupulous as to the methods used to obtain that *inward* knowledge. Mr Cartwright, according to the usual custom of evangelical divines, had his village matron, ostensibly only a merchant of apples, gingerbread, and lollypops, but entrusted with as many secret missions of inquiry as the most jealous pontiff ever committed to a faithful and favoured nuncio on quitting the gates of Rome. She could tell, and was not ill paid for that precious knowledge, how often Betty Jackson went to buy baccy; and how many times in the day Sally Wright looked over her shoulder at the passers-by while walking out with her master's children; and how many pots of porter were carried to one house, and how many times the ladies walked forth from another; besides innumerable other facts and anecdotes, which, though apparently not of sufficient importance to record, were nevertheless of great value to the vicar and to his curate, as themes to lecture upon in private, and preach upon in public.

Sources of information such as these had never been overlooked or neglected by Mr Cartwright at any period of his ministry; but hitherto he had held them to be important rather to the general welfare of the Christian world than to his own family: no sooner, however, did he find himself placed in the responsible position of master of a large household, than, besides taking the butler into a sort of evangelical partnership for the discovery of petty offences, and having moreover an elected stable-boy, who made a daily report of all that he saw and heard, and a little more, he determined that all letters addressed to any member of the family should pass through his hand; and in like manner, that all those put into the letter-box in the hall, of which he kept the key himself, should be submitted to the same species of religious examination before they were deposited in the post-bag.

In the execution of this part of his duty Mr Cartwright displayed, to himself at least, considerable mechanical skill – for the letters were excellently well re-sealed – and likewise great equanimity of temper; for, scanty as the family correspondence proved to be, he chanced to fall upon some few passages which might have shaken the philosophy of a mind less admirably regulated.

In former times, if any Mowbray had wished to send a note from the Park to the village, a groom or a groom's helper would have taken it: but, now, though the establishment was greatly increased, there was no such privilege allowed them; and in order to escape the ceremony of asking permission to employ a servant they all resorted to the post-bag.

One of the letters thus sent and thus examined was from little Mary Richards to her friend Fanny; and many more important documents had passed through his hands without exciting an equal degree of emotion. It ran thus:

'I cannot express to you, my dearest Fanny, how anxious I feel to open my whole heart to you on a subject that has long occupied us both with, I believe, equal depth and sincerity of interest; – I mean, as I am sure you will instantly anticipate, that inward call to especial grace and favour in the sight of God which Mr Cartwright taught us to expect would be the sure and certain consequence of unbounded faith in *himself*; for so only can we interpret the language he used to us. If I were to live a thousand years, dear Fanny, I should never cease to regret the dreadful, but, I thank God, brief interval, during which I firmly believed that I had received this call. While this frightful and most presumptuous notion had possession of me, I looked upon my dear and excellent mother – ay, and, to my bitter sorrow, treated her too, as a being almost unworthy of communion with me! Is not this of itself enough to prove the unholy tendency of the doctrine? Now that the madness is passed, I look back upon it with as much astonishment as sorrow; and can so clearly trace in it the workings of the most paltry vanity and egregious self-love, that while remembering how sincerely I believed myself *the better* for all the hateful crimes of impious presumption and filial ingratitude of which I was guilty, I cannot but think that the most contemptible follies into which vanity and fine speeches ever plunged a girl in the ordinary routine of this world's nonsense must be considered as innocent and respectable, when compared to those committed (oh! fearful impiety!) in the name of the Lord.

'Though we frequently meet, I have never yet been able fully and clearly to state to you how completely I have made a recantation of all my evangelical errors. It is singular how Mr Cartwright contrives, either by himself or his satellites, to be always hovering near us. For the three last Wednesdays I have set off for the Park with a firm determination to speak to you on this subject; but I have each time found it impossible. I believe that my countenance or manner must have expressed some part of the anxiety I felt to converse with you, and that my eagerness to obtain my object defeated it. On one occasion, as I think you must remember, Mr Cartwright himself, though constantly drawn here and there to perform his gracious hospitalities to the rest of the company, ceased not again and again to return with his soft "Well, dear children! what are you talking about?" – on another, it was his curate and deputy who performed the office of interrupter; and last Wednesday, that very unaccountable person Mr Jacob seemed determined that no one should speak to you but himself. I have therefore, dearest Fanny, determined to write to you. I think it likely that I may soon leave this neighbourhood: Major Dalrymple, who has been greatly the means of bringing me back to happiness and common sense, will, I believe, undertake the charge of me for the rest of my life. This, I find, has long been my dear, dear mother's wish. Had I been quite sure of this a year ago, I think I should have been saved this wild interlude of fanatic raving. However, it is over; and greatly as I have been the worse, I hope and believe that for the future I shall be the humbler Christian and the better woman for it.

'Major Dalrymple is at present in Scotland, attending the sick – I believe the dying hours of his cousin Lord Hilton. After his return, it is probable we shall leave Wrexhill; and I am therefore most anxious to make you acquainted with my present state of mind, for I cannot but suspect that we have run the farther into this lamentable folly because we ran together.

'You have already said enough to make me hope that you too are recovering from your delusion; but I cannot be easy without telling you explicity, that I am again the same unpretending little Church-of-England Christian that I was in the days of our good Mr Wallace; that I am once more a loving and dutiful daughter to the best of mothers, and ever and always your very

'Affectionate friend,
'MARY RICHARDS.'

'P.S. Pray let me hear from you.'

This letter was wormwood to Mr Cartwright from one end to the other. Had it rehearsed the kissing story, he would have liked it infinitely better. He was quite aware of Mary Richard's 'falling off,' and attributed it, as well as that equally evident in Fanny, to jealousy – woman's jealousy, and drew thence a species of gratification that almost atoned for their secession; the more so perhaps as the all-important business of the will rendered it absolutely necessary that, cost what converts it might, he should bestow his love-making wholly and solely upon his lady.

But to find that this pretty little girl really appeared to have forgotten the kiss altogether, and yet that she had escaped from his net – at the very moment too when, as it seemed, she was on the very verge of becoming a viscountess, was a mortification so cutting, that he actually ground his fine teeth together with rage at it.

His first impulse was to destroy it. But he recollected that by suffering it to reach Fanny, he should obtain a sight of her answer; and feeling considerable curiosity to discover how he should fare in the hands of the little melancholy poetess who had of late evidently avoided all tête-à-tête communication with him, he carefully re-sealed it, and sedulously pinching its folds into unsuspicious-looking flatness, put it aside to be delivered according to its address.

The event proved that he was quite right in believing that Fanny Mowbray would answer this letter; but whether the perusal of her reply increased his satisfaction in being master of Cartwright Park, may be doubted.

Fanny's reply was as follows:

'My very dear Mary,

'I am most thankful to have received your letter; for one source of the mental misery I have endured has arisen from believing that I first led you to fix your attention on Mr Cartwright, and your faith on the hateful dogmas he taught. You are freed – you have escaped, you are restored to the mother you love, and *you* will be happy! I thank God, Mary, that my heart is not wholly perverted by all the unnatural struggles it has gone through; for I do rejoice, my dear friend, at your felicity with a pureness and freshness of joy that I have never felt at anything since the death of my poor father came and blighted all our joys. Neither am I surprised at the end of your history. May you through life be as happy as I wish you, and you shall have no reason to complain.

'Of myself I know not how to speak; and yet I am sure that you will not be easy without knowing something of the present state of my mind.

'Yes, Mary, the mad fanaticism has passed away; but it has left me weak as a child recovered from the delirium of a raging fever; and I feel very doubtful if I shall ever wholly recover it. I am thankful that you have suffered less than I have done; indeed the mischief wrought so differently with you, that I almost doubt my power of making you understand all I have suffered. I cannot explain even to myself what species of feeling it was which took possession of me when first I became acquainted with Mr Cartwright. Of this, however, I am quite sure, that I believed with all the simplicity of truth and innocence, that all I felt proceeded from the immediate influence of the Deity working within me to secure my eternal salvation. Had I seen the Holy Ghost descend bodily upon Mr Cartwright, I could not more firmly have believed that he was God's appointed agent on earth; and everything he did and everything he said appeared clothed in a sort of holiness in my eyes which would have rendered it impious to judge him as another would have been judged. During the first two or three months of our acquaintance, I was happy – oh! much more than happy; I lived in a sort of ecstasy. I believed myself the chosen of Heaven, and that all the agitating but delightful emotions which Mr Cartwright's admiration and praises excited were only so many heavenly assurances that I was indeed one of the elected few predestined to eternal and unspeakable happiness. He caressed me – very often he caressed me. But even now, Mary, that I see clearly much that was then concealed, I cannot comprehend the sort of effect this had upon me. I think that had he asked me to marry him, I should have been conscious of the disparity of his age; and I think, too, that I should have been startled and shocked at discovering that his love, always so fervently expressed, and often shown by tender endearments, was in any way an earthly love. And yet, weak and inconsistent creatures that we are! when I discovered that the object of my mother's last sudden journey to town, in which I accompanied her – when I discovered that her purpose was to marry Mr Cartwright, the sick faintness that seemed to seize upon my heart and creep over all my limbs convinced me for a moment that I loved him . . . not as I fancied I did, dear Mary, as a lower angel might love one of higher order, but with the love of a weak sinful woman. The tortures that I endured that night can never be obliterated from my mind; a terrified conscience and a wounded heart seemed struggling together, as if to try which could torment me most. But the struggle did not last long. My heart – at least all that was tender and womanly in it – appeared to turn to stone, and was tranquil enough as far as any feelings connected with love for Mr Cartwright were concerned; but religious terrors, frightful, hideous, almost maddening, took possession of me. I believed that the crime I had committed in loving the man whom God had ordained to be my spiritual teacher, was a sin against the Holy Ghost. I now felt certain – or, in the language of the sect, an inward assurance, that I was pre-doomed to eternal perdition; and that the belief I had once entertained, exactly contrary to this, was of itself a damning sin never to be atoned, and only to be punished by eternal flames. Is there another torture of the mind equal to this? I do not think it; for true and reasonable remorse for crimes really committed cannot approach it. Not all the sins that man ever laid upon his soul could equal in atrocity what my guilt seemed to me. I suppose I was mad, quite mad; for as I now recall the hours that passed over me, and all the horrid images of the avenging fury of an angry God which entered and rested upon my spirit, I can call the state I was in nothing short of madness.

'This state lasted, with little variation in the amount of suffering, during the first week after my mother's marriage; and then its feverish violence gave place to sullen, heavy gloom. The cure however was near, very near me, for I found it in Mr Cartwright himself.

'It was some trifling instance of contemptible artifice which first drew aside the veil from my mental vision, and caused me to see Mr Cartwright, not as he is – oh no! that has been a work of steady study, and some length of time, – but as something of a very different species from that to which I had fancied he belonged.

'One must have been under a delusion as complete as mine has been, to conceive the sensation produced by once more seeing things as they are. I can compare it only to walking out of a region peopled with phantoms and shadows into a world filled with sober, solid realities. It is the phantom world which produces the strongest effect on the imagination; and the first effect of the change was to make everything around me seem most earthly dull, stale, and unprofitable. I was still, however, a fanatic; I still believed the impious doctrine of election and reprobation, and still deemed myself one of those foredoomed to eternal destruction. But one blessed day, some time after I had become convinced that Mr Cartwright was a very pitiful scoundrel, I chanced to hear him in sweet and solemn accents expound HIS scheme of providence to one of our distant neighbours who came here to pass the morning, and who seemed well disposed to listen to him. I saw that every word he said, rendered soothing and attractive by the gentle kindness of his manner and the eloquent commentary of his eyes, was making its way to the poor lady's soul, just as a year before the self-same words and looks had worked their way to mine.

'It was at that moment I felt the first doubts of the truth of the doctrine I had imbibed from him. For himself I had long felt the most profound contempt; but I had hitherto shrunk from the impiety of confounding the doctrine and the teacher. Something artificial and forced in his manner recalled by the force of contrast the voice and look of our dear Mr Wallace; and then came the bold and blessed thought that the awful dogmas by which he had kept my soul in thrall, might be as false and worthless as himself. My recovery from my mental malady may be dated from that hour. Every day that has passed since has led me back nearer and nearer, I hope, to the happy state (of religious feeling at least) in which Mr Cartwright found me. But the more fully I recover my senses, the more fully I become aware of the sad change he has wrought in everything else. Not only do we all creep like permitted slaves through the house that we once felt to be our own, but he has stolen our mother from us. Poor, poor mamma! how dearly did she love us! how dearly did we love her! Where is the feeling gone? She has never quarrelled with us; with me, particularly, she has never expressed herself displeased in any way; – and yet her love seems blighted and dried up, as if some poisonous breath had blasted it: – and so it has – placid and fair as is the outward seeming of this hateful man, I question not but every hour brings forth some sorry trick to draw her farther from us. Poor, poor mamma! I know this cannot last; and when she finds him out – how dreadful will her feelings be!

'Then, too, I have another sorrow, my dear Mary, which tarnishes, though it cannot destroy, the joy of my return to reason. While the fit lasted, I believed it a part of my dark duty to keep Helen and Rosalind, and our poor exiled Charles, as much at distance from me as possible; and now I hardly dare to hope that this can ever be quite forgotten by them. I have not courage to enter with them into an explanation as full as this which I have now given you; yet, till I do this, I cannot hope that they will either understand or forgive me.

'If Charles were at home, I think the task would be easier; but Rosalind and Helen both seem to avoid me. I believe they are too miserable themselves to look much at me, or they might see that I no longer turned from them as I did some months ago. All this, however, may some day or other come right again. But what is to become of poor

Charles? I feel convinced this hypocrite will never rest till he has robbed him of his inheritance; and I sometimes think that as the doing this must be the act of my mother, it would be right in me to put her on her guard against his machinations. But this can only be done by opening her eyes to his real character; and though I think I could do this, I tremble at the misery into which it would plunge her. – But this is going beyond your request, dear Mary. You cannot be ignorant that my unhappy mother's marriage has plunged us all in misery; and there is little kindness in impressing this truth upon you when your own bright prospects ought to occupy you with pleasant thoughts of future happiness. Forgive me! and believe me with every wish that this happiness may be as great and as lasting as the nature of human life can permit,

'Your ever affectionate friend,
                                      'FANNY MOWBRAY.'

Some people might have found the perusal of these letters sufficient to damp the ardour of their curiosity in the pursuit of private information; but it had not this effect upon Mr Cartwright. He even doubted whether he should not suffer this letter of Fanny's to reach its destination for the same reason that he had permitted that of her friend to reach hers – namely, the procuring a reply. But upon a reperusal, for he gave himself the gratification of reading it twice, – he tore it into tiny atoms, and then lighted a bougie to set fire to the fragments.

The next letter of any importance which fell into his hands by the same means must also be given to the reader, as it contains some important information which, as it immediately shared the same fate as that of Fanny's, remained for a considerable time unknown to the person it most concerned, as well as to all others.

This letter was addressed to Helen from one whom beyond all others in the wide world it would best have pleased her to receive any token of remembrance or attention. It came from Colonel Harrington, and contained the following lines:

'Were Miss Mowbray placed in other circumstances – were not all proper access to her barred by the hateful influence of an alien and a stranger to her and to her blood, I should not thus venture to address her. All application to your mother and natural guardian would be, we know but too well, in vain: nay, there is every reason to believe that any application to yourself through her would never be permitted to reach you. But, rascal as this Cartwright has proved himself, I presume he does not tamper with the post; and it is therefore by this vulgar and ordinary medium that I determine to make known to you what it is great misery to conceal. Yet, after all, in saying, "*Helen, I love you*," I think I say nothing that you do not know already. But, nevertheless, it is delightful to say it; and were I, sweet Helen, once more within reach of being heard by you, I might perchance weary you with the repetition of it.

'But this is not all I have to say, though it is only in the supposition of your listening to this without anger that I dare proceed. I believe, Helen, I ought to say something – a great deal perhaps about my presumption – and my fears, and I know not what beside, – but the simple truth is, that being quite conscious I loved you, and not feeling the least reason or wish to conceal it, my manner and words, too, I believe, must have let you into the secret the last time we met; and those dear eyes, with their long eyelashes, so constantly as they are before me, would long ago have looked me into despair if the memory of one soft glance at parting had not permitted me to hope. My father and mother, Helen, know that I love you, and that all my future happiness hangs on your consenting to become my wife, *even without your mother's consent*. Why should I conceal from you that I know it will be refused? – Why should I not frankly and fairly tell you at once, my beloved Helen, that something very like an elopement must be resorted to before you can be mine? – But what an elopement! It will only be to the house of your godmother, who already loves you as her child; and who not only sanctions my addressing you, but has commissioned me to say that she shall never know anything approaching happiness till she can take you in her arms and call you her real daughter and her William's wife. For my father, – you know his oddities, – he declares that if you will come to Oakley and frankly consent to be his daughter, it will be the happiest moment of his life when he puts your hand in mine, and calls you so. But he swears lustily, Helen, that no application to your mother shall ever be made with his consent. This is rough wooing, sweet one! But do I overrate the generosity of your temper when I express my belief that you will not suffer what is inevitable, to destroy hopes that smile so sweetly on us?'

'Address your answer to Oakley, Helen: write it, if you will, to my mother. Dear and precious as one little line of kindness would be to me, I will not ask it if your proud heart would find it easier to open itself to her than to me. But keep me not long in suspense; before I shall have sealed my letter, I shall feel sick because the answer to it is not come. My regiment is not going abroad. This change in its destination was only known to us on Friday last. – Farewell! How wholly does my fate hang upon your answer!

'Ever, ever yours,
'WILLIAM HARRINGTON.'

The destruction of this letter was attended with a feeling of pleasure greatly superior both in quality and extent to that which he received

from watching spark after spark die away from the fading embers of poor
Fanny's long epistle. That was merely a matter of mawkish sentiment; this
was an affair of business.

'But Miss Helen shall have a lover, nevertheless.' It was thus he ended
his cogitation. 'My cousin Stephen will not fail me. This evening he will
be here with what will make the young lady's hand worth just as much as
I please, and no more: and if my worthy cousin likes her, he shall have
her.' And as he thought these words, a smile curled his lips, and he
playfully blackened the paper, and singed it, and finally set it in a blaze,
uttering aloud as the flame expired, 'A lieutenant-colonel of dragoons
versus the Vicar of Wrexhill.'

CHAPTER XXXIX

THE WILL EXECUTED

The evening was pretty far advanced when at length the house-door bell
was loudly rung; and immediately afterwards Mr Stephen Corbold
entered the drawing-room looking more assured, and, as Helen thought,
more detestable than ever.

Having deliberately sipped his tea, and indulged himself the while in a
long steady stare in the face of the unfortunate object of his passion, he at
length rose, and with an air of much confidential importance, raising
himself on his toes, and playing with his watch-chain, approached Mrs
Cartwright, and whispered something in her ear.

'Have the kindness to ring the bell, Mr Hetherington,' said the lady,
addressing the curate, who, according to his frequent custom, had taken
his tea at the Park, partly for the advantage of receiving the instructions
of his principal upon sundry little points of Church and village discipline,
and partly for the hope of finding some one among the young ladies less
cruel than the inexorable Henrietta, who had never appeared to see him,
from the moment they parted in the shrubbery.

'Tell Curtis to carry lights to my dressing-room,' said Mrs Cartwright
to the servant who answered the bell.

The vicar's heart gave a bound. One hour more and he should clutch
it! One short hour more and he should at last be master of his own
destiny, dependant on no fond woman's whim, trembling before no
children's power to change her purpose.

'Once let her sign this will,' thought he, 'and if I ever leave her long
enough unwatched to make another, the fault will be my own, and I will
abide the consequence.'

With a placid countenance that manifested no emotion of any kind, Mr Cartwright amused himself for a few minutes in examining a drawing just finished for the Fancy Fair, by the light of a lamp on the chimney-piece; and as he passed behind his cousin to set it down, he condescendingly stopped to show it to him, pointing out its merits with affectionate admiration, for the artist was no other than his accomplished lady.

'Is not the expression of this head beautifully holy, cousin Stephen? Just look at the eyes. . . . Chivers the butler, her maid Curtis, and my valet can witness it. . . . Charming, is it not?'

In a short time afterwards Mrs Cartwright rose; the attentive attorney sprang to the door, opened it, and silently followed her out of the room.

Henrietta's eye followed them, and she sighed heavily. 'You do not seem well to-night, Miss Cartwright,' said Helen, 'and I do not feel gay; what say you to our keeping each other in countenance, and both going to bed though the clock has not yet struck ten?'

'A comfortable, and very wise proposal,' replied Henrietta, rising at once. 'I am much more inclined to be in bed than up; for I would rather be asleep than awake.'

'It is very right for you, Henrietta, who are an invalid, to be indulged in your wish to retire early,' said her father. 'Good night! I am sorry that the accidental absence of your mother renders it impossible for me to hasten the hour of evening prayer. But you shall have my blessing. May the Lord watch over your slumbers if you close your eyes in faith! If not, may he visit you in the night season, with such appalling thoughts as may awaken a right spirit within you! But for you, my dear child,' he continued, turning to Helen, 'I cannot suffer you to leave us so prematurely. We shall have prayers within an hour, and I do not permit any member of my family to absent herself from the performance of this sacred ordinance, without very good and sufficient reason for so doing.'

'I conceive that I have very good and sufficient reason for so doing, sir,' replied Helen, approaching the door: 'I wish you all good night.'

'She shall pay for this!' whispered one of the little demons that nestled in the vicar's heart. 'Stephen must absolve me of my promise for to-night; but if I do not keep it with him nobly on some future occasion, I will give him leave to tear in fragments the parchment which at this very moment is growing into a rod wherewith to scourge the insolence of this proud vixen.'

It was probably not so much the failing to keep his promise with Corbold, which the late hour might readily excuse, as the displaying to his slave and curate that his power was not absolute, which galled him so severely. His wife and cousin, however, soon returned; they both looked placidly contented, as those do look, who, having had important business to transact, have done it well and thoroughly. Soon afterwards the numerous household were summoned to appear, and the labours of the day were closed with prayer, Mr Hetherington uttering the extempore invocation, and the vicar pronouncing the blessing: an arrangement, by the way, approved by the master of Cartwright Park for three especial reasons. First, it gave to his establishment very greatly the effect of having a domestic chaplain at its head.

Secondly, it afforded an opportunity, which the worthy Mr Hetherington never neglected, of calling down sundry especial blessings on the vicar's own particular head, and, which was perhaps more important still, of pronouncing a lofty eulogium on his transcendent virtues.

Thirdly, the having to rise from his knees and pronounce the final blessing, never failed to soothe his spirit with a delicious foreboding that he might one day do so likewise in his own cathedral, and from his own proper throne: this being an object of ambition to him as dear, or dearer still, than the possession of the precious will itself.

Rarely indeed did he seat himself in his own soft chair, in his own noble library, without seeing in his mind's eye a mitre, as distinctly visible as Macbeth's air-drawn dagger was to him; and the hope that this crowning blessing would one day fall upon his favoured head, not only cheered every waking, and often every sleeping hour, but made him so generously come forward upon all occasions when a penniless Whig was to be accommodated with a seat in Parliament, or any other subscription set on foot to help the radical poor and needy into political power and place, that he was already considered in the high places as one of the most conscientious and right-minded clergymen within the pale of the Established Church, and almost supernaturally gifted (considering he was not a Roman Catholic priest) with the power of judging political characters according to their real value.

As soon as the prayers were ended, the blessing spoken, and the servants dismissed, Mr Corbold, whose eyes had vainly wandered round the room in search of Helen, approached the vicar, and said in a very firm and intelligible tone, 'I wish to speak to you, cousin Cartwright.'

'Certainly!' replied his kinsman in a voice of the most cordial friendship. 'Come into my library with me, cousin Stephen.'

And into the library they went; and almost before the door was shut Mr Corbold exclaimed,

'How am I to see Miss Helen, cousin Cartwright, if you have let her take herself off to bed?'

This very pertinent question was, however, only answered by another.

'Have you got the will, cousin Stephen?'

'Yes, I have,' answered the attorney with more boldness than he had ever used in speaking to his cousin since he became a great man. 'But a bargain's a bargain.'

'I know it is, cousin, – and the Lord preserve to me my lawful rights and inheritance, as I faithfully keep to you the word I have given!'

'And how is it to be managed then? . . . Am I to go to the girl's bedroom?'

'Give me the will, cousin Stephen,' said the vicar, holding out his hand to receive it, 'and I will satisfy you fully upon this matter.'

Mr Corbold, however, looked extremely rebellious, and no corner of parchment could be descried about any part of his person. 'A bargain's a bargain, I tell you, cousin William,' he repeated doggedly; 'and you may as well remember that a lawyer that is entrusted with the keeping of a will is no way bound to give it up; particularly to the party whom it chiefly concerns.'

Mr Cartwright measured his contumacious relative with his eye, very much as if he intended to floor and rifle him; but wiser thoughts prevailed, and he gently replied, seating himself in his own peculiar chair, and making a sign to his companion that he should place himself opposite: 'May the Lord, cousin Stephen, whose professing servants we are, save and deliver us from quarrelling with one another, especially at a blessed moment like this, when everything seems fitted by his holy providence, so as to ensure us peace and prosperity in this world, and doubtless, everlasting glory in the life to come!'

'All that's very true, cousin Cartwright; and if your cloth and calling set you to speak of heavenly things, especial grace, years ago manifested in me, makes me nothing behind you in the same. But, for all that, I know well enough, that there's many a worldly-minded, unprofessing lawyer who would gain credit and honour both, by taking care to let young Mowbray know what that pious lady his mother has been about, instead of keeping the thing as secret as if it were a forgery of my own; and it is but common justice between man and man, to say nothing of cousins and professing Christians, that conduct so every way convenient and considerate as mine, should not go unrewarded. I have set my heart upon having that girl Helen, and I don't wish for anything in the end but lawful wedlock before God's altar, and all that; and the more, because I take it for granted that you don't mean altogether to leave the young woman without fortune; – but she's restive, cousin, and that you know, and we are therefore called upon, as men and Christians, to make use and profit of that wit and strength which it hath pleased the Lord in his wisdom to give us over the weaker vessel; and all I ask of you is so to put it within my reach and power to do this, that the righteous ends we have in view may be obtained through the same.'

'I have heard you to the end, cousin Stephen, which will, I trust, considering all things, be accepted by the Lord in token of an humble spirit. What you have said, however, excepting that it was needless, is altogether reasonable, and betokens that wisdom of which the Lord hath seen fit to make you an example upon the earth. But you find that my conscience needed not your reproof. Few hours have passed since I gave proof sufficient of the sincerity with which I desire to strengthen the ties between us. By the accident of the post-bag's being brought into my room, I was made aware that it contained a letter addressed to Helen Mowbray, evidently in the handwriting of a man. And what could it be to me, cousin Stephen, whether that unconverted girl got a letter from a man, or went without it? Nothing, positively nothing. But I remembered me of you, cousin, and of the tender affections which you had fixed upon her, and, fearless of consequences, I instantly broke the seal, and found, as I expected, a very worldly-minded proposal of marriage, without the decency of any allusion whatever to my will, or the will of God, in the business; and I therefore of course felt it my duty to destroy it both for your sake and that of the Lord, whose blessing the impious young man did not deem it necessary to mention. Nevertheless, the proposal came from one of the first families in the county, and the girl would have been my lady in due course of nature, a thing not altogether without value to her family and father-in-law. But I never hesitated for a moment, and you may see the ashes of Colonel Harrington's love-letter under the grate.'

'That was acting like the good and chosen servant of the Lord, cousin William, that I have long known you to be. But, such being the case, why have you scrupled to let me speak to the young girl this night in private?'

'For the good and sufficient reason, that she chose to go, even though I told her to stay, and, without exposing myself to a very unpleasant scene before my curate and the rest of my people, I could not have detained her. Besides, at the moment of her departure I knew that the will, which you still keep from me, cousin Stephen, was not either signed or executed, – another good and sufficient reason, as I take it, for not choosing to keep the girl back by force. But fear nothing; what I have promised, that I will perform. Give me the will, cousin Stephen, and I will tell you what my scheme is for you.'

'Tell me the scheme first, cousin William; that is but square and fair. We lawyers have got our ceremonies as well as the clergy, and I don't see why they should be broken through.'

'I don't very well know what you mean by ceremonies in this case, cousin, and I don't think you take the best way to oblige me; however, I am not going to shrink from my word for that. All I expect, cousin

Stephen, is your word pledged to me in return, that, let what will happen, you will bring no scandal or dishonour upon my family, for so doing might be of the greatest injury to my hopes.'

'I mean nothing but honour, cousin William,' replied Corbold eagerly: 'let me have but a fair opportunity given me, and you shall find that, though I use it, I will not abuse it. Tell me, then, what is your scheme?'

'You know that on the 12th of this month a Serious Fancy Fair is to be held in my grounds. Not only will all the rank and fashion of the county assemble on the occasion, but my park-gates will be open likewise to the people. At two o'clock a very splendid collation will be ready in five of my saloons; and it is after the company have risen and left the tables to resort once more to the booths in order to assist in the disposal of the remaining articles, that I shall permit every servant in my establishment to leave the mansion, and repair to witness the busy and impressive scenes in the booths. It will be a very impressive scene, cousin Stephen, for I shall myself pronounce a blessing upon the assembled crowd. From this I fear, my dear Stephen, that you must on this occasion absent yourself; but be assured, that as I speak those words of power, I will remember you.

'When you shall see a rush of my hired servants pour forth from my mansion upon my lawns, it is then that I shall counsel you to retire, enter the house by the library windows, and if questioned, say you are sent there on an errand by me. From my library, find your way up the grand staircase to the small apartment which I permit my wife to appropriate as her dressing-room, – the same in which you have this night executed, as I trust, her will. There remain, concealed perhaps behind the curtains, till Helen Mowbray enters. I will deposit in that room something valuable and curious for sale, which shall be forgotten till you are safely hidden there, and then I will command my very dear and obedient wife to send Miss Helen to seek for it. Does this plan please you, cousin?'

Before speaking a word, Mr Corbold drew the will from his long coat pocket, and placed it in the hands of the vicar. This was a species of mute eloquence most perfectly understood by the person to whom it was addressed.

The Vicar of Wrexhill received the parchment with much solemnity in his two hands, and bending his head upon it, exclaimed, 'May the blessing of the Lord be with me and my heirs for ever, world everlasting, Amen!'

* * *

It may possibly appear improbable to many persons that such a phrase as this last should recur in ordinary discourse so frequently as I have represented it to do. But to those not belonging to the sect, and therefore not so familiarized with its phraseology as to be unconscious of its peculiarity, and who yet have been thrown by accident within reach of hearing it, I need offer no explanation; for they must know by experience that this, or expressions of equally religious formation and import, are in constant use among them.

Sometimes, especially in the company of the profane, they are uttered *sotto voce*, as if to satisfy the secret conscience. Sometimes, even in equally un-elect society, they are pronounced aloud and with most distinct emphasis, as if to show that the speaker feared not the ribald laugh of the scorner, and held himself ready to perform this, or any other feat likely to ensure the same petty, but glorious martyrdom, despite any possible quantum of absurdity that may attach thereto.

★ ★ ★

The two kinsmen being now mutually satisfied with each other's conduct, shook hands and parted; Mr Corbold ruminating, as he walked slowly back to Wrexhill, on the happy termination to which he was at last likely to bring his hitherto unpropitious wooing, and Mr Cartwright gazing with unspeakable delight on the signatures and seals which secured to him, and his heirs for ever, the possession of all the wealth and state in which he now revelled. Having satisfied himself that all was right, he opened a secret drawer in his library table, laid the precious parchment within it, and having turned the lock, actually kissed the key that secured his treasure. He then carefully fastened it to his watch-chain, and returned to escort his lady to her chamber.

CHAPTER XL

THE SERIOUS FANCY FAIR

There were but few families within an ordinary visiting distance of the Park who had not called on Mrs Cartwright upon her marriage. Some went from simple curiosity, – some expressly to quiz her, – a few from feelings of real kindness towards the young people, whom it would be, they said, a shame to give up merely because their mother had played the fool and ruined all their prospects: – not a few, for the fun of seeing Mowbray Park turned into a conventicle, and the inhabitants into its congregation; and the rest came principally because Mr Cartwright was such a pious man, and likely to do so much good in the neighbourhood.

Among all these, the Fancy Fair announced to be held there on the 12th of July, created a lively interest. All the world determined to attend; and half the world gave themselves up to the making of pincushions and pen-wipers with as much zeal as if the entire remnant of the Jewish people, as well as the whole population of Fababo, were to be converted thereby.

The mansion and grounds of Mr Cartwright's residence began to give note of very great and splendid preparation for this serious fête. Never had the reverend vicar been seen in such spirits on any former occasion;

'His bosom's lord sat lightly on his throne;'

and (due allowance being made for the evangelical nature of the proceedings) it might safely be averred, that no entertainment ever given in the neighbourhood had caused more sensation, or been prepared for with a more lavish expenditure.

The whole of the 9th, 10th, and 11th days of the month were entirely employed by the majority of the Cartwright household in receiving and arranging the different works of fancy contributed by the neighbouring ladies for the sale. By far the greater half of these articles were pincushions, and for the most part they packed and unpacked well and safely; but amidst the vast variety of forms into which this favourite vehicle of charity was turned, some among them were equally ingenious in design, delicate in execution, and difficult of carriage.

There were harps, of which the strings were actually musical, and the foot a pincushion. Old women of pasteboard, washing their feet in a pasteboard tub, but with knees stuffed for pincushions. Pasteboard hunch-backs, the hunches being pincushions. Babies dressed with the nicest taste and care, their plump little necks and shoulders forming pincushions. Pretty silken volumes, lettered 'pointed satires,' and their yellow edges stuffed for pincushions. Ladies very fashionably dressed, with the crowns of their bonnets, and their graceful backs, prepared as pincushions. These, and ten thousand more, of which a prolonged description might probably prove tedious, formed the staple commodity of the elegant booths, which stretched themselves in two long rows from one extremity of the beautiful lawn to the other. Tracts, so numerous that it would be impossible to give their measure or their value by any other calculation than that of their weight, were made by the ingenuity of the fair and pious contributors to assume a very tempting aspect, bound by their own delicate hands in silks and velvets of every hue to be found between earth and heaven, green and blue inclusive.

It would be quite impossible to give anything deserving the name of a catalogue of the articles contributed to this charming exhibition; and it will therefore be better not to attempt it. It will be sufficient to observe, that, by a sentiment of elegant refinement which seemed to have pervaded all the contributors, every article to which the idea of utility could attach was scrupulously banished; it not being fair, as some of the ladies very judiciously observed, to injure the poor shopkeepers by permitting the sale of anything that anybody in the world could really wish to buy. One instance of very delicate attention on the part of Mrs Cartwright towards the hero of the fête deserves to be recorded, as showing both the natural kindness of her temper, and the respect in which every feeling of this celebrated character was held. Among the almost incredible number of devices for winding silks, or for converting them into bobbins, or for some other of the ingenious little contrivances invented for – one hardly knows what, was a very pretty thing, more in the shape of a Jew's harp than anything else. The instant Mrs Cartwright cast her eyes on this, she ordered it to be withdrawn, observing that, as the Reverend Isaac Isaacs himself was expected to honour the entertainment with his presence, she could by no means permit anything bearing such a name to appear.

It may be feared that it was with a far different spirit Mr Jacob Cartwright, on hearing his stepmother mention this exclusion, and the motive for it, proposed that all the cold chickens and turkeys to be eaten at the banquet, should appear without their usual accompaniment of cold hams, – a pleasantry which, though it won a smile from his indulgent father, was by no means well received by Mrs Cartwright.

The twelfth day of July itself arrived at last, and fortunately was as fine a day as ever shone. Helen asked Rosalind if she remembered the day on which Charles came of age, and the question brought tears to the eyes of both: this, however, was but a trifling exception to the general cheerfulness; all the world really looked as gay as if the Fancy Fair were not a serious one. In one of the long and elegantly decorated booths, indeed, one silly young girl was heard to exclaim, 'Oh! what a beautiful place this would be for dancing!' – but the levity was checked by Mr Cartwright, who, happening to overhear her, replied,

'My dear young lady, there is no dancing in Heaven!'

It had been settled among the ladies of the neighbourhood, on the first announcement of this pious and charitable undertaking, that no *young* ladies, either married or single, should be invited to sell the articles; and for some time after the circulation of this decision, it appeared to be very doubtful whether there would be any ladies found (not actually too decrepit to endure the fatigue) who would be willing to undertake it. This circumstance threw poor Mrs Cartwright into great embarrassment. The idea of having advertised a Fancy Fair, and then to be unable to procure ladies to preside at it, was a vexation almost beyond what even a professing Christian's patience could bear.

When at length it appeared evident that every middle-aged lady for ten miles round had, for some excellent good reason or other, declined the office, Mr Cartwright proposed that gentlemen, instead of ladies, should perform it. But to this Miss Charlotte Richards, who happened to be present when the difficulty was discussed, entered a violent protest, declaring that she was quite sure, if such a measure were resorted to, not one hundredth part of the goods would be sold. Neither Jew nor Gentile, she assured them, would ever make anything by it, if such a project were resorted to; and in short she pleaded the cause of the ladies so well, that after some time it was agreed that the original principle should be altogether changed, and that the youngest and prettiest ladies should be selected, only with this condition annexed – that they should all be dressed in uniform, the form and material of which were to be specified by Mrs Cartwright.

The circular letter announcing this alteration was composed by Mr Cartwright himself, and proved perfectly successful, although it contained but few words.

'It having been decided at a meeting of some of the senior supporters of the South Central African Bible Association, that the cause of the poor inhabitants of Fababo was one which ought to be peculiarly interesting to the young and lovely, inasmuch as it is beyond all others the cause of piety; it was THEREFORE strongly recommended that they should be especially chosen and elected to serve the office of vendors or sellers at the Fancy Fair instituted by the Reverend William Jacob Cartwright, and by him appointed to be held on his own premises.' – After which followed a request that such ladies as were kindly willing to undertake the fatigues of the office, would forthwith forward their names to Mrs Cartwright, that they might receive from her instructions respecting the uniform to be worn on the occasion.

The number of applications for permission to sell, which followed the circulation of this letter, was quite extraordinary, and so greatly exceeded the number required, that the task of selection became difficult, if not impossible; so it was finally decided that a description of the uniform should be sent to them all, and that those who arrived first, should be installed in their office under condition of permitting a relay to succeed them after the enjoyment of two hours of duty.

The consequence of this was, that at a very early hour, not only all the young and handsome part of the company expected, but all who considered themselves as belonging to that class, were seen arriving in their very becoming sad-coloured suits, with their smooth braided tresses, and Quakerish bonnets and caps.

'Let all the ladies in the serious uniform stand up together behind the stalls if they like it,' said the accommodating Mrs Cartwright: 'it would be so very difficult to select; and they will all look so very well!'

As the stalls were all ready, having been walked round, through, and about, by Mr and Mrs Cartwright, Mr Hetherington the curate, Chivers the butler, Curtis the lady's maid, as well as all the other serious servants, and all agreeing in the opinion that it was impossible anything could be more beautiful, the uniform ladies were ushered into them, and begged to decide among themselves the order in which they should stand.

The manner in which this self-regulating system worked, was amusing, and Rosalind Torrington stood by, and enjoyed it greatly. As soon as it was notified to the young and pretty ladies that the booths were all ready, the prices of every article marked, and all things prepared so that they might take their places behind the stands in such order as they should agree among themselves, any one who had witnessed and watched the sweet universal smile with which each one regarded the other, and the charming accents in which all exclaimed as with one voice, 'Oh! it is exactly the same to me where I stand,' would have been ready to declare that even their youth and beauty were less attractive than the sweet temper which seemed to be so universal among them.

The fair bevy, amounting to above fifty, poured themselves by various entrances into the booths, which were in fact a succession of very handsome tents, against the sides of which were ranged the elegantly decorated stands; while through the whole extent, a space of nearly thirty feet was left for promenading. In the centre of the range, the gaily painted canvass rose into a lofty point, from which, to the extremity of the circle round it, depended graceful draperies, festooned with large bunches of flowers. In the middle of this noble circular tent stood a lofty frame, supporting the finest green-house plants, and the stalls which here skirted the sides of the enclosure were decidedly more distinguished by their elegant decorations than the rest.

'Oh, dear! how lovely!' was the universal exclamation uttered by the ladies on entering this beautiful circle.

'Well! I think I will stand here,' said one of the most lively and enterprising among them, placing herself at the same time behind a world of many-tinted paper and silk commodities, close to which was a side entrance arched with evergreen boughs, and gay with a thousand blossoms.

'And I will take this stand!' cried a stout and long-limbed demoiselle, stepping out with great activity to secure the one opposite.

'This will just suit me!' said a third, popping into another of the enviable stations which flanked the garlanded entrances, and immediately taking possession of its lofty seat and comfortable footstool.

Up to this point the universal smile continued, with an almost unabated display of charming teeth; but to the fourth place, promising equal affluence of passers-by to the three already taken, no less than four ladies rushed at once. And then began the civil war which in a greater or less degree, as circumstances may excite or assuage it, rages at all fancy fairs, bazaars, and charity sales of every class and denomination whatever.

Some folks, uninitiated in such matters, may suppose that there is less of this at a serious fancy fair, than at one professing to be gay. But a little experience will rapidly undeceive them. Whether the benevolent sale-ladies be beautiful saints or beautiful sinners, the inclination to show off Nature's gifts to the best advantage is pretty nearly the same; and whether the sweet graceful thanks, so softly uttered, be constructed after one form or another, the pleasure of speaking them is the same likewise. What matters it, whether a bright eye laugh from beneath a drapery of pendant curls, or is raised to heaven with no twisted meshes to obscure its upward ray? What matters it whether ruby lips open to say, 'The Lord reward you, sir! Our poor missionaries shall pray for you!' or, 'Thank you!' (with a familiar nod) 'some dear Spanish whiskerandos shall buy a sword with this!' In both cases the speaker would indisputably prefer having a well-frequented stand to speak from; and if it chance to be placed beside some avenue through which the crowd must pass and repass incessantly, why so much the better.

The four ladies that met together with more of haste than inclination at the last of the doorway stands, as above described, were really, considering all things, exceedingly civil to each other. At the early part of a busy day, the temper can bear much more without wincing, than after it has been battered and bruised by all the little *contretems* that are almost sure to beset it before the close of it.

'I beg your pardon, ma'am, but I believe I was here first.'

'Oh, dear! I hope I did not hurt you, but this is my place.'

'You must let me stand here, dear ladies, for I have set my heart upon it:' – comprised very nearly all the spoken part of the contest. A few sidelong glances there might have been, and one or two almost invisible *nudges*; but after all, the person who finally got possession of the desired post, was a tall, thin, pale, and remarkably pious maiden, who having laid her hand upon the board, and her foot upon the stool, moved them no more, but who from first to last did not pronounce a single word.

Though these four favourite seats were thus rapidly taken possession of, there was still a good deal to be struggled for. It appeared indeed for some time that all the fifty young and handsome ladies had firmly made up their minds to station themselves in the circular tent, and nowhere else.

Greatly did the peaceable Mrs Cartwright rejoice that she had from the first desired the ladies to please themselves; for it soon became evident that it would have been no easy task for her to please them. Very continuous buzzings made themselves heard around the canvass walls; and lady-like remonstrances were occasionally audible.

'Really, ladies, I think we are very close here.'

'Would it not be better for some of the ladies to move on?'

'I believe, ma'am, that you will find no room just here,' and,

'Upon my word I must beg you not to press upon me so!' – were sentences distinctly repeated in more places than one.

At length things, or rather ladies, began to arrange themselves in tolerable order, the difficulty being got over at last, as always happens upon such occasions, by the best tempers taking the worst places.

It was an almost simultaneous rush of carriages through the Park Gates, and the approach of many persons on foot by various entrances, which at last produced this desirable effect. Mr Cartwright now came forth in all his glory from beneath the shelter of a sort of canvass portico that formed the entrance to the principal line of tents. Almost innumerable were the hands he shook, the bows he made, and the smiles he smiled. It is perfectly impossible that he could have sustained so radiant and benevolent a graciousness to all sorts and conditions of men, had not his animal spirits been sustained by the ever-present recollection that the little key which dangled from his watch-chain, and with which he constantly dallied when any of his ten fingers were disengaged from hand-shaking, kept watch and ward over his lady's will.

Mrs Cartwright, meanwhile, not being in a situation to endure the fatigue of standing, sat with some dozen chairs around her, waiting for the most distinguished guests, within the flowery shelter of this same pretty portico, round which were ranged orange-trees, and various other fragrant plants, reaching from the ground almost to the roof.

Whenever any person arrived of sufficient importance to be so distinguished, the Vicar of Wrexhill himself ushered them to the presence of his lady, and those so honoured at length filled all the chairs around her. To all the rest Mrs Cartwright bowed and smiled as they passed onward; as they all most obediently did, in compliance with the mandate of their host, who continued to utter with little intermission, 'Straight on if you please – straight on, – and you will reach the centre pavilion.'

Between the spot at which the carriages set down the company, and the entrance to this portico, four servants in rich liveries were stationed to pass their names to Chivers, who stood within it. At length a party, who had walked across the Park and entered on the lawn by the little hand gate, (to pass through which, the present master of the domain had once considered as his dearest privilege,) approached the entrance at a point by which they escaped three out of the four reverberations of their names, and were very quietly stepping under the draperied entrance, when the fourth now stopped them short to demand their style and title.

'Mrs and the Miss Richards, – Lord Hilton,' answered the trumpet-mouthed London-bred domestic, who, it may be observed in passing, had, like most of his fellows, answered one of Mr Cartwright's advertisements headed thus –

'Wanted
to live in the country
A SERIOUS FOOTMAN.'

No sooner did the title reach the vicar's ears, than he dropped pious Mr Somebody's hand which he was affectionately pressing, and turning short round met the cold glance of the honest-hearted Major Dalrymple, who advanced with Mrs Richards upon one arm, and his affianced Mary on the other. A moment of rather awkward deliberation ensued, as to whether the man, or the man's title, should modify the manner of his reception; but before the question could be decided, the party had quietly passed on, without appearing to perceive him. The two elder Miss Richards followed, both of them having been obliged to relinquish their hopes of presiding at a stand in consequence of the expensive nature of the uniform. These two young ladies, who from the first hour of their conversion had really been among the most faithful followers of the Vicar of Wrexhill in all ways – ready to be in love with him – ready to pray with him – and now ready to bow before him as almost the greatest man in the county, were not perhaps greeted with all the distinguished kindness they deserved. Unfortunately for their feelings, Mr Cartwright was more awake to the fact that they were sisters to little Mary, than to their very excellent chance of becoming sisters-in-law to a nobleman: – and so they too passed on, without pausing, as they had intended to do, for the expression of their unbounded admiration for him and his Fancy Fair.

Nearly the whole of the invited society were already assembled, and the Park was beginning to fill with the multitude which was to be admitted to the tents after the collation, when, at length, the Reverend Isaac Isaacs was announced.

The arrival of the hero of the day produced, as may be supposed, a very powerful sensation; his name was no sooner pronounced by the servants than it was caught up by the company, and borne along from mouth to mouth till every individual of the crowd which filled the tents was made acquainted with the interesting fact, that the Reverend Isaac Isaacs was approaching. The effect of this was for some moments really alarming; every Christian soul turned back to welcome the converted Jew, and something nearly resembling suffocation ensued. Indeed when the throng which pressed back to meet him, met that which had turned to follow him as he laboured to make his way between the stands, the crush was really terrible: and had there not fortunately been many lateral exits through which those escaped who loved their lives better than the gratification of their curiosity, the consequences might have been very serious.

Not all, however, whose strength and whose zeal induced them to remain, could get a sight of this desired of all eyes; for, as Mr Isaacs was a very short man, those only who were very close could distinguish him. The effect of this procession, however, through the double row of stands, still thickly studded with pin-cushions, every one of which had been made for his sake, was very impressive, and rendered greatly more so by every fair sales-woman mounting upon the high seat with which she was furnished for occasional rest, and thus looking down upon him as he passed in attitudes that displayed both courage and enthusiasm.

The weather was intensely hot, and more than once he appeared nearly overcome by his emotions. He expressed the greatest concern for having arrived so late, and especially for having missed the opening prayer, which, as he imagined, had been pronounced by Mr Cartwright himself; but when it was explained to him that this was not the case, and, moreover, that he was not too late to share the blessing to be given by that gentleman, he became more reconciled to the accident which had detained him, and gave himself wholly up to the enjoyment of the striking spectacle that surrounded him.

After he had remained for some time in the central pavilion, gazing, and gazed at, in a manner which it was extremely interesting to watch, some one well acquainted with the best method of carrying on the business of such a meeting as the present, suggested that it would be advisable that the acolyte should retire till the sale of the goods was pretty well completed: for if the feeling among the charitable crowd were permitted to exhaust itself in affectionate glances towards Mr Isaacs, no more money would be collected: and it was also judiciously remarked, that it might be as well to circulate through the company the assurance, that as soon as the stalls were about two-thirds cleared, the banquet would be announced.

The effect of these suggestions was speedily visible: Mr Isaacs stood in the enjoyment of space and fresh air before the entrance to the portico, engrossing the almost undivided attention of his great patron, while ladies peeped at him from a respectful distance; and Chivers himself, with a look as reverential as if he were waiting upon an apostle, approached him with Madeira and soda water.

The sale, meanwhile, benefited equally by his near presence and his actual absence. Enthusiasm was raised without being disturbed in that great object of all English Christian enthusiasm – the disbursing of money; and by four o'clock such a report was made of the general receipts, that the selling ladies were waited upon by as many clergymen as could be collected to hand them from their stands to the banquet, and, when these were all furnished with a fair partner, the most serious gentlemen among the company were requested to take charge of the rest.

Mrs Cartwright herself was led to the great dining-room by Mr Isaacs, and for this reason, or else because it was the great dining-room, the crowd which followed her became so oppressive that the doors of the room were ordered to be closed and strictly guarded. This measure was equally serviceable to those within and without; for no sooner was it fully understood that this decisive mode had been resorted to, than the other tables were instantly filled, and nothing could be more satisfactory than the activity with which eating and drinking proceeded in all directions.

The champagne flowed freely; and whether it were that the sacred cause for which the meeting was assembled appeared to justify, or at least excuse, some little excess, – or that nothing furnished at Mr Cartwright's board but must bring a blessing to him who swallowed it, – or that the fervent season led to thirst, and thirst to copious libations: – whatever the cause, it is certain that a very large quantity of wine was swallowed that day, and that even the most serious of the party felt their spirits considerably elevated thereby.

But, in recording this fact, it should be mentioned likewise, that, excepting in some few instances in which thirst, good wine, and indiscretion united to overpower some unfortunate individuals, the serious gentlemen of the party, though elevated, were far from drunk; and the tone of their conversation only became more animated, without losing any portion of the peculiar jargon which distinguished it when they were perfectly sober.

The discourse especially, which was carried on round Mr Cartwright after the ladies retired, was, for the most part, of the most purely evangelical cast: though some of the anecdotes related might, perhaps, in their details, have partaken more of the nature of miracles than they would have done if fewer champagne corks had saluted the ceiling.

One clerical gentleman, for instance, a Mr Thompson, who was much distinguished for his piety, stated as a fact which had happened to himself, that, in his early days, before the gift of extempore preaching was fully come upon him, he was one Sabbath-day at the house of a reverend friend, who, being taken suddenly ill, desired Mr Thompson to preach for him, at the same time furnishing him with the written discourse which he had been himself about to deliver. 'I mounted the pulpit,' said Mr Thompson, 'with this written sermon in my pocket; but the moment I drew it forth and opened it, I perceived, to my inexpressible dismay, that the handwriting was totally illegible to me. For a few moments I was visited with heavy doubts and discomfiture of spirit, but I had immediate recourse to prayer. I closed the book, and besought God to make its characters legible to me; – and when I opened it again, the pages seemed to my eyes to be as a manuscript of my own.'

This statement, however, was not only received with every evidence of the most undoubting belief, but an elderly clergyman, who sat near the narrator, exclaimed with great warmth, 'I thank you, sir, – I thank you greatly, Mr Thompson, for this shining example of the effect of ready piety and ready wit. Though the cloth is removed, sir, I must ask to drink a glass of wine with you, – and may the Lord continue to you his especial grace!'

There were some phrases too, which, though undoubtedly sanctioned by serious usage, sounded strangely when used in a scene apparently of such gay festivity.

One gentleman confessed very frankly his inability to resist taking more of such wine as that now set before them than was altogether consistent with his own strict ideas of *ministerial* propriety. 'But,' added he, 'though in so yielding, I am conscious of being in some sort wrong, I feel intimately persuaded at the same time, that by thus freely demonstrating the strength and power of original sin within me, I am doing a service to the cause of religion, by establishing one of its most important truths.'

This apology was received with universal applause: it manifested, as one of the company remarked, equal soundness of faith, and delicacy of conscience.

One of the most celebrated of the regular London speakers, known at all meetings throughout the whole evangelical season, having silently emptied a bottle of claret, which he kept close to him, began, just as he had finished the last glass, to recover the use of his tongue. His first words were, 'My king has been paying me a visit.'

'Indeed!' said Mr Cartwright, whose attention was instantly roused by this very interesting statement; 'where was the visit made, Mr White?'

'Even here, sir,' replied Mr White solemnly; 'here, since I have been sitting silently at your hospitable board.'

'As how, sir?' inquired a certain Sir William Crompton, who was placed near him. 'Do you mean that you have been sleeping, and that his Majesty has visited you in your dreams?'

'The Majesty that I speak of, sir,' replied Mr White, 'is the King of Heaven, and the Lord of Hosts.'

'What other could it be!' exclaimed Mr Cartwright, showing the whites of his eyes, and appearing scandalized at the blunder.

'I wonder, Mr Cartwright,' said a young man of decidedly pious propensities, but not as yet considering himself quite assured of his election, – 'I wonder, Mr Cartwright, whether I shall be saved or not?'

'It is a most interesting question, my young friend,' replied the vicar mildly; 'and you really cannot pay too much attention to it. I am happy to see that it leaves you not, even at the festive board; and I sincerely hope it will finally be settled to your satisfaction. But as yet it is impossible to decide.'

'I shall not fail to ride over to hear you preach, excellent Mr Cartwright!' said a gentleman of the neighbourhood, who, though not hitherto enrolled in the evangelical calendar, was so struck on the present occasion with the hospitable entertainment he received, that he determined to cultivate the acquaintance.

'You do me great honour, sir!' replied the vicar. 'If you do, I hope it will be on a day when you can stay supper with us.'

'You are excessively kind, my dear sir!' answered the guest; 'but as my place is at least ten miles distant from yours, I fear, if you sup in the same style that you dine, it would be somewhat late before I got home.'

Mr Cartwright bowed, dropped his eyes, and said nothing.

'Oh, sir!' said Mr Hetherington, who, though he had drunk more than any man at table, excepting the cousin Corbold, had as yet in no degree lost his apprehension, – 'Oh, sir! you quite mistake. The supper that the excellent Mr Cartwright means, is to be taken at the table of the Lord!'

'Dear me!' exclaimed the squire, who really meant to be both civil and serious, 'I beg pardon, I made a sad blunder indeed!'

'There is nothing sad but sin, Mr Wilkins!' replied the vicar meekly. 'A mistake is no sin. Even I myself have sometimes been mistaken.'

'What heavenly-minded humility there is in Mr Cartwright!' said Mr Hetherington in a loud whisper to his neighbour: 'every day he lives seems to elevate my idea of his character. Is not this claret admirable, Mr Dickson?'

Just at this moment Chivers the butler entered the room and whispered something in his master's ear.

'Indeed!' exclaimed Mr Cartwright, 'a very disagreeable accident, upon my word.'

'What is it, sir?' inquired several voices at once.

'The head cook, gentlemen,' replied Chivers, 'has fallen off the larder-ladder, and has put out his shoulder.'

'A very disagreeable accident indeed,' echoed the guests.

The butler whispered again.

'Certainly, Chivers, certainly. I am very glad Mr Bird the surgeon happens to be on the premises. Let him immediately set the joint, and when this is done, and the poor fellow laid comfortably in bed, come for Mr Hetherington, whom I will immediately order to awaken him.'

'God bless my soul, sir!' exclaimed the good-natured Sir William Crompton; 'won't that be rather injudicious? If it should please God that the poor fellow get a nap, I should think it would be the worst thing in the world to awaken him.'

'Pardon me, Sir William,' replied the vicar with great respect, 'but persons of the world do not well understand the language of those who are not of the world. No accident, no illness ever occurs in my house, Sir William, but my first effort is to awaken the soul of the sufferer to a proper sense of his sins. I always take care they shall be told that the jaws of the tomb are opening before them, and that, as death comes like a thief in the night, they should be watching for him. This, in the language of a pious and professing Christian, is called an awakening; and needful as it is at all times, it is of course more needful still in sickness, or danger of any kind.'

Sir William Crompton filled his glass with the wealthy vicar's admirable wine, and said no more.

The time was now approaching at which the populace were to be admitted to the tents on the lawn; and Mr Cartwright having looked at his watch, rose and said,

'Gentlemen, – It is distressing to me to be forced to disturb you, but the business of the meeting requires that we should all repair to the lawn. The populace are about to be admitted, and it is expected that our estimable Mr Isaacs will benefit very considerably by the eagerness with which the farmers' wives and daughters will purchase the articles which remain of our Christian ladies' elegant handiworks. One bumper to the success of the Reverend Isaac Isaacs! and to the conversion and salvation of the people of Fababo! – And now we will return to our duty in the tents.'

'To your tents, O Israel!' shouted a young man, with more of wine than wit, as he turned towards the converted Jew; 'for myself,' he added, 'I'll be d——d if I stir an inch till I have finished this bottle.'

Mr Cartwright stopped short in his progress towards the door. He turned a glance, more inquiring perhaps than stern, on the face of the intoxicated speaker, and perceived that he was the nephew of an earl; the sole reason indeed which had procured him the honour of a seat in that distinguished circle.

The vicar balanced for a moment whether he should reprimand him or not. Had he been the son, instead of the nephew of the noble lord, he would certainly have passed on in holy meditation, but, as it was, he stopped. There were many serious eyes upon him, notwithstanding the claret. He remembered that the earl had a 'goodly progeny,' and that consequently his nephew would never be likely to succeed to his title; and therefore with great dignity, and much pious solemnity, he thus addressed his curate, who, in his capacity of domestic chaplain, was ever near him.

'Mr Hetherington! you have heard the awful words spoken by Mr Augustus Mappleton. Remember, sir, that his repentance and conversion be prayed for at our concluding service this evening, and also in your extempore prayer before sermon on next Sabbath morning.'

These words had a very sobering effect on the company, and the whole party made, all things considered, a very orderly exit from the dining-room, not however without Mr Cartwright finding an opportunity of whispering in the ear of his cousin –

'Now is your time, Stephen, to go into the dressing-room.'

CHAPTER XLI

THE 'ELOPEMENT'

When the gentlemen reached the lawn, they found it already covered, not only with the company from all the other rooms, but likewise with crowds of people from the Park, who came rushing in through different entrances from all quarters.

In the midst of all this bustle and confusion, however, Mr Cartwright remembered his engagement with Mr Stephen Corbold, and, only waiting till he saw that the servants of his house were among the throng, he sought Mrs Cartwright, and finding, as he expected, her daughter close beside her, whispered in her ear,

'Oblige me, dearest Clara! by sending Helen to your dressing-room for a small packet of very important papers which I left on the chimney-piece. I cannot go myself; and there is not a servant to be found.'

Mrs Cartwright immediately spoke the command to Helen, and the vicar had the satisfaction of watching her make her way through the crowd, and enter the window of the drawing-room.

Poor Helen was not happy enough to have enjoyed in any degree the splendid bustle of the day, and the total repose and silence of the house was quite refreshing to her. She passed through the drawing-room into the hall, from whence not even the loud buzz of the multitude without could reach her; and untying her bonnet, and throwing that and her scarf on a slab, she sat down to enjoy for a few moments the cool quiet of the lofty silent room.

At length she reluctantly rose to perform her mother's bidding, walked slowly and languidly up the stairs, along the spacious corridor, and into Mrs Cartwright's dressing-room. This little apartment was no longer the dear familiar scene of maternal fondness that it once was, or Helen might here again have been tempted to sit down for the enjoyment of temporary repose. But, in truth, she no longer loved that dressing-room; and walking straight to the chimney-piece, she took the packet she found there, and turned to retrace her steps.

It was with a start of disagreeable surprise, though hardly of alarm, that she saw Mr Stephen Corbold standing between her and the door. The persevering impertinence of his addresses had long ago obliged her to decline all communication with him, and it was therefore without appearing to notice him that she now pursued her way towards the door. But hardly had she made a step towards it, when the odious wretch enclosed her in his arms. She uttered a loud shriek, and by a violent effort disengaged herself; but ere she could reach the door, he had closed, locked it, and put the key in his pocket.

A dreadful sensation of terror now seized upon her; yet even then she remembered that she was in her mother's house, and a feeling of confidence returned.

'You are intoxicated, sir!' said she, drawing back from him towards the bell. 'But you surely cannot be so mad as to insult me here?'

'I will insult you nowhere, Miss Helen, if you will behave as you ought to do to the man whom the Lord hath chosen for your husband. But as for your ringing the bell, or screeching either, I'll fairly tell you at once, it is of no use. There is not a single human being left in the house but our two selves; so you may as well give me satisfaction at once, and promise to marry me without more trouble, or else, as the Lord liveth, I will make you thankful for the same, without my ever asking you again.'

'Open that door, sir, and let me out instantly,' said Helen, pale as death, yet still not believing that the monster before her would dare to attempt any outrage. 'Even Mr Cartwright,' she added, 'would resent any impertinence offered to me under my mother's roof. Let me pass, sir: believe me, you had better.'

'Believe me, I had better not, Miss Helen. You have been playing the fool with me long enough; and as to my cousin Cartwright, he is quite of the same opinion, I assure you. Charming Helen!' he exclaimed, again stretching out his arms to enclose her, 'be only half as kind as you are beautiful, and we shall be the happiest couple in the world!'

'At least, sir, you must let me consult my mother about it,' said Helen, contriving to keep the table between them, and believing that he was there only in consequence of his being intoxicated. 'Let me ask my mother's consent, Mr Corbold.'

Corbold laughed aloud. 'You think me tipsy, my sweet girl; but if I am, trust me it's no more than just to give me courage to teach you your duty. My charming Helen! let go the table, and understand the thing at once. My cousin Mr Cartwright is under some obligations to me, and he means to settle them all by giving me a pretty fortune with you; and as he knows that unhappily you are not converted as yet, and have shown yourself not over christian-like in return for my love, it is he himself who invented this scheme of having you sent up here when all the servants were out of the house – and of my being here ready to meet you, and to teach you your duty to him, and to your mother, and to your heavenly father, and to me; – and so now you know all and everything, and I have got the key of the room in my pocket. – And will you consent to be my wife, beginning from this very minute?'

Dreadful as Helen's terror was, her senses did not leave her; on the contrary, all the strength of her mind seemed to be roused, and her faculties sharpened, by the peril that beset her. She doubted not for a moment that his statement respecting Mr Cartwright's part in this villany was true, and that she was indeed left in the power of this detested being, with no help but the protection of Heaven and her own courage. She fixed her eye steadily on that of Corbold, and perceived that, as he talked, the look of intoxication increased; she therefore skilfully prolonged the conversation by asking him, if indeed she must be his wife, where they were to live, whether her sister Fanny might live with them, whether he ever meant to take her to London, and the like; contriving, as she did so, to push the table, which still continued between them, in such a direction as to leave her between it and the door of her mother's bed-chamber. Corbold was evidently losing his head, and appeared aware of it; for he stopped short in the replies and professions of passionate love that he was making: exclaiming with an oath that he would be trifled with no longer, he suddenly thrust the table from between them, and again threw his arms round Helen's waist.

She was not, however, wholly unprepared to receive him. On first approaching the table that had hitherto befriended her, she perceived on it a large vial of spirits of hartshorn: this she had taken possession of, and held firmly in her hand; and at the moment that Corbold bent his audacious head to kiss her, she discharged the whole contents upon his eyes and face, occasioning a degree of blindness and suffocation, that for the moment totally disabled him. He screamed with the sudden pain, and raised his hands to his tortured eyes. Before he removed them, Helen had already passed through her mother's bed-room, and was flying by a back staircase to the servants' rooms below. Without waiting to see if she were pursued, she opened a back door that led into the stable-yard, and, after a moment's consideration, proceeded across it, into a lane which led in one direction to the kitchen gardens, and in the other into the road to Oakley.

Even at that moment Helen had time to remember that if she turned her steps towards the kitchen gardens, she should pass by a park gate which would immediately lead her to all the safety that the protection of an assembled multitude could give. But she remembered also that in a few hours she should again be left in the hands of Mr Cartwright, and, inwardly uttering a solemn vow that nothing should ever again make her wilfully submit to this, she darted forward, unmindful of her uncovered head, and, with a degree of speed more proportioned to her agitation than her strength, pursued the short cut across the fields to Oakley, and entering the grounds by the gate which led to the lawn, perceived Sir Gilbert, Lady Harrington, and their son, seated on a garden bench, under the shelter of a widely spreading cedar-tree.

Helen knew that she was now safe, and she relaxed her speed, slowly and with tottering steps approaching the friends from whom, not-withstanding their long estrangement, her heart anticipated a warm and tender welcome. Yet they did not rise to meet her.

'Perhaps,' thought she, 'they do not know me;' and it was then she recollected that her hair was hanging dishevelled about her face without hat or cap to shelter it. She was greatly heated, and her breath and strength barely sufficed to bring her within a few yards of the party, when, totally exhausted, she sat down upon the turf, and burst into tears.

Colonel Harrington had not written the letter to Helen which the Vicar of Wrexhill destroyed without having put both his parents in his confidence. Lady Harrington's fond affection for her god-daughter, which her enforced absence had in no degree lessened, rendered the avowal of her son's attachment a matter of unmixed joy; and though Sir Gilbert declared that he would as soon stand in the relation of brother to his Satanic majesty as to Cartwright, he at length gave his apparently sulky consent with perhaps as much real pleasure as his lady herself.

Both the one and the other, however, knew perfectly well that their son would have been an excellent match for Helen, even when her father was alive, and would, as it was supposed, have given her a fortune of forty thousand pounds; and they felt some degree of triumph, neither unamiable nor ungenerous in its nature, at the idea of securing to one at least of poor Mowbray's family a station in society that not even their connexion with Mr Cartwright could tarnish.

The whole family understood the position of things at the Park too well to be surprised at no answer's being sent express to Colonel Harrington's letter, and the following post was waited for with pleasurable though impatient anxiety. But when it arrived without bringing any answer, and another and another followed with no notice taken of a proposal of marriage, which, as Sir Gilbert said, the proudest woman in England might have been glad to accept, the misery of the young man himself, and the anger and indignation of his parents, were about equally vehement.

Considering the opinion entertained by Sir Gilbert of what he was pleased to term Mr Cartwright's finished character, it is surprising that no idea should ever have occurred to him of the possible suppression of this important epistle; but, in truth, the same interpretation of it had suggested itself to the minds of them all. They believed that Helen, from a sense of duty, had submitted the proposal to her mother, and that, forbidden to accept it by the vindictive feelings of the 'parvenu priest,' she had been weak enough to obey even his commands to leave the letter unanswered – a degree of timidity and want of proper feeling, productive of almost equal disappointment to all three.

Impressed with such feelings against her, it is perhaps not very surprising that neither the heart-stricken lover, nor his offended parents, rose to welcome the approach of poor Helen.

'Some family quarrel, I suppose,' said Lady Harrington. 'They seem to have turned her out of doors in some haste.'

'I will promise her that she shall not now find an entrance into mine,' said Sir Gilbert. 'Perhaps the young lady thinks better of it, and that it may be as well to contradict pa and ma a little for the sake of being Mrs Harrington. Those who will not when they may, when they will they shall have——' But, before Sir Gilbert could finish his stave, Helen Mowbray was stretched upon the turf.

Colonel Harrington, not too well knowing what he did, ran to the spot where she lay, and hardly daring to look at her, stammered out –

'Miss Mowbray! Gracious Heaven, how fearfully she changes colour! So red, and now so deadly pale! Speak to me, Helen – What has happened to you? – How comes it that you are here? After – Oh, Helen, open your eyes and speak to me! Mother! mother! she is very ill!'

Lady Harrington now rose slowly and gloomily from her seat, and walked to the place where Helen lay, her head supported by the arm of Colonel Harrington; every tinge of colour fled from her cheeks, her eyes closed, and no symptom of life remaining, excepting that tears from time to time escaped from beneath her long eyelashes.

It is difficult to see a person one has ever loved, asleep, and yet retain anger towards them; they look so helpless, so innocent, so free from all that could have ever moved our spleen, that not the most eloquent defence that language ever framed could plead their cause so well as that mute slumber. Still more difficult would it be to look at a fair creature in the state in which Helen now lay, and retain any feeling harsher than pity.

'There is something more in all this, William, than we yet understand,' said Lady Harrington, after gazing silently at Helen for some minutes. 'This poor child has not fainted, her tears prove that; but she is suffering from bodily fatigue and mental misery. – Helen! rouse yourself. Let us understand each other at once. Why did you not reply to my son William's letter?'

Helen did rouse herself. She opened her eyes, and fixing them on Lady Harrington, while the colour for a moment rapidly revisited her cheeks, she said in a voice so low as to be scarcely audible, 'A letter from Colonel Harrington? – To me? – A letter to me? – I never received it.'

'Thank God!' cried Colonel Harrington, springing from the ground, for Helen's head no longer rested on his arm. 'Oh! what suffering should we have been spared if we had done her but the justice to think of this!'

He hastily returned to his father, who, though he had not advanced a step, had risen from his seat, and, to do him justice, was looking towards Helen with great anxiety. 'She never received it, sir!' said he, in a voice husky from agitation: 'Oh! come to her; soothe her with kindness, my dearest father, and all may yet be happiness amongst us.'

'What, Helen! – Helen, my poor girl, are you come to us with some new trouble? – And did you indeed never get William's letter, my dear child?'

The mention of such a letter again dyed Helen's cheek with blushes; but she raised her eyes to Sir Gilbert's face, with a look that seemed to ask a thousand questions as she replied,

'I never received any letter from Colonel Harrington in my life.'

'I am devilish glad to hear it, my dear, that's all. So, then, you don't know that——'

'Hold your peace, Sir Knight,' said Lady Harrington, interrupting him. 'And you come with me, sweet love. I'll lay my best herbal to that dead leaf, that you are the only one perfectly faultless among us: and that one, two, and three of us deserve to be – I can hardly tell what – in the power of the vicar, I think, for having been so villanous as to suspect you; and worse still, for having lived so close to you without ever having found out whether you were really watched like a state prisoner or not.'

'Has the rascal dared——?' cried Sir Gilbert. But, before he could finish his sentence, Lady Harrington and her son were leading Helen between them towards the house, her ladyship laying a finger on her lip as she passed her husband, in token that he was to say no more.

Having reached what Lady Harrington called a place of safety, where, as she said, the men could neither come nor hear, she made Helen lay herself upon a sofa, and then said,

'Now, my Helen, if you are ill at ease in body, lay there quiet, and try to sleep; but if you are only, or chiefly ill at ease in mind, let your limbs only remain at rest, and relieve yourself and me by telling me everything that has happened since we parted last.'

'It is a long and sad history, my dearest friend,' replied Helen, kissing the hand which still held hers, 'but I am very anxious that you should know it all; for so only can the action I have committed to-day be excused.'

'What action, Helen? – what is it you have done, my child?'

'I have eloped from my mother's house, Lady Harrington.'

'But you have eloped alone, Helen?'

'Yes! alone.'

'Well then, my dear, I will give you absolution for that. Perhaps there are those among us who may not find it so easy to absolve you from all blame for not doing it before. But now for particulars. – Will you have a glass of water, Helen? Mercy on me I believe it must be a glass of wine. What can you have got to tell? You change colour every moment, my dear child.'

Helen's narrative, however, being of necessity less full than that contained in the preceding pages, need not be repeated. It was given indeed with all the force and simplicity of truth and deep feeling, and told all she knew of Mr Cartwright's plans and projects; but excepting what she had that day learned during her dreadful interview with Corbold, she had little to add to what Lady Harrington knew before.

This interview, however, was itself fully enough to justify the 'elopement,' of which Helen still spoke with such dismay; and, together with the fact, again asked for, and again repeated, that no letter from Colonel Harrington had reached her hands, was sufficient to make her ladyship burst forth into a passion of indignation against the Vicar of Wrexhill, and to make her, while overpowering Helen with the tenderest caresses, bless her again and again for having at last flown to seek shelter where it would be given with such heartfelt joy.

Smoothed, consoled, and almost happy as Helen was made by this recovered kindness, her anxiety to know why, and upon what subject Colonel Harrington could have written to her, was becoming every moment more powerful. There was something so very fond, so very maternal in Lady Harrington's manner to her, – something that seemed to say that she was of more consequence to her now than she had ever been before, – something, in short, quite indescribable, but which gave birth to such delicious hopes in the breast of Helen, that she almost feared to meet the eye of the old lady, lest all she guessed, and all she wished, should be read in her own.

It is possible, that with all the care she took to avoid the betraying this anxiety, she did not succeed; for, in answer to some very delicate and very distant hint, that it was extremely disagreeable to have one's letters intercepted, Lady Harrington, though she only replied, 'Yes, it is, Helen,' rose and left the room, only adding as she closed the door,

'Keep yourself quiet, my dear child: I shall return to you presently.'

'Presently' is a word that certainly appears, by common usage, to admit of very considerable variety of interpretation; and it was evident that on the present occasion the two parties between whom it passed understood it differently. Long before Lady Harrington again appeared, Helen felt persuaded that some important circumstance must have occurred to make her so completely change her purpose; yet the good lady herself, when she re-entered the room, looked and was perfectly unconscious of having made any delay at all inconsistent with her 'presently.'

She held a folded paper in her hand. 'You have not asked me, Helen,' she said, 'on what subject it was that my son wrote to you; and yet I suspect that you have some wish to know. I have been down stairs to consult him on the best mode of repairing your precious vicar's treachery, and he suggested by putting into your hands the copy of the letter which has been so basely intercepted; which copy, it seems, has remained safely in his desk, while its original has probably fed the flames in Mr Cartwright's secret chamber, kindling thereby a sympathetic and very consuming fire in the breast of the writer.'

Helen stretched forth a very trembling hand to receive the paper; her eyes were fixed upon it, either to read through its enclosure the characters within, or to avoid at that moment meeting the eye of her godmother.

'I shall leave you, my love, to peruse it alone; and presently, when I think you have done so, will return to ask if you cannot in some degree comprehend what must have been felt at its not obtaining an answer.'

Having said this, Lady Harrington retired without waiting for a reply, and leaving Helen unable for a moment to learn what her heart throbbed with such violence to know.

The letter of which Helen now held the copy has been already presented to the reader; and if she chance to be one of Helen's age, having at her heart a love unbreathed to any human ear, she may guess what Helen's feelings were at finding such love had met an equal, an acknowledged return. Such a one may guess Helen's feelings; – but no other can.

Lady Harrington's *presently* now seemed to Helen as much shorter than it really was, as the last had seemed longer. She had read the letter but four times through, and pressed it to her heart, kissed it, and so forth, not half so much as she desired, and it deserved, when a knock was heard at the door, and the old lady again entered.

The happy, but agitated girl stood up to receive her, and though she spoke not a single word, the manner in which she rushed into her maternal arms, and hid her face upon her bosom, spoke plainly enough that the gallant colonel had no reason to despair.

'What must he have thought of me!' were Helen's first words. – 'And you? – and Sir Gilbert? – Such a letter! Dearest, dearest Lady Harrington, you could not really think I had ever received it?'

'You have struck the right chord there, my Helen. We all deserve to have suffered ten thousand times more than we have done, for having for a moment believed it possible you should have received that letter and not invented some means to answer it – let the answer be what it might. And this answer? – you have not yet told me what it is to be. I do not know how much, or how little, you may happen to like William, my dear; but in case you should have no insuperable aversion to him, the business is made delightfully easy by this adventure. The elopement is done and over already.'

Helen only pressed Lady Harrington's hand to her heart, but said nothing.

'Yes, – you have found the way to let me into your secret, without speaking. This little heart throbs violently enough to prevent any suspicion of indifference. But what am I to say to my impatient hero below? – That you will, or you won't marry him, as soon as the lawyers will let you?'

'Oh! Lady Harrington!'

'Come down stairs, my dear; – you had better come down, I do assure you; for I expect Sir Gilbert will be up in a moment, and you cannot suppose that William will remain behind; and my bed-room would by no means be so dignified a scene for the denouement as the great saloon. Come, dear, come.'

And Helen went – trembling, blushing, with tears in her eyes, and such palpitation at her heart that she was very sure she could not pronounce a word. But what need was there of words? The happy colonel was soon perfectly satisfied, and thanked her on his bended knee for a consent more looked than spoken.

Even Sir Gilbert himself, though singularly attached to plain speaking, seemed well content on the present occasion to dispense with it; and pressed Helen to his heart, and kissed her forehead, and called her his dear daughter, appparently with as much satisfaction as if she had declared herself ready to accept of his son in the very best arranged words ever spoken upon such an occasion.

When the first few decisive moments were past, and each one of the party felt that all things were settled, or about to be settled, in exact conformity to their most inward and earnest desires, and when Helen was placed as the centre of the six loving and admiring eyes that were fixed upon her, she closed her own; but it was neither to faint, nor to sleep, but to meditate for a moment with the more intensity upon the miraculous change wrought in her destiny within the last few hours.

'What are you thinking of, my Helen?' said the colonel, jealous, as it should seem, of losing sight of those dear eyes, even for a moment.

'I am endeavouring to believe that it is all real,' replied Helen with beautiful simplicity.

'Bless you, my darling child,' said the rough baronet, greatly touched. 'What an old villain I have been to you, Helen! – abusing you, hating you, calling you all manner of hard names, – and your little heart as true as steel all the time.'

'Real? – real that you are beloved by me, Helen?' cried Colonel Harrington, absolutely forgetting that he was not tête-à-tête with his fair mistress.

'And how is she to answer him, with you and me peering in her face, my lady? Ought we not to be ashamed of ourselves? – Come along this moment.'

'Very well, – I will go, but only upon one condition, Helen. Remember, William, she is to indulge in no disagreeable reminiscences, and no melancholy anticipations, but look just as beautiful and as happy when I come back, as she does now.'

This farewell advice was not thrown away; for it assisted Colonel Harrington to baffle, or to banish, all the fears and regrets respecting her mother's displeasure at her conduct, which came like a cloud across the bright perspective of Helen's hopes for the future. Her lover showed himself, indeed, sufficiently adroit, both in turning to account all the favourable circumstances attending their sudden engagement, and in using his mother's authority to prevent her dwelling upon what was unfavourable. 'Might not a second home,' he asked, 'be of great advantage both to Fanny and Miss Torrington? Might not the connection tend to keep Mr Cartwright in order, and prevent his finally injuring Charles? And lastly, did she not think it would give pleasure to that Charles himself?'

To Lady Harrington Helen had frankly recounted the history of Corbold's hateful persecution, from its first beginning in London, to

the fearful outrage it had led to on that eventful day; but she had
begged her to repeat no more of it to Sir Gilbert and the colonel than
might be sufficient to render her running away intelligible; and this
request having been strictly complied with, for Lady Harrington
seemed as unwilling as Helen to trust her men-folk with this history;
Colonel Harrington, in conversing with her on all she had felt and
suffered since her mother's marriage, spoke of him only as a
presumptuous man who had dared to persevere in addressing her after
she had refused him.

It was, probably, the heightened colour of Helen as she listened to
this mention of his name that excited a greater degree of interest and
curiosity concerning him, than her lover had at first bestowed upon
him.

'Were these hateful addresses repeated by letter, or in person, Helen?'
said he, fixing his eyes upon her agitated face.

'In person – in person,' answered Helen, impatiently.

'Did your mother know, Helen, how greatly these addresses annoyed
you?'

'I have often attempted to tell her; but she has always evaded the
subject, telling me strangely enough, and Heaven knows, not very
correctly, that it was plain I did not know my own mind, or else that I
was guilty of affectation.'

'Your mother, then, Helen, would have approved of this man's
addresses?'

'I fear so.'

'It was, then, to avoid her importunity that you left her house to-day?'

Helen looked uneasy and distressed under this questioning, but
answered, 'No, Colonel Harrington; not her importunity, but his own.'

The blood mounted to the young soldier's face, and an angry glance
shot from his eye, as if he suspected something approaching – but at great
distance – to the truth.

'He surely did not dare to be impertinent? Helen, you have not told
me all: you came here in a state of dreadful agitation; tell me, I conjure
you, all that has happened to you. – You will not, Helen? What am I to
think of this? – that you have been insulted in a manner that you will not
repeat to your affianced husband? For Heaven's sake, put an end to this
torture; I must know all.'

'Your mother does know all, Colonel Harrington; make me not repeat
the hateful history again.'

'Will you refer me to my mother? Will you permit me to tell her that
you have done so?'

'Why, Colonel Harrington,' replied Helen, 'should you wish to know
more than I have told you? But of course I cannot object to your

knowing all that has passed between us, – only I think he does not deserve the trouble you take in speaking of him.'

Much to the surprise of Sir Gilbert and his lady, who were very amiably undergoing a real penance, by absenting themselves from the sight of happiness which touched them so nearly, Colonel Harrington was seen hurrying towards them, where they were beguiling the time as they could, by inhaling the cool breath of evening under the cedar-tree.

'Take a turn with me, mother, will you?' said he in a voice not quite as gay as they expected to hear from him.

Lady Harrington immediately rose, and passing her arm under his they walked off together at a rapid pace to a distant walk.

'Mother!' he said, stopping short and looking earnestly in her face 'tell me, I beseech you, everything that you have learnt from Helen respecting that wretch Corbold. For some reason or other which I cannot understand, she is averse to entering upon the subject with me; but she assures me that you know everything that has passed, and she has authorised my asking you for the particulars.'

'Has she, William? Then she is a silly girl for her pains. But it is your fault, I dare say. You have been tormenting her with cross-questions about a vulgar villain that neither of you ought ever again to call to remembrance. Say no more about him or his precious cousin either. Surely we can find more agreeable subjects to talk about than the vicar and his cousin.'

'Very likely, mother. But I cannot be easy till I know exactly what it was which caused Helen to leave her mother's house in the manner she did this afternoon. Have I not a right to inquire? – can you blame me for doing so?'

'No, my dear William, I do not. But heavily shall I blame you if you make an extorted confidence the source of quarrel between an officer of rank in his majesty's service and a pettifogging methodist attorney of Wrexhill.'

'Is it possible, mother, that you know me so little as to think there can exist the slightest chance of my doing this? Pray do not keep me in this fever for the sake of protecting me from a duel with Mr Stephen Corbold.'

'There you are, hot-head, – your father's own son beyond all question. Now listen then to this infamous story, and take care that you do not renew a sorrow that is past, by improperly resenting it.'

After this preface, Lady Harrington ventured to repeat to her son the narrative she had heard from Helen. He listened with very exemplary tranquillity, only occasionally biting his lips, but uttering no single word of any kind till it was concluded. He then said very quietly, – 'Let us return to poor Helen, mother. – How admirably has she behaved throughout!'

Lady Harrington looked up into her son's face as if to discover whether his calmness were genuine; but his pocket-handkerchief at that moment concealed his features, and, as he walked rapidly towards the house, she could only take it for granted that all was right, and follow him.

Having reached the door of the room where he had left Helen, he opened it, but waited outside till his mother overtook him.

'Go to her, mother,' said he, 'and confess that you have told me everything. I would rather you did this than me; – tell her too, that she has behaved gloriously, and, when I think you have put her at her ease about me, I will come to you.'

So saying, he passed on, and entered a small parlour that was called his own at the front of the house.

Sir Gilbert soon followed his lady, and, without going again over the disagreeable narrative at length, the whole business was made sufficiently intelligible to the baronet to make him extol in high terms the courage and presence of mind of his future daughter. This occupied a quarter of an hour excellently well, but still the colonel came not: and Helen, though with no feeling of alarm, certainly kept her eye upon the door with more steadiness than she was herself aware of. At length, Lady Harrington began to show evident symptoms of that state of mind usually called fidgeting. She rang the bell and asked if the colonel were at home. The servant did not know. Tea was ordered, and when it came the same question was repeated; but the same answer was not given, for the man said that the colonel had been seen to go out about half an hour ago.

'Who saw him go, John?' said her ladyship; 'did you?'

'No, my lady, – it was the colonel's own groom.'

'Send him here.'

The groom came, and was questioned as to how and when he had seen his master go out.

'I was in the harness-room, my lady, and the colonel came in, and took down, one after another, all the coachman's whips from the pegs, and at last, my lady, he chose the newest and the stoutest, and carried it away with him: – but he said never a word.'

'Wheugh!' whistled Sir Gilbert with very considerable continuity of sound. 'That will do, Dick – you may go. And so, his colonelship is gone forth with the stoutest and the best horsewhip he could find. Well, upon my word, I do not think he could have done better.'

'Foolish boy!' exclaimed Lady Harrington. 'He will get into some abominable scrape or other!'

'Yes, my lady; – he will horsewhip the lawyer, you may depend upon it: – and then he will have damages to pay. But for an only son, William is far from extravagant, and I really don't feel inclined to begrudge him this little amusement.'

'Nor I, either, Sir Gilbert, provided he takes care not to get into a downright vulgar brawl.'

'Come, come, Helen,' said Sir Gilbert, turning towards her, 'you must not look pale, my child, for this. You are not afraid that there will be any blunder, are you? and that the attorney will horsewhip the soldier? – No harm will be done, depend upon it, – except to my new horsewhip.'

CHAPTER XLII

MR CORBOLD'S ADVENTURES

It was some time before Mr Stephen Corbold recovered sufficiently from the efforts of Helen's libation to enable him to see where he was, or to perceive that where he was, she was not. The ceremony had, indeed, been a painful one; but it at least did him the good service of dispelling the effects of the wine he had taken; and after a few moments more of winking, and blinking, and wiping his smarting eyes, he descended the stairs to seek his cousin, a soberer, if not a better man than when he mounted them.

Everything was at this time in full activity on the lawn. Above two thousand people were assembled there, all more than decently clad, and presenting altogether a very striking spectacle. Those who before dinner had been the company, were now converted into spectators: many of them accommodated with seats in the shade, from whence they watched the chequered movements of the motley crowd. This cool and quiet position was in every way beneficial to those who had been tempted to heat themselves by drinking somewhat too freely of the vicar's wine. Among these Mr Corbold introduced himself; probably, more sober than any of them, – except, perhaps, the vicar himself, – but bearing in his 'altered eye,' and general discomfiture of aspect, more visible traces of intemperance than any individual amongst them.

Mr Cartwright rose to meet him with sensations of considerable alarm. He fancied, from his appearance, that he was quite intoxicated, and feared the utterance of some folly which might explain the cause of his having absented himself more fully than was at all necessary.

This idea was by no means lessened when his cousin beckoned him from the party amidst whom he sat, and gravely assured him that Miss Helen had very nearly murdered him.

'Compose yourself, cousin Stephen – compose yourself. Where have you left her?'

'Left her? – She left me, I tell you, blind, and almost suffocated. If you don't wish to have the whole county set gossiping about Mrs Mowbray's will – your wife's will, I mean, – you had better let me see that vixen properly punished, cousin. As I live and breathe I will have revenge somehow.'

'You shall, you shall, Stephen,' answered the vicar, endeavouring to quiet him. 'She shall be treated in any way that you like, only don't make a noise now.'

'Will you give orders that she shall be confined to her room and kept on bread and water?'

'To be sure I will, if you desire it. She shall be locked up as soon as the place is cleared: and you shall see it done, Stephen, if you will only step in, and take a nap in my library to recover yourself a little.'

This proposal was, on the whole, a very tempting one; for Mr Stephen Corbold's head ached with considerable violence, not to mention that he had hardly yet recovered his eyesight, and was otherwise very ill at ease. So, without arguing the matter farther, he retreated to the comfortable station recommended to him, and soon fell into a slumber that lasted till the whole business of the day, prayers, blessing, and all, were done and over, and the place as solitary and forsaken as if no Serious Fancy Fair, no Israelitish missionary, and no Fababo had ever been heard of.

It was then that the Vicar of Wrexhill remembered his cousin Stephen. And it was then that Fanny Mowbray, looking round the room in which the whole family was assembled, said, 'Where is Helen?'

This question, which, as it seemed, no one could answer, and the recollection of his library guest, coming at one and the same moment across him, made Mr Cartwright start. Poor man! He was most heartily fatigued and worn out by the honours, glories, and hospitalities of the day, and wished for nothing on earth so much as soda-water and a bed-room bougie. But he felt that his labours were not over, though not exactly aware how much remained to be done.

Having furnished himself with a light, and commanded that Miss Mowbray should be desired to meet him in the library, he repaired immediately to that room, where he found, as he expected, his serious and legal relative as fast asleep in his favourite arm-chair, as he himself wished to be in his bed.

The ceremony of awaking him was soon performed; and when he once more stood on his feet, and had rubbed his still suffering eyes sufficiently to perceive where he was, the vicar addressed him thus, in the most gentle voice imaginable, hoping to soothe and get rid of him.

'Well, cousin Stephen, you have had a nice nap; and now you had better go home. It is getting quite late. Good night, Stephen.'

'What have you done with that murderous vixen, cousin Cartwright? I won't stir till I know you have locked her up, as you promised to do.'

'I have ordered her to come here, Stephen, that you may yourself hear what I mean to say to her.'

'I don't want to see her, cousin Cartwright,' replied the attorney, in a tone that betokened as much fear as dislike; 'I only want to have her punished.'

'And punished she shall be, depend upon that; but if you really do not wish to see her, cousin Stephen, you had better be off, at once, for I expect her here every moment. Come along – I will walk with you myself as far as the lodge.'

Whatever vengeance he wished executed on Helen, that he had no inclination to be present at it himself, was proved by the alacrity with which the attorney acceded to this proposal.

'Only let me get my hat – it's quite a new hat, – and I'll come with you this moment, cousin Cartwright.'

The hat was found, and the two serious gentlemen set off together across the lawn; from that point, to within a few yards of the lodge, the lawyer entertained the minister with such an account of Helen's attack upon him, as convinced the latter, that it would be quite necessary in his parental character, to exercise such a degree of authority as might speedily bring the rebellious young lady to reason. It was already as dark as a fine night in July ever is, and the fine large oaks which in many places overhung the road, rendered some spots particularly sombre. At one of these, and just before they arrived at the Park gates, they heard the steps of a man whom they appeared to be overtaking.

'Who can this loiterer be?' said Mr Cartwright. 'My people had orders to see that the grounds were cleared, and all the gates locked before this time.'

'We shall be able to see him when we get beyond these trees,' replied Corbold.

He was quite right: a few steps farther brought them to an open space, and there, as if waiting for them, stood the intruder, as still and silent as if he had been a statue.

'We are two to one, however,' observed the attorney, 'but he is a monstrous tall fellow.'

The next breath that issued from the lips of the vicar's cousin came not in words, but in a most dismal, hideous, and prolonged yell; for the 'tall fellow' had seized him by the collar with one hand, while with the other he brandished and applied a huge horsewhip to his shoulders with such energy, activity, and perseverance, that his howling startled the dull ear of night, as well as the frightened organs of his astonished kinsman. Though Mr Cartwright had not the slightest intention of doing so unclerical a thing as interfering in the fray, he drew a little nearer to it than was quite prudent, from a natural curiosity to know who the bold mortal was who dared thus belabour his cousin.

The light was quite sufficient to enable him to discern Colonel Harrington in the aggressor; but it should seem that it was not equally effective to the eyes of that gentleman himself, or he would hardly have ventured to permit a few apparently random, but very sharp cuts to visit the reverend shoulders of the owner of the soil on which he stood. This prodigious impiety, however, certainly took place, upon which the vicar, very properly anxious to put the earliest possible stop to such indecent proceedings, ran off as fast as his legs could carry him, and in about half an hour returned again with eight stout serving-men, armed with bludgeons, broom-sticks, and the great kitchen-poker.

That he had not, in his agitation, forgotten the spot on which he had left his unfortunate cousin, was quickly made manifest to the ears of all who accompanied him; for dismal groans made themselves heard exactly from the place where the operation had been performed, and on examination, the bruised body of Mr Stephen Corbold was found extended on the grass, apparently too stiff and sore to have much power of movement left.

Even during the hurried interval which Mr Cartwright spent in his house while waiting for the gathering together of his host, he had found time to inquire of his wife if she had seen Helen, and being told in reply that she was nowhere to be found, the extremely disagreeable truth immediately suggested itself to him. In one short, sharp moment he remembered Colonel Harrington's suppressed letter, Corbold's permitted outrage, Helen's escape, and the degrading lash that had so vigorously saluted his own shoulders.

How was it possible, that being, as he most undoubtedly was, the lord and master of Cartwright Park, and all the wealth annexed thereto, and holding his lady's comprehensive will, signed, sealed, and duly executed, in his own possession, – how could it be that he should feel so utterly beat down, overpowered, and degraded?

The bitter pang, however, lasted but a moment. What was the gossip of an hour, or a day, when set against the solid happiness of wealth? This was still his, to have and to hold; and after one little pinch at his heart, as he thought of the longed-for mitre, he struggled manfully to despise the paltry annoyance, and hastened, with all the speed he could make, to the rescue of his cousin, and, if the Lord so willed, to inflict vengeance, even unto death, upon his enemy.

The Lord, however, did not so will; Colonel Harrington having given the attorney exactly the quantum of flogging he intended, stuck his card, with his name and address both in town and country, into the groaning man's pocket, laid him down very gently on the grass, and departed.

The disposal of the flogged gentleman's person was now taken into consideration. Some cousins, perhaps, might have thought that a bed at Cartwright Park would have been the best thing to propose for it; but it appeared that such was not the opinion of Mr Cartwright; for having quickly ascertained the situation of affairs, and assured himself that Colonel Harrington was no longer within his reach, he instantly ordered the coachman and stable-boy, who were among his suite, to return with all possible haste to the house, and prepare a carriage instantly to take his ill-used cousin home.

'Take me to your house, cousin!' murmured the smarting man, 'I shall die if you send me to Wrexhill!' But Mr Cartwright did not happen to hear him; and indeed his time and attention were wholly engrossed till the carriage arrived, and his kinsman lifted into it, by a strict examination of the people at the lodge, as to when Colonel Harrington had entered the Park, and whether they were at all aware that he was still lurking there.

To all which inquiries he of course received for answer − 'Law! your honour, upon such a day as this, how was anybody to mark who went in, or who went out of the Park?'

Mr Stephen Corbold was therefore safely conveyed to his own dwelling in Wrexhill; and the vicar returned to tell his lady, that from circumstances which had transpired, there could be no doubt but her daughter Helen had eloped with Colonel Harrington.

'On my word, my dearest Cartwright, I hardly know how to be sorry for it. William Harrington would be an excellent match for any woman. They were very fond of each other when they were children; and Helen has been so miserable and moping ever since I married, that it has been quite a misery to see her. I thought she was in love with your cousin? However, I suppose she has changed her mind again, and that it was a fit of jealousy on the part of Harrington that made him attack poor Mr Corbold. But we can't help it, you know. I am tired to death, my dear Cartwright; − do not let us stay up any longer talking about it; I dare say Helen will be very happy.'

So ended the eventful day of the Fababo Fancy Fair.

*　*　*

It is not necessary to inquire what were the reports, or what the gossipings to which this day's events gave rise. The papers announced that a very large sum had been collected for the interesting missionary;

and all the Hampshire world soon said that Colonel Harrington was going to be married to Miss Mowbray. But the attention of the Park family themselves was at this time greatly engrossed by Henrietta. She had long been in a very delicate state of health, but, probably from some cold caught at the late fête, her symptoms had become rapidly more alarming; she was soon confined to her bed, and the most skilful physician in the county gave it as his opinion that she could not live many weeks.

Rosalind was indefatigable in her attentions to her; and when the awful judgment of the physician was made known to her, she at once resolved that Henrietta should be made acquainted with it, in the hope that the prospect of approaching dissolution might soften her heart and lead her to seek and receive the only consolation of which such a situation admits.

Rosalind was too truly attached to Helen not to rejoice at the unexpected step she had taken, though her surprise at it was unbounded. She knew Helen's character well, she knew too how implicitly they had trusted each other; and that this known, trusted and trusting friend should have eloped without having even hinted to her that Colonel Harrington had confessed the love which in happier moments she owned she hoped he felt, was inconceivable! Still it was true. And though no line of explanation had ever been permitted to reach her, still she rejoiced; and with all the trusting confidence of her nature believed that whatever appeared wrong or unkind, would some day or other be explained.

She now rejoiced yet more at Helen's absence. Henrietta had never admitted her even to the uncertain and capricious degree of friendship which she had bestowed on herself; and had she been still at the Park, it would have been difficult for Rosalind to have devoted herself so wholly to the poor sufferer as she now did. Mrs Cartwright's situation prevented her from being much in the room. Fanny was still less there. She and Henrietta had never loved each other. At first Fanny disliked her because it was easy to perceive that she was neither beloved nor approved by Mr Cartwright; and Henrietta despised her in return for the easy weakness with which she had become her father's convert. So that, in this awful hour, Rosalind was the only friend who drew near her with affection; and most tender and constant was the care she bestowed upon her.

To the communication which she so much dreaded to make, though she considered it her duty to do it, Henrietta only replied by assuring her that for more than a year she had been fully aware that death was rapidly approaching her. 'Alas! how lightly have I listened to you, dear Henrietta, when you have said this!' replied the weeping Rosalind. 'But the reason, dear friend, why I did not, why I could not believe you were in earnest, was——'

'Speak fearlessly, dear Rosalind – was – that you thought I was unfit to die. But so are many, Rosalind, who yet must go when Nature bids them.'

'But now, now Henrietta! Oh! tell me that you do not still doubt all things – doubt even the being of the eternal power that made you; tell me, I beseech you, that you have read and thought on these things since that dreadful day that I overheard you make the confession to Mr Hetherington which has rung in my ears ever since.'

'Yes, Rosalind, I have read, and I have thought – but not now only, my kind friend. My short life, Rosalind, has been but one series of perturbed thinking – my brain has been racked by it. But I have gained nothing.'

'I have no power, Henrietta, no learning, no strength of reason to remove the doubts that so fearfully darken these your last hours. Yet what would I not give that you could taste the ineffable comfort of perfect hope and perfect faith in God!'

'Perfect faith!' repeated Henrietta impatiently – 'why do you have recourse to the slang I hate? Teach me to hope – oh! that you could! but let me not hear the hateful words, the false use of which has been my destruction.'

'Henrietta! dearest Henrietta! will you consent to see a clergyman who can speak to you with the authority of age and wisdom?'

'A clergyman?' she replied, scoffingly. 'Perhaps you will propose that I should see the Reverend Mr Cartwright?'

'No, no. You do not think that it is such as him I would wish to send to you.'

'Yet he is my father, Miss Torrington. And there it is, you see – there lies the difficulty. Name a clergyman, and Mr Cartwright seems to rise before me. And shall I use my dying breath to say that I would hear with reverence what such as he could say? Leave me in peace, Rosalind. Let me sleep, I tell you. If there be a God, he will pity me!'

There was so much feverish excitement in her manner of speaking, that Rosalind, terrified lest she might hasten the hour she so earnestly wished to retard, in the hope that light might break upon that darkness which it was so terrible to witness, forbore to answer her, and tenderly arranging her pillows under her head, kissed her pale cheek and set herself down behind the curtain, in the place that she now almost constantly occupied.

After a moment, however, Henrietta spoke again, but it was gently and calmly. 'Leave me, my most kind Rosalind,' said she; 'leave me for an hour or two; you must want the fresh air, and I want perfect solitude. Rosalind, I will think. Let no one come to me till I ring my bell. Go, my dear friend!'

Rosalind, greatly affected by the changed voice and manner, pressed to her lip the emaciated hand held out to her, and retired.

Rosalind did indeed require the refreshment of air and exercise, from which she had almost wholly debarred herself for above a week; and such refreshment will certainly do more towards restoring the exhausted strength, both to body and mind, than any other remedy which can be devised. Yet, though it acts well, and almost infallibly, on the system, the benefit does not at once reach the consciousness of the weary watcher. Rosalind, as she slowly dragged her languid steps along, felt none of the pleasurable effects of the sweet breeze that blew in her face, for she was not aware of it. Her heart and soul were still in the chamber of the dying Henrietta; and though greatly too well taught to believe that a few feverish moments of changed opinions can put the passing spirit into a state of fitness for heaven; still she clung to the hope of hearing the unhappy girl avow better thoughts and feelings than those which had so long brooded over her misguided spirit. Fully occupied with these meditations, Rosalind walked for an hour, almost mechanically, through the shrubberies, unmindful of the sweet voice of nature that greeted her in the songs of birds and in the breath of flowers, and thinking only of what she might say or do to make the light of truth send one cheering ray upon the last hours of her unhappy friend.

When she re-entered the house, her maid, who was watching for her, said that Miss Cartwright had rung her bell, and requested to know when she returned.

Blaming herself for her long absence, Rosalind hastened to the sick room, and found Henrietta seated upright in her bed, with rather more animation and brightness in her eyes than she wished to see, for she thought it betokened fever; but her voice and manner were gentle and composed.

'Your words have not fallen to the ground, my most kind Rosalind,' said she; 'and if it be possible, during the short period that remains for me to live, that I should attain a clearer knowledge of what I am than I have hitherto possessed, I shall welcome it most gladly. But of all the attributes with which the beautiful idea that you call God, is invested, the only one that I conceive it possible for mortals to share with Him, is TRUTH. Power, alas! we have none – of knowledge very little, of wisdom less – and as to perfect goodness, perfect benevolence, we are not framed to feel it. But TRUTH, clear, pure, beautiful, and bright, we can know and we can feel! It can make a part of us, even as it makes a part of Him; and by this only, as it seems to me, can we approach Him, touch Him, and, as it were, be part of Him. For truth in a mortal, Rosalind, if it exist at all, is perfect as in a God. It is therefore, my dear friend, that though I feel, ay, and have always felt, that there may be an existing cause, endowed with will, productive of all the wonders of creation – and though this wondrous existence, if it be! deserves all worship – and though I (more sinned against than sinning) have offered none, yet still I feel that I may be forgiven. If I have kept far off from him my worship and my thoughts, at least I never have approached him with falsehood on my tongue or in my heart; and, to my judgment, this is the only crime relating to our intercourse with God at which we need to tremble. If such a Being be, can our blundering theories so touch his greatness that he should deign to frown upon us for them? No, no, no! WE CANNOT KNOW HIM; and those who guess the nearest, can guess but very darkly. But truth and falsehood are as much within the compass of man's nature as of God's, and therefore are they, as concerning Him, the only virtue and the only sin.'

Henrietta spoke these words with her eyes closed, slowly and deliberately, as if her mind, like a cloud that

– 'Turns forth its silver lining to the night,'

sought in the midst of darkness to show the faint gleam within.

But every word she uttered made Rosalind more deeply feel the necessity of letting her hear the truths of religion from some one who had made its laws the study of a holy life. She longed that she should hear with more authority than she could lend to it, the voice of God himself, as revealed to man in records enduring as the world; – but where was she to seek such a one? As poor Henrietta had said, the name of a minister could to her suggest no other image than that of her father; – and from him she ever seemed to turn with horror.

Yet still Rosalind could not endure to abandon the hope that such a one might be found, and only waited till Henrietta would promise to see him before she took measures for the purpose. In answer to this request, the dying girl replied,

'But my permission is not all that is necessary, dearest Rosalind. What would my father say if you were fortunate enough to obtain for me a visit from such a one as you describe? He would not bear it. He would not admit his approach. I know he would not.'

'Let me ask him, Henrietta.'

'No!' cried the invalid with sudden energy, as if she had at that moment conceived and decided on her line of conduct. 'I will ask him myself! This doubt, this darkness, this fearful mist that seems to hang about me, is terrible. Why should I feel not hopeful and assured as you do? Send to him, Rosalind – send to my father; and send too for his besotted wife, and for the poor, weak, wavering Fanny. Send for them all. –

But don't you leave me, Rosalind. I have a strange, anxious fluttering at my heart. It will be better when I have spoken to him.'

Rosalind delayed not a moment to do her bidding. There was an inequality in her manner that frightened her. She feared her time was short; and so worded the summons she sent to Mr Cartwright and his wife, that they came instantly. Fanny entered the room nearly at the same moment; and it was evident from their manner that they all thought they were come to receive her last farewell.

The feeble Henrietta asked Rosalind so to arrange her pillows that she might sit upright. Rosalind did so, and then kneeled down beside the bed.

Mr Cartwright stood with his back leaning against the bed-post, and his eyes fixed on the ground: his wife entered leaning on his arm, and had not quitted it; but for some reason or other, Henrietta, who rarely took notice of her in any way, now asked her to place herself in a chair beside her bed.

'You had better sit,' said she. 'You are not very strong in any way.'

Fanny stood apart, and alone; and having looked round upon each of them, the dying girl fixed her eyes upon her father, and thus addressed him,

'I have heard you say – a thousand times perhaps – that religion was the business of your life; and for that reason, sir, its very name hath become abhorrent to my soul! Oh, father! – you have much to answer for! I would have given my own right hand to believe in a good, a merciful, a forgiving God! – and I turned my young eyes to you. You told me that few could be saved, and that it was not what I deemed innocence could save me. You told me too, that I was in danger, but that you were safe. You told me that God had set his seal upon you. And then I watched you – oh, how earnestly! – I spied out all your ways! – I found fraud, pride, impurity, and falsehood, mix with your deeds through every day you lived! Yet still you said that God had set his seal upon you, – that your immortal soul was safe, – that happiness eternal was your predestined doom. I listened to you as a child listens to a father; not a word was lost; no, nor an action either. And then it was, father, that I became an unbeliever! an hardened infidel! a daring atheist! If it were true that God had chosen you, then it was true my soul rejected him! – Yet Rosalind, dear Rosalind, do not hate me, – do not shudder at my words. It was because I found no truth in him, that I could not, would not believe his doctrine true. But you – good, kind, and innocent, – I believe you.'

The harsh and awful accents of her voice changed into a tone of the deepest tenderness as she continued to address Rosalind. 'When did you ever lie? You tell me there is a God, and I may trust you. You do not prate of grace, and then labour to corrupt the innocence that looks into your face to ask the way to Heaven. You do not bid me wear a mask of feigned assurance of salvation; nor will you bind my hands, nor keep me from the light of day, when I refuse to kneel, and sigh, and play the hypocrite. You will not bid me lie, and tell me that so only I can find the way to Heaven. You will not——'

With slow and stealthy pace Mr Cartwright at this moment began to creep from his station and approach the door. But Henrietta, whose eyes were half closed – for the lashes seemed heavy with tears – instantly opened them, and cried aloud, 'Stay! I have a right to bid you. – Father! – This good girl is kind and innocent; but she is young and very ignorant. – What can she know of Heaven? Is there – speak truly, these are the last words you will ever utter to me – is there within our reach some pious, holy, humble man of God, – such as I have read of, – but no saint, no saint? Father! is there such a one? – and may he come and pray with me?'

Every eye in the room was fixed on Mr Cartwright, as his daughter made the appeal. For some moments he did not answer; but upon Henrietta's repeating loudly, and almost wildly, 'May he come?' he answered in a low, husky voice, 'This is mere bravado! You have lived a scoffing infidel, – and a scoffing infidel will you die. If, indeed, you wished for prayer and pardon, you would turn to me for it. – My curate may pray with her, – but none else.'

And with these words he turned away without looking at her, and quitted the room.

The silence of death seemed already to have settled on the chamber; which was broken, at length, by the deep sobbings of the unfortunate Mrs Cartwright.

'Poor soul!' said Henrietta, turning towards her. 'She is not wholly bad, but more unfit to judge and act than a baby; – for they can do nothing, and she, alas! can do much dreadful mischief. With my dying breath, unhappy victim of a most finished hypocrite, I do conjure you not to wrong your children, to enrich him. Poor soul! – He loves her not; no, not even so much as, silly as she is, she well deserves from him. He will have a child born to him here, and another at Gloucester, much at the same time. Do not ruin your poor helpless children for him!'

Mrs Cartwright sat with her eyes immovably fixed on those of Henrietta, even after she had ceased to speak: she sighed deeply, but uttered no syllable in reply.

'Take her away, Rosalind. I have no more to say to her. And poor Fanny too. God bless you, Fanny! – You may go now, my dear. All go, but Rosalind.'

Her commands were instantly obeyed, and once more the two strangely-matched friends were left alone together.

'It is too late now, my Rosalind! My strength is failing fast. I can hardly see your sweet, kind eyes, dear Rosalind! – but I can hear. Read to me, dearest; – quick, open the Bible that you left for me: – open it where the man says to Paul, "Almost thou persuadest me to be a Christian."'

Rosalind opened the precious volume, and read to her, slowly and distinctly, that exquisite passage of heaven-taught eloquence, which produced in reply the words she had quoted.

Henrietta's eyes were closed; but now and then a gentle pressure of the hand she held in hers, persuaded Rosalind that she heard and understood each powerful word of that majestic pleading.

When she had reached, and read the words Henrietta had quoted, she paused, and in a moment afterwards the now expiring girl uttered in broken accents,

'Yes, – stop there. It has reached my soul – from your lips only, Rosalind!'

Then suddenly her dying eyes opened, and fixed themselves on Rosalind; she clasped her hands as if in prayer, and then with a strong effort pronounced these words,

'Lord! I believe! – Help thou my unbelief.'

Her head sank on her breast. The breath that uttered these words, was her last.

CHAPTER XLIII

A CHANGE COMES O'ER THE SPIRIT OF HER DREAM

Helen had been nearly six weeks at Oakley without receiving a single line or message from any individual at the Park. She had written to her mother, fully explaining the reasons which had led her so suddenly to absent herself; and also, in the most respectful and affectionate manner, announced to her the proposal of Colonel Harrington and the approbation of his parents, – adding her earnest entreaties that her mother would not withhold her consent to their marriage. To this letter she received no answer; a circumstance which would have occasioned her the most cruel uneasiness, had not the fate of Colonel Harrington's letter to herself enabled her to guess that of her own to her mother. To Fanny and to Rosalind she likewise wrote, and with the same ill success; but, fortunately for her tranquillity, their silence was reasonably interpreted in the same manner: and though this could but ill console her for the separation existing between them, it at least prevented her from feeling the pang of neglected affection.

From her brother she received the only letter that had reached her since they parted; and though it was written in a strain of very melancholy despondency respecting himself, it spoke of her prospects with an energy of satisfaction and hope that it was delightful to have inspired.

The report of Henrietta's death reached her through the servants; and though no cordial intimacy had ever existed between them, she felt as a gentle-hearted young creature must ever feel on hearing that a companion of her own age and sex was gone hence to be no more seen.

More than ever did she wish for tidings of her family; and of Rosalind, perhaps, more than of any other: for she knew that if her feelings for the poor Henrietta had not amounted to affection, she had inspired a very powerful interest in her bosom, and that Rosalind was likely to feel her early death very painfully. It was therefore with the strongest emotions of joy that one morning, rather more than a week after the event, she saw Rosalind approaching the principal entrance of the house alone and on foot.

Helen flew down stairs, through the hall, and out upon the steps to meet her, opening her arms to receive her with all the eager warmth of welcome natural after such an absence. But before Rosalind returned the embrace, she exclaimed,

'You have seen your mother, Helen!'

'Alas! no!' replied Helen. 'Would to Heaven I had, Rosalind! What is it makes you think I have had this great happiness?'

'Because I have just met her, – just seen her with my own eyes driving down the avenue.'

'Impossible! Rosalind, you must be mistaken. I have been sitting in my own room these two hours, copying a long act of parliament for Sir Gilbert; and if any carriage had been here, I must have seen it.'

'No, no, you would not: I observed that the carriage drove direct from the stable-yard, and out into the avenue below the second gate. When I saw the carriage, spite of my astonishment, my first feeling was terror lest I should be seen myself; and accordingly I retreated behind one of the enormous trees, which I am sure hid me effectually, but from whence I had not only a full view of the Cartwright equipage, but of Mrs Cartwright in it, looking, I am sorry to say, even paler and more ill than usual.'

'Is my mother looking ill, Rosalind?' said Helen anxiously, and seeming for the moment to be unmindful of the strange circumstance of her having been at Oakley. 'Is she unwell?'

'I grieve to say that I think she is. A scene which took place in poor Henrietta's room only a few moments before she died, and at which Mrs Cartwright was present, has, I think, shaken her severely. But what can have brought her here, Helen, unless it were her wish to see you? – And yet she has been, and is gone, without your hearing of it.'

'It is indeed most strange,' replied Helen, ringing the bell of the drawing-room, into which they had entered. 'Lady Harrington is, I know, in her closet, – perhaps my mother has seen her.'

'Has my mother been here, Thomas?' inquired Helen of the old servant who answered the bell.

'Oh, dear no, Miss Mowbray: that was noways likely.'

'Likely or not, Thomas, I assure you she has been here,' said Miss Torrington; 'for I myself met her coming away.'

'Then if that is the case, young ladies, there is certainly no use in my telling any more lies about it; for that's a job I don't like to be put upon, seeing as I am not over and above used to it. And so, as you know it already, I'm quite ready and willing to tell you the truth. – Mrs Mowbray, – I ask your pardon, ladies, but I really can't call her by no other name, – Mrs Mowbray has been shut up in the library for above two hours with my master.'

'How very strange!' exclaimed Rosalind thoughtfully. 'Then I am sure she has chosen this day for the same reason that I did. Mr Cartwright was sent for last night by the Earl of Harrowmore. Though he is not very communicative about his adventures in general, he could not resist mentioning this flattering circumstance at tea last night; adding, that he could not refuse the excellent and pious old nobleman, who probably was desirous of obtaining the benefit of his advice on some business of importance. And this morning he set off in his travelling-carriage and four post-horses, with two out-riders, leaving word, as Judy told me, that he should not return till to-morrow. But, good Heavens! what can Mrs Cartwright have to say to Sir Gilbert? and how in the world did he come to admit her, Thomas?'

'Since you know so much, you may as well know all, ladies. The carriage, sure enough, did not venture to drive up even to the back door without leave asked of Sir Gilbert; – at least I suppose it was to ask leave, that one of the new Park servants brought a note for him first. I took it in myself to him, and said, as I was bid, that the man was to wait for an answer. Never did I see mortal face screw itself up funnier than Sir Gilbert's when he was reading that note: he looked for all the world as if he wanted to whistle; howsomever, he did no such thing, but only scrawled a bit of an answer as grave as a judge; and then it was, Miss Mowbray, that he ordered me to say no word whatever of the Park servant's coming, or of the carriage coming after, as it was likely to do; and he sealed up his answer, and told me to give it to the man, and then to go into the garden to look for you and the colonel, Miss Mowbray, and bid you come in, as you know I did, miss; and after a bit you went up stairs, miss, and the colonel's horse was ordered; and when he was off and all clear, then, and not before, the carriage drove into the stable-yard; and your poor mamma, Miss Mowbray, looking as white as a sheet, went tottering and trembling in to Sir Gilbert, and there she stayed till about ten minutes ago, when the bell rang and out she came again, but looking, I thought, a deal less miserable.'

'Thank you, Thomas,' said Helen. 'This is, I believe, all we wish to know.'

The venerable serving-man took the hint and departed.

'What can all this mean, Rosalind?' said her friend the moment the door closed behind him. 'Has anything happened at home that can account for it?'

'I hardly know how to answer you, my Helen, without appearing to know more than I really do – for in honest truth I know nothing. Your mother, it would be wrong to conceal it from you, Helen, is certainly very much out of health, and for some weeks past has appeared I think, out of spirits and unhappy.'

'Oh, Rosalind! Do you think it is I who have made her so? Do you think that my coming here has made her really unhappy?'

'Indeed I do not: on the contrary, I am firmly persuaded she rejoices at it. You know, dearest, that since her marriage I have never been in great favour; and no wonder, considering the very particular aversion I have ever felt, and perhaps manifested, towards her bridegroom. But more than once since you left us, she has spoken to me in a manner which reminded me of the days that are gone; and once she said, when that hateful cause of all harm, her Tartuffe husband, was not in the room, 'You must greatly miss poor Helen, my dear Rosalind.' I involuntarily caught her hand and kissed it, earnestly fixing my eyes on hers to discover if possible what she thought and felt about you. She guessed as much, I fancy, for she turned her head away from me; but she pressed my hand, and said almost in a whisper, 'Dear Helen! I trust that the step she has taken will end in her happiness.' He entered just as she had uttered these words; and the manner in which she started and withdrew her hand when the handle of the door turned, told me plainly enough that her love for her holy spouse was not of that perfect kind which casteth out fear. There was, moreover, Helen, a tear in her eye when she named you.'

'Oh! my dear, dear mother!' cried Helen, her own eyes overflowing with freshly-awakened tenderness. 'To hear this, Rosalind, is a joy far greater than I can express: and yet if this returning love is obtained at the expense of her own happiness, I am a wretch to rejoice at it.'

'You would be a wretch to purchase it at that price perhaps,' replied Rosalind, – 'but not for rejoicing at it, now that, poor soul! she has already paid the penalty, as in truth I fear she has, of peace of mind for returning reason.'

'And what has occurred, Rosalind, to make you think her less happy than heretofore?'

'It is not very easy to answer that question, Helen. Excepting the death of poor Henrietta, and the awful scene which preceded it, in which she accused her father in the presence of Mrs Cartwright, Fanny, and myself, of pretty nearly all the sins and iniquities of which a man can be guilty; excepting this, I can hardly say that any particular circumstance has occurred which can account for the evident change in your mother's spirits, which was quite as evident before the death of Henrietta as since.'

'You have observed no unkindness towards her on his part, Rosalind?' said Helen anxiously.

'N . . . o; certainly I have witnessed nothing that could be called unkindness. You know, Helen, he can smile, and smile – but he seems, I think, to watch her. More than once, when I have been going to her, I have met him coming away; and when he has seen me, he has turned back and re-entered her room with me. I know I have been savagely cross to her ever since her hateful marriage; but since I have seen her looking ill and miserable, my hard heart has softened towards her, and I have sought instead of avoiding her; and I am quite sure that from the moment he perceived this change he has been on the *qui vive* to prevent our being alone together.'

'My poor dear mother! I fear, I fear that she may live to deplore this marriage as much as we have ever done. You know, Rosalind, that we never believed Mr Cartwright to be the holy man he proclaimed himself; but since I have been here, I have heard dreadful stories of him. Lady Harrington's maid is a prodigious gossip; and though I really give her no encouragement, she never dresses me without telling me some new report respecting him. He has, however, a very strong party at Wrexhill, who appear firmly to believe that he is a perfect saint. But here, you know, they are literally and figuratively of another parish, and seem to make it a matter of duty to their own pastor to believe all the tales they can pick up about him. There is one very shocking story indeed, that is, I think, quite incredible. They say that Mrs Simpson has been seduced by him, and only went away to be confined.'

'Incredible. No! – this story is a commentary on one part of Henrietta's dying accusation. She said he would have a child born to him at Gloucester nearly at the same time as that expected here.'

'And it is to Gloucester she is gone!' exclaimed Helen. 'Gracious heaven, what a wretch!'

'That this at least is true, I have not the slightest doubt,' rejoined Rosalind: 'and what is more, I am certain your mother has heard it. You know that this precious vicar invited Mrs Simpson's child to pass the period of her absence at the Park; and you must remember how very fond of the poor little thing your mother seemed to be, actually listening to her parrot performances in the evangelical line as if she had been inspired. It was before you went, I think, that I laughed at her so immoderately for saying that she prayed for currant pudding every night, and that Mrs Cartwright was so very angry with me about it. Well! observe the change, and account for it as you will. For the last two or three weeks she has hardly spoken to the child, or taken the least notice of her: and if I am not greatly mistaken, it is for about the same period that her health and her spirits have appeared to droop. Depend upon it, Helen, some one has carried this report to her.'

'It certainly seems probable. Poor, poor mamma! How terrible her feelings must be, Rosalind, if from thinking this man something half-way between heaven and earth, she has really found out that he is a hypocrite and a villain!'

'Terrible indeed! I would that she had not so well deserved it, Helen. But now comes the question: *what has brought her here?*'

'I think I understand that perfectly,' replied Helen. 'No sooner are her eyes opened to the real character of this man, than her tenderness for us returns. I have little doubt that she came here to speak of me. Perhaps, Rosalind, she has heard, and you too, of my engagement with Colonel Harrington?'

'Perhaps we have, Helen,' replied Rosalind, laughing: 'and I think it likely that you have partly read the riddle right, and that she may have taken advantage of her watchful husband's absence to express to Sir Gilbert her approbation, – which, you know, is necessary before you can be married, Helen.'

'I know it is,' replied Helen, colouring; 'and if indeed she has given this consent, she has removed the only obstacle to our immediate marriage.'

'Then heartily I wish you joy, sweet friend!' said Rosalind, kissing her. 'Novice as I am, I found out long ago – did I not, Helen? – that you and Colonel Harrington, or Colonel Harrington and you – I really do not know how to express myself to spare your beautiful blushes, my dear friend, – but I am very, very glad of this – in every way it is so desirable. Poor dear little Fanny, whose hair is gently creeping down into ringlets again, will find a fitter home with you, Helen, than Cartwright Park can be for her.'

'How fast your fancy runs, Rosalind! How do we know that my mother's visit,' (and Helen's bright blushes all forsook her as she spoke,) – 'how do we know that it was not to forbid this marriage that she came, and not to permit it?'

'Two months ago, had the same thing occurred, I should have thought so: now I cannot think it. However, Helen, this suspense cannot last long. Although Sir Gilbert forbad his servants to mention your mother's visit, for fear perhaps that it should reach the ears of her husband, you may depend upon it that he will inform you of it himself. But I must go, dearest! – I by no means wish this instance of positive rebellion to the commands of my guardian should be known. You must remember the command I long ago received not to carry on any correspondence with the family at Oakley; and this command has never been rescinded. So adieu, my dearest Helen! – I am quite persuaded now that nothing which you could write would reach me at the Park; but unless I am positively locked up, we may surely contrive to meet without my again performing this desperate feat of disobedience. Could you not wander in the fields sometimes?'

'I have done so constantly, dear Rosalind; but ever and always in vain.'

'That has not been because you were forgotten; but I have seldom left poor Henrietta, and never long enough to have reached the fields. But now I certainly can manage this. I should like to bring poor Fanny with me: but this I will not do, for fear of drawing down the anger of Mr Cartwright upon her – which she would not bear, I think, so well as I. – But ought I not, before I go, to ask for Lady Harrington?'

'Oh yes! – I am sure she would be so very glad to see you!'

A message was accordingly sent to my lady's closet, and the two girls requested to go to her there. Helen was not without hope that she would mention to her Mrs Cartwright's visit; but she was disappointed: nor was there the slightest reason to believe from her manner that she was acquainted with it. She appeared exceedingly pleased at seeing Miss Torrington, and told her that whenever she could venture to repeat the visit without endangering the tranquillity of her present irksome home, they should all be delighted to see her.

It was now, however, high time for her to depart; but while returning through the breakfast-room in her way to the hall-door, she met Sir Gilbert. The remembrance of her last interview with him, and its abortive result, brought sudden blushes to her cheeks. She remembered, too, that she had never offered any explanation to Sir Gilbert for so suddenly changing her mind; and altogether she felt so painfully embarrassed, that she hardly ventured to raise her eyes to his face. The voice in which he greeted her, however, soon chased every feeling of embarrassment, or anything else that was not agreeable, for it spoke nothing but welcome and hilarity.

'What! – The bright-eyed Rosalind? Come to look after the runaway? – But I hope you have not scolded her, Miss Torrington, for leaving you all in the lurch? Upon my honour, young lady, she was very right. Take my word for it, she never did a wiser thing in her life. But has she told you the scrape she has got into, Miss Torrington? Poor child! – no sooner ran away from a snake of a stepfather, than she has got noosed by a tiger of a father-in-law. – Ask my lady else. Has she told you all about it, my dear?'

'Perhaps not quite all, Sir Gilbert; – but quite enough to make me very happy, and wish her joy, and you too, most heartily.'

'Thankye, my dear; – I am very much obliged to you. I feel very much inclined to wish myself joy, I assure you, and my pretty daughter too. Kiss me, Helen! God bless you, my dear child, and Charles too! That's a fine fellow, Miss Torrington! And God bless your pretty Fanny! – especially as her soul, you say, has found its way out of Limbo. It is a remarkably fine, pleasant day, Miss Torrington: such a day as this always puts one in spirits.'

Rosalind turned to give a farewell embrace to her friend, whispering in her ear as she did so, 'At least there has been no refusal of consent, Helen! – Adieu!'

CHAPTER XLIV

IN WHICH SUNDRY VISITS ARE MADE

Whatever kind or remorseful feelings had led Mrs Cartwright to make this unexpected visit to Oakley, she seemed to consider this one visit enough – for it was never repeated: and however tenderly she might watch over the fate of Helen, it was evident that she could only venture to do so secretly; for Sir Gilbert never mentioned her visit to any one. But, knowing she had been there, Helen's heart was satisfied when Sir Gilbert, joining her hand and his son's together, said,

'Make haste, children; – get your courting done without loss of time; or you may find yourselves married before it is finished, and so continue lovers after the knot is tied, – a thing never heard of in civilised society.'

' – But very likely, nevertheless, to happen to my Helen's husband, let her marry when she will,' said Colonel Harrington.

To her affianced husband Helen could have no secrets, and accordingly he had been made acquainted with all that she knew respecting her mother's most unexpected appearance at Oakley. He drew the same inference from his father's joyous manner after it that Rosalind had done: and when Sir Gilbert alluded to their marriage as an event which was speedily to take place, no doubt remained either on his mind, or on that of the happy Helen, that Mrs Cartwright, having learned, from some source which her husband could not impede, the proposal that had been made her, she had proved her maternal feelings not extinct, though they had seemed obscured, and ventured to make this secret visit for the purpose of formally giving her consent, and thereby removing the only obstacle to their marriage.

Instructions were accordingly immediately given by Sir Gilbert in person, for he declared that he must see the lawyer himself; and everything relating to settlements was speedily put in train. The day after the baronet's return to Oakley, he sent to Miss Mowbray, requesting that she would meet him in the library; and having greeted her on her entrance with even more than usual affection, he said,

'Do you think, my dear Helen, that you should have courage to make your mother a visit even in the lion's den? Do you think you could have courage to spend half an hour at the Park? I don't think it likely that Master Corbold has forgotten his horse-whipping as yet; – so I own I think you may venture.'

'I will go anywhere, or do anything that you think I ought to do, Sir Gilbert; and to see my dear mother and poor Fanny once more would indeed be a pleausre to me. We have met Rosalind twice since you went to London, and she gives a very indifferent account of mamma's health.'

'Poor thing! you shall go immediately, my dear child, if you have no objection. I have ordered the carriage. William and I will go in it with you as far as the Lodge, and there we will wait your return. If you delay it above an hour, we shall drive up to the house to inquire what is become of you; but you may return to us as much sooner as you like.'

The carriage drove to the door as he spoke; but Helen kept it not waiting long, and on returning from her room to the hall found Colonel Harrington waiting to hand her into it. The two gentlemen stepped in after her, and in a moment she found herself on her road to *Cartwright* Park, accompanied by Sir Gilbert and Colonel Harrington.

The strangeness of this came upon her so forcibly, that she exclaimed, almost unconsciously,

'Is it possible!'

'I don't wonder at your saying that, my dear,' said Sir Gilbert: 'it is very natural. But you see, Helen, that as your mother has testified no dislike to your approaching marriage, or taken any steps to oppose it, I feel that she may expect, perhaps, – in short, I think it is very right that you should call upon her; and to prove that, angry as I have been, I do not bear malice, you may give her this little note from me, Helen. But for your life, child, do not let that wretch her husband see her receive it. I believe, in my soul, he would be the death of her if he thought she could touch a bit of paper from me. – But the truth is, Helen, I think she has suffered enough; and, in short, my dear, I forgive her with all my heart; and I should like her to have this bit of a note from me, and to get a friendly word of answer in return, if I could. But for God's sake be careful, child!'

'Fear not, Sir Gilbert, that I should run any risk of bringing more misery upon her than, I fear, she has already. I will be very careful, – and most thankful am I to be the bearer of a word of kindness to her from you!'

'Well, well, Helen, that's all right, – bygones are bygones. Here we are

at the Lodge. Look at your watch, my dear; and remember, if you do not
return in an hour, we shall come and fetch you. I fear nothing, for the
fellow knows you are under the protection of the Oakley horsewhips;
only it is as well to leave nothing to chance. If you cannot in any way
escape the eyes of the villain, bring my note back again. – There, now,
dear, get out. Goodb'ye!'

The colonel was already at the door to assist her, and whispered
earnestly as he quitted her hand, 'You will not stay the full hour, Helen,
if – you love me.'

With a step as light as Camilla's, Helen traversed the Park, and, with a
heart throbbing with many feelings, wound her way through sundry
well-known twistings and turnings that brought her to the same door by
which she had quitted the house on the memorable day of the Fancy
Fair. From what Rosalind had told her, she thought that if she could find
her way unannounced to her mother's dressing-room, it was probable she
should find her alone, and thereby be enabled to perform her errand
without danger. In the stable-yard she saw one of the vicar's regenerated
stable-boys; but he did not appear to take much notice of her, and she
succeeded in reaching her mother's dressing-room without interruption.

She had calculated rightly. Mrs Cartwright was sitting, or rather lying,
alone in her dressing-room; for she was stretched upon a sofa, totally
unemployed, and appearing so ill that Helen almost uttered a cry as she
looked at her.

At the sight of her daughter, Mrs Cartwright started violently, and
rising from her recumbent posture, threw her arms round her with even
passionate fondness. But dear, inexpressibly dear as was this moment to
Helen's heart, she did not forget her commission; and while her lips still
rested on her mother's cheek, she drew Sir Gilbert's note from her pocket
and placed it in her hand.

'Read it quick, dearest mother! I know not what it contains; but Sir
Gilbert charged me to let no one see you read it.'

Mrs Cartwright seemed not to require any stimulant to caution, for,
reading it rapidly, she tore it into atoms, and then, removing some of the
fuel from the grate, which though not lighted was prepared for fire, she
carefully placed the fragments on the rest, and covered them up so that
no speck remained visible. While thus employed, she said to Helen
almost in a whisper, 'Thank Sir Gilbert; tell him I am better, – at least
well enough to take an airing.'

Helen had reason to rejoice that she had lost no time in executing her
commission; for scarcely had her mother in all haste resumed her place
upon the sofa, when Mr Cartwright entered.

By some means or other her arrival had certainly been announced to
him, for his countenance and manner expressed agitation, but not

surprise. He looked keenly first at his wife, and then at her; but they were prepared for it; and excepting that Mrs Cartwright's pale cheek was slightly flushed, and Helen's brow contracted by an involuntary frown, they neither of them betrayed any symptom of agitation.

The Vicar of Wrexhill uttered no word of salutation or of welcome to his unexpected guest; nor did Helen address him. He placed himself, without any pretext of occupation whatever, in a chair commanding a full view of his wife and her daughter, and folding his arms, fixed his eyes first on one and then on the other with the most undisguised determination of watching them both.

The first words spoken were by Helen.

'May I be permitted to see my sister Fanny?' said she.

She addressed herself to her mother, but received her answer from Mr Cartwright.

'Most assuredly no! – You have stolen into my house by a back entrance, and by the same you may leave it; you are used to the mode, it will not puzzle you; and, if I may venture to give my opinion on the subject, the sooner you again make use of this appropriate mode of retreat the better.'

'I believe you are right, sir,' replied Helen coldly; adding very judiciously, 'The reception I have met with has not been such as to give me any inclination to repeat the visit. Good morning, ma'am, – good morning, Mr Cartwright.'

Mrs Cartwright, inexpressibly relieved by this happy stroke of policy, stiffly bowed her head; and Helen retreated, very literally obeying the mandate of the imperious master of the mansion, and returning by the way she came, soon rejoiced her friends by her unhoped-for re-appearance before half the allotted time had expired. Helen most accurately reported every word and look; which seemed not only to satisfy, but perfectly to enchant Sir Gilbert. He laughed, rubbed his hands, made her repeat every word again, and literally chuckled with delight as she dwelt upon the fortunate rapidity with which she had seized the only available moment to do his bidding.

On the following morning, Sir Gilbert, when asked by his lady what he was going to do with himself, replied that he thought he should ride over to Wrexhill. He did so, and returned only in time to dress himself for dinner. The following day, and again the day after, the same question, answer, and result occurred; it being quietly remarked moreover by the rest of the party, that the particularly sweet temper which the worthy baronet had brought from London appeared day by day to be wearing away, and something of what his lady called his 'tiger mood' taking its place.

On the fourth morning, her ladyship's daily inquiry having received in very sullen accents the same reply, Colonel Harrington remarked upon it as soon as he was gone; adding, that he had a great inclination to go over to Wrexhill, in order to discover, if possible, how his honoured but mysterious father employed himself there.

'I really shall be very much obliged to you, William, if you will find this out,' said Lady Harrington. 'It is the first time since we two became one that I have ever suspected him of having a secret; and the consequence is, that I am like to die of curiosity.'

'Thus encouraged, I shall be gone instantly. Take care of Helen, mother, till I come back.' And with these words he departed, leaving the two ladies leisure and inclination to discuss at length the many singular caprices of which Sir Gilbert had been lately guilty.

At about four o'clock Colonel Harrington returned; but his report tended rather to thicken than to elucidate the mystery. He had, without being remarked himself, seen his father walking up and down the town apparently in a state of the most perfect idleness; and then the Cartwright carriage drove by the shop in which he had fixed his look out. Mr and Mrs Cartwright were both in it. It stopped at the next door, which was that of the haberdasher, and they entered the shop together. In about ten minutes Mr Cartwright came out; and he heard him say to his lady, (as he supposed,) 'Get your business done as quickly as you can: I shall be back in ten minutes.' He then re-entered the carriage and drove off. The instant he was gone, Sir Gilbert came out of the post-office, into which he had darted as the carriage passed, and entered the shop in which Mrs Cartwright was left. The interview, if he had sought one with her, certainly did not last above five minutes: when he reappeared, followed by the master of the shop making innumerable bows. Sir Gilbert cut his obsequious civilities short by heartily shaking hands with him, and then departed.

'Where he went next,' continued the colonel, 'I know not; but not choosing to meet him, and feeling somehow or other perfectly persuaded that he had seen Mrs Cartwright, and that this interview, short as it was, had been what he waited for, I got my horse and galloped home as fast as I could.'

Scarcely had he finished his narrative, when Sir Gilbert arrived. He said not a word, however, to throw any light upon his own adventures; yet was he neither silent nor sad.

* * *

Several weeks elapsed after this without bringing to Helen any tidings of her mother. Her appearance and manner during their short interview had indicated so much languor and ill-health, that her anxiety respecting her became very acute, and daily did she haunt every spot where it was probable she should meet with Rosalind, but in vain – no Rosalind came, and nothing was left but to inquire through servants and tradespeople the news of the Park. Nothing, however, obtained in this way afforded her satisfaction: for not only did every report so obtained tend to confirm the idea that Mrs Cartwright was an invalid, but notwithstanding they were on many points uncertain and contradictory, they all agreed in representing the conduct of Mr Cartwright as being strangely altered, and giving ground of fear to those who loved or pitied his unfortunate wife, that he would every day become a harsher and more jealous tyrant to her, for that of late he appeared fearful of leaving her for an hour alone.

Happy therefore as Helen's individual prospects appeared to be, a heavy weight and sad foreboding hung upon her spirits. Her brother's letters, too, though eloquent in affection, and in every expression of joy at her approaching marriage, spoke of himself in a tone of such hopeless despondency as dashed her happier destiny with bitterness. It was no slight augmentation of these sorrows that she felt herself in a great measure obliged to conceal them. To Colonel Harrington, indeed, she ventured to confess that her anxious solicitude for those she loved tarnished her happiness: but this confidence brought with it more sorrow than comfort, for she perceived but too plainly that she had blighted his happiness while confessing the imperfection of her own.

Lady Harrington, though all kindness and even tenderness to her, seemed almost cautiously to avoid every subject that led her to talk of her family: and as for Sir Gilbert, he appeared to be enjoying a state of spirits so enviable in their uniform cheerfulness, that to mention fear or sorrow to him would have been wanton cruelty.

At length, from the butcher, or the baker, or some other of those indispensable functionaries who know all things concerning those who live, move, and have their being, by means of their ministering ambulations, and who fail not to make all they know to circulate as freely as they do themselves, – at length, from some such the news arrived at Oakley that Mrs Cartwright had presented her husband with a son; and moreover, that the mother and child were as well as could be expected.

To Helen this intelligence brought the most unfeigned joy. She believed that all her fears for her mother's health had been unfounded; and that, though it seemed certain that she must live banished from her recovered love, she might at least enjoy the comfort of believing that she was well and happy.

On Sir Gilbert the intelligence produced a very different effect. As Helen regained her spirits he lost his; and though he was still gentle and kind to her, he was upon the whole as cross, crusty, and disagreeable as it is easy to imagine.

One morning, while Colonel Harrington and Helen were sauntering in the avenue, he enjoying her improved cheerfulness, and she secretly blaming herself for having ever suffered him to pine for the want of it, they perceived a servant in the Cartwright livery galloping towards the house. The same idea, the same terror, though felt in a most unequal degree, struck them both. Helen turned deadly pale; and so persuaded did she feel that her mother was dead, that when they stopped the man and received from him a verbal notice that her mother was very ill and wished to see her, the words, though alarming enough in themselves, seemed to be a relief. They returned with all haste to the house to order the carriage for her; and while she was preparing for this sad and most unexpected expedition, the colonel questioned the servant, and learned from him that Mrs Cartwright's infant having died in convulsions in her arms, she had fallen into a state considered by her attendants as extremely dangerous; that during the whole of the last night she had remained nearly insensible, but having recovered her intellects and speech, her entreaties to see Helen were so urgent that Mr Cartwright (who, as the man said, never left her bedside for an instant,) consented that she should be sent for. Miss Fanny and Miss Torrington were also with her, he added, and young Mr Mowbray had been written to; but he believed, from what the people about her said, that there was little chance of her surviving till he arrived.

Having learned these particulars, the colonel sought his father, not only to communicate them, but to ask his opinion as to the propriety of his accompanying Helen on this sad visit.

'I cannot bear,' he added, 'that she should go alone.'

'Of course, young sir, you cannot,' replied Sir Gilbert, with a sudden, and, as his son thought, not very feeling return of cheerfulness, 'I should as soon think of letting her walk thither on all fours: but your lovership must excuse me if I declare that it is my intention to accompany the young lady myself. I am sorry for you, William; – but so it must be. There's the carriage; – go to my lady's closet, and let her hear the news.'

So saying, the baronet, without waiting to receive any answer, hastened to the door, and reached it just as Helen was stepping into the carriage. Without consulting her on the subject, he stepped in after her, and they drove away.

It would be doing an injustice to the essentially kind feelings of Sir Gilbert not to avow that his manner expressed very tender sympathy with Helen's natural and heavy sorrow: but the minds of both were full, and few words passed between them during their drive.

The lodge gates were standing wide open, and they dashed through them without seeing any one of whom the trembling Helen could make inquiry; but once arrived at the house, all suspense was soon over: Mrs Cartwright had breathed her last about ten minutes before they got there.

Poor Helen's first burst of grief was terrible. The remembrance of her poor mother's last embrace, though it became the most soothing comfort

to her during her after life, seemed at that moment only to soften her
heart to greater suffering. Passive, and almost unconscious, she suffered
Sir Gilbert to lift her out of the carriage and lay her on a sofa in the
drawing-room: and there, her tears flowing fast, and her very soul, as it
seemed, melting within her, she might probably have long given way to
her absorbing grief, had not surprise acted on her faculties more
powerfully than salts or hartshorn, and forced her to open her eyes and
her ears to witness the scene that passed before her.

Having seen her placed on a sofa with a female servant standing by her,
Sir Gilbert turned his attention from Helen, and politely requested
permission to wait on Mr Cartwright.

Many, many things of an ordinary nature might have passed around her
without rousing Helen from her deep and most true sorrow; but this
request, and still more the tone in which it was spoken, awakened all her
attention to what followed.

The servant to whom Sir Gilbert addressed himself executed his
commission promptly and effectually; for almost immediately after closing
the drawing-room door, he threw it open again, and his master entered.

Mr Cartwright walked into the room with a proud and lofty aspect, and a
something both of sternness and of triumph on his brow, which Helen
thought Sir Gilbert would not easily endure; but, to her extreme surprise,
the baronet accosted him with a degree of almost servile civility, bowing low,
and uttering a few words of respectful condolence with as much deference
and ceremony as if addressing a sovereign prince on the loss of his consort.

Mr Cartwright replied with equal decorum; but the glance of pride
and triumph, not quite unmixed with something that gleamed like
malice too, shot from his eye, and Helen shuddered as she looked at him.

'I presume that you are aware, Mr Cartwright,' said Sir Gilbert with
imperturbable suavity, 'that your late lady's eldest daughter, Miss Mowbray,
is about to contract a marriage with my son. Her remaining therefore a
member of my family will certainly be very agreeable to us all; but at this
painful moment, it would doubtless be a consolation to the sisters, as well
as to their friend, Miss Torrington, could they be together. Will you
therefore permit me, sir, to convey the three young ladies to my house
together, there to await the opening of the late Mrs Cartwright's will?'

'For this young lady, sir,' replied the Vicar of Wrexhill, pointing to
Helen, 'as she has chosen to exchange the protection of her own mother
for that of your son, I have nothing to say, – excepting, perhaps, that the
sooner she leaves my house, the better satisfied I shall feel myself. But for
Miss Torrington and Miss Fanny Mowbray, I must think further of it
before I resign them to any one.'

'Well, sir,' replied Sir Gilbert with, if possible, still-increasing urbanity,
'we must in this and all things submit ourselves wholly to your will and

pleasure. But may I, in testimony of my respect to the memory of a lady towards whom perhaps I have behaved with some harshness, – may I hope, Mr Cartwright, that you will permit me to attend her funeral?'

'Of this too I must think further,' replied Mr Cartwright with much haughtiness.

'And her son?' rejoined the humbled baronet: – 'I trust he will be present at the last sad ceremony?'

'It is probable I may permit him to be so,' replied the vicar, drawing himself up into an attitude that might really have been called majestic. 'But permit me to observe, Sir Gilbert Harrington, – such is, I think, your name, – that I require not in the arrangement of my affairs counsel or advice from any man, – and least of all – from you.'

So saying, he turned on his heel and stalked out of the room.

'Come, my poor Helen!' said the repulsed baronet with great gentleness, and not in the least, as it seemed, resenting the insolence with which he had been treated, – 'Come – I would have wished to have taken your poor little sister and your friend Rosalind home with us. But God's will – and the vicar's – must be done!'

CHAPTER XLV

MRS CARTWRIGHT'S LAST WILL AND TESTAMENT

It was probably the love of seeing an enemy mortified, – which, it may be feared, is too common to all men, – which induced the Vicar of Wrexhill, notwithstanding the deep aversion he felt for Sir Gilbert Harrington, to suffer him not only to be invited to attend Mrs Cartwright's funeral, but also to be present at the opening of her will.

To both invitations the baronet returned a gracious acceptance, and accordingly once more found himself at the Park on the day that its gates were again to open to the funeral array of its owner.

Charles Mowbray, as Sir Gilbert's carriage drew up, stood ready on the steps of the mansion to receive him: and tears moistened the eyes of both as they silently shook hands and entered the drawing-room, where the funeral guests were assembled.

The room was full. Not only all such saintly scions of the new birth as the evangelical esprit de corps always brought together were present there, but as many of the neighbouring gentry as he could collect were now assembled to witness the proud fanatic's crowning triumph. One circumstance only tended to damp the happiness of this full success, this great conclusion to all his hopes and wishes, – his son was not present at it: and indeed so great had been the licence granted him, that he was at this time wandering, his proud father knew not where.

Nothing however, notwithstanding his deepfelt happiness, could be better got up than Mr Cartwright's sorrow as he watched his wife laid in the tomb: never was white cambric used with better grace. Poor Charles the while sheltered himself behind the stalwart figure of Sir Gilbert, and wept unseen.

Nearly the whole of the company who attended the funeral were invited to be present at the ceremony of opening of the will, which it was the pleasure of the bereaved widower should follow immediately after it.

Again the large drawing-room was surrounded by a circle of sable guests; not one of whom but felt more than usual curiosity at the opening a will upon which hung so large a property, and concerning which there were such conflicting interests.

Sir Gilbert considerately led his friend Charles into a corner where he was not conspicuous, and placed himself beside him; both of them being in good part concealed by the tall and portly person of a gentleman whom young Mowbray had never seen before, and whom indeed several persons, not too much interested in the scene to note what passed, had observed to enter with the funeral train after its return from the church, although he had not been present at the interment.

It is probable, however, that the master of the house himself was not aware of this; for he took no notice of him, and was in fact too fully occupied by the business afoot to know more or to think more of those around him than that they were there to witness the proudest and happiest moment of his life.

All the company being seated, and mute attentive silence hovering over all, Mr Corbold, after bowing to two or three distinguished personages, whose seats were placed near the table at which he had stationed himself as if to assure their attentive witnessing of the act he was about to perform, broke open the seals of the parchment he held in his hand, and having spread it fairly open upon the table, read its contents aloud with a clear voice.

Never man had a more attentive auditory; no sound or movement interrupted the lecture; and when it was concluded, a murmur only, of rather shame-faced congratulation from the particular friends of Mr Cartwright, broke the continued silence.

Something, meanwhile, very like a groan burst from the breast of the unhappy Mowbray; but Sir Gilbert Harrington hemmed so stoutly at the same moment, that no one heard it.

The company had already risen from their seats, and some were crowding round the meek and tranquil-looking vicar, – nay, one active carrier of evil tidings had slipped out of the room to inform Miss Torrington and Fanny of the nature of the departed lady's testament, – when the tall gentleman who sat before the disinherited son arose, and with great politeness requested the attention of the company for one moment before they separated, for the purpose of hearing a document which he should be happy to have the pleasure of reading to them, and which, if not of so extraordinary a nature as the one they had just listened to, and therefore less likely to excite general attention, was at least of later date.

Every one appeared to listen to this address with interest, and nearly the whole company immediately reseated themselves. Some keen-eyed persons fancied they perceived the Vicar of Wrexhill change colour; but they were probably mistaken; for when Mr Corbold whispered to him, 'In the name of the Lord, what does this mean, cousin! – You never left her, did you?' he replied, also in a whisper, but in a steady voice, 'Never for time enough to draw a codicil, – it is impossible!' And having so spoken, he too reseated himself in the attitude of a listener.

The tall gentleman then drew forth from his pocket another parchment, purporting to be the last will of the same lady, containing even more skins than the first; and running over with technical volubility a preamble, only important as describing the testator's state of mind, he proceeded to the more essential portion of the document, and then read slowly and loudly, so that all men might hear, the bequest of all she died possessed of to her beloved son Charles Mowbray; the only deductions being legacies of fifty thousand pounds to each of her younger children, and her jewels to her daughter Helen, provided that within one year from the date of the will she should marry, or have married, Colonel William Harrington, of His Majesty's —— Dragoons.

The name of Cartwright appeared not in any shape; probably because the provision for her younger children would have included the infant yet unborn when this will was made, had it survived her.

This document was as fully and satisfactorily signed, sealed, witnessed, and delivered, as the former one; the only difference being that it was dated some months later.

The pen that has traced these events is too feeble to portray the state into which this change of scenery and decorations threw the Vicar of Wrexhill. It would have been a great mercy for him if he had altogether lost his senses; but no symptom of this sort appeared, beyond a short paroxysm, during which he called upon the Lord to witness his promise of going to law with Mr Mowbray for the purpose of setting aside his mother's will.

After the first buzz produced by this second lecture had subsided, Sir Gilbert Harrington arose and addressed the company with equal good taste and good feeling. A few minutes' conversation with his young friend Mr Mowbray, he said, authorised him to assure the Vicar of Wrexhill that whatever private property he could lay claim to (a wag here whispered, 'Sermons, surplices, and the like') should be packed up and sent to the Vicarage, or any other place he would name, with the utmost attention and care. He added very succinctly, and without a single syllable unnecessarily irritating, that the circumstances connected with the situation of the ladies of the family rendered it necessary that the reverend gentleman should not continue in the house; a necessity which, it might be hoped, would be the less inconvenient from the circumstance of his former residence being so near.

While his old friend was uttering this extremely judicious harangue, Charles escaped by a side door from the room, and bounding up the stairs to Rosalind's dressing-room, where (though as yet he had hardly spoken to her) he pretty well knew she was sitting with his sister Fanny, he burst open the door, rushed in, and fell on his knees before her, clasping her most daringly in his arms, and almost devouring her hands with kisses.

Fanny stood perfectly aghast at this scene. During the few days that Charles had been at home, she had truly grieved to see the decided coldness and estrangement that was between Rosalind and him; and what could have produced this sudden change she was totally unable to guess.

Not one of the family party had entertained the slightest doubt that the will, which Mr Cartwright had more than once alluded to, was such as to render his late wife's children wholly dependent upon him; and this painful expectation had been already fully confirmed: but even if it had proved otherwise, Fanny knew no reason why this should so change the conduct of Charles towards Miss Torrington.

Not so, however, the young lady herself. The vehement caresses of Mowbray explained the whole matter to her as fully and as clearly as the will itself could have done; and if she did bend forward her head till her dark tresses almost covered his – and if under that thick veil she impressed a wild and rapid kiss of joy upon his forehead, most people would forgive her if they knew how well she had all the while guessed at his misery, and how often her young heart had ached to think of it.

This impropriety, however, such as it was, was really the only one committed on the occasion. Sir Gilbert was an excellent man of business, as was likewise the tall gentleman his attorney; so seals were put upon all plate-chests, jewel-cases, and the like, except such as were proved satisfactorily by Mr Stephen Corbold to have been purchased since the marriage of the widow Mowbray and Mr Cartwright. All such were given over to the packing-cases of the serious attorney and the serious butler, and at half-past nine P.M. the Vicar of Wrexhill stepped into his recently-purchased (but not paid for) travelling carriage, and turned his back on the Park – once more *Mowbray Park* – for ever.

* * *

But little remains to be said that may not easily be guessed at by the accomplished novel reader: – and for such, of course, these pages are prepared.

Little Mary Richards speedily became Lady Hilton; and Fanny Mowbray, during a visit of some months at her Scotch castle, learned to think of her religious sufferings with sufficient composure to enable her once more to look forward, as well as around her, with hope and enjoyment. And who is there that can doubt that the lovely Fanny Mowbray, with recovered senses and fifty thousand pounds, even though she did for ever abandon her poetic pursuits, met, at no very advanced age, with a husband worthy of her?

The two tall Misses Richards ceased to be evangelical as soon as it became decidedly *mauvais ton* at Wrexhill to be so: and in process of time they too married; leaving their charming little mother leisure to cultivate the friendship of Rosalind, who retained her partiality for her, and enjoyed her friendship and society for many happy years.

Need it be said that Rosalind and Helen were married on the same day? – So it was, however; and Mr Edward Wallace performed the ceremony, the Vicar of Wrexhill being indisposed. Indeed, the air of the Vicarage evidently disagreed with him; but, by the influence of some of the most distinguished of his party both in religion and politics, he soon obtained an exchange with a gentleman who held preferment in the Fens. He did not, however, obtain a mitre, though a great many serious people declared that he deserved it: a disappointment which was perhaps the more cutting from the circumstances of Mr Jacob's having joined a troop of strolling players; and as he was not sufficiently successful amongst them to add any glory thereby to the family name, the loss of episcopal honours was the more severely felt.

Everything else, I think, went just as it ought to do. Poor Miss Minima was sent off to her mamma, who never again ventured to show her face at Wrexhill; probably fearing that she might cease to be considered as the principal person of the village.

Mr Mowbray speedily re-established Mr Marsh in his school; the old lawyer and apothecary returned; the newly-hired serious servants retreated before the returning honest ones – and, in short, a whole flight of evangelicals followed their incomparable vicar, till the pretty village of Wrexhill once more became happy and gay, and the memory of their serious epidemic rendered its inhabitants the most orderly, peaceable, and orthodox population in the whole country.

THE TROLLOPE SOCIETY

Anthony Trollope wrote 47 novels, three times as many as Dickens, including such well-known works as *The Warden*, *Barchester Towers* and *Phineas Finn*. Today, Trollope is probably the most widely-read and the best loved of all the great Victorian novelists. Yet by 1987, no complete edition had been published and Trollope had not even achieved the dignity of a memorial in Westminster Abbey. The Trollope Society, founded in that year, sought to put that right. In 1994 a memorial to Anthony Trollope was unveiled in Poets' Corner by John Major, and the first volumes of the Complete Edition had been published (the remaining volumes continue to appear at the rate of four books a year, so the edition will be complete by the year 2000).

New members joining the Society can take advantage of the generous subscription prices on each year's new titles in the Complete Edition and also receive FREE each year a full-length hardback book, four copies of the literary quarterly *Trollopiana* and the right to attend the Annual Lecture and the Annual Dinner. Membership requires an annual payment (currently £20/$40).

For full details of The Trollope Society please fill in the form below:

-- ✂ -----

I would like to receive more information on The Trollope Society. ☐

I would also like to receive further information on Pocket Classics. Please add me to your mailing list. ☐

Name ....

Address ....

....

....Postcode ....

Please return this form to: Regina Schinner, Alan Sutton Publishing Ltd, Phoenix Mill, Far Thrupp, Stroud, Glos GL5 2BU.